KT-873-045

CLAIMING HIS BOLLYWOOD CINDERELLA

TARA PAMMI

For Megan—for your endless patience,
and for helping me make this story sparkle
while the world was in chaos.

CLAIMING HIS BOLLYWOOD CINDERELLA

TARA PAMMI

HIS SCANDALOUS CHRISTMAS PRINCESS

CAITLIN CREWS

MILLS & BOON

All rights reserved including the right of reproduction
in whole or in part in any form. This edition is published
by arrangement with Harlequin Books S.A.

This is a work of fiction. Names, characters, places, locations
and incidents are purely fictional and bear no relationship to
any real life individuals, living or dead, or to any actual places,
business establishments, locations, events or incidents.
Any resemblance is entirely coincidental.

This book is sold subject to the condition that it shall not,
by way of trade or otherwise, be lent, resold, hired out
or otherwise circulated without the prior consent of the publisher
in any form of binding or cover other than that in which it is published
and without a similar condition including this condition
being imposed on the subsequent purchaser.

® and TM are trademarks owned and used by the trademark owner
and/or its licensee. Trademarks marked with ® are registered with the
United Kingdom Patent Office and/or the Office for Harmonisation
in the Internal Market and in other countries.

First Published in Great Britain 2020
by Mills & Boon, an imprint of HarperCollins*Publishers*
1 London Bridge Street, London, SE1 9GF

Claiming His Bollywood Cinderella © 2020 Tara Pammi

His Scandalous Christmas Princess © 2020 Caitlin Crews

ISBN: 978-0-263-27838-5

MIX
Paper from
responsible sources
FSC® C007454

This book is produced from independently certified FSC™ paper
to ensure responsible forest management.
For more information visit www.harpercollins.co.uk/green.

Printed and bound in Spain
by CPI, Barcelona

CHAPTER ONE

VIKRAM RAAWAL WALKED up the steps of Raawal Mahal, his family's two-hundred-year-old palatial ancestral bungalow. It was the only property his parents had left unsullied by their still-tempestuous marriage of forty years.

The muggy October afternoon was redolent with the pungent aroma of the jasmine creeper that his grandfather had planted for his wife all those years ago.

His grandparents had shared a love story that couldn't be recreated by all the glittering sets and stars of Bollywood. If not for the fact that Vikram had very clear memories of them—Daadu and Daadi sitting side by side listening to ghazals on the gramophone, sharing stories with him and his younger brother and sister, Daadi keeping silent vigil by her husband's side as he vanished away into nothing…he would have scoffed at even the idea of such a love.

But he had seen it. He'd been a part of it. He'd found comfort and joy in its shadow. And today, at the age of thirty-six, memories of that love hit him hard.

He was lonely, he admitted to himself, as he walked through the gated courtyard toward the main bungalow. The strains of an old ghazal played on the gramophone player, sinking sweetly into his veins, slowly releasing the pent-up tension he'd been carrying. He laughed at the mural his younger brother, Virat, had painted on one wall where a profusion of plants and flowerpots sat on an elevated concrete bench.

The cozy bungalow, full of sweet memories and peaceful childhood associations, was his favorite place in the world. And yet, he had avoided visiting for almost two months, using out-of-country shoots and overloaded scheduling as excuses.

But here in this place where he was just Vikram and not Vikram Raawal, Bollywood star, and the chairman of the family production company Raawal House of Cinema, he couldn't lie to himself.

He hadn't wanted to expose himself to his *daadi*'s brand of perceptiveness. He hadn't wanted her to see how unhappy he'd been of late. How…*unsettled* in his own skin.

The raucous burst of a man's laughter punctured his thoughts. It was Virat.

For a few seconds, Vikram considered turning around and walking out. His recent argument with his brother had been far dirtier than their usual headbutting over projects for Raawal House. Being called arrogant and dominating by a brother that he loved and respected had…shaken him.

The laughter came again and Vikram's curiosity trumped his reluctance. He walked through the grand salon, filled with his grandfather's trophies and accolades from a career that had lasted close to five decades in Bollywood.

Vijay Raawal had not only been a celebrated actor and director but had built his career from the ground up after traveling the country with a theater group for years. Started his own production company, and taken the industry in a new direction. Made mainstream films, art projects, and careers of many stars and never once lost his integrity.

How had his grandfather sustained such a glittering career in such a superficial and cutthroat industry? Had it been simply the unconditional support Daadi had offered him through everything?

After fifteen years and numerous box office hits in Bollywood, Vikram had suddenly found himself filled with a strange feeling of discontent all of a sudden. But it was more than creative burnout. In a cinematic twist, he'd found himself wanting the same kind of support and affection from someone that Daadi had given Daadu while knowing that he wasn't actually capable of returning it.

In a crazy moment of impulse, he'd asked his best friend Zara to marry him. Thankfully, Zara had instantly said no. That he had even considered marriage in the first place—even if it was to his oldest and longest friend, showed how unlike himself he was currently feeling.

He nodded at Ramu Kaka—his grandfather's old man-servant, as old and comfortingly familiar as the bunga-low itself.

The first thing that hit him as he entered the expansive sitting room was the subtle scent of roses. Every inch of him stilled as he stood over the threshold, his long form hidden from his *daadi* and Virat by the L-shaped angle of the hall. They were lounging on the divan, while a number of their servants stood huddled by the other door that led to the huge kitchen. Every mouth twitched in varying degrees of smiles.

In the middle of the room, kneeling on the rug, was a young woman with her face in profile to Vikram. Evening sunlight filtered through the high windows in the room and lit up her silhouette. The first thing he noted was the dark halo of her hair, curly and thick like her very own crown, that swung from side to side every time she moved her head, and huge glittering earrings that reminded him of the crystal chandelier Mama had spent thousands of dollars on in some Italian boutique.

The earrings swayed enchantingly every time the young woman moved her head. And she did it a lot. His mouth curved.

Wide eyes, pert nose and a lush mouth moved in constant animation, along with her plump body. Almost anesthetized by seeing size zero bodies on movie sets, he let his gaze return to the voluptuous lines of her body with a curious fascination. A white cotton kurta hugged her breasts, a long chain of glittery beads dancing over them.

White stones on tiny half-moon gold hoops glinted in a perfect line over the shell of her left ear, winking mischievously in the waning sunlight. With her multihued skirt spread out around her in a kaleidoscope of colors, she was a gorgeous burst of color against a gray landscape.

Full of life and verve and authenticity he hadn't seen in a long time.

A thrilling sliver of excitement bloomed in his gut even as he frowned at the oversized stuffed teddy bear on the floor in front of her. Suddenly, the woman opened her mouth and screamed.

The cry was deep rather than shrill, perfectly modulated, and eerily familiar.

Vikram watched in increasing fascination as she extended her arms and bent to scoop up the stuffed toy from the ground into her arms. The gold and silver-colored bracelets she wore on one wrist tinkled at the moment, adding their own background score to the entire scene.

And then it came to him.

She *was* enacting a scene. From a recent movie. *His latest action thriller.*

She was…mocking him?

She was imitating the cheesiest line he'd ever said in

front of a camera and she was doing a fantastic job of pinpointing everything he'd hated about the movie and in particular, that scene.

But instead of putting an end to what felt like a mockery of his talent, his choices, and even him, Vikram continued to watch. Still curious to see what else she'd do. Bizarrely hungry for the spectacle the woman was making of him.

No wonder Virat was having the time of his life. In their recent argument, his younger brother hadn't packed his punches when he'd criticized that action thriller and every other career choice Vikram had made in the last fifteen years with the brilliant wit and rapacious tongue that he was famous for throughout the industry as a top Bollywood director.

It seemed his brother had been sitting on a mountain of complaints that had suddenly blown up in Vikram's face. The argument had begun after he'd confessed to Virat about his ridiculous proposal to Zara. Virat had unexpectedly gone ballistic about that, then moved on to an old disagreement about their sister Anya's future, then the script for a film Vikram had rejected last year…and finished with his brother calling him a control freak who just didn't know when to stop.

The woman hugged the imaginary person to her chest and bent her head, a low growl building out of her petite form. A couple of seconds passed as she buried her head in the stuffed toy's neck. Just as he'd done to the heroine in that scene. Even the theater hadn't had this kind of pin-drop silence from the audience that she did.

His chest burned with embarrassment, even the beginnings of anger but there was something else too. He continued to watch, as captivated as the rest of them.

The low growl erupted from the woman's throat as she let the huge toy roll away from her lap and, in a movement that was creepily close to his own movements, she raised her head, pushed her fingers to the back of her neck, and screamed again in simulated fury and anguish.

She managed to pitch her voice pretty low, sounding almost as a man might. And then, she looked up.

"I will avenge you, Meri Jaan, in this life and the next. I will destroy everyone that harmed you. I will paint the world with the blood of the man that wronged you. I am the destroyer."

The wretched woman even started humming the soundtrack that followed those horrible lines of dialogue. Who was she?

Applause broke around her. With a familiarity that Vikram found annoying on a disproportionate level, Virat wrapped his arm around the woman and pulled her into a hug against him. Even Daadi laughed.

And then it clicked. This was his grandmother's new personal assistant. The wonderful Ms. Naina Menon that Daadi couldn't stop singing praises of. The one who'd been hired by his grandmother around two months ago, after she'd done some work for Virat. Vikram had never met her.

"You could give most of the leading ladies a run for their money, darling," said Virat.

She shook her head. "Thanks, Virat. But I'm not made for acting. I...this was just—"

Pushing his hands into the pockets of his trousers, Vikram stepped into the room. "My brother's right, Ms. Menon."

The cheerful atmosphere died an instant death. The servants disappeared like rats at the sight of a big cat. Slender fingers pushing away at her unruly cloud of hair in a nervous gesture, the woman turned to face him.

Large, wide eyes alighted on his face, and there was a tremble to that pink mouth. "Hello, Mr. Raawal. I can't tell you how excited I am to finally meet you." It should have sounded pandering, syrupy, and yet the sentiment in her words was clearly genuine.

The fascination he'd felt as he'd taken in her plump curves morphed into a rumbling growl inside his chest, not unlike the one she'd just done in imitation of him. "I wish I could say the same of you, Ms. Menon," he said, his tone betraying nothing but icy disdain.

"I'm sorry if that performance offended you, Mr. Raawal. It was meant to just be a bit of fun…" She looked incredibly young as she visibly swallowed. "I wasn't mocking you."

"No? It sounded like you were," he retorted softly, childishly put out that he was Mr. Raawal while his brother was Virat. Of course, Virat had been charming women since he'd been in *langotis*, so it wasn't much of a surprise. "You *are* wasting your talents here. If not the silver screen, you should be on one of those talk shows, making money from doing the caustic commentaries that are all the rage now, mocking every artist, and bringing them down for the world's glee."

The moment the words were out of his mouth, Vikram regretted them. Even before he noticed her stricken expression. He'd been called arrogant, blunt, even grumpy, but never cruel, not even by the media that kept looking for dirt underneath the shield of his public persona.

But that had been downright cruel.

She went from laughing and glowing to a pinched paleness that punched a hole in his bitterness.

Virat interrupted. "*Bhai*, Daadi and I insisted that she—"

"What do you do with that talent?" he cut in, once again disproportionately riled by Virat's protective stance toward this relative stranger. For some reason, Vikram was far too invested in this woman's opinion of him.

Ms. Menon continued to stare up at him, big eyes wide, tension swathing her petite frame. He moved closer to her and felt that tug again. She was pretty in a girl-next-door way, but the expression in those eyes, the rapid change from anger to desire to confusion…it made her utterly gorgeous.

God, she only looked about twenty.

"Lost your ability for words now?" he murmured, more to hear her speak again than anything else.

She glared at him. "I don't understand your question."

"You're clearly talented, Ms. Menon. What do you do with it all? I mean, other than making a mockery of others?"

"I was… I was just showing them my mimicry. I even did a few other actors earlier too. Like Big B."

"Ahh…so you're one of those critics who makes fun but has never done a minute's worth of creative work themselves or shared it with the world? It's so easy to hide on the sidelines and mock the person out in the public arena, no? Can I ask why you pinpointed that particular scene?"

Her spine straightened and she charged forward. The scent of roses filled his nostrils and he felt a thrill run down his spine. God, she was gorgeous when she was all riled up.

"First of all, I'm not ill-equipped to make such comments. Not when I've studied film history all through college. Secondly, are you sure you want to know why I picked that scene to reenact?"

"I'm a big boy, Ms. Menon. I assure you I can take it."

"Can you though? When you've turned a minute of comedy into a huge insult to your own ego?" He didn't answer and the resolve tightened in her face. "Fine, here's my honest opinion, for what it's worth.

"You cater to the lowest denomination of the mass population with these action blockbusters, and you offer a warped image of what a hero should be with your revenge and destroy plotlines. You perpetuate the same tired old trope of being the macho guy who's a 'true man' just because you can supposedly beat up more guys than anyone else. That movie was not only gratuitously violent but offensive on every level to women, from your leading lady to your blind sister to even your overdramatized female best friend. They only exist in the film to make you their savior."

Every word of her criticism was justified. Every word was utter truth.

And he'd asked for it, so he couldn't even blame her for saying it, could he?

If Vikram didn't hate the idea of true physical violence on every level, he would've sucker-punched his brother for the low whistle that ran around the room.

"I make movies to make money, Ms. Menon. Having clearly inveigled yourself into my grandmother's household, I'm sure you've a really good idea that it's wealth which makes the world go around. So please don't tell me that all artists create just for the purpose of art."

He had no idea why he'd just said that because his grandmother was a great judge of character. And if she thought Ms. Menon was the newly rising sun, then Vikram would normally have believed her, no questions asked.

"Inveigled myself?" she repeated in a low tone, her body vibrating with her anger. "I can't… I can't believe I used to have a teenage crush on you! Of course, I know wealth makes the world go around probably far better than you do—because, believe me, I don't have any.

"As for art… I'm not asking you to throw away any of your considerable wealth making artsy movies that might bomb at the box office. I know you have to keep growing this amazing dynasty…" she threw her arms around and those damn bracelets of hers tinkled again "…to enable the generations of Raawals that might come after you to sit around on their bums."

She slapped her hand over her mouth and groaned. Vikram felt the insane urge to drag her hand away and taste that groan. As much as she was skewering him with her painful truths, he wanted to hear her go on tirade after tirade. God, he could listen to that throaty voice of hers for hours.

She turned to address his grandmother. "I'm sorry, Daadiji. I didn't mean to insult your family."

Virat and Daadi laughed and even Vikram's chest filled with a burst of irreverent joy.

"Never mind, *beta*," Daadi crooned, her perceptive gaze on Vikram. "No one else would dare rip into my grandson quite so well as you just have. Please go on. You have my blessing." The last he knew was added for his benefit.

Not that she believed he would harm Ms. Menon in any way.

"I don't think she has the guts, Daadi," Vikram taunted deliberately. "She's too scared to say anything else to my face."

Fury coated her cheeks, and her brown eyes danced with fire.

"You're not just wealthy, you wield power and influence. Directors and producers change story lines for you. They hire and fire people at your say-so. They create these multi-crore elaborate sets for you. You have the chance to steer things the right way in the industry. You could use your star power to create a new kind of hero, Mr. Raawal. Because, believe me, the world needs to reexamine what makes a man a hero."

Vikram knew he should leave it at that. She hadn't said anything he hadn't already faced up to in the dark of the night. And yet to be so thoroughly reduced to the sum of his flaws grated at his ego. To be thought of in such poor terms by a woman that stirred his interest like never before...pricked his male pride.

"Why should I give your cutting opinion any weight? What have you done so far that's so important and worthwhile? You're clearly both educated and talented because even Virat sings your praises, and yet you're hiding here playing PA to my grandmother, hiding from your own life!"

"That's unfair," she threw back at him and yet he could see from her reaction he'd hit the nail on its head. He hadn't become the king of an industry without being perceptive.

"Ah... Ms. Menon, you can dish it out, but you clearly can't take it," he drawled.

"You don't know anything about my life," she retorted and he had a horrible feeling he'd truly wounded her.

Regret filled his chest. He desperately wanted to touch her, to hold her trembling body. Instead he stepped back.

For the entire world, even for his family who knew him well, he was a coldhearted businessman, the head of Raawal House. And nothing else. With no shades or flaws.

"And yet you presume to know everything about mine," he said softly, his frustration with himself, with the world seeping into his tone. "Because I live my life for your entertainment and God forbid I make mistakes like every other person on the planet. God forbid anyone even wonders that there's more to me than the company or this bloody family or being a successful star. Right?"

Silence met his own outburst. Virat and Daadi stared at him with stunned expressions. As for Ms. Menon, he had no words to describe the look in her eyes.

It wasn't pity or sympathy. It was something else, something he wanted to drown in. Something he wanted to demand she give voice to.

Which was crazy enough in itself.

Vikram turned around and walked away from the damned woman with her far-too-blunt opinions and big eyes and from the house with its insistent mockery of what he should've been and what he had become instead.

Damn it, how had the woman gotten under his skin so easily? Why had it taken someone like her to point out the obvious truth of how far off course he'd veered? To make him suddenly understand the reason for his recent burnout?

Because he'd surrounded himself with yes-men and women. Because he'd made himself so powerful, so untouchable that there wasn't anyone who would dare dig into him like she just had. Except Virat. And he hadn't really listened to his brother.

Because in the pursuit of trying to fix everything their father had destroyed, he'd sold his soul in the process.

CHAPTER TWO

"YOU'RE HIDING HERE…"

One bitingly truthful comment from Vikram Raawal had been enough to make Naina ache to take action. One small tidbit of gossip from her stepsister, Maya, that Naina's ex was getting engaged had propelled her into doing this…

And now she was here. At a masked ball in borrowed glad rags, determined to have fun. The minute Naina had asked him, Virat had agreed to bring her to his parents' latest charity ball, a mischievous smile lighting up his entire face. He'd always been friendly, charming but since her tirade at his older brother, he'd positively showered her with affection.

They'd arrived not two hours ago, waved in through the high gates into a beautiful winding pathway toward yet another bungalow the Raawals owned.

Naina took a glass of some frothy pink cocktail as she moved around the dance floor in the expansive ballroom.

Her eyes were going to be permanently stuck in a wide-eyed position from all the celebrities she had spotted so far. Even with elaborate, custom-designed, gem-encrusted masks, the stunning features of more than one actor and beautiful actress were obvious. And yet, there was a strange thrill in the air as most of the A-listers pretended as if they didn't know each other.

Was that the attraction of a masquerade ball? Were these people so jaded that a pretend dress-up party passed for excitement in their frenetic, under-the-microscope lives?

Looking like one of them, even if every inch of her had been pinched, pushed, molded, painted, had been much easier than she'd imagined. Especially since Daadiji had tasked an entire team to dress Naina for the party.

The baby-pink A-line dress in chiffon, one of Anya Raawal's own creations, had initially reminded Naina of a birthday frock her stepmother, Jaya Ma, had bought her when she'd been twelve. Full of layers and gauzy material, that frock had made Naina look like pink bubblegum. But since the elegant Ms. Raawal had been doing Naina a favor with this dress, she'd kept her mouth shut.

Once she had stood in front of the full-length mirror, Naina had quickly realized that Anya was a genius. The dress hugged her body from chest to waist and then flared wide, making the most of her short stature. With her unruly hair straightened to within an inch of its life, it fell to her waist in a long silky curtain.

With her hair not stealing the focus from her face and with cleverly applied makeup, her eyes seemed huge in her face. Even Naina had thought she looked almost beautiful.

After two dances and an introduction to one of her favorite writers, she'd insisted that Virat do his own thing. She'd realized from Daadiji's sharp surprise he was even attending this party, that Virat usually gave a wide berth to anything related to his parents.

"I feel like I'm releasing an innocent doe into a horde of stampeding beasts," Virat had said when she'd demanded if he was going to stick to her like last week's gum.

"If you stand by me the entire time, shooting glares at

any man who even looks at me," she said with a smile, "I might as well freeze in place and look like one of these priceless sculptures that are dotted around. Please, Virat. I'm not as helpless as I look."

That had done it.

She'd kissed him on the cheek, nodded obediently when he gave her strict instructions to text him when she was ready to leave, and then he disappeared into the crowd.

For the next half hour, Naina stayed on the steps going out into the balmy night, standing on the fringes of a group, listening to them argue the finer points of why remake mania had taken over the industry.

"You're hiding, Ms. Menon," said a deep voice in her head and she took a long drink of her cocktail in defiance. Damn Vikram Raawal. She wasn't going to let the man have the last word.

Spotting another young actor that she thought was particularly cute, Naina edged along the perimeter of the dancing crowd, determined to introduce herself.

It wasn't until an hour and a half later when Naina reached the huge library and closed the door behind her that she took in a deep breath. The last thing she wanted was another confrontation with Vikram Raawal.

No matter that he stood so separate from the crowd at the party, almost as if he was as out of place among these people as she herself. Which was ridiculous.

For one dazzling second, their eyes had met across the room, the rhythmic beat of the music around them in concert with her own heart. For one insane second, Naina had felt as if he'd actually seen her. The real her.

The usually dull, plump, bookish Naina Menon who stood on the sidelines and watched life pass her by. It felt as if he'd known that it was she beneath the mask.

Luckily, his attention had been quickly drawn away by a costar of his. And whatever spell, imagined or real, had woven between them, had been broken.

"And yet you presume to know everything about me..." Those words of his haunted her.

He had been right. Who was she to moralize to anyone else? She had not only criticized him, but she had attacked his worth as a person.

Naina sat down on a comfortable lounger and pulled her cell phone out of her clutch to text Virat. She'd had enough of the party and the loud music.

She had introduced herself to a lot of people, she'd danced, she'd shamelessly fan-girled over one Urdu poet that Papa and she had adored for years by reciting his own poem back at him, she had laughed at the not-so-funny joke by an actor who had been called the latest wonder boy to breeze into the industry. The same one she'd thought was cute.

For all his gorgeous features and ripped body, Naina had found him deeply boring. Really, the man-child had talked about himself—his workout regimen, his Instagram followers, the love letters he received from his rabid, female fans professing undying love to his perfectly chiseled abdomen—for more than half an hour. Without saying anything of significance concerning the arts or films or theater or anything.

Holding her arm up, she moved her phone around to get a signal. She was about to go find Virat in person when the huge double doors of the library opened. And in walked *the very man* she'd wanted to avoid, not just for tonight, not just this week, but for the rest of her life.

Vikram hadn't noticed her yet. She'd turned off most of the lights, leaving only the dim lamp next to her switched on. Not until he reached the pool of soft light thrown by the lamp did he see her.

"I didn't realize anyone else needed to escape that madness," he said after a beat of silence. In the near dark, his voice sounded impossibly deep, sliding over her skin like a note of music.

She didn't answer. She couldn't. Couldn't find the words past her dry mouth and the rapid drumbeat of her heart in her ears.

"Are you all right?" he asked, concern filling his voice.

Naina took a deep breath and pitched her voice lower than usual. "I am. Thank you. I just…"

"You were clearly not enjoying the party."

"I was. I mean, I am. How do you know, anyway?"

"I was watching you in the other room." He raised his hands and backed up a step when she frowned. "In a non-creepy way, that is. There's something very familiar about you and I was trying to remember if we had met."

Heat poured into Naina's cheeks and she ducked her head. That feeling of being consumed by his gaze returned. She looked up to find him studying her intently and she was immensely grateful she'd kept her mask on when she'd walked into the library. "No. I don't know you." She smiled at her own words. "I mean I *do* know who you are."

She pointed a finger at his unmasked face. He was wearing a white shirt, unbuttoned at his throat, his hair a little bit on the longer side right now. The subdued light from the lamp only served to highlight the beautiful symmetry of his features. "I wondered why you clearly touted the rules of the party. But then I realized you'd have been recognized even with a mask on. Your face is certainly perfect enough," she blurted out and then instantly regretted it. "I'm sorry. I didn't mean to push myself and my compliments into your space. I've learned recently how much I presume..." She cleared her throat and looked away. "Sorry."

"Since I was the one who intruded on your solitude, shall we call a truce?"

She nodded.

"May I sit down?"

"Yes, but it's literally your parents' house. I should be the one to—"

"No, please stay. That way, we can be alone together. Instead of being forced to socialize."

Her suddenly teenaged heart went pitter-patter at that. "Why are you hiding?"

"I usually come to these parties just to keep an eye on...things." He folded his tall, lean form next to her with movements that were sheer poetry in motion. "I promised my brother I'd give his friend a lift home. He had to leave suddenly."

She straightened instantly. "Wait, Virat already left? But he said..." She flushed furiously when he saw Vikram studying her with a raised brow.

"Ah...that's why you were waiting for him here? In the dark. In secret. You should know, Virat is notorious for changing his girlfriends as easily as he changes actors for his projects."

"What?"

"He left with that new pop singer."

There was a strange gentleness in his voice that enveloped her. "Why are you telling me that?"

"It's better to cut your losses now rather than have your heart trampled later on by Virat. He's ditched you and whatever exciting, private tryst you'd both planned and gone home with another woman."

Naina looked around the quiet, shady nook she'd chosen in the vast library, the rest of which was enveloped in darkness. "You think I was waiting here to meet Virat so that we could...for some secret...to have a private..." The longer she stumbled over her words, the more she blushed and the wider the dratted man's smile grew.

"Virat is well known for his...adventurous exploits."

"I'm not waiting here for your brother so that we can get it on in some kind of secret, silly seduction game."

"No?"

"No. And stop smirking at me in that condescending way."

His mouth straightened but the smile lingered in his eyes. *Gorgeous* did not do the man justice. "I'm not smirking or condescending. I just find you adorable."

"I'm no such thing and how...what?" Apparently, the night was full of surprises.

"You apologized for invading my personal space and for complimenting my perfect features. You're trying very hard to sound all sophisticated about men and seduction yet it's clear you're not, and the effect is very endearing."

"My ex did say I was far too old-fashioned." Naina sighed. The temptation to pull off the mask was overwhelming but it meant whatever this camaraderie between them was...would disappear in a breath.

It was strange how life worked. She had covered her face with a mask because she wanted to be someone else for one night. And yet, even with the mask in place, she felt seen for the first time in a long time. By the very man she'd torn into not a few days ago for his insensitive portrayal of women.

If he realized who she was, there was no doubt he'd walk away without a backward glance. He might even think she'd...*tricked* him. She couldn't bear the thought of tonight ending like that, the thought of him thinking ill of her.

She wanted more from tonight. From him. From herself.

"Are you old-fashioned?"

Naina shrugged. "What does that even mean? Who decides what's modern and what's old-fashioned anyway? And why are all those stupid, arbitrary constructs only applied to women? You and Virat are praised as playboys whereas every move your sister Anya makes is held to some vague standards of behavior no one else in your family is held accountable to."

"Ah...now I know how you became close to my brother." His arm went around the chaise lounge. "Also, your ex sounds like a jackass who wanted to push you into things you were not ready for. And because he's probably a mama's boy used to getting what he wants, he attached a label to you to make you feel bad about it. You should be glad you dumped his ass."

"I didn't. He dumped me," Naina replied automatically, stunned to her core at this seemingly arrogant man's astute summary of Rohan. Hadn't Jaya Ma always said the same? Why hadn't Naina seen it? Why had she let him hurt her like that?

She looked at Vikram with new eyes.

"Then I'd suggest you be thankful for whatever brought that around."

"He had started a new job in Delhi last year, and asked me to move in with him. First Papa got really sick, so I had to postpone it. Then after Papa died, we discovered we were up to our neck in debt. So my ex decided he didn't want to be held back any longer by my dead weight. He had places to go, careers to achieve."

Thankfully, he didn't offer any meaningless platitudes to fill up the silence like Maya had or say *I told you so* like Jaya Ma. He simply honored her feelings of grief and betrayal. Naina didn't know how long they sat quietly like that. But she absolutely knew she liked being alone together with him.

"He's not a bad guy really," she finally said into the silence.

He snorted. She glared at him.

"So if you were not waiting for Virat for a secret seduction, what did you want with him?"

"Oh, he…he was only supposed to give me a lift back home, that's all. I'd had enough of my wild crazy night. Did he really dump me onto you to take home?"

He shrugged. "Virat has a weird sense of humor. Was the party everything you imagined it might be?"

"I… I wanted excitement and drama. And I certainly got more than enough to last me for a decade."

"I saw you dance earlier with that hot young actor. I tried to keep an eye on you but I got distracted. He didn't act…inappropriately with you, did he?"

Naina colored at his direct question. "Oh, no, nothing like that. I got the impression that I was far too beneath his usual standards to be the object of his lust. The dance he indulged me with was, I believe, his charity act for the year. Maybe for the decade."

Those beautiful brown eyes of his swept over her face as if taking inventory. Naina felt as if he had actually touched her. "Charity act?"

"Apparently, he doesn't date anyone who's not at least eight inches taller and twenty kilos lighter than me. Or alternately a few crores richer than I am.

"But he decided he could be generous enough to give me a taste of how it felt to be in his arms. A treat to remember when I return to my unglamorous, unhappening life, as he put it. God save me from men who want to save me from my apparently pitiful existence!"

Laughter burst from him so suddenly that Naina startled.

She pushed back into the lounger until her legs were crossed away from his and she could study this gorgeous man with his stunning smile. All evening, she'd thought whatever magical quality she'd been chasing tonight had been nonexistent. That she was foolish to have expected life to be more exciting just because she'd entered a different world for a few hours.

But sitting here with Vikram, and seeing his irreverent smile and knowing that she'd caused it, this was the magic she'd been looking for. This moment, with its explosive, exciting possibilities.

"I'm glad my life is a source of entertainment to you, Mr. Raawal."

"Vikram." A simple command.

She shook her head. "I won't know you long enough to be so presumptuous."

"Try," he urged, with a half smile around his mouth, and she found herself nodding. If he smiled like that and asked her to follow him into hell, Naina had a feeling she would do it without a blink.

Was that why so many women—actresses and models and businesswomen alike—fell for him year after year, even knowing that he would never commit to any of them? In-depth details of his love life, if it existed, never graced any magazine or TV channel. Only frequent speculations about his relationship with actress Zara Khan—which by its long-standing nature made the media hungry for more.

"I'm sorry your exciting evening turned out to be… exhausting."

"It isn't a complete waste." She ran her palms over the soft chiffon of her dress and smiled. "I got to dress up and play a star for one evening. I danced with more than one gorgeous stud, I saw things that I never thought I would. I met Husainji, although I'm afraid I made a fool of myself by reciting his own poem back at him. Papa would have loved to be here. For that alone, I'm happy I came tonight."

He smiled.

"And I got to look beautiful for one night."

"I have a feeling you look beautiful whatever you're wearing, Ms....."

False names came and went from Naina's lips. "Please don't ask me to tell you my identity. I don't want to return to the real world just yet."

"Tell me why you came tonight then."

"I just heard that my ex is engaged to be married. He... found a girlfriend a mere month after he dumped me and now she's his fiancée. The other night, I got into an argument with...someone and what they said, it really shook me. I took a good look at my life, at myself, and I just... I became angry with myself.

"Since Papa died, I've been flitting from job to job, situation to situation, letting circumstances and other people push me around. For one night, I wanted to be in control. I wanted to...not be in control too. I just didn't want to be the boring N...girl that people left behind."

Something shimmered in his eyes, something that looked like desire. But no, that wasn't possible. This man, this gorgeous superstar couldn't be attracted to her. For all the makeup and the dress and the glittering mask, she was still only Naina.

Naina Menon, whose sole accomplishment so far had been running away from her own life. Despite the smiles and down-to-earth attitude of his, Vikram was used to seeing perfection from sunup to sundown.

"I'm sorry," she said, looking away. "I don't think I'm making much sense."

His hand reached for hers on the back of the sofa, barely touching the tips of her fingers. The slight contact was teasing, yet grounding. As if he saw her clearly even in the darkness. "You're making perfect sense.

"I'd give anything to not be Vikram Raawal for one day. To forget that my every breath, every look, every step is hounded by the media. To make mistakes like any other man and not be vilified for it. To throw off the shackles of…" He looked away, his fingers roughly thrusting through his hair. A laugh, full of self-mockery burst from his mouth. "God, you're a dangerous woman. And believe me, I have known enough of them."

Her smile faltered and he instantly caught it. "What have I said wrong?"

"I don't like the way you lump women together, as if we all share the same brain. The same thoughts. Have the same agenda."

"That's the second time this week I've been criticized by someone for my bias against women." He rubbed a hand over his face, as if he was truly tired. "As galling as it is to admit, I owe both of you an apology," he said, stealing away the ground from under her feet.

Another teasing smile. "Now you're shocked that I even know the meaning of the word."

"No, I just…"

"It's okay. Even with that mask on, you have the most expressive face I've ever seen. Your eyes flash like glittering gems when you're angry and your mouth…" His gaze dipped to it and a flash of electricity seemed to strike them both simultaneously.

Suddenly depleting the air from the room. Filling her skin with a restless energy. Filling her mind with impossibly wanton desires that could never come true.

Dreams and desires that had to be impossible, didn't they? She wasn't actually thinking of kissing Vikram Raawal, was she? She couldn't.

"You've got that feverish glint in your eyes again. Tell me what you're thinking."

"That this day couldn't get any more bizarre. That I had no idea what I'd signed up for. That wanting to kiss you has to be the most impossible thought to ever cross my mind."

He didn't flinch at her statement. He didn't even blink. He just sat there and stared at her with those eyes that seemed to devour her.

Naina could feel her cheeks burning. Mortification, she'd tell Maya, had a special kind of sting. If only the earth could burst open like it did so often in his blockbusters and swallow her whole. Closing her eyes didn't change reality. He was still there, solid as ever, watching her.

It caused fast words to spill out of her without her permission. "I don't know what just got into me. I'm thoroughly ashamed of myself and not that this makes it any better, but believe me, my desire to kiss you doesn't arise from the fact that you're *the* Vikram Raawal, Bollywood superstar, eligible bachelor and one of the wealthiest men in the country."

"No?" he said.

He didn't sound accusatory. It encouraged her to carry on.

"No. I mean, I know I can't just isolate the movie star part of you, but that's not the draw for me," Naina clarified breathlessly. She didn't know why it mattered so much that he believed her. That she wasn't some mindless groupie that wanted to live out a kind of warped fantasy here.

"Tell me what it is then?"

His question had a curious thirst to it. As if he desperately wanted to know why she wanted him. As if hearing a woman's admiration for him wasn't a regular thing in his world, only she knew that it was.

"I want to kiss the man that saw me across the room

this evening. The man that can laugh at himself, who is maybe just as lonely as I've been, for all that he has the world at his feet. The complicated stranger with whom I've found a connection in a quiet, darkened room made for secret trysts," she finished with a smile, loving this fearless version of herself.

Their gazes held, a live wire of electricity sparking into life between them.

For a long time, he didn't say anything. And Naina was okay with that too. He had given her something tonight, something precious. Self-confidence. And she wanted to give something back to him, this man who had everything in the world.

"Then come kiss me. I'm all yours."

Her heart went thud against her rib cage. "What?"

"Kiss me," he repeated and as if to underscore his invitation, he spread his legs apart, making room for her. "Have your way with me. Do with me whatever you will."

Naina had never felt more terrified and more thrilled in her entire life. Not even when Papa had taken her and Mama to see snow for the first time when she'd been six and they'd stood at the top of a snow-covered mountain, both majestic and terrifying in its presence.

"Why?" she managed to ask, trying to cling to the last remnants of any sanity that might be left.

"Shall I speak my mind? I'll probably be blunt."

"You're a gentleman to ask permission. I believe I crossed that line long ago."

"I want to see if that lovely mouth of yours tastes as good as it looks. I want to tear that mask and that dress off and touch every inch of you. I want to cover those gorgeous breasts with my hands and mouth until you're begging me for more. I want to be inside you while you laugh with your beautiful eyes and strip another layer of clothing off me."

"Oh." Her clutch slipped from Naina's hands, falling onto the floor in a sinuous whisper. "Why?"

He sighed. "Because when a man thinks a woman is incredibly sexy, he wants to do things to her. With her. Wild, wicked things. He wants to—"

"I said I don't have much experience, not that I'm lacking basic common sense," Naina interrupted, feeling a tingle of excitement all over her skin. The chiffon suddenly felt like a tight cage against it.

He smiled and shrugged. "I warned you I'd be blunt."

It was the kind of smile that made girls like her put posters of him up on their walls after his debut movie. There was charm and mischief in that smile. She hadn't seen it that day at his grandmother's house. A little glow erupted in her chest that she'd made him smile like that again. As if it were a prize to be won.

"Honesty seems to be the best policy when you want to do all those things with someone," she agreed and again, he laughed.

Naina felt as if she was the richest person in the world. She wanted to spend entire eons making him laugh like this. While he whispered filthy things in her ear and made her damp between her legs.

"Says the woman who won't reveal who she is."

"If I reveal myself, I can't be this wild, crazy woman."

"But I have to call you something." He swept his gaze over her with a scorching intensity that put paid to any doubts she harbored. "I've got it. Dream Girl."

She laughed. "That name is for beautiful divas like Hema Malini," she said, naming the star of the seventies who'd taken both the industry and her leading men by storm. There was even a song with that title.

"It suits you just as well it suited her." He shook his head when she'd have protested. The moment stretched and she finally nodded, taking the compliment with a grace she didn't usually possess. "You don't feel it? This thing between us?"

"I do. Absolutely." She had felt the tension between them even the other day. When they'd been busy lobbing verbal grenades at each other. "But I…" She licked her mouth and his gaze immediately focused there. "I'm not good at reading the signals. I didn't want to assume that you'd be attracted to someone like me."

"Ah…who's stereotyping now?"

"There's a certain truth to stereotyping," she protested, feeling flustered.

"In yours but not in mine?" he said gently, calling her out.

"It's just that… I'm not what you call conventionally beautiful. Please, I'm not asking for compliments. And I'm fully aware that conventional beauty is also an arbitrary standard. It's just that you're used to being with incredibly sophisticated, beautiful, accomplished women. Like we established earlier, I'm little more than a novice when it comes to men and their desires."

"I've definitely never met a woman who disagreed with me so much."

A shaft of joy blew through Naina. She loved how he made her smile. Even when she was mostly attacking him. "I couldn't bear it if you were laughing at me. Or worse, condescending to me like that arrogant young stud earlier."

"You think I'm asking you to kiss me out of some sense of pity?"

"If not pity, at least as an experiment."

"Every kiss is an experiment. Sometimes, the result is that whatever chemistry you had burning between you just fizzled out. Sometimes, you find that flame in the strangest of places with the last person you'd have ever thought of."

"See? Because I'm not your type."

"No, because I don't know you. Not even your name. Should I tell you the risk I'm taking right now?"

Naina snorted inelegantly. "There's nothing you risk by indulging the silly woman who wants to kiss you senseless. Who wants to muss you up so thoroughly with her hands that she's shaking. Who wants to…" She trailed off at the unholy glint of wickedness in his eyes, then swallowed and found the courage to continue. "Press her mouth against the hollow at your throat and make you feel as crazy as she does."

"Kiss me senseless… Ahh…love, now you're just winding me up." He smiled, his teeth digging into his lower lip, grooves in his cheeks and a dark twinkle in his eyes. Energy vibrated from his frame. As if he was thoroughly excited at the thought of her kissing him senseless. "If you could see yourself as I see you right now, threatening all kinds of delicious sensual attacks on me…"

Anticipation licked through her body, releasing a restless hunger. "Tell me, what great risk are you taking right now?"

"You know who I am. You know pretty much everything about me. My favorite color, my favorite car, my favorite dish, probably even my favorite position with a partner." He sounded close to disgusted, and Naina realized he was right. What she was doing was not a risk at all. Not when compared to him. "Tomorrow morning, you could go to any media outlet you want and tell them all about this moment. You could repeat everything I said to you tonight. You could sell this story and probably make enough money to last the rest of your life."

Naina vibrated with anger and hurt. "I would never do that. Ever. Revealing to anyone what might happen between you and me tonight would be a total betrayal of myself."

Those long fingers of his slid against hers until they were entwined. His touch sent a jolt of warmth up her arm. "I believe you. You've no idea how fantastic that is."

"How?"

He sighed. "I am Vikram Raawal. From the moment I could understand the world, it meant something. It meant more to other people even before I understood what it meant to me. Privilege and power and pride, yes. But so much more that the world doesn't see. Everybody wants something from me. My family, my friends, my fans…apparently even my critics. There are so many expectations that they feel like shackles around my ankles."

He pressed a finger against her mouth when she opened it. "Hear me out before you give me another speech about my civic duties, please. I'm more than happy to lend a word or a hand when I can. But it's not every day that someone comes to me with no expectations of me. Expect maybe what my mouth can do for her."

Naina let her gaze fall to study it. "It *is* a gorgeous mouth," she whispered on a long sigh and it came again.

His laughter. Deep and rumbling. Turning his face into a thing of beauty. That need between them shimmered into life again, gaining in intensity, until it was a peal ringing deep inside her body. He tugged and she scooted closer to him on the sofa. The warmth of his body was a tempting caress against her bare arms.

"I want to join you in your fantasy and escape. So for tonight, I'm all yours, Dream Girl."

"I can muss you up however I want?" Naina asked, stunned by her own daring.

Again, he dug those teeth into his lower lip and nodded.

"I can take this however far I want?"

"Yes."

"And if I…"

"If you want to stop, we will stop. This is absolutely your show, baby. In fact, how about I don't touch you unless you ask me to?"

"I was going to say what if I don't know what to do next?" she murmured.

"Then you can ask me to help you along."

Her heart beating a million to the dozen, Naina covered the small distance that still remained between them. It was akin to flying off a cliff. But she wanted this kiss. She wanted this man, so she took a deep breath and shoved herself off the edge.

CHAPTER THREE

SHE HAD THE silkiest-looking skin Vikram had ever seen. And as he'd said, he'd seen a number of stunning women during his career. There was a glow, a suppleness to it that he knew no amount of makeup could achieve. It made him want to lift his hand and stroke his knuckles softly down one cheek. It made him want to nuzzle his nose into the hollow underneath her ear and test for himself if she was also that silky to the touch.

Eyes wide, breathing shallow, she shuffled herself toward him slowly, carefully.

The scent of her hit him first. A subtle blend of jasmine and her that he'd remember for the rest of his life. And equate with honesty and irreverence and passion and laughter. There was a joy about this woman, despite her insecurities and vulnerabilities, that he found almost magical.

The mask she wore was black satin with elaborate gold threading at the edges and was woven tightly into her hair, leaving just enough of her beautiful dark brown eyes visible. The bridge of her small nose was revealed as was the slice of her cheekbones. For a few seconds, Vikram had the overwhelming urge to tear it off. He wanted to see her face. Not because he wanted to find out her identity.

He wanted to see her face because he wanted to know this woman. He wanted to know everything about her.

He wanted… With a rueful shake of his head, he pushed away the urge. It was more than clear that men had only ever disappointed her. He was damned if he was going to be counted as one of them. He wanted to be different in her memory.

When she remembered him after tonight, he wanted her to smile. He wanted her to crave more of him. Just as he would crave more of her. He knew this before their lips even touched. And he would find a way to discover her identity. He was just as sure of that too.

Her mouth was completely uncovered. Her lipstick was mostly gone leaving a faint pink smudge that he wanted to lick away with his tongue. He was already half-hard and he hadn't even touched her. Or been touched. He hadn't felt this excited at the prospect of a simple kiss in so long. Not since he'd been a boy.

She held the edge of her silk dress with one hand and as she'd lifted it to move, he got a flash of a thigh. Soft and smooth and silky. It was like receiving a jolt of electricity, with every inch he discovered of this woman. The dress swooped low in the front, baring the upper curves of her breasts in a tantalizing display.

He wanted to lick the line of her cleavage until she was panting against him. He wanted to sneak his hand under that neckline and push her breasts out until he could uncover the tight knots of her nipples that were thrusting against the silk now.

And then there she was, within touching distance. Sitting with her legs folded beneath her, looking straight into his eyes. One arm held the sofa while the other smoothed repeatedly over the slight curve of her belly. She was nervous and he found it both endearing and incredibly arousing. She wanted to please herself. And him. And he'd never wanted more for a woman to discover pleasure with him.

Her warm breath hit him somewhere between his mouth and jaw in silky strokes that resonated with his heartbeat. This close, he could see the tiny scar on the other corner of her mouth.

"Are you going to do anything?" she asked after a couple of seconds, sounding completely put out.

He wanted to laugh and tug that pouty lower lip with his teeth. Instead he forced himself to take a breath. He was never going to smell jasmine and not think of her ever again. "It's your kiss, darling. You take it."

She looked at him as if he was her favorite experiment. "Okay, here goes," she whispered, her brow knotting in concentration.

His breath hitching in his throat, Vikram waited. Small hands cradled his jaw and cheek and then there she was, leaning forward. Pressing those lovely lips against his. Soft and tentative and incredibly lush against his mouth. Warm and smelling of mint and sherbet. A quick slanted press. Then another. A quiet drag of that wide mouth, this way and that. A tentative flick of her tongue against the seam of his lips. An exhale that played his nerve endings like the strokes of a piano. And then she pulled back.

She stroked his lips with a featherlight touch. "You're not participating," she protested.

"Say my name."

She frowned and sighed. And mumbled something to herself. Something like "If you want to do anything properly, you have to do it yourself."

He chuckled.

The minx pressed her palm to his chest. His heart thundered away at her touch. Her gaze intent, she moved the hand down to his abdomen. And then lower, until her fingertips rested against the waistband of his trousers.

A burst of strange sensation erupted around his heart

and he groaned. She studied their bodies some more, as if it was as complex as rocket science. He wondered if she was just plain torturing him. But no, clearly, the woman didn't have a manipulative bone in her body.

It was the hardest thing he'd ever done to sit still. When all he wanted was to push her down onto the sofa and show her what kissing someone senseless really meant. He wanted to cover her luscious body with his, lick his way into that tart mouth and grind his growing erection into the cradle of her legs. "Do you need help?" he asked and barely recognized his own voice.

Her head jerked up, her fingers still pressing against his lips. He licked the tip of one that was peeking into his mouth. And then nipped it gently with his teeth. "What was that for?" she gasped.

He shrugged. "You have thirty seconds to act, Dream Girl."

"If not?"

"If not, I simply get up and walk away."

"You're a cruel, cruel man, Vikram Raawal. And no, I won't let you walk away. Not yet."

Her weight shifted forward. A graze of those gorgeous full breasts against his chest. The tips of her fingers dug into his abdomen for purchase when she slipped slightly. She frowned some more. With a curse, she lifted the hem of her dress. Flashed her toned thighs at him and blushed furiously. And then she was straddling his legs, the soft curves of her body leaning forward at an angle and pressing against his in a completely delicious torture. He went from half-mast to fully hard in an instant.

"You know," she said, between humming a tune against his cheek, tracing every inch of his face with that mouth, "Papa used to say, if you do something, you should do it right." She opened her mouth and continued her foray, up one cheek, down the other, his neck, and then back up, leaving little pockets of warmth on his skin. Leaving him panting for more.

Vikram wondered if she could hear the hard thud of his heart. And then she was kissing him properly. Hot and hard and honest. Like thunder on a stormy evening. Like the earthy scent of the world after rain. All magic and mayhem in the air.

He'd expected her to be sweet, a little bumbling maybe. He'd thought he'd have to show her how to kiss him properly. Arrogant stud indeed!

She licked and nipped at his lips until he opened his mouth. Her gasp seemed to burrow into his very cells. And then there she was, dueling her tongue with his, running away, and then catching him back again. Teasing him by licking at the tip of his tongue. Taunting him by retreating.

She sucked at his tongue and a jolt of current burst through his nerve endings. Soft and warm, her body moved in a tantalizing rhythm that goaded his.

Vikram released his hands from behind him and went for her with a mindless need he didn't understand. He ran his hands, fingers wide, all over the dips and valleys of her body, greedy to touch all of her. Desperate to not miss an inch. Her arms were around his neck, her weight settled onto his legs.

Damn, the woman really knew how to kiss. There was no tentativeness, no holding back. She let herself fly free with a voraciousness that fueled his own.

"How's that?" she asked him innocently, while she paused, her teeth nipping at his neck, sending a bolt of pleasure down his spine.

"You kiss like a woman who knows what she wants," he managed somehow, while her tongue licked at the tiny bruise she'd just given him.

"I like kissing. I used to do it for hours and it drove—"

He sank his fingers into her hair and tugged gently, and she got the hint. "You're right. No ghosts of the past allowed here."

"Talk to me," he whispered, drowning in the luscious scent of her. Usually, he wasn't into chatting during sex. But this encounter with this woman was the farthest thing from his usual anything. He didn't even know what it was. "Tell me what you love about kissing so much."

"I love the anticipation of what comes next. I like how you can do it slow and soft or fast and hard and how your entire body starts thrumming like this…" she punctuated each word with a long kiss with slow flicks of her tongue and Vikram felt as if she'd been sent to steal his sanity. He wanted to tell her they could do a lot of other things like that too fast or slow, soft or hard. That he would be more than happy to help her discover all of them. That he wanted her name and her address and that he wanted her in his bed tomorrow night too.

Instead, he kept quiet and let her drive him mad.

She dragged her mouth to his jaw, then to his neck again.

His fingers tightened on her hips when she caught the skin at his shoulder between her teeth and sucked. A groan ripped through him, his erection pressing painfully against his trousers.

And then she was back to claim his mouth again. This time, it was a soft melding of mouths, an exploration after the initial frenzy. She cupped his cheek and tugged until he looked up.

Her eyes looked like molten pools of desire, her breasts rose and fell in concert with his own breaths. Her mouth was swollen from kissing him, and Vikram wanted more.

"This is good, isn't it? Between us?" she asked.

Vikram dipped his finger into her mouth. His body hummed for the same caress somewhere else when she licked his finger and wrapped her tongue around it. "It's better than good, Dream Girl. It's…fantastic. The number of dirty things I could do to you while you chat away in my ear… I can't wait to discover all of them."

Naina ducked her face into his neck and took a deep breath.

He smelled like leather and whiskey and something else, far too decadent to be anything other than pure Vikram. His heart thundered against hers, his body a lean fortress of warmth and hardness combined. He wasn't rippling with overdeveloped muscles as every other Bollywood hero seemed to be these days, but rather there was a lean, wiry strength to him that surrounded her. She ran her hands over those taut muscles now, loving the solid feel of him.

His mouth, God, she couldn't believe how good it felt against hers. Couldn't believe how he'd let her take the lead. Play with him. Tease and taunt him. And not once had he pushed for more. Not once had he prodded her along as if the kiss was nothing but a precursor to something else. As if it was a necessary punishment he was sitting through just to get to the end result.

No, she wasn't going to compare him to anyone else in her life.

Vikram Raawal, she was realizing, was more of a hero than the world realized. And he was here with her, fully, in this moment. Hers to do whatever she wanted with. But only for tonight. Only now.

There was no future, no happily-ever-after. Not with Vikram Raawal. Not for her. And she wanted more. She wanted everything tonight.

She sent her fingers on a query up his neck, into his thick hair. "Vikram?"

His head jerked up, his light brown eyes intent on her face. His nostrils flared, something almost like victory dancing in his eyes before he turned his gaze back to her fingers. As if he couldn't allow himself to be distracted for too long from her body and its secrets. He kissed, licked and tongued each knuckle with an erotic thoroughness that sent tremors through her lower belly. "Yes, Dream Girl?"

"All those things you mentioned you wanted to do to me, with me…" She licked her suddenly dry lips when he looked up. "Can we do them? Like, right now?"

He straightened up from his lounging position with a grace Naina knew she'd never have. When he'd walked in earlier, he'd looked so polished, sophisticated, so out of her reach he might as well be the sun to her earth. Now, she could see that his lower lip had a small bump where she'd bitten it, his collar had a stain of her lipstick on it and his expensively cut hair stood up in all directions after she'd pulled her fingers through it.

He looked…suitably rumpled. A little changed. More approachable. As if she'd left her mark on him.

Tomorrow, even a few hours later, all those changes would be gone. He would go back to being Vikram Raawal, the man who had a multi-crore industry at his feet, worshipping him, wanting a piece of him. But Naina wanted him to remember tonight—and her—for a long time to come.

He licked her lower lip, before tugging it gently between his teeth. "Are you sure?" he whispered against her mouth.

"Yes, please. One hundred percent," she said fervently.

"How old are you, Dream Girl?"

"Old enough to know my own mind."

"Answer me."

"Twenty-four."

He blew out a breath and shook his head.

"Oh, come on, Vikram, I know you're a few years older than me, but don't go all honorable on me now. I'm all keyed up. If you leave me hanging tonight, I might have to go knock on my ex's door and beg him—"

He pressed his palm to her mouth and Naina licked it. She tasted salt and sweat, and she felt as if she was drunk on a heady cocktail that was all him.

"No, you won't. That rat doesn't deserve you. And I—"

"Do you want the whole lecture about arbitrary constructs again? Because the first one was just a warm-up."

"God, no!"

"This is an experience I want to have with you, not a gift I'm bestowing on you. Not a thing that will devalue me if I give it away. If you think my ex should have respected my no, then you should respect my yes."

"I don't have condoms on me, but I swear to you I'm clean."

She blushed. "I'm clean and on the pill. Have been for a while."

"In preparation for the rat?" he asked, scrunching his face distastefully.

She shrugged. "He dumped me just as I was ready to make that commitment. Finally. Poor guy put in two years' worth of hard work and persuasion and never got to reap the results."

"He's a fool, Dream Girl. And don't talk about yourself like that." He took her mouth in a rough kiss so full of passion that it clearly told her how much control he'd exerted when she'd been all over him earlier. How much he'd let her explore him. His forehead pressed against hers in a gesture that spoke of a tenderness she wouldn't have associated with this man. "So you've never done this before?"

"I hated being constantly pressured. But I knew my mind when I didn't want it. Just as I know for certain that

I do now. I want to have sex. With you. Right now, Vikram, if you please?"

"It pleases me a lot. And if you want to stop, anytime, all you have to do is say so."

She nodded, and bit her lip. Excitement fizzed through her like the bubbles in a bottle of the best champagne. She was nervous too, of course.

He was used to women who were size zero and highly sophisticated. She was…nowhere close to either. The dark couldn't hide her little ice-cream bulge, could it? And for all the kissing she'd practiced, she hadn't ever been anywhere near a man's…thing.

His long fingers wrapped around her nape, drawing her down toward him. Another hard, purely possessive kiss that made her breath ragged in her throat. The kiss held promise and demand in equal measures.

She traced her fingers over his collarbone, mesmerized by the play of light on his skin. "Hey, Vikram?"

"Hmm…" he said, licking her lip. "God, I can't get enough of you saying my name."

"Will you tell me how to make it good for you?"

His hand, that had been pulling the hem of her dress up, up and away, stilled. On her highly sensitive knee. His other hand, playing over the overtly bare neckline that her dress exposed, like she was the strings of a guitar, also halted its movements. "What?" His voice sounded so husky that she barely heard him.

"I want this to be really good for you. And except for some bad porn, I don't know my way around a man's… bits. So some instruction would be much appreciated."

"Yeah?"

"Don't you dare laugh at me. This is important to me."

"Move further up on my thighs then. All the way into my lap."

Naina felt fire run down her spine at the command in his voice. There was something to be said for being ordered by the Bollywood heartthrob Vikram Raawal, to climb atop him, like he was her favorite two-wheeler.

"What are you laughing about?"

She let him see the pleasure she was getting out of every minute of this. "Just that, it is kind of fun being ordered around by you."

His nostrils flared, he threw his head back and let out a groan. "I was wrong in my estimation of you."

Keeping her fingers on the solid breadth of his shoulders, Naina did as she was told. He jerked her close the last inch. Her thighs now grazed the muscular sides of his abdomen and beneath her...he was clearly rock hard. And growing.

Head thrown back, Naina let out a soft moan, her hips wriggling until he was at the exact place where she needed him. At the aching place between her thighs. Hands on his shoulders, she rocked back and forth until their combined moans filled the air.

"You feel that, Dream Girl?" he groaned.

"In every cell of my being," Naina replied, a glorious feeling of warmth and desire running through her veins.

"This is already good for me, love. If it gets any better, it will be over too soon."

"Who... What?" Naina managed to say, when every cell in her being was focused on his questing fingertips. Both of his hands were busy under her dress. He had found the supersensitive skin of her inner thighs and was tracing mesmerizing circles without moving any further north. "You should know, my IQ has already been reduced to half."

Again, another quick swipe of his fingers, and Naina gasped when this time the tip of an index finger grazed the seam of her panties. And then, he was there. Or rather, his wickedly clever fingers were. Playing peekaboo with the seam of her panties. When one finger snuck in under the elastic, Naina went rigid. Anticipation was a concentric yearning in her lower belly. When his fingers teased through the curls at her sex, she buried her face in his neck. "I… I didn't shave down there." She thought she might die if he mocked her.

"I told you before, Dream Girl. I want you exactly as you are. As whoever you are." And then he flicked her most sensitive place in a move that sent shivers through every inch of her. His fingers, she realized, were not just clever. He was a maestro expertly playing his instrument of choice. His thumb stayed loyally at that aching center of her entire being, while his other fingers busied themselves, dipping into the wetness she could feel there. "Oh…" She kept saying the same word, all other faculties reduced to only feeling. She went up on her knees to facilitate his fingers exactly where she wanted them. His mouth, pressed against her neck, erupted into a smile and the vibrations of that laughter rocked through Naina, just as arousing as the fingers he was thrusting into her wet heat.

"Look at me, pretty girl," he said then, and Naina flicked her eyes open, despite the fact that all she wanted to do was drown in the sensation he was creating in her sex. All she wanted to do was focus on it, chase it to its end, until she was nothing else but pleasure.

But there was something to looking into the eyes of the man who was more committed to ensuring your pleasure than you had ever been yourself. There was something to locking eyes with a man who wanted you just as much as you wanted him. Vikram's eyes told her silently, said so many things that his mouth didn't. And Naina was okay with that.

"Keep looking at me, and move. Trust your instincts. Tell me what you want me to do. Tell me how fast, or how slow, or how deep. Tell me where you want my fingers. Tell me where you want my mouth. I'm entirely at your disposal, pretty girl."

His words, in concert with his fingers, pulled at the ever-tightening knot in her lower belly. Naina sent her own hands up her belly to her breasts, already achy and desperate for attention, and she tugged down the bodice of the dress. "Here," she whispered. "I need those clever fingers here too."

"My fingers are far too busy right now." His deep voice had an edge to it. A dark, slumbering quality. "Will my mouth do?"

"Yes, please."

He gave her what she asked for. And even more than that.

In the blink of an eye, Naina found herself drowning in sensation that Vikram created. His mouth painted erotic images over her tight nipples. The sound of him licking them was one she'd never forget. He alternated between them as if he was determined to evoke, to conjure, to pull every inch of sensation out of her body that it was capable of feeling.

His mouth, his fingers, his entire body worked in tandem to push her up and up and up. Her spine arched. And then she was there, thrown into a kaleidoscope of colors and sounds and sensations. Her sex contracted and released and still he kept up the relentless rhythm, dragging it out, prolonging the acute pleasure until tears filled her eyes.

She flopped forward onto him, her arms going tight around him, her face dripping with tears and sweat. She didn't care that she was clinging to him. In this moment, he was hers. She needed an anchor, to come down from the cliff she had just jumped off.

But of course, in her moment of vulnerability, she had misjudged him again.

He held her just as tight as she did him, whispering sweet nothings at her temple, telling her how sexy and how thrilling it was to watch her climax. And she knew he was telling her the truth. Because it was there in his voice. Need rippled through him—his words, his tight body, even in the tension across his face. Naina pulled back. It wasn't enough that she had found satisfaction unlike she had ever known before. She wanted him to find it too. She wanted him to remember her forever. She reached for the seam of his trousers and slowly undid the button and the zipper. She refused to look away from him and he held her gaze too, as if he intended to see into her soul. "I need your words, pretty girl. I need to know you still want this. I need to know you're as desperate as I am in this moment."

"I want you inside me, Vikram. I want you to find satisfaction in my body just as I found it in yours. I want you to wake up tomorrow and think *Oh, my God, that girl rocked my world.*" She dropped her nose against his and smiled up at him. "Is that clear enough?"

"It might hurt. For just a little while."

"I trust you will make it all better after the hurt," she said, a taunt in her tone.

"Of course I will, Dream Girl. Kiss me again," he said simply and Naina complied.

Their kisses went from soft to intense in a matter of seconds. She went from loose and sated to greedy and aroused in minutes. With his hands and mouth, Vikram was everywhere on her skin. Kissing, nipping, licking, until she was a single mass of thrumming sensation. Slowly, he built her up again, until she was panting. Until she was so close to the edge that she could taste it.

He lifted her up and over him, and in the next blink, he was inside her, in a single thrust.

Naina gasped at the thread of pain.

"Shh…look at me, love. Stay here with me," he said, and Naina let his words wash through her. Over her. In this way, he felt as if he was everywhere inside her.

He didn't move. Or even wiggle his hips.

Eyes closed, Naina ran her hands over him. Over that sharp blade of a nose, the surprisingly sweet-tasting mouth, the line of his jaw, to the thud of his heart, to the tautly fascinating map of his abs…her fingers boldly moved down further, to where they were joined together.

Digging her fingers into his shoulders, she pushed up with her thighs and rose up a little, then sank back down. The friction was amazing, the pinch of pain already fading. She did it again, gasping at the thrill that shot through her spine, the tightening knot there…

He moved his palms all over her, just as she'd done to him. Those clever fingers molding and squeezing… "How do you feel now, Dream Girl?"

"It's like a sweet ache, a sense of overwhelming fullness. Vikram?"

His tongue licked at the rigid knot of her nipple. Then he closed those lips over it and tugged, repeating the action, again and again. "Yes, baby?"

"I want to come again," she declared, without an ounce of shyness this time.

She felt his smile near her heart, felt his fingers abandon her breast and when she protested, he took her mouth in such a rough kiss that she felt burned. And then she felt him there, rubbing at her bud, whispering into her ear. "I wish I was a man of beautiful words, Dream Girl." With every word, he thrust up, while pushing his finger down at her center, creating sensations that were amplified a thousand times. "I wish I could describe to you in this moment how beautiful you are…the flush on your skin, the tremble of your lips, the pulse at your neck.

"But I can give you what you want. Tell me again, Dream Girl."

"I want everything. Tonight. Everything you can give me."

And before she could blink, he was lifting her up again, this time pressing her back onto the lounger. And then he was moving inside her again, more deeply than before.

A slow, hard thrust that would have thrown her off the lounger if he wasn't holding her. A swivel of his hips, then another slow drag and every time he did it, the slab of his muscles rubbed her in just the right place and Naina thought she might die if she didn't climax soon.

As if he heard her unsaid plea, his movements became faster, harder, his fingers digging into her hips, causing delicious points of pain that made all the other sensations she was feeling even sharper and brighter.

When Naina would have screamed in ecstasy at the top of her lungs, he covered her mouth with his and swallowed up her pleasure. "Look at me, Dream Girl," he whispered and Naina did and saw his own explosion of pleasure transform his face into a thing of beauty that she would never forget.

This night, this man, these moments of pure, joyous pleasure… Naina knew she was forever changed by it.

CHAPTER FOUR

"VIKRAM RAAWAL'S LATEST blockbuster is nothing more than a cheesy, gratuitously violent, sexist romp…"

"Hell, Rita, turn the bloody radio off!"

Without waiting for a reply, Vikram hung up the phone and then slammed his hand against the steering wheel.

God, he'd just snapped at his very pregnant secretary for no fault of hers. But listening to the same lousy headlines that had been on every TV and radio station for the last week meant his temper was hanging by a thin thread.

Pulling his Range Rover onto the unpaved land at the back of his grandmother's bungalow, he called Rita back, and begged for forgiveness. He laid his head back against the seat and exhaled. Of course, the media was having a field day with the criticism being showered on his latest hit, even though it was raking it up at the box office.

But for once Vikram didn't really give a damn about the bad publicity even, if the entire world thought he was a sellout. If the whole lot of them boycotted his movies.

He *should* care, however.

This was business and he'd always looked at it without getting bogged down by sentiment or ego or prejudice.

But he couldn't give a damn, if he tried. *That* was more worrying than any of the cutting reviews.

"Your life is going to turn upside down."

The grave announcement the astrologer his sister Anya visited every month had made after looking at Vikram's star chart came back to him now. He'd only gone because Anya had insisted. And because Anya had been rather quiet recently and that had worried him.

Worrying about his crazy family's antics was second nature to him ever since he'd found out as a young man that in just a few short years his father had gambled away the entire fortune his grandfather had amassed and that Raawal House was on the verge of collapse. Then came the worry about Virat's daredevil ways after the huge fallout between him and his parents. Then it had been Daadi's heart attack. Then discovering his eighteen-year-old sister was pregnant with a fortune hunter's child, who'd hightailed it out of town the minute he'd realized Anya wasn't the easy express train to fame and fortune.

He *didn't like* involving himself in their lives, as Virat had claimed during their recent fight. He was not a *"pain in the backside control freak who got his kicks from directing his family members' lives as if they were his expensive ivory chess pieces."*

Virat had always had a way with words. But Vikram refused to feel guilty.

Their own parents' incapability of actually acting like parents had forced him into that surrogate role. For as long as he could remember, he'd protected Virat and Anya. Was he supposed to suddenly stop doing it now? Of course, he'd been angry and defensive when he'd asked Virat to prove with his actions that he could be responsible for himself. Which had spiraled into yet another row over what was the definition of respectability and responsibility.

You've forgotten what it is to take risks, Vikram. You've forgotten what it means to live.

Having spent his entire childhood with parents who

thrived on drama and chaos, Vikram loathed losing control. He hated the chaos that emotional vulnerability brought with it. He hated being dependent on anyone else for his happiness. God, he'd lived his life like that all through his childhood and adolescence.

He'd worked hard to bring order to the chaos, and yet suddenly, he felt like he was losing it all now. In both his professional and personal lives. His agent had recently informed him that the music director Vikram had wanted for his production company's next film had refused to be involved in the project. The man was brilliant and had always hated Vikram's guts.

The only silver lining from the entirety of this year had been the few hours he'd spent with Dream Girl at the party last week. He rubbed a hand over his face and laughed. God, he was actually referring to her as Dream Girl in his own head now. Surely he was going insane.

It had been a one-night stand. He'd had one-night stands before. God, yes, the sex, the connection between them had been extraordinary.

But the woman and the memory of the few hours he'd spent with her wouldn't leave him alone. He wanted her. Again. But she clearly didn't want him. Not for anything more than a few hours of fantasy. Because she hadn't got in touch with him. And he still didn't know who she was. He'd fallen asleep for just a couple of minutes in the quiet darkness of the library and when he'd jerked awake, she'd vanished into thin air.

However, what had become inconveniently clear to him over the last week was how much he wanted to believe her when she'd assured him she'd keep their tryst a secret. And his cynical assumption that she'd reveal herself to him, to the whole world, sooner or later.

After all, he was Vikram Raawal. Every woman wanted a piece of him.

God, he could just see those twinkling eyes widen and her mouth narrow in disapproval before she told him he shouldn't believe his own egotistical hype so much.

A strange cocktail of relief and disappointment coursed through him. Relief because their strange encounter couldn't be unmarred by reality now.

He'd seen enough of life to know the kind of visceral connection they'd shared couldn't be sustained. A few more hours together and she would have surely disappointed him. And he'd have disillusioned her with his own cynical nature.

He should be thankful she hadn't reappeared.

He was thirty-six and clearly in the middle of a midlife crisis. On a good day, he was cynical, grumpy and an unsentimental bastard who only cared about his family's reputation and creating the next hit for Raawal House. He didn't know what a healthy relationship between a man and woman even constituted. For all his stardom, and wealth and "stunning good looks," he wasn't any woman's best chance at a long, happy relationship.

Dream Girl...wasn't just any woman, though. God, she was only twenty-four, a veritable novice when it came to life experience. And yet, she'd been so mature. So funny. So...full of life. So damn sexy. So...out of his reach, for all the power and privilege he held in his palm.

And for the first time in his life, he really wanted something very badly and yet couldn't have it.

His mood went from grumpy to downright crabby when he entered his grandmother's bungalow and discovered Virat had stolen away Daadi for the day. He accepted

Ramu Kaka's offer of a cup of chai instead of immediately heading out.

Daadi's yearly pilgrimage to London meant she'd leave tomorrow. Since he had to be on a flight to the Maldives in a few days, he wouldn't see her again for three months.

Three months was a long time when one's grandmother was eighty-three years old. A flash of fear struck him straight in his chest at the thought of the world without Daadi in it. It was infuriating to realize some things would always be out of one's control. Especially the things that mattered the most.

Like Daadi, and Dream Girl.

He laughed so hard that tears pricked his eyes. Daadi and the Dream Girl sounded like the title of one of those artsy, cutting comedy films that a brilliant genius like Virat would make. His cell phone rang.

He yelled at Virat, got scolded by Daadi for yelling, and then made her promise she'd be back in two months this time rather than three.

"Vicky, *beta*, look after Naina for me, *haa*?" Daadi said, finally getting to the point. "She's trying to find work in the film industry and it's not like you to be harsh toward someone so innocent."

He hung up, after promising Daadi he would look after that "poor innocent lamb" with the decidedly cutting tongue. But like it or not, he did owe the woman an apology, for more than one thing. Grumpy and arrogant he might be, but he knew when to admit he was wrong. And he had been kind of nasty to her.

The creaky whine of the old gramophone player and an old, slow song cut into his quiet reverie. He thought the language might be Tamil, but he didn't understand the words. The soulful melody suited his own mood perfectly. He took the winding stairs up, toward the sound coming from one of the back bedrooms, anticipation building inside him, just as the melody came to a crescendo.

He found Naina Menon crooning softly along with the song, her small nose noticeably red, wrapping a beautiful, expensive-looking green sari in layers of tissue paper with the utmost care. A battered-looking suitcase lay open behind her, with a rumpled duffel bag. The bracelets she wore on one wrist tinkled every time she spread out another layer of tissue paper.

The song went through a particularly maudlin stretch. Ms. Menon laid her head against the wall, bringing one knee up. Losing herself completely in the song. She wasn't crying and yet Vikram felt as if she was on the verge of it. He couldn't move, transfixed by the simple and yet stunning beauty of the woman.

He'd always considered the expression of too much emotion to be a vulgar display. Maybe because he'd been exposed to such excessive amounts of it while growing up. Every day, there had been some unavoidable drama with his parents, until Daadi, who'd been living with them since his grandfather died, had moved out again, bringing Vikram with her back to this bungalow.

But Ms. Menon…it was obvious she was struggling with something. Her entire body seemed to move as one with the song.

She wore another oversized yellow kurta over blue jeans, with those dangling earrings again, and her untamed hair was held together by a small clip that was clearly losing its fight. Jet-black corkscrew curls framed a halo around her face. A colorful, flimsy scarf hung around her neck, a long, beaded necklace with a metallic pendant moving every time she took a deep breath.

She looked like the words from the song given beautiful

form. Words he didn't understand technically and yet the meaning they conveyed sank deep into his bones.

Loneliness. A desperate need for comfort. The very human need for companionship.

The song thrummed through him with a familiarity he didn't understand. He looked anew at the woman, marveling at how easily he could sense her own confusion, pain and something else.

His first impression of her had been of a deceptively plain woman. And the flash of attraction he'd felt for her had blindsided him. She wasn't his type.

Although, after the encounter with Dream Girl, he was rethinking arbitrary constructs like types. Questioning everything he'd been conditioned to think from a young age thanks to his constant exposure to the film industry. About beauty and art and authenticity. About the masks they all wore.

Now, in this moment, he realized calling Naina Menon plain was like calling a sunflower boring compared to some exotic, temperamental flower. Slowly, the song came to an end. The deep breath she took sent her breasts rising and falling and he watched, far too fascinated.

A breeze flew through the open windows, and the scarf flew away from her neck, revealing a fading pinkish-blue smudge on the area between her neck and shoulder.

Vikram stiffened, a thread of something piercing him with a sudden intensity.

She looked up and jerked. "How did you find…"

Coming away from the wall, she slammed her palm against her mouth and launched onto her feet so fast that she stumbled over the open suitcase lying at her feet.

It sent her toppling forward.

Vikram reached for her instantly, trying to overcome her momentum. She fell onto him with a thud that knocked her head into the underside of his chin. His teeth rattled inside his mouth and a wave of pain vibrated up his jaw. But even through the jarring sensation, there was a familiarity in the way her body pressed against his. A subtle wisp of a jasmine scent teasing his nostrils. A fragment of sound that had fallen from her mouth that reminded him of how Dream Girl had sounded when she…

"Let me go." He heard the words as if through a long tunnel, while scents and sensations poured through him. "Please. I'm fine," she said, louder this time, and Vikram released his hold.

She rubbed at her wrist as though his touch had burned her. "I'm sorry," he said, not surprised to find his voice gruff.

Did this midlife crisis mean he was going to behave like a randy goat with every woman he came across? Hadn't Virat teased him he was turning grumpier than usual because *"your testosterone levels are falling and you clearly aren't the powerful, macho guy who attracts all the women anymore"*?

With Naina Menon's warm imprint still on his own body, Vikram felt no lack of testosterone flowing through him. In fact, it felt like his libido was working overtime for the short contact had made his every nerve ending sing with desire.

"No, don't apologize." Ms. Menon cleared her throat, and when she spoke again, she sounded different, in control. "Thanks for catching me. You saved me from a bad fall."

He didn't say anything. Just stared at her, a hint of premonition gathering at the base of his neck, tightening it unbearably.

This uptight, self-righteous, morality inspector couldn't be his fun, bold, sexy Dream Girl, could she?

"What were you about to say when you saw me?" he demanded, the words coming out of his mouth in a rush.

A slight dusting of pink claimed her cheeks and she turned away. "Nothing. My thoughts were somewhere else." She threw a look at him over her shoulder. As if to confirm he was still there. "Daadiji left with Virat and your sister. Anya kept saying you wanted to see your grandmother, but he didn't listen. They won't be back tonight and Daadiji is leaving for London tomorrow."

When he didn't show any sign of leaving, she turned around again, folding her arms under her breasts. "Is there anything else I can help you with?"

"Are you dismissing me from my own home, Ms. Menon?" he said, suddenly feeling a lot more comfortable. Riling her up, he was realizing, was making his own grumpy mood better.

She opened her mouth, closed it, then opened it again.

"You're upset. What's happened?" he asked softly. Something was off about her reaction to him. About his reaction to her. About this whole thing.

"I'm not upset," she denied, her voice full of a shakiness that belied her words. Her dark brown gaze met his briefly and again, he felt that jolt of electricity thrum through him. Another pair of beautiful eyes the exact same dark brown as hers had held his gaze boldly while he'd lost himself in her warmth.

He walked across the room, and leaned against the wall. He wanted to sit down but he saw the panic in her eyes, the tensing of her shoulders with every breath he took. She was nervous in his presence.

Because they had argued with each other last time he'd been here? Because she didn't like him? Or for another, much more sensational reason?

She sighed. "I got some news today that upset me a

little… On top of learning that Daadiji's leaving for London tomorrow. It's been a too much kind of day."

He nodded absently.

She was the right height for Dream Girl, though that's all he had in the physical arena to go by. There was no way he could have missed that mass of curly hair. But hair could be straightened and he knew first-hand the miracles makeup could achieve.

Not that this woman needed makeup to look stunning.

So if it was her, why all the secrecy? What did she hope to achieve by pretending as if they didn't know each other in the most intimate way? Had it truly been a fantasy of a few hours? Damn the woman, why did she have to complicate this by not admitting it?

"I have her permission to stay here tonight. You can call Virat and confirm that if you would like."

"You think I'm waiting to throw you out right now?"

She shrugged.

Vikram bit his lip and then went for it. "I apologize for speaking harshly to you the first time we met. And for assigning cheap, utterly unfair motives to your presence here. I have had enough calls from Daadi to understand that she really appreciated your company and assistance these past two months."

"It was my pleasure," she added, without really acknowledging his apology.

So, the woman held grudges, huh? "What were you doing for Virat before you came here to help Daadi?"

"Just some research for another one of his projects. I have a half-finished PhD in film history so I was qualified."

He swallowed his frustration and nodded at the gramophone player.

"What was the song you were listening to?"

"Oh, it's from the nineteen-fifties. I found the record while sorting out your grandfather's old things." For the flash of a second, excitement lit up her face. And he saw that same incandescent quality that had held him breathless in the dim light of the library. "Some of those records are priceless. Your grandmother said I could have this one. But if you want it—"

"I don't give a rat's ass about that old record. Stop casting me as some mustache-twirling villain."

Her mouth twitched, but she still didn't meet his gaze.

"Tell me what the song means," he said, wanting to see that joy return to her eyes.

She frowned. "Why?"

"There's no ulterior motive, Ms. Menon. I know most songs from that era but I'd never heard of that one."

"It's in Tamil," she said.

"I do know songs outside of Hindi. Raawal House used to produce a lot of South Indian movies at that time."

"It's by this lady who didn't find a lot of commercial success. In fact, I think it's the only film that she sang for."

"How do you know so much about it?"

"Oh, it was my mother's favorite song. I heard it all the time growing up. She would play it and walk around our house acting out the song. She was very… Do you understand the words?"

He shook his head.

"She's saying goodbye to someone she loves. Mama always said the best thing we could do for ourselves was to understand what we were feeling. It's hard to acknowledge our own emotions sometimes. Especially when they make us realize something uncomfortable about ourselves. It's strange, isn't it?"

The restlessness within him this last year, this constant need for something more in his life and yet not knowing what the more was…her words suddenly made him understand himself a little better.

She wasn't aware of him anymore, caught up in whatever put that look in her eyes. "What's strange?" he asked quietly.

"Even until last year, that song was a big source of comfort to me. I'd play it and go back to those happy times where I trailed behind her through the house. Now, it feels like the song doesn't have that same sense of comfort and familiarity that I associated with it for so long.

"I feel like I've lost her all over again."

"Maybe it's just your perception of yourself that's changing, Ms. Menon. Maybe you simply aren't that heart-broken little girl anymore. Maybe you're coming into your own and no longer need the false comfort of an old song," he said, holding her gaze.

Falling into those beautiful brown depths one word at a time. There was honesty and intelligence and such strength in those eyes. Such heart and heat in them. Just like that, suddenly he knew. In his heart, of all places, which he could truthfully say had never before known anything with such certainty.

Naina Menon was his Dream Girl.

"Are you mocking me?"

He blinked. "Not at all."

Thoughts and consequences ran through his head like a film on fast forward. What did it mean? Why had she done it? Was he simply supposed to behave as if that night hadn't happened? Was that what she meant to do? The idea of leaving it up in the air, the idea of just…letting that night remain between them like some fantasy illusion made the hair on his neck stand up. "In fact, this is probably the second most meaningful conversation I've had in years."

Her head jerked up, her eyes searching his face with an

intensity that bordered on interest. No, something more. Not fear, no. She wasn't afraid of him. The last thing he wanted was for Naina to think he'd abuse his power in this, his knowledge of her identity in any way. "Then that sounds incredibly wise."

"I'm not all perfect good looks," he said wickedly, wondering if by repeating what she'd said to him that night, he could draw out a confession from her.

"Wow, looks, a sense of humor and a deep understanding of my psyche. I almost want to put your poster up on my wall again."

"Did you have my poster up on your wall, Ms. Menon?" he asked smoothly.

She blinked and it was all Vikram could do to stop himself from reaching for her.

He tucked his hands behind him to arrest the overwhelming impulse. Damn it, the woman had been playful and funny at the ball and he'd lapped it up. Today, she looked bashful and wary and he still liked her. Whatever facet she revealed of herself, he had a feeling he would appreciate it.

"A long time ago, yes. After your first movie. Most of the heroes were older men for decades and then there was suddenly you, the boy next door, the college student, the idealistic young man. No wonder it launched you into stardom.

"I'm not that schoolgirl anymore. And you're not perfect hero material, this larger-than-life boy whose broad shoulders could carry every girl's dreams. You're…"

Their eyes locked and Vikram had the strangest sensation. As if anticipation was his breath, ballooning up in his chest. Waiting for more words from this woman who seemed to see through him with such unsettling ease. Waiting for more of her devastating insight.

"What am I now, Ms. Menon?"

"You're…human," she said simply. "Like the rest of us."

A lightness filled his entire being and Vikram felt as if he had moved from the shadows into bright sunshine. As if, after living in the harsh, unnatural spotlight of fame all his life, he was suddenly being seen for the very first time.

"Which also means you're my equal." He laughed at the relief that poured through him. "Not that it was ever in question."

A hint of pink crept up her cheeks. He felt like he'd won something for the simple fact of surprising her. "Did I render you mute? Then I guess I'm not as bad with words as Virat would like us all to believe."

"I don't think you're bad with words at all, Mr. Raawal. I think you just don't feel people are usually worth using that skill on."

"How did she die? Your mother?"

She turned to him and the ache of grief in her eyes almost knocked him flat. "She didn't. She walked out on my father and me when I was ten. Left a note saying her heart wasn't in the life we had and disappeared in the middle of the night."

He felt a burst of such fury on her behalf that he couldn't speak for a few minutes. "I'm sorry about that." He racked his mind for more words. The right thing to say. "There were days I wished my mother or father had walked out in the middle of the night," he finally said.

She laughed and then sobered up, all before he could blink twice. "Oh, that's such an awful thing to say. Thanks for trying to make me feel better, Mr. Raawal, but you're absolutely horrific at it."

"I really wasn't joking."

"Of course, you…" Her mouth fell open and she closed it with a click. "I'm sorry about…that."

He shrugged, pretending to not show how shocked he was by his own admission. He could see it in her eyes too. He never ever spoke to the media about his family. It was none of their business. His parents had provided enough fodder for the gossips with their high-profile separations every time his father was unfaithful and the subsequent reunions every time his mother forgave him, resulting in an endless vicious cycle of hate and love.

In the beginning, fixing the reputation of Raawal House had been an act of survival. With all the company's assets tied up in sinking films and unwise investments, the only thing he'd had to start with was the respect and prestige his grandfather Vijay Raawal's name still commanded in some circles. Producers and investors had trusted him, his word, had seen something in him that had reminded them of Daadu.

For fifteen years, he'd forced his family by every means available to him, to behave. Constantly herding them to walk a respectful line so that he could rebuild the reputation of Raawal House.

But somewhere along the line, he'd lost his own way. He'd started believing in his own invincibility. He'd started overcompensating for all the negative attention his parents had brought to the family by keeping Virat and Anya on too tight a leash and then condemning them for any missteps they might take. By stifling them. His need to keep them safe and secure, to protect them from the same kind of chaos that had disrupted his childhood and adolescence had been somehow twisted up and morphed into needing to control every minute detail of their lives.

Of his own life.

But with Naina, it was easy to speak of his family. Easy to share the tales of dysfunction and drama that had made up most of his childhood. Though he had absolutely no idea how they'd ended up trading childhood pain of all things. Crossing swords was more their style, wasn't it?

And if this woman was his Dream Girl too…she'd unraveled him not once, but twice now. Every rational instinct in him, every voice he'd honed to be in total control of himself warned him to get the hell out of there. To walk away from her and never return.

Instead, he said, "My mother wasn't the most spectacular actress in Bollywood over the span of two decades for nothing. After a while, I think she saw no distinction between her public persona and the private one. Anyway, I survived. I had Daadi at the worst of times." Thinking of this fierce woman in front of him as a lost, motherless little girl made his chest tight. "I hope you had someone too."

"I had Papa." She scrunched her brow. "Or rather he had me. He was devastated by her leaving. We somehow muddled through. Later, he married my stepmother. She and her daughter Maya…" She smiled, and there was that fleeting happiness in her eyes again. "We became each other's saving grace. Have you heard of my stepmother Jaya Pandit? She's also an actress, although she's not hugely successful."

He nodded, vaguely remembering a short, pretty woman with intelligent eyes and a colorful personality. "She's the one developing a reputation for being difficult and abrasive. Didn't she get into a mad scuffle with some producer and that ridiculous TV channel got it all on camera?"

She winced and Vikram regretted the distaste he was sure had shown on his face. "It's easy for you to look down on her. But that's the only way Jaya Ma knows how to survive in your horrid industry. She put on fifteen kilos for a role only to be told by the producer that he'd given it to his wife's cousin. It's been…hard for her. If she isn't being turned down for being too loud, she's simply forgotten."

"The other news you got to make it a 'too much kind of day'…is it about her?"

"No, my stepsister Maya got accepted to a university in the States. She'll be leaving soon." She tried to hide the pain in her eyes with an empty smile. But one thing was certain; this woman was no actress.

She wore her emotions on her face with such an artless honesty that Vikram found it hard to look at. It was like looking straight at the sun and you couldn't do it for too long. You simply closed your eyes and basked in the warmth of it. "I'll miss her…she's my sister and best friend rolled into one. I'm thrilled for her though." A forced chuckle this time. "She's the brilliant one in the family. And the beauty, too, actually."

"You had no idea that she'd even applied to study abroad, did you? And yet you value her so much."

She shrugged. "Maya's always talked about pursuing a career in academia, getting into one of the prestigious research laboratories. Which segues perfectly into…" She looked up. Shoulders straight, she took a deep breath. Readying for battle? "Daadiji mentioned your secretary is going on maternity leave early because of complications, and that you're looking for an urgent temporary stand-in until her proper replacement arrives. Give me the chance to work for you."

"What?"

"I want to come work for you. You're going on a writing trip to the Maldives for a few weeks, right? With Daadiji going to London for the next two months, I'm available and I'm also kind of cash-strapped."

"You must be desperate if you're willing to work for me, Ms. Menon."

She picked up the notepad that had been sitting on the bed. Vikram saw the numbers she'd been adding up and scratching out, before she hid it behind her back. Even with the quick glimpse he got, it was clear the second column far outweighed the first. "I have a lot of expenses," she said evasively.

"Why can't your sister get a job?"

"I told you. She just got admitted into a renowned university. She can't give up her education."

"What was it you said about your half-finished PhD?"

"I had to quit when Papa became very ill because someone had to nurse him; Maya was too busy and Jaya Ma too distressed to do it. Now, with the medical bills and the loan payment on the house, without Maya earning a paycheck, it will be very tight. I can't afford to go back and finish my PhD."

He reached around her to grab the pad. Embarrassment filled her cheeks. "We've all been there, Ms. Menon. What's the loan for?" he asked, tapping the big number.

"Papa took a loan against the house to pay for Jaya Ma's cosmetic procedures to enable her to get more film roles, but she still hasn't found enough work. If I don't keep up with the payments, the bank will seize the house I grew up in. We rent it out because it's cheaper for us to share a flat."

Ten different ideas rose to his mouth about how she could cut these expenses in half. But he kept them to himself. The last thing he wanted to do was make her defensive again. "You will have no…problems taking orders from me? Haven't you heard the horror stories about how this industry treats personal assistants?"

"None of them have been about you. In fact, you have the stellar reputation of being a fair boss. Even Jaya Ma has nothing bad to say about you and believe me, she has an opinion on everyone."

"Ahh…but none of my staff has ever laid into me with such cutting condemnation about my life."

She nodded. "Of course, I said things to you that I had no right to."

He crossed his legs and smiled. But deep inside, he was sorely disappointed. Was she going to turn out like the rest of the damn world now? Pander to him just because she wanted something from him? Stroke his ego all out of proportion because he was in a position to help her out financially? "I'm all ears if you want to apologize."

"I agree that I had no right to say those words to you. But it doesn't mean that what I said was untrue. Even if I say sorry, it won't really be genuine. So do you still want my apology?"

A thrill shot through him at the defiant tilt of her chin.

There was an undeniable attraction between them. He'd known that before she'd bitten into him that very first time. But the interesting thing was that it was still there, shimmering in the air between them. In the way she greedily studied his face but looked away when he met her gaze.

In the way the air charged between them.

That was two unusual women that had snared his attention in less than one week. Not a coincidence at all—seeing as they were the same person.

But Dream Girl had made it clear that she'd been looking for a fantasy for only one night.

"You're consistent, Ms. Menon. I'll give you that."

"I couldn't stand it if you thought I was a hypocrite."

"For God's sake! Don't be ashamed of wanting a better life. Of using the opportunities and people that come your way to build that better life. Or you'll be left behind while they all use you to climb up their own ladder. Like I assume your stepmother and stepsister are doing."

"That's a horrible thing to say about them! Jaya Ma and Maya are my family."

"And you think family doesn't manipulate and use you?"

"Please, don't. You don't know us. If you want me to say sorry for everything I've ever said to you and beg you for this job, then I will do it. I'm—"

He pressed his hand against her mouth in a sudden move that surprised even him. His heartbeat was loud in his ears as the incredible softness of her mouth pressed into his palm. The warmth of her lips singed his skin. The skin of her jaw was silky under the pads of his fingers and he wanted to keep them there forever.

Eyes wide, she stared at him. The same sensual shock traveled through him. There was something about this woman that undid him on a level he didn't understand. That made excitement thrum through his blood.

"No, Ms. Menon," he finally said, pulling away his hand. No movement had ever cost him as much willpower as he'd just had to exert to pull away from her. "I will not be responsible for bringing you that low. I won't have that sin at my feet."

For once, she said nothing. Only continued to stare at him as if she meant to eat him up.

He moved away from her, wondering if he was going mad. Was he actually considering her request? This woman knew him like no one else did. She wanted to go on pretending that they had not been intimate with each other on a level that moved beyond just the physical. She...had the knack of twisting him up, of shaking up rules he'd lived by for years. And still...

If he took away this opportunity from her when she clearly needed it, what kind of a man did it make him?

Was he going to hold the insanity of that night against her? Was he going to be a petulant little man, a shadow of his father, just because she wouldn't admit to him that she wanted him?

God, no!

And even if she admitted to him that it had been her, what would he do with that information? Offer her another one-night stand? A fling that would only hurt her in the end? A relationship that he would walk away from as soon as he became bored? Because, it was inevitable that he would.

He turned around to face her. "If I agree, there will be a clear hierarchy between us. I would be your boss and you my assistant. Not my personal morality advisor. Neither will I allow a repetition of those lectures you're really fond of spouting."

"Right, of course! You won't even know I'm there, except to say yes to whatever you say." She took a deep breath. "And after it's over, you'll never hear from me again."

"What the hell does that mean?" he said with a frown, not liking that idea one bit. Just like that, she got under his skin again. Made dust of his own damned rules. "I thought your aim was to work in the film industry. Or did I misunderstand Daadi?"

She shrugged. "It's clear that you're doing this to honor Daadiji's wishes to look after me, Mr. Raawal. I won't take advantage of her good nature or your sense of obligation. I don't like lingering where I'm not wanted."

"No, you prefer to hide from real life, don't you? From your stepmother, from your stepsister, from…anything that's uncomfortable, no? You prefer to escape. Live life in stolen moments under darkness and disguises."

Her hands fisted by her sides, her eyes glinting with a brightness that made them look like large pools. Anger vibrated from her, as honest and pure as the laughter she'd delighted him with that night.

He waited, breath on hold, for her to lose the tightly held control, to come at him, cutting words and all. His heart beat at a pace that drummed loud in his ears. It shook him to realize how much he wanted her to admit it had been her that night at the ball.

How much he wanted to see the same laughter and desire in her eyes when she looked at him now. Whatever common ground they'd achieved unwittingly in the last hour was gone now. And maybe it was for the best, he realized, especially if they were to spend several weeks together in close quarters.

"You don't know anything about me," she said finally, her breasts still rising and falling. "Not my fears, nor my dreams."

With that fierce statement, she firmly slammed the door on the self-indulgent drama he was forcing on them both. Not by a flicker of an eyelid did she show that she got his pointed remark about living life under darkness and disguises. But... Vikram knew that face. He'd witnessed the most intimate pleasure and joy and irreverence written on it even while it had been more than half covered by the mask she'd worn.

And that was for the best. There was no permutation of events in which he could see her in his future on a permanent basis.

"Your days and nights will be mine, Ms. Menon. I will ask you to fetch coffee, dry cleaning, send gifts to friends and family, even break up with my exes. Are you quite sure you have the constitution to quietly take orders from me without any further preaching?"

There was a minute hesitation he'd have missed if he wasn't obsessed with every nuance of her face. "I'll just pretend that you're the most fascinating man I've ever met. And keep any criticism to myself."

"Oh, I wouldn't want you to curb your opinions, Ms. Menon. What would the world be if it didn't have your tart tongue in it?"

He walked out of her room, leaving her steaming mad. His own mouth was curved into a wide smile and Vikram realized he hadn't felt this good in a long time. If ever.

CHAPTER FIVE

"YOU PREFER TO live life in stolen moments under darkness and disguises."

Vikram's parting shot still haunted her as the taxi drove along a narrow, winding road on the outskirts of the city leading to a private airfield.

Had he already realized she was the woman from the masked ball?

No, he couldn't. She looked so different, he couldn't possibly have recognized her.

That comment had to be his way of aggravating her, as he'd done from the beginning. Getting under her skin just because she'd criticized him.

Why would he give her a job if he knew she was Dream Girl? If he had, he'd have thrown her out of his grandmother's house because he'd automatically assume she was cooking up some nefarious scheme to trap him. At best, he'd have openly asked what her game plan was.

The man that the world saw, and who she had seen initially, was a hardened cynic. Except he hadn't been on the night of the party or a few days ago when he'd asked her about the meaning of her mother's favorite song.

When he'd talked about his own family, when he'd asked after hers, he had been genuine. Oh, of course he was still arrogant, coming to the conclusion that her family were taking advantage of her. But beneath that arrogance, there had been understanding too.

Which had prompted her to blurt out this idea of working for him.

For a few weeks, in gorgeous Maldives, all she'd need to do was keep her head down. Figure out where her future lay after what had happened with Rohan and now that Maya was moving on. Think of how best to save the house.

She paid off the taxi driver, wincing over all the crisp notes she pressed into his hand. It was the price of her pride. Of course, her new boss had offered to pick her up on the way to the private airport on the outskirts of Mumbai that she'd had no idea even existed.

But that meant spending more time in Vikram's company while that gaze of his drilled into her. Being coherent while he permeated the space around her with his vital masculinity was too much to ask of herself right now.

Before that night, her old teenage infatuation with him had been silly, one-dimensional, completely based in fantasyland. Fueled by her mooning over him for years.

Yes, he'd been funny and approachable and let's not forget, hot. But now...now she knew the man and she found him even more fascinating, to say the least.

The taxi driver mumbled something about living the high life and Naina turned away with a smile. He'd no idea how much she wanted to crawl back into the taxi and run away from the man waiting for her on the plane.

That night in the library had been just an accident of nature—like the meteor that hit earth every hundred years. It had shaken up the very foundation of her life and she was still processing the tremors it had left behind. But she knew she couldn't survive a second impact.

With that resolve sorted in her head, she walked up the airplane stairs just as it started to rain, anticipation thrumming through her.

Elegant cream-and-white leather greeted her as she stepped inside, the main cabin more spacious than the entire flat she shared with her stepmom.

Seven pairs of eyes focused on her for a few seconds, took in her pink blouse and colorful skirt and then promptly ignored her. Somehow, she kept her squeal locked away when she recognized her favorite playwright.

From all the information Vikram's secretary had told her over a long phone call, Naina knew she'd be working hard for every rupee she earned over the next few weeks. But talking to Rita without Vikram staring down at her had also helped her realize she could do this job well.

For so long after Mama had left, it had been she who had tried to wrangle the household accounts into some semblance of order, despite her young age. Papa had been so lost without his wife. It had been all he could do to hold onto his tenure at the university.

When he had married her stepmother, Naina had given up control of the family finances to her. Looking back, she should have realized Jaya Ma had no impulse control, whether it came to emotions or finances. She had felt so betrayed when her father had died and she'd discovered the extent of the debts but had shoved the negative emotion away, because really, what was the point? There had been so many things to take care of after he'd died that indulging in her feelings would have been nothing but a petty waste of time.

She handed her pathetic-looking duffel bag into the all-too-elegant flight attendant's hands. After requesting a cup of coffee, Naina settled down into her luxurious, buttery soft leather seat and looked around the unusual assortment of people onboard.

As well as the playwright, there were the Sharmas, who were a writing team of husband and wife, a septuagenarian cinematographer that she recognized only because her father had made it a point to show Naina the vintage movies the man had made, a well-known female novelist, with a man Naina didn't recognize cozying up to her, and the last, a smartly dressed young man around her age with fashionable spectacles and a sharp nose. And a dazzlingly hot smile.

Grateful for a friendly face, Naina joined him.

It took three minutes for them to discover that Ajay was the son of a friend of a colleague of a cousin of Papa's and that he also believed it a great loss that many fabulous filmmakers from South India were barely known outside of their region.

Ajay was even more nervous than her, because while Virat had recommended him to Vikram, he'd never worked for the big Mr. Raawal before. He'd also gathered from industry gossip that Vikram and Virat butted heads quite a lot, so he wasn't sure how long his employment might last.

Naina did her best to allay his fears, by distracting Ajay with questions about his work. His portfolio—Ajay was an artist and set designer—was magnificent.

Whatever this project was, she was thrilled to see its conception. "Your work speaks for you," she said, after gushing over all the period costume pieces and sets in his sketchbook.

"These are just rough sketches. Virat mentioned this film is going to be a period blockbuster with an all-star cast. It's actually Mr. Raawal's dream project that he's been trying to get off the ground for years." Ajay chuckled. "As if anything's impossible for Mr. Raawal. The entire industry bends its knee to him if he so much as blinks in their direction."

Naina didn't like the censure in his voice. Maybe because it's what she had thought too. At first.

"Everyone wants a piece of me," Vikram had said.

"For what it's worth, I've heard Mr. Raawal is a demanding but fair man to work for," she said, incapable of staying quiet. "I'd say this is your big chance."

Gratitude filling his eyes, Ajay reached for her hand on the table between them and squeezed it. Naina returned his clasp, feeling much better herself. The flight attendant opened the luggage hatch opposite them and put Ajay's bag next to hers.

"At least our bags have each other," he whispered with a wink.

As if on cue, Vikram stepped inside the plane, right at that precise moment.

His broad shoulders filled the not-so-narrow expanse of the aisle. The white shirt he wore was plastered to his chest from the now torrential downpour outside, and he was dripping water all over the floor. The outline of his hard chest reminded her of how delicious it had felt against her naked breasts. His black trousers molded to his strong thighs. His hair was pushed away from his forehead. He looked like her dreams given form.

Naina urgently wanted to go up to him and press her mouth to the pulse beating at his neck. She wanted to push her hands through his wet hair.

A number of greetings rang out around the cabin, cutting into her reverie. His gaze swept through the cabin, slowly, methodically. Her tummy went into a slow roll, every cell prickling with awareness. She knew who he was looking for.

Those dark brown eyes finally landed on her. Their

gazes held, for no more than a few seconds. His, hot and demanding. A jolt of answering hunger rose in her, her body thrumming with anticipation.

Oh, God, how many times had she made fun of seeing lightning in the sky when the hero and heroine met in one of those cheesier romance movies? And yet, lightning striking the jet because of the energy sparking between them didn't seem quite so far-fetched right now.

And then his gaze moved to her hand in Ajay's, to their heads bent together, to the smile that had frozen on her face.

His disapproval was instant. As if the flight attendant had flipped the air-conditioning switch from warm to chilly in a few seconds. A guilty flush of heat climbed up her cheeks. Her smile slipped, but she refused to pull her hand from Ajay's just because Vikram didn't like it.

With a muffled curse, Ajay jerked away from her and buried his face in his portfolio. Naina wanted to throw something at the man still staring down at her as if he owned her.

It wasn't going unnoticed by the rest of the team either. She much preferred their earlier indifference to this sudden curiosity.

Her pulse returned to a normal pace as Vikram finally strode past her. Three long minutes later, he called out her name. She felt like a disobedient child being called to the headmaster's office.

The front cabin had nothing on the sheer luxury that was the rear one, separated by a sturdy beige door. There was a bed in here with cream sheets, that was bigger than the one she'd shared with Maya when they'd been teenagers. A compact en suite bathroom was in one corner, the door slightly ajar to show her a tiny glimpse of a shower with sleek gold fittings. Her mouth was going to perpetually stay open at this rate.

Vikram sat down on the bed and bent over to undo his shoelaces. The wet shirt did wonders to the musculature of his back and all Naina wanted to do was to trace her finger down the line of his spine. And maybe then follow it up with her tongue. And then maybe sink her teeth into that area where his shoulder met his neck. Like he'd done to her just before he'd climaxed inside her.

She didn't want to lose the slight mark he'd given her so she'd been standing lopsided in her shower ever since that night in the library, trying to not let anything that could make it go away touch her skin there. Her fingers went to the spot now.

The wet gurgle of his shoes as he yanked them off made her pull her hand away.

He had caught her watching him. The knowledge was there in his eyes.

"I'm sorry, what?" she said extra politely, realizing he'd said something.

"I asked you if you've—"

"I've gone through the entire to-do list with Rita and run every errand you requested."

He pulled his shirt out from his trousers, pulled it over his head and threw it into a small basket.

"Where's my luggage, Ms. Menon?"

"What?" Naina muttered, now faced with the amazing prospect that was his naked chest. As she'd thought that night at the masked ball, he didn't have one of those stupidly ripped bodies that reminded her of weightlifters pumped up on steroids. What he did have was hard, beautifully defined pectoral muscles, with a sparse coating of hair that converged into a line running down his abs.

Tight, equally well-defined abdominal muscles. That she hadn't touched or licked or kissed yet.

So much wasted opportunity.

"Ms. Menon?"

"What?" she snapped at him.

Towel in hand, he stilled. A wicked glint appeared in his eyes. "You're muttering about wasted opportunities. Do you want to clarify?"

"No," she whispered, face aflame.

"It's clear you're not used to seeing half-naked men. But I was shivering in that thing, which is not very manly of me and I'd hoped you'd bring my stuff in here."

"First of all, I *too* am used to seeing half-naked men," she retorted. *"All the time."*

He waited with a raised brow and a twitching mouth. She sounded like her friend Pinky who'd boasted to have French-kissed a boy when they'd been twelve. Pinky, it turned out, had been licking away at her favorite teddy bear's mouth.

"Secondly, it's entirely manly to shiver when you're in wet clothes. And thirdly, what stuff?"

"My luggage. You were supposed to pick it up."

Mortification painted her face with heat. "Of course, that's why you called me in here. I..." She opened the door, went back to the front cabin, found where the attendant had put it and dragged it back to him. She'd acted like a complete bumbling idiot. And she liked herself the least when she did that.

"Look, you're..." She moved her hand to signal his body. "I just lost my head there for a second. It won't happen again. I'm sorry."

"Are you going to apologize every time I catch you staring at me?"

Affront filled her, like air pumped into a balloon. "I will

not… I…" Her shoulders slumped. "I don't stare at every good-looking man, okay? It's just that you…"

"What about me, Ms. Menon?"

The interest in his voice caught her before she admitted what she absolutely couldn't. "I told you, I had a silly little crush on you as a teenager. It catches me out sometimes. That's all."

"That's all, yeah," he said, nodding. He sounded disappointed. "Can you step out for a moment and let me change out of these wet clothes?"

"Sure." She stood outside the door, called herself a hundred names and then walked back in. When she was absolutely certain that he was done showing off his glorious body.

He was stretched out on the bed, a sheaf of papers all around him. A pair of glasses with bifocal lenses rested on his nose. He was wearing a worn-out T-shirt with a comic print on it and sweatpants. And his big feet were bare. He had nice, long toes and square nails.

Even the man's feet were cute and sexy.

He looked up. "Sit down please."

She sat at the edge of the bed on the opposite side from him. As far away as possible, with one butt cheek hanging off. The whir of the plane's engines filled the background and she scooted up so she didn't fall off.

"I'll allow you a certain amount of leeway for today since this was all very sudden." It was as if he'd amassed patience from the entire world and filled his words with it. "Remember that you're here as my assistant. To be at my beck and call. Not for a vacation or to stir up gossip and definitely not to socialize."

"I was only being friendly," she said hotly, knowing that his lecture had more to do with her chatting to Ajay than any of his other points. "Any gossip in there, you started it. You're the one that looked at me as if you…"

Those beautiful brown eyes trapped hers. "As if I what, Ms. Menon?"

"As if I was the most interesting thing you've ever seen. Now you've got them all riled up with unnecessary curiosity."

"Ahh…yes, that was my fault. You reminded me of someone for a moment." His gaze swept over her—from her hair in a professional-looking bun on top of her head to her knees folded primly and tucked against the bed. Heat licked through her even though it wasn't an invasive perusal. Raising his arms, he laced them behind his head. A casual grace filled his every movement.

"Of someone so interesting that even after nearly a fortnight, I'm still thinking of her. But after a few moments, it became clear that you're not her. Not even remotely like her."

God, the man was a genius at baiting her.

Naina looked up at him, a hot declaration dancing on the tip of her tongue.

It was me you kissed as if you couldn't get enough.

This was a cat-and-mouse game they were playing. A game she was insisting on. He knew she'd been the woman that night. She suddenly knew that he knew. Without a doubt.

Whatever lies she'd told herself not an hour ago didn't hold up now when the truth was shining in his eyes. When it was clear from the challenge in the tilt of his square jaw. When the air charged up every time they looked into each other's eyes.

So why had he hired her then?

To make sure she didn't sell her story to the media?

Or because he'd taken pity on her situation after she'd

practically begged him to give her a job because she was so desperately in need of funds?

It had to be one or the other. And, more importantly, she had to be okay with either of those reasons. "Oh, I wouldn't dream for a second that I could hold your interest for even that long, Mr. Raawal. Now, shall we get on with the list of tasks still waiting for you?"

CHAPTER SIX

VIKRAM KNEW HE'D been very thoroughly and very politely steered toward work. Which should make him elated. One of them, at least, needed to keep their cool and focus on the job in hand. Needed to remember that there was no future in whatever this was between them.

But the hunger with which she'd watched his body, as if he were her favorite ice cream…the woman had no idea how obvious her expressions were. How artless she was in her desire.

He'd never particularly cared one way or the other that he had, as everyone stated, "stunning" looks. It had been an accident of a genetics pool contributed to by two of the most self-absorbed, destructive people he'd ever known. Yes, it had come in handy in his career. But it had only been one tool in a whole arsenal he'd been given to save his family from the huge hole his father had dug them into.

To save the prestigious Raawal name from becoming synonymous with scandal and shame.

But for the first time in his life, he found he was more than fond of his symmetrical features. More than happy to go through the rigorous exercise regimen his trainer had created.

Just because this woman looked at him as if she wanted to lick him up.

He pushed his fingers through his hair, a smile curving his mouth. He felt like a teenager, waiting to pass a note to the girl he liked. But without the burden of being the family's last saving grace.

For the first time in his life, he found a distinct pleasure in this chase. This attraction that was more than a simple need to slake his lust or scratch an itch. For the first time ever, he felt as if there was more to him too.

He was still smiling when she looked up from her notepad. Again, those eyes stayed on his mouth for a few seconds too long before they finally met his. "Why are you smiling?"

He shrugged.

Her mouth pursed. "As I've told you, I've already tackled the to-dos Rita had for next week. The remaining are a list of tasks I'm not sure how to deal with."

He nodded and pulled forward the tray of fruit the flight attendant had left him. "Did you catch up to Virat, Anya and Daadi like I asked before they left for the airport?" he said, reaching for a plump orange.

"Yes. I delivered the medicines she left behind. Although…"

"What?"

"Virat said you'd made me take an unnecessary trip across the city. He'd already picked up all of Daadiji's medication from another medical store." She turned the pages back on the notepad. Her eyes danced with laughter when she found the page. "He made me note down a message for you."

"And?"

"And what?" she said, batting her eyelashes innocently.

"What's the message?"

"It's a little…colorful."

"You know you're dying to read it to me, Ms. Menon. So go ahead."

"He said, and I quote, 'My brother needs to get his interfering nose out of everyone else's business.' Anya then added, 'TBH, he really needs to get laid.'"

Vikram plopped the orange segment into his mouth. "Ah...what my brother and sister don't know is I've already taken their advice. Only..."

"Only what?" she demanded, suddenly all fire and sass.

Vikram blinked. "I'm sure you'd like nothing better than to hear salacious details about my sex life but I don't kiss and tell. Let me just say I'd have a hat trick record if this were cricket."

Her face lost all its color. "So you're boasting that you've had..." there was that pink along her cheeks again, "that you've been with three women in the last what? Month? Week? Day?"

He shrugged, thoroughly enjoying the overt displeasure on her face.

Jealousy had never looked so beautiful to his eyes before. He could practically see her launching herself at him, all fists and curses, demanding an explanation. And he would tell her the truth. That all he'd been able to think of was her. Her laughter, and her kisses and her eagerness and her hot mouth and her even hotter need. And then she would beg him to kiss her in that delicious throaty voice of hers and he would press her down into this very bed...

The sound of a page being ripped from the notepad made him look up. She balled the torn-out paper in her hand with a vicious energy that made him smile.

"Is something wrong, Ms. Menon? Are you thinking up a lecture for me again?"

She straightened her shoulders, but didn't meet his gaze.

"No, it's your life. If jumping from woman to woman is what brings you happiness, then…" She ended it with a shrug.

But Vikram saw the disappointment in her face before she shielded those big eyes with her thick lashes.

She looked down at her notepad for a long time and Vikram let the silence build between them. Gave her the space to ask him if his boasts were really true.

To ask him if she'd just been one in a row of other women. To ask if he…

God, what was he doing with her?

He had no idea why he was egging her on like this. Yes, some of it was the fact that he absolutely didn't like that she seemed to have control of this thing between them. But some of it was also the fact that he didn't really know her. Or himself when he was with her.

Every look, every word, every exchange felt like a thrilling ride. Leaving him either laughing at himself or her, or drowning in desire. Ever since he'd agreed to let her take Rita's job for the next four weeks, he'd been on tenterhooks the entire time.

Wondering if she would back out. Wondering what she'd do when she saw him again. Wondering if she…

The fact that he was turning into the cliché that he most abhorred—a cynical, hardened thirty-six-year-old man panting after an innocent woman more than a decade younger than himself, who to all intents and purposes didn't want anything to do with him in a personal way, which was the script of his father's most notorious scandal—still didn't stop his thoughts about Naina. Or the thrill he felt when she looked at him with just as much hunger as he did her.

When she looked back at him, her eyes were devoid of any expression. "Shall we start?" she said in that polite voice and he nodded. It was probably best she thought he was a bed-hopping playboy.

"Your father and mother called separately about nine times each. Rita told me that under no circumstance was I allowed to let them reach you until we looked over the subject of their calls first."

There was a question in her tone and Vikram answered it first. "She's right. Only Daadi, Virat, Anya, Zara, and now you…as well as Rita, of course, have access to my private number. It's not to be given out to anyone else. Including my parents."

Her eyes went wide. "Zara as in Zara Khan, the spectacular actress I adore who doesn't let anyone tell her how to live her life? The Zara Khan who's won three national awards, the Zara Khan who runs a shelter for abused women, that Zara Khan, right?"

"Yes. Zara's my oldest friend."

"I'll not do this to anyone else I meet but please, if we run into her over the next few weeks, will you introduce me? I'd love to ask for her autograph. I know it's childish but Zara's just amazing and I love her."

Zara was the most amazing woman he'd ever known. The one constant in his life. "It's not in the schedule but if she comes, yes, I'll introduce you, Ms. Menon." And since teasing her was like breathing, he said, "You don't want my autograph?"

"Not really," she said immediately, scrunching that adorable nose at him. "I've got what I want from you, Mr. Raawal."

The outrageously bold declaration made him tip back his head and laugh loudly. Vikram had to fist his hands at his sides or he'd be grabbing her with both hands and scaring the hell out of her. Desire was a tiger clawing under his skin. "What exactly is that, Ms. Menon?"

"This job," she said sweetly, challenge in her expression. Ha! So the minx wanted to do battle, did she?

"So back to—"

"Anybody else who wants to contact me calls you on the line Rita gave to you. Every call needs to be—"

"Screened by me first. No one can reach you, yes, I know. Even if your mother's—"

"Even if my mother's screaming threats of destruction at you." He sighed. "Like I said, her penchant for drama pervades everything she says and does. But she doesn't have a vicious bone in her body."

"To be honest, I wasn't afraid of what Mrs. Raawal might do to me. I was worried more that she might find out that my stepmother is Jaya Pandit. Jaya Ma doesn't need any more bad luck and your mother's a woman of considerable influence in the industry."

"You have my word that no one will harm you or your loved ones in any way because of your...association with me." He cleared his throat. "It's important to me that you believe that, Ms. Menon. No actions of yours, past or future, will be used against you. I'd never abuse my position of power like that. If I fire you, it will be because you either violated the NDA you've signed or because you're not up to the job. Is that clear?"

The confusion in her eyes cleared. But she didn't look away. She didn't play coy. The truth of their night shimmered in her eyes. Along with her conviction in him. And the furor in his chest calmed at her absolute trust in him.

She looked back down at the list, though she remained quiet for a while. The silence lingered on, but it didn't rush at Vikram like it had done. It had a comforting quality to it now.

"So there's a woman who's contacted your mother

who's claimed that she's…" She cleared her throat and tried again. "That she…"

Whatever pleasure he'd felt instantly siphoned out of Vikram, leaving only hardness behind. He popped another sliver of orange into his mouth but the sweetness felt like nothing on his tongue. He chewed and swallowed, forcing himself to speak. "Whatever it is, Ms. Menon, just say it. If you hesitate like this every time my father creates a new problem for me to solve, we'll get nothing done."

"Your mother has been receiving notes and calls from this anonymous woman claiming to be pregnant with your father's child. She said she's tried to deal with it on her own but hasn't succeeded."

"Is the woman demanding money?"

"Something like that, yes." She turned the page on the notepad and tapped her pen. "The gist of your father's messages was that he'd never met this lady before. At the time of…" She ran her fingers through her hair a couple of times, and Vikram watched bemused as it sprang back exactly as it had been before. "He pointed out that at what would have been the time of conception, he'd been in Paris with a different lady love of his. He also got pretty upset…"

"You're to hang up immediately if he's being—"

"He was drunk, I believe. Not aggressive. I couldn't hang up on him, Mr. Raawal. He sounded close to tears." She held up a palm, ordering him to be silent when he'd have interrupted again. "So I did call the hotel in Paris for confirmation he was with that other woman. I also crawled through that particular lady's social media account and while she doesn't come out and say she was with your father at the time, there's enough information to figure out that he's telling the truth. As per Rita's instructions for what to do in these scenarios, I passed on the blackmailer's information and all the other evidence I'd gathered to your lawyer. I mentioned it now just to keep you informed."

She didn't wait for him to say anything. He hated that he had to be grateful to her for the intense awkwardness. But then most of his adult life had been like this. "Shall we move on to the next thing?" she asked, still all business and he nodded.

"There's a report from your sister's PA that I'm to pass on to you." He heard the curiosity in her voice but she didn't indulge it. "There's a conflict between an awards show in Mumbai you promised to appear at and the charity youth program that you, Anya and Virat oversee in Delhi."

"Cancel my appearance at the awards show. I go to enough of the damned things; there's one in the Maldives while we're there."

She made a note, flipped through the notepad a few more times and made more notes on the two phones. "Those are the most important ones for now. Oh, and I heard from the retired actress you wanted on this project, Mrs. Saira Ahmed. She said, 'Tell your boss I'm not coming out of retirement just to help his self-indulgent, masala pop trash movie become a reality. His grandfather Vijay would be turning in his grave at what his grandson has done to his beloved production house.'"

Vikram sighed. There was no amount of money or gifts that would change Mrs. Ahmed's mind. Damn it, he'd tried. He'd even hoped that throwing around Virat's name—after all, to the true artists among them, his brother was a better Raawal than he, might sway the stubborn old goat's mind. "That's that then."

"That's *not* that however," Naina piped up. "Rita told me how disappointed you'd be to hear Mrs. Ahmed's decision and so I tried something else."

He sat up, noting the glint of pride in her expression. She was practically vibrating with excitement and it tugged at Vikram. He wanted to shake her and demand she tell him immediately. He also wanted to grab her and kiss her hard as if he could fill himself with that joy of hers. "What did you try, Ms. Menon?" He forced himself to say her name formally, as if it could kill this constant need inside him.

"When I went into the city to drop off the medication for Daadiji, I dropped by this old library that Papa and I used to visit. The owner is this eighty-year-old man Chaudharyji with a private collection of books like you would not believe. Papa and he talked history for hours and he'd let me browse through his collection. I asked him to let me borrow the first edition of a poetry collection that Mrs. Ahmed's father wrote in 1935. I remembered seeing a feature on TV about how most of their possessions had been destroyed during the migration after independence. She was close to tears.

"I took the edition to her, and told her you went to a lot of effort to locate it and borrow it for her. I cannot describe her joy when she held that old edition in her hands. She hugged me and said it was clear that you had more sense than she'd previously credited you with if you had someone like me work for you, so," she took a deep breath, her eyes twinkling, "she said she will give you one chance. The script, she said, will have to be magnificent. I sat down with her secretary, hashed out some dates and she wants a look at the script in four weeks."

Vikram didn't, couldn't, say anything for long minutes.

She looked up and smiled. "Thank you—that's the phrase you're looking for."

He smiled. "Thank you, Ms. Menon. It's been my dream

to have Mrs. Ahmed on this project and you brought us a chance. Now, is that all?"

"I called the resort and changed one of the reservations. Mr. and Mrs. Sharma would prefer to be in separate villas. The only member I haven't heard back from so far is Virat."

She closed the notepad and sighed. "Can I ask why you've gathered them all here? They seem like a very…"

"Eccentric, self-centered bunch of old has-beens?"

She smiled. "Those are your words. I was going to say interesting group of people."

"I've been trying to pin down a script for more than two years. Usually, Raawal House will just buy a spec script but this is close to my—" he cleared his throat, as if he couldn't admit that he had a heart or that it felt things "—that's important to me. There's a skeleton script ready but it needs fleshing out. And this bunch of self-important snobs are who I need to do it. But it's a pain to get them to work together.

"This is my last attempt at bringing this project to fruition, which is why we're holed up here in such stunning surroundings. I also have no doubt it's the reason Virat is MIA. He absolutely doesn't believe in coddling anyone or pandering to anyone's superiority complex. He'll turn up to contribute eventually, either in person or via video link."

"So it's a project you're going to take on together? You as lead actor, he to direct it?"

"Yes."

"To be released in time for the seventieth anniversary celebrations of Raawal House, right?"

"You're very quick, Ms. Menon."

"Yeah, we can often surprise you like that, us women."

"Ahh…still getting those hits in whenever you can, I see."

She clapped her hands together, the excitement on her face contagious. "This is amazing. I adore everything Virat has ever made. I can't believe you've never worked together before. I mean, you've both had unprecedented successes with everything you've ever touched."

"Like you, my brother thinks I'm a populist sellout."

"I never said that. I just…" She colored, and he decided to take pity on her.

"We need this group to produce what they're capable of, Ms. Menon. It's just a matter of getting them to communicate together. With Mrs. Ahmed wanting a look at the script, you know now what's on the line. I should have a history expert here, too, but the professor had an accident not two days ago."

"I have a master's degree in history and theater, and history of theater in India. Of course, I didn't get to finish my PhD in film history but that's all I've ever studied. I can help with anything in that area."

"It's all hands on deck at this point. I need a script of some sort at the end of four weeks, if I want to keep the investors I've attracted."

"What's the subject?"

"It's a biopic about my grandfather Vijay Raawal. With India's Independence struggle as the background."

"Oh, my," Naina said, dropping onto the bed. "The scope of it, the history of it…wow…just wow! That sounds magnificent. I can't believe I'm here to see its inception, to see history in the making.

"I mean, can you imagine? The struggles he had to face, the traveling theater stories, the increasingly charged atmosphere…" She suddenly looked at him, her heart in her eyes. "Will you be playing him?"

"That's the idea."

"That's…that's the role of a lifetime. And I have no

doubt you'll be absolutely fantastic at it, Mr. Raawal. With Virat in the director's chair, the industry will see what you're really made of."

"Thank you for the vote of confidence, Ms. Menon. I wish my brother had the same confidence in me as you do."

His husky whisper in her ear made Naina realize, that in all her excitement, she had got really close to him on the bed. The arc of heat between them was instantaneous. All-consuming. All the excitement about the project seemed to have found new sources inside both him and her.

There was a stillness to him that felt like it was tearing at the edges. As if it were a deceptive front and one word from her would fracture his façade. This close, she could see the slight curl to his hair, helped along by the moisture of the recent downpour. She wanted to reach out and push it back, and keep her fingers there.

Her gaze drifted to his mouth, as if it were her true north. As if she could still feel the soft, hot weight of his lips on hers. She could vividly remember the corded strength in his thighs, the rough dig of his fingers into her hips.

The sounds he'd made when he'd climaxed inside her... The memories all beat through her with a tempting force that shook her. In that minute, all she wanted was to climb fully onto the bed, push him back against the covers and beg him to kiss her again. To make love to her again. To make her feel as if she was the most desperately needed woman in the entire universe.

But she couldn't.

Because he was her boss and she didn't want to mess up this job. She was only just discovering how much she wanted to work in the film industry. And while she believed that he'd never harm her reputation or prospects in any way, a relationship between them had nowhere to go, except to crash and burn. He wasn't a man who wanted marriage and babies and all the things she wanted.

There was no future for her with him.

Yes, Vikram Raawal was not the egotistic, privileged, arrogant ass she'd thought him at their first meeting. But he was still the superstar who had the reputation of breaking women's hearts. The confirmed bachelor. The control freak. The man who absolutely didn't believe in love or marriage.

But of course, she was tempted. She was more than tempted. With him, she'd been bold, beautiful, brazen even. She'd been a different Naina. She'd been a Naina she was proud of. But that Naina existed only in darkness and disguises. He was absolutely right about that.

Slowly, feeling as if she couldn't trust her own limbs to follow her commands, she got up from the bed and walked toward the front cabin. "I can't tell you how much this opportunity means to me, Mr. Raawal. I wouldn't do anything that would jeopardize this. Not for anything."

She didn't wait to see if he understood. This thing between them…would just have to fizzle out. It had to stay a fantasy.

CHAPTER SEVEN

EVEN AFTER TEN days, Naina still wasn't used to the magical splendor of the island. She had never seen a blue like that of the ocean before. The small island was tiny with one main resort building in the middle and cozy two-bedroom villas interspersed around. Crystal-blue water floated as tiny wood walkways connected the villas and the main resort as if they were glinting sapphires on a beautiful necklace.

Though working sixteen to seventeen hours a day keeping up with the supercharged life of Vikram Raawal meant she'd barely had the chance to do anything more than take a quick glance at the stunning beauty around her.

Fifteen minutes during every morning's catered breakfast—which was a veritable feast of North Indian, Continental and South Indian delicacies—sitting atop the veranda with a view of blue lagoons was still more than enough to fill her with a quiet sense of well-being she hadn't had in a long time.

Lunch, an informal buffet served at the main villa, was usually a working affair. During dinner, the team often dispersed and she'd gotten into the habit of bringing something to her room to eat while she finished up the day's communication.

She was sharing a villa with Vikram and the first morning, her main concern had been about stepping into the kitchen area and running into Vikram and his sexy masculinity before she'd even had the chance to have a cup of coffee. But by the time she'd showered and ventured out, he'd already left for the main villa. However late Naina stayed up during the evening, typing up notes, scheduling meetings and video calls for the next day, he worked later than her.

The team worked at the main villa with two bedrooms designated as workspaces for Vikram and Virat, who was still not here in person, although he had video-called several times. Vikram read the script nightly after Naina sent it to him and discussed revisions with the team first thing in the morning.

Despite the rift between them, the brothers were clearly committed to the project. She loved watching the arguments and discussions amongst the team about the main plot, dialogue and the two main characters, while Vikram played the referee.

Outside of the script, there were casting sheets to go through, video conferences with potential investors, sketches he oversaw with Ajay, and they were also combing through an incredible amount of research each evening.

They'd had Chaudaryji and Mrs. Ahmed on two conference calls—informal, sprawling discussions about that time period. Naina loved those calls—even Vikram seemed to light up from within at the long, leisurely walk down memory lane.

Naina followed Vikram into the open lounge area after one such call, pulled toward him despite every rational voice that warned her differently. They'd finished early today, and twilight bathed the open lounge area with a grayish-blue tinge. With the soft swish of the water and a balmy breeze, the quiet had an otherworldly feel to it.

Fingers laced through each other behind his back, he

was standing at the balcony looking out into the deep blue
expanse of the ocean. The white linen shirt fluttered up
in the breeze, baring the hard slab of his lower back muscles. Her fingers itched to touch him, her body suddenly
flush with that cocktail of thrill and need whenever she
was near him.

Naina couldn't help wondering at how greedy she became when it was him. True to their unspoken truce, they
had both been nothing but professional in both their words
and looks. And yet, the silence between them possessed
a strange quality—as if it was hungry for words, tinged
with anticipation.

Waiting and wanting.

This attraction to him, it hungrily ate up any rational
excuses she threw at it.

She knew she should retire for the evening. If she hur-
ried, she could join the rest of the team on their hunt for a
nightclub. And yet she stood rooted to the spot. No luxury
experience, no celeb spotting, nothing, she was beginning
to understand, would hold more appeal than a simple, quiet
conversation with this complex man.

Telling herself she'd already had her once-in-a-lifetime
fantasy night with him, warning herself that this job was
too important to jeopardize…nothing was helping. All her
life, she'd carefully lived within the confines of others' expectations and now…now it was as if everything within her
was rebelling against taking a sensible course of action.
Everything in her, selfishly, wanted him. More of him.

She must slowly be going crazy, because she easily convinced herself that he needed her too.

Naina joined him at the small balcony, leaving enough
distance between them just to prove she could.

Vikram cast her a look of surprise. Those eyes didn't

miss the distance she'd put between them. His mouth twitched. "Not into the club scene?"

"I'm not into it, no, and Ajay's working late anyway," she replied, somehow managing to sound rational.

He frowned.

She wondered if he found her company that distasteful. "I didn't mean to intrude. I'll say good-night—"

"Stay, Ms. Menon."

She bristled at the way he invoked her last name. As if it was an incantation that immediately imposed distance between them.

"You were in a bit of a strange mood earlier tonight. On the call with Mrs. Ahmed," she said, as if it was the reason she had sought him out.

He held her gaze and again, she knew she was just finding excuses to be near him. Even that knowledge didn't send her on her way. He sighed and looked back at the ocean. "I'd forgotten that little tidbit she mentioned. That Daadu had been rejected at least fourteen times before he got his first role."

"You miss him," she said, full of a giddy relief that he was talking to her. That he was sharing a private moment with her. That despite the game they were playing, he still considered her close to him.

God, she was going mad, if him just talking to her was making her this happy.

"I never got to know him that well before he died. All I remember is the rows he and my father would have, the disappointment in his eyes afterwards. One time, though, when things were really bad with my parents and I went to live with Daadu and Daadi for the summer, every night after dinner, we would lie on this handwoven cot in the courtyard, old *gazals* playing on the gramophone, look up at stars and he would tell me stories of brave kings and courageous queens and clever poets, and cunning spies in our history…he was a magnificent storyteller, with a true love for theater and cinema."

Just like that, everything that made this man into Vikram Raawal clicked into place for her. "I owe you an apology," she said, aware now that she'd deeply wounded him the first time they'd met. The shame of her judgmental words stung her.

Brows raised, he turned to her. Focused that intense gaze on her for the first time in days. "This should be good."

She shook her head at his lighthearted tone. "I was wrong. It's easy for the likes of Mrs. Ahmed and me to sit atop our judgmental horses and call you a sellout.

"But you never had the luxury to make the movies that met the vision of the company that your grandfather established. To simply take over and walk in his footsteps." She didn't have to mention the calls with his parents, the constant back-and-forth over finances, the better understanding she now had of his reign over the Raawals after only ten days. He constantly juggled a million responsibilities in addition to his own acting career and being the creative head of Raawal House. "You had to dig the production house from a financial hole really quickly, and then salvage its reputation when you took over. Have I got it right so far?"

He shrugged. "It wasn't simply the prestige of the company I was saving. Daadi would have lost her bungalow, the house Daadu built for her. We'd have lost the studio and gone into bankruptcy. So many livelihoods depended on me. All our employees—both at the studio and all the various mansions, they'd have been on the streets. Virat and Anya would've had to give up their higher education.

"My father sank all their personal fortunes into unwise

investments and my mother lost hers on three huge movies that were supposed to give her career a second wind but then were major flops.

"They would have had to sell their cars and their mansions and everything. They'd have lost their entire way of life, and believe me, they wouldn't have survived it. They do not possess the strength of character to retire to simpler lives." She could still see the weight of that decision in his eyes.

"My first movie was my first and final gamble, with everything riding on it. I used everything I knew about mass appeal and made sure I created the most commercial blockbuster I could. And I never looked back."

"Why doesn't Virat get that?" she asked with a frown. "Why doesn't he understand that you've spent the last fifteen years of your career righting the mighty ship of Raawal House? What right does he have to call you a sellout when he's reaping the benefits?"

He studied her face with bemusement but she was far too gone. "Such anger on my behalf, Ms. Menon?"

"It's so unfair that you've carried this burden for so long."

"Virat simply thinks I should have walked away from the mess my father and mother created. That the prestige of the Raawal family didn't deserve to be preserved. Virat, you must understand, had a childhood that was eons different from mine. Mine was child's play compared to the… challenges both he and Anya faced with them, as they were quite a bit younger than me."

"Did you ever consider walking away? From the studio and your…family?"

"I did, for all of five minutes. But those long summer nights with my grandfather, the vision he had built into a reality with nothing but hard work, his love of family above all else…it didn't sit well with me. Walking away would have been cowardly."

"And you never regretted it?"

"Not the choice I made. For what it's worth, Raawal House stands as a symbol of one man's vision of cinema. My fortune is a hundred times what my grandfather ever made. If I say I regret building an empire and being rich, then I'm lying through my teeth. But…"

"But what?"

"Why such curiosity about all this, Ms. Menon?"

Heat claimed her cheeks. "I misjudged you. Some of it is the easy, casual cruelty with which we judge celebrities, delving into their private lives, standing on higher moral ground, combing through their every mistake, drawing satisfaction when they flounder. I honestly thought myself above all that.

"And some of it is just that I've come to…" Naina considered and rejected words that rose so easily to her lips, expressing feelings she wasn't ready to examine "…respect you. I feel as if I owe it to you."

"You don't owe me anything," he said, his gaze holding hers. For once, she didn't understand the look there.

"Then I owe it to myself, I think." Before he could analyze that, she said, "What do you regret?" In that moment more than any others, she wanted to call him Vikram. She wanted the feeling of intimacy it would give them, she wanted the right to demand answers from him.

She wanted…so much she couldn't even put it all into words.

He combed his fingers through his hair, his shoulders tense. "Not regrets so much as niggles. Certain recent events…have made me realize that there are consequences to my actions that I hadn't foreseen."

"Like what?"

"Like the fact that taking control of everyone's lives to fix a sinking ship has turned me into a control freak who can't keep out of his family's personal business. Like the fact that I seem to have lost my soul somewhere along the way in the pursuit of wealth and security. Like the fact that I…" He rubbed a finger over his temple and then shook his head. As if deciding that those niggles weren't important. "I've become so arrogant that maybe I don't even know myself anymore."

"I'd venture that most of that arrogance is innate rather than a byproduct of all the problems you've had to fix," she offered lightly, her heart heavy at the remoteness of his expression.

"Touché, Ms. Menon," he said with a laugh. "Guess you think you know me very well now, huh?"

She said nothing, suddenly finding her breath far too shallow under his intent gaze.

"I'm too practical to pine over a future that never really existed for me," he said finally. "Virat is the genius, the thinker who lives in alternate story lines and potential futures. I'm a hardheaded businessman. When you've had to make decisions for everyone, life-changing decisions at such an age as I did, it becomes a deeply ingrained habit. It becomes a part of you—that controlling nature, the arrogant assumption that you know best for everyone. You stop listening to anyone, you think yourself invincible. You…become distant from your family friends, maybe even your own heart."

"But if you have this self-awareness now, if you know that you need to bend sometimes…"

Naina heard the self-deprecation in his laugh. How had she ever thought this man a one-dimensional cardboard cutout?

"Knowing that I've become a controlling, arrogant man

is no help when it comes to changing, Ms. Menon. Most of the time, I think I'm too set in my ways to even want to change.

"Would you walk away from your stepmother and your stepsister even though they demand and take without a thought to your own happiness?"

She reared back from that softly worded comment as if it was a slap. "I told you. They're not burdens. They're…" She smiled once the sudden burst of anger died down. "This is what you've been talking about, isn't it? This knowing what's best for everyone. This belief in your own superiority? This is why Virat and Anya are often angry with you."

He shrugged.

"Tell me then," she demanded. "Tell me your opinion of my family. Of me. Of how I should be fixing my life."

"No, Ms. Menon," he replied calmly but with a hint of steel in his tone. "I've just crawled back into your good graces. I should like to stay there. Especially since we do make a rather spectacular team."

She preened at the praise. And she knew she should heed his warning. But a desperate need to know what he thought of her took hold of her. A self-indulgent yearning for his regard. "I'm a big girl, Mr. Raawal, I can take it," she said, mimicking his words from that first day. "Do your worst."

"You'll not like me for it," he said, coming closer. And then, he sighed. "Why? Why are you so bent on hearing what I think of you?"

"Let's just say curiosity is my number one sin."

"You never got over your mother abandoning you as a child. And to be honest, maybe it's not a thing one ever gets over. Add to that a father who at best sounds like the absentminded, messed-up sort, at worst, a man who should've paid more attention to his little girl instead of his own feelings of loss and devastation, and you had to grow up too fast.

"I know how that feels. I know what it means to have to take hold of the family reins when you don't even understand yourself. Only our innate natures are such that it appears I have to control everything and everyone around me and you…"

"I…what?"

"You…you make yourself indispensable to everyone in your orbit. You're afraid that if you don't move everything to not only anticipate what your stepmother and stepsister need, but lay it at their feet, they will abandon you too. That they will stop loving you."

"And what is it that you think I should do to fix it?" she demanded, thrusting her face into his, so angry that tears filled her eyes. "Cut them out of my life? I'm not like you. I can't screen my family's calls. I couldn't bear it if they were mad at me. I couldn't…" And just like that, she confirmed everything he'd said about her.

He came closer then, his fingers reaching for her face. Even knowing that she should jerk away from his touch, Naina didn't move. He'd given her enough time to retreat from him. He clasped her jaw with such reverence that something inside her burst open.

She wanted to crawl into his arms and weep. She wanted to beg him to hold her so tight that she didn't have to acknowledge the painful truth in his words. She wanted so much from a man who could dispassionately arrange his own life to mitigate emotional pain.

"Remember that I said it is one thing to know one's weaknesses and a whole other thing to actually do something about them?" His smile was all teeth and no real warmth. "I never said you should give them up, Ms. Menon. Only that you shouldn't let them hurt you.

"Why leave yourself vulnerable to people who have a high chance of hurting you? Why not protect yourself?"

"How would you do it then? Draw boundaries around what they're allowed to do? Create rules for them to follow? I can't live like that." She wanted to walk away from him then because she was angry with him. Angry with herself. "Keeping everyone out, being cold and calculating like you are, loneliness eating away at me. Isolated from both joy and pain, with nothing to show for my life but material success and wealth and mansions," she practically yelled at him, fury and pain stealing away any rational sense.

She froze, disgusted and astonished with herself in equal measures.

Bracing for him to either cut her down to size or to laugh and tell her he didn't need her pity because lonely was the last thing he was. She wasn't even sure it was true. Only an impression she'd formed of him. Mostly full of delusion, maybe.

He simply stood there, without blinking, staring at her, waiting for the storm that was her temper to pass. As if he were one of the tall palm trees that bent and swayed during tornados but never broke.

After what felt like an eternity, he said, "Are you less lonely than I am, Ms. Menon? Truly not hurt by your stepsister's selfishness, your stepmother's thoughtlessness? Lie to me all you want, but I thought you weren't the kind to lie to yourself."

With that simple, softly spoken question, he made her look at herself. At all her patterns and behaviors. At her dreams and fears.

"You don't have to take my word as law, Ms. Menon," he said, when she just looked at him, still hurt and angry.

His voice was full of a gentleness that felt like a lash against her skin.

His gaze did one final sweep of her, from her tear-filled eyes to her trembling mouth. When his eyes met hers, the look of resignation was so absolute that she wanted to beg him to not shut her out. "My obligation to you as your employer doesn't stretch that far. And beyond the basic courtesy, I don't have a personal concern in your well-being.

"Believe me, I have enough messed-up people to take care of."

And just like that, she was reminded, not undeservedly, that she was only his employee. He left before she could offer him an apology.

She'd offered him an apology for an earlier insult and had then immediately committed a new offense against him. But it was only with him that she lost her usually placid temper.

Only him who from the first moment of meeting her had challenged all her own beliefs and made her reexamine everything in her life. And every time he did that, she ended up not liking what she discovered.

CHAPTER EIGHT

COLD AND CALCULATING...

She'd made it clear what she thought of him when she'd told him that a few days ago. It wasn't as if Vikram didn't already know that about himself. But it had never bothered him this much before, like a shard of wood stuck under his skin.

She'd also proved that she was no match for him, for all that she boldly bandied words with him. Not when he didn't temper his words or his personality. He'd hurt her. Especially when she'd sought him out in the first place so she could express her concern at his restlessness.

Damn it, what did the woman want from him? Why did she look at him with those big eyes in which he could clearly read longing and desire and hurt? Why didn't she stay away?

Because that's what he was trying his damnedest to do.

He hated this obsession with her, that was slowly but surely spiraling out of control.

It wasn't as if he could have a fling with her and work her out of his system. For one thing, she worked for him. He absolutely wasn't going to engage in some torrid affair with an employee and then throw her away like his father had done several times over. For another, she was...no sophisticate who knew the name of the game.

She was the kind of girl around whom epic love stories were written. And he wasn't a hero on his very best day.

So, the last thing he needed to do was to seek her out.

But ever since Mrs. Sharma had pointed out that Naina had missed the team dinner he'd organized this evening, he hadn't been able to focus. It was strange enough that she'd deviate from anything he asked of her professionally.

She usually made it a point of retiring to her room long before he returned to their villa and it was already past eleven. Once he found her bedroom empty, there was no stopping him.

He walked out of their villa, already a strange thrill gripping him with each step. Why was it that even a confrontation with the woman held more appeal than a night of hard sex with someone else?

He would be professional if it killed him. He would keep his distance from her even if it was the hardest thing he'd ever had to do.

Because there was no way he could have Naina in his life. Not with the way he was wired and definitely not with the way she seemed to weave people into the very fabric of her life with such unconscious ease.

Which meant, this madness, this obsession with her, had to end.

Naina was sitting with her back to Ajay's side, her legs dangling over the armrest of the sofa, in the open lounge of the main villa, while he was sketching on his pad. He was one of those people who didn't fill every minute with unnecessary chatter and she loved seeing the sets and the costumes come to life from his clever fingers.

The huge plasma screen was playing Vikram's second movie, in which he'd played two different roles—of father and son.

Ajay, she knew, was watching it for research. She was watching it because she was…fixated on the man. There was no avoiding the fact anymore that all she thought of was Vikram.

Of how to be that bold Naina with him again, even if it was for just a night, a day, a week. Of how to have him, for herself, just one more time.

She knew she owed him another apology. And yet, if she sought him out for such a personal discussion again, she was afraid of what she might say. Of what she might do and demand of him.

So she was avoiding him. Which was a joke since she worked so many hours each day next to him. She felt as if she was standing on the cusp of something vast and important. As if something inside of her was changing and she didn't even know if she wanted to stop it. Or maybe it was already far too late to do so.

The younger Vikram on the screen took off his shirt and was doused with colored water in a Holi celebration. Naina sighed.

Ajay laughed, and pulled at the messy braid she'd caged her wild hair into. But his concentration was unbroken. She liked sitting by him when he sketched because he never tried to poke his nose into her thoughts. His rapidly moving fingers on the page sent vibrations up his arm and into her back. She stared at the emerging picture of Vikram—the sharp bridge of his nose, the deep-set, soulful eyes, the high forehead, and the mouth that could be languid and sexy in one breath and hard and calculating the next.

"You've got the lower lip all wrong," she said, when Ajay made it too flat. Too thin. Too…cynical. "It's much more…forgiving." She bent down and traced her finger along that lower lip, making it wider, thicker. "You also missed the crease he gets here when he smiles. You've made him far too brooding, too..."

"That's the man I see every day," Ajay said, his tone matter-of-fact.

"That's only one version of him. There's so much more to him than you..."

Ajay's fingers stilled on the paper. The sudden tension in his lanky shoulders transferred to Naina and she looked up.

Vikram stood just inside the doorway of the expansive lounge, looking down that arrogant nose of his at them. And he was angry. She didn't know how she knew that but she did. She quickly did a run-through of all her to-do items in her head. No, she hadn't missed anything.

Ajay turned off the television and stood up, as if he'd been caught doing something inappropriate. Naina fell onto the sofa with a soft thud. Feeling like the most ungainly creature ever, she pushed herself up and into a sitting position, her skin prickling under the intensity of Vikram's scrutiny.

She'd never been so aware of every inch of her own skin—from the breeze kissing her bare legs, the embroidered hem of her loose shorts against her thighs, to the silk of her pink sleeveless chiffon blouse fluttering against her skin.

She felt as if he'd run those long fingers over every inch of her in that thorough way of his.

"Hello, Mr. Raawal. Did you need anything?" Ajay prompted, his spine ramrod-straight.

Naina refused to stand to attention. Refused to let him make her feel guilty. But her heart sped off anyway as she wondered just how much he'd heard her singing praises of his lower lip.

Vikram's gaze didn't shift to Ajay, not even for a second. "If I could borrow my assistant for a few minutes?" Politeness oozed from his every word as he held open the door.

Ajay picked up his sketch pad and pencils and disappeared under Vikram's outstretched arm, the coward.

Naina stood up as Vikram closed the door behind Ajay and ventured in. She hated it when he looked down at her from his great height. The light brown shirt and beige-colored khakis did wonders for his broad-shouldered frame and long legs. He looked effortlessly sexy in even casual clothes.

For long moments, he just stared at her face. It made her feel anything but uncomfortable. Already, during the time they'd been here, she'd become entirely familiar with how he weighed each word before he spoke, how he studied every nuance in his audience.

"I don't think I've ever seen you in anything outside of your usual colorful skirts, Ms. Menon. Maybe once. Definitely once."

Heat flared across her skin, the memory hitting her right in her lower belly. As strongly as if they were back in that darkened library, their fingers and mouths communicating for them.

She pulled the loose strap of her blouse back into place. His gaze followed her every movement, every breath until she felt like she was one giant string of tightly tuned need. One touch from him and she would burst into...ecstasy.

"It was too hot earlier. I..." Naina had no idea what was going on inside his head. "Is there something I can do for you?" she prompted, and then wished she'd worded it differently.

But he didn't notice. There was a strange tension in his face.

"Why weren't you at the team dinner?"

"I didn't realize it was mandatory," she retorted, defensive rather than defiant.

His gaze roved over her. "Are you unwell?"

He knew she was not. Even with the busy workload, the island and the schedule had done wonders for her. For the first time in months, she didn't feel weighed down by grief or fear. She'd never looked as good as she did now.

"Mrs. Sharma said you had a headache."

"Oh, that. I made it up when it looked like she would stay back with me. She's sweet but I didn't feel like company."

Naina watched in bewilderment as he pushed off from the wall, sauntered closer and picked up a sheet of paper at her feet. It must have come loose from Ajay's sketch pad.

Shock rooted her as she looked at the sketch. She hadn't realized Ajay had drawn her too. He had rendered it with his usual artistic brilliance, capturing such intimate details for a black-and-white sketch.

Her mouth was curved into a tentative smile, her hair its usual mess. But her eyes and mouth…he'd caught the wistfulness and the longing and the desperation with such crystal-clear clarity that she felt exposed, raw. As if things about herself even she didn't fully understand had been captured on paper for all the world to see.

She reached out to grab it. Her hand landed on Vikram's arm as he held the paper out of reach. Taut muscles clenched under her fingers, the side of him hard and warm against her front. Her breath became shallow as she realized how close they were standing. If she moved her head one inch, she could kiss his stubbled chin. If she leaned forward, her chest would graze his.

His harsh exhale was a warm stroke against her cheek. Her tummy began a slow roll as their gazes held, a million questions ping-ponging between them.

Naina knew in that moment what Ajay had seen with his artist's eye even before she had.

She would do anything if it meant she could touch, hold, kiss this man with the sort of freedom she'd had that night at the ball. And the depth of her longing went beyond physical attraction, beyond the need to be the center of his attention. So much beyond the powerful prize he represented.

She pulled away, sudden fear making her jerky.

Vikram's expression shuttered, the earlier tension swathing his frame again. "But Ajay was here with you. So it's only certain company you wanted to avoid."

Still too shaken, Naina couldn't summon the energy to rise to the bait. She felt as if she'd simply unravel if he said one wrong word. "Mrs. Sharma chatters constantly. Ajay missed the dinner because he had a call with Virat. I jotted down notes for him. Virat was in one of his brilliant moods…" She rubbed her temple, feeling a real headache setting in. "I'm sorry I didn't realize that the team dinner tonight was so important."

He stepped back. Naina had a feeling he'd come to some sort of decision. About her?

When he spoke, he was all formality. "Zara's flying in first thing tomorrow morning and seeing as she's coming, I've asked her if she'll do a photoshoot with me. She'll join us all at the resort afterwards. Tell the team they're free for a couple of days."

"I didn't know Ms. Khan was flying in. I'll let Virat know he can do her screen test. He said he might be here—"

"This isn't really a work trip for Zara," Vikram said, cutting her off. "She's mainly coming to see me. Virat and I haven't yet reached a consensus on whether she'll play the role of the prostitute spy yet."

"But she's perfect for the role. Virat doesn't approve

of Ms. Khan?" she asked to keep the conversation going more than anything.

Thoughts swirled through her head like a whirlpool, sucking her in.

Why was the actress coming if not to join the project? Had Vikram specifically invited her? How long was she going to stay? Were they going to re-ignite their well-publicized on/off affair?

She wanted to demand answers from him even knowing that the answers might not be bearable.

"Virat and Zara have never seen eye to eye," he said, still staring at the sketch. "But I'll get my way in the end. See to the arrangements for her stay, will you? Clear my calendar."

"What about the call with—"

"Cancel everything for tomorrow and day after. You won't be needed either. Feel free to explore the islands with...the rest of them."

The command felt like a slap in the face. She couldn't help feeling as if she'd somehow failed him. "Wait, Mr. Raawal," she called out.

He turned, his expression even more closed off than usual. "Yes, Ms. Menon?"

"Did I do something wrong? Did I—?"

"No. You've been your delightful self, as always," he said with a smile that didn't reach his eyes.

It didn't feel like a compliment. She pointed to the paper in his hand. "Can I have that?"

He looked at the paper in his hand for long seconds. As if it was the most fascinating thing he'd ever seen. As if... Then he looked at her, his expression completely shuttered. "No. You may not," he said, and walked out.

Zara Khan arrived at the resort the next afternoon, straight from the morning photoshoot, arm in arm with Vikram.

Naina would have given anything to hide, but the entire team had been determined to welcome the actress, their enthusiasm contagious.

She looked like an island queen in a two-piece yellow bikini and a bright white sarong wrapped around her waist as she walked over the wooden bridge, flanked by water all around, her beauty one of strong lines and angles rather than something that would fade with age.

In contrast to her extravagantly sunny look, Vikram was the perfect foil for her with his sculpted features and un-shaven jaw. Dressed casually in khaki slacks and a white linen shirt rolled back at the sleeves, he was darkly sexy, his appeal a byproduct of his arrogance and power. That intensity of his presence, which was always a huge draw on the screen came from how deeply he felt about things. To call him cold and calculating had been unfair on so many levels, Naina knew.

She'd learned that the photoshoot was for an exposé that would feature Vikram and Zara as long-standing top Bol-lywood stars, their rise to stardom, their long-sustained careers, and their coming together for a behemoth project for the biggest project Raawal House had taken on in its seventy-year history.

At exactly the same time as the article ran, the sensa-tional news about Vijay Raawal's biopic would also hit the industry.

Just because it was the project of his heart didn't mean it wasn't a huge, commercial machine that he was setting up to succeed at every level. With the knowledge of how many employees were involved, Naina was relieved that he was at the helm.

"So many livelihoods depended on me," he'd said, and she could see it in action now. But at the end of the day, she wanted to be the one he leaned on, for pleasure, for

laughter. She wanted to be the person with whom he could be just Vikram. The strength of that feeling increased with every passing moment.

As the rest of the team surrounded them, Naina stayed back.

From a PR point, it was sheer brilliance to use the long-standing rumors about their possible romantic association to fuel the news cycle. Naina had never paid much attention to the gossip about them, but with them standing front of her right now, it was unavoidable.

Impossible to miss the ease and affection between them, to not see their gazes meet in wordless communication. Impossible to not notice that Zara Khan enjoyed a level of intimacy that Vikram didn't even allow his family.

Naina couldn't even hate her because the woman was graceful and down-to-earth when introduced to the team. Fresh fruit tasted like ash in her mouth when Naina returned to lunch.

Had he already lost interest in her then? Was it as simple as switching from her back to Zara?

Could Naina blame him when she'd made it so clear that she wanted nothing to do with him? When she continued with the pretense that night at the ball had been a one-off?

What would happen if she openly admitted to him that she was his Dream Girl? If she met him in the daylight as his equal? If she walked up to him and said, *I want more than a few hours of stolen kisses. I want to see where this will go. I want to make you laugh again like I did that night. I want you to kiss me again.*

What would happen if instead of doing what was safe, Naina reached out for what she really wanted?

CHAPTER NINE

CURSING HERSELF, NAINA picked up what felt like twenty pairs of earrings she'd thrown around the room when she heard someone come in.

"I'm almost done packing. You can start in the—"

"Where the hell do you think you're going?"

She straightened up to see Vikram and Zara standing at the entrance to her room. Damn it, she'd meant to leave before they returned from wherever they'd gone. For most of the afternoon and the evening. All seven hours of which she'd been acutely aware, down to the last minute.

Zara was dressed in a beautiful white pantsuit that made her look as if she'd just stepped off the pages of a magazine. Vikram, however, looked much more casual in a white linen shirt tucked loosely into blue jeans that hugged his lean hips and muscular thighs. He still hadn't shaved. He looked deliciously scruffy, but there was also a look of resolution in his eyes.

"Ms. Menon?"

Naina jerked her gaze to his. Barely banked impatience shimmered there. It made her own hackles rise. She'd waited all afternoon to approach him. To...take her chance. And he'd been...gone. With the woman who occupied the closest familiarity with him.

Jealousy was a vile taste on her tongue. She closed her

fingers over the *jhumka* she was holding, the sharp metal of the earring digging into her palm. "I'm vacating the villa."

His jaw clenched. "Why?"

Naina busied her hands and her eyes with trying to close the zipper on her bag. "Ms. Khan and you will have more privacy here without my constant interruptions."

"You're a beast to throw the poor girl out, Vicky," Zara said softly.

"This is not on me, Zara. All I asked her to do was to make arrangements for your stay. Ms. Menon prides herself on anticipating every need anyone in this team might have and bends over backwards to fulfill them."

Naina dragged on the stuck zipper, fury rattling inside her. "You're the only member of the human race who thinks being nice to people is a serious character flaw."

"There's nice and then there's naive," he retorted.

She rounded on him. "Admit it, my 'innate goodness' that you sneer at so much is what finally healed the rift between Mr. and Mrs. Sharma and made them create that brilliant plot twist in the script. I'm the one who got Saira Ahmed to give this project another chance. I'm the one who—"

"No one's saying your contributions aren't valuable. But you don't even realize that half the team is taking advantage of you. You run their errands, you take notes for them, you…act as their champion to me and Virat. They've got you wrapped around their collective little finger."

"What's wrong with wanting to help?" Naina took a step toward him. "You've no idea how good I feel working on this project, working for you. Why is it that you're constantly—"

"Thank you for arranging that chat with Mrs. Ahmed. I've been a fan of hers for so long," Zara cut in, clearly jumping in to defuse an escalating situation. "Will you have dinner with me soon—tomorrow, perhaps? Or the following evening?"

"It was a small favor, Ms. Khan," Naina said, turning her attention to the woman studying her intently. If her heart wasn't in her throat, she'd have wondered what the gorgeous actress found *so* fascinating about her. "Dinner isn't necessary."

"I insist. I want you to come work for me, Ms. Menon."

"What?" Naina whispered, feeling as if the ground had just been stolen from underneath her.

"Vicky said he can spare you in as soon as three days."

Naina swallowed, keeping her gaze away from him. It felt as if he'd dealt a punch to her gut. "I... I can't accept your offer, generous as it is." She swallowed again. "Mr. Raawal's arrogance, as I'm sure you very well know, has no bounds. He likes to believe he knows me and my life better than I do myself."

Zara's mouth dropped open and then she laughed. The sound filled the stifling silence. "She definitely knows you well, Vicky."

To Vikram's angry gaze, it seemed no one but Naina existed. "You don't have to flee the villa in the middle of the night. As cold and calculating as I am, I don't throw my assistants out to sleep in the open."

"Ajay's okay with me bunking in his villa for the next week. Or until whenever it is that you're actually throwing me out."

"Like hell you're sharing with him," he declared, coming into the room and grabbing her bag.

"Why are you so angry with me?" Naina blurted out. "I should be the one who's... In fact, I *am* mad at you."

His head jerked back. "Go on, Ms. Menon. Don't get shy now."

Her skin prickled at his tone. "If this is about me calling you cold and calculating the other day—" Ms. Khan's stifled laughter filled the air "—I—"

"I don't want your bloody apologies."

"Then what *do you want* from me?"

"The truth." With one more stop, he came closer, the heat of his body singeing hers. "What will it take to get you to stop pretending?"

"Fine." Naina poked him in the chest, every emotion she'd been struggling to bury ever since that night they'd made love finally erupting out of her. "I'm leaving because from where I stand, it looks like the moment you lost interest in me, you invited *her*! I'm leaving because you know damn well it was me that night at the masked ball and I... want more. More of you and me."

Her face flamed as if someone had lit up lights under her very skin. Her fingers were shaking, her knees felt like pudding. And yet, Naina also felt as if a huge weight had been lifted. As if she had finally walked into the sunlight after stumbling around in the dark.

The tense silence that followed made her wish she could take a running jump into the ocean. Maybe swim her way across the Indian Ocean back to Mumbai. Or at least drown trying.

Vikram just looked as if he'd finally won the Best Actor award he kept being shunned for by the national film committee, every year. Now sitting on the bed, legs crossed at his ankles, mouth pressed into satisfaction, he was arrogance personified. She wanted to kick him as much as she wanted to kiss him.

Instead, she forced herself to make eye contact with Zara. This was not how she wanted to begin her associations in an industry in which she wanted to build her career. "I'm so sorry, Ms. Khan. I assure you I'm not usually so unprofessional."

"Oh, psshh…" Zara said, waving an airy hand. "This is the most fun I've had in a long while. I don't think I've seen Vicky jealous in…forever, actually. He's been terrible company the whole day. As for the villa, I'm afraid I was far too preoccupied with my own troubles to inform him before I arrived that I made my own accommodation reservations. Vicky and I don't need that kind of privacy, Ms. Menon. Forgive me for the confusion I created."

Naina didn't miss the nugget of information the actress had purposely offered. "I'll move out anyway," she said numbly, feeling like a fool.

"Zara, please leave us."

Vikram's quiet request cut through the tension like the crack of thunder split a calm, blue sky. Zara left without a word.

Naina's heart pounded in her chest as he got up and closed the door. She opened her mouth to speak but nothing came out. She swallowed and tried again. "I'm not leaving until the script is finalized. In fact, I've even figured out what Virat thinks is missing from it. I know how to—"

His soft curse exploded in the thick silence. "This is not about your job and if you were anyone else, you'd know it." He pushed his fingers roughly through his hair. "You fight me when I call you naïve, and yet you turn down Zara's job offer instantly?" His chest rattled with a sound that was half growl, half sigh. "God, you need a damned keeper."

Slowly, the full meaning of his words sank in. Of course, he was the one who'd recommended her to Zara. Why? To what end? Naina felt as if she was standing in a fog of unknowns—mostly created by her own feelings. But she had nothing to hide anymore.

"I don't want to work for her."

"Why not?"

"I don't want to be associated with anyone you know."

"That's most of the bloody industry then," he snarled, coming closer. Impatience etched into the lines around his mouth. He looked nothing like the suave, coldhearted businessman she'd called him that first day. "I won't have your joblessness on my conscience." He closed his eyes, sighed and then skewered her with his gaze. "Has it become so hard to be near me?"

"I don't need to be rescued. By you, especially." After months of being directionless, she knew what she wanted to do now. The last few weeks had filled her with a renewed purpose, with new zeal. Working with him on this concept had filled her with inspiration and energy. "Why are you so intent on kicking me off this project? Did I do such a bad job?"

"You've done a fantastic job of everything I've thrown at you. I just…can't have you working for me. Not anymore. It's too distracting.

"And FYI, you're selling yourself short if you think Zara's doing you a favor."

"And if I don't want to leave you?"

He raised a brow, and took in her resolute expression. She thought he'd ask her why she wanted to stay. It wasn't as if he hadn't stripped her to the core already.

She knew this was what being with him would mean. There would be no lies between them, no games, nowhere to hide, even if she wanted to. There was something about him that brought out the boldest, best version of her and she loved being that Naina. Not a flicker of fear touched her.

He leaned back against the large window frame, his fingers wrapped tightly over the sill. "Why were you moving in with that…graphics guy?" he bit out.

"I don't want to move in with him so much as…" Naina looked at him, without her own emotions blinding her.

"It's been forever since I've seen Vicky jealous," Zara had said. He *was* jealous. Of her friendship with Ajay?

"You think I'm interested in Ajay?" she said, taken aback.

"Are you?" When she looked blankly at him, he sighed. "You've been spending a lot of time with him since we got here. Maybe you decided you've wasted enough of your life moping after your useless ex. Maybe you're making up for lost time, since you've discovered that men find you irresistible. Maybe you've decided you want more and more of those fantasy nights like the one we shared.

"I've been told by Virat and Anya and now Zara that I need to ask first and then act. So, I'm asking you first. Instead of just having him thrown off the project on some flimsy excuse."

"That's not funny, Vikram," she said, reaching for his folded arm. His muscles were taut under her fingers. "Promise me you won't do any such thing. You can't—"

He closed his other hand over hers, the contact sending a shock wave of pleasure through her. His fingers were warm and tight over hers, and she wanted to lean into the touch even more. Until she was burrowed into his warmth. "That's what I need to do to get you to say my name? Threaten your latest boyfriend?"

"You've always been Vikram in my thoughts…"

Folding her arms, she gazed at him, the panicked thunder of her heart slowly settling down into calm acceptance. Standing here with him, discussing where this was going between them…shouldn't have felt so natural. But it did.

It felt easy and right and inevitable, since the second he'd walked into her room at his grandmother's house and asked her what was wrong.

"You won't fire Ajay," she said with confidence. "You're

not the type to ruin a man's career because you're jealous. *If* you're jealous in the first place."

"Ahh...such faith in me, Naina?" He sighed, and this close, she could feel the tension in him. "Yes, I'm jealous. I spent the entire photoshoot imagining you being with him like you were yesterday evening. I was short with Zara for needing me right now. I've cursed Virat for recommending the guy in the first place.

"Then I cursed you for making me jealous. Every time, you called me Mr. Raawal, I wanted to drag you back into my bedroom and show you how familiar we are with each other.

"You've been driving me crazy, Dream Girl."

"I'm not interested in Ajay in that way. He's easy to talk to. Maybe because he doesn't dictate what I should be doing with my life."

He groaned and turned away from her. "Are you going to hold that against me forever?"

"I don't know," she whispered softly, her pulse zigzagging through her entire body.

Forever...was that where he saw this thing between them going? Or was it just a slip of the tongue? Or his definition of forever could be completely different from hers. It could mean a week, a month. It could mean just tonight, could mean just long enough for them to reach climax.

And yet it didn't deter her one bit. Whatever he gave, for however long, she wanted it. She wanted him. And for the first time in her life, she was going to do precisely what she wanted. Take what she wanted.

She took a step forward and leaned her forehead onto his back, loving the solid feel of him so close. For long seconds, they stood like that, with just that small contact, their breaths tuning into the same rhythm. "Can I ask you something?" she whispered, before taking the final plunge.

His hands fisted by his sides and she felt his exhale as if it were her own.

"Ask away, Dream Girl."

Her smile felt like it came from her stomach, spread upward, filling her with indescribable joy. She was such a fool. Why had it taken her so long to reach out and ask for this familiarity? This intimacy? "You...you didn't invite Zara here because you're kick-starting your relationship with her?" She felt small, naïve, exactly the woman he called her asking that question, but she had to know.

"No. You know there's an awards show on the island coming up. She wasn't initially going to attend but I persuaded her to change her mind and come a few days early so we could do the photoshoot at the same time. Zara and I have no relationship to kick-start because we have never been involved like that."

"I'm sorry for assuming that you simply switched from me back to her."

He shook his head. "You're the only woman I've slept with for months, regardless of what I said to you on the flight here. But I'm not going to apologize for thinking you were with Ajay. It only says another man can also see what I see."

"Ahh...there's my old friend. Your mighty arrogance. Just when I think I couldn't like you any more, it shows up. Saving me from toppling headlong at your feet."

He turned his head, offering her his profile. "Let's hope you always think that."

Always and forever...she knew he didn't throw out words like that with everyone. He wasn't even that voluble with the general public. But neither was she going to build castles in the air. He clearly wanted her. For now. And that was enough for her, for however long it lasted.

The tight knot in her stomach was already melting, the

sun-kissed scent of him coiling around her with a familiarity that comforted her, with a thrill that unraveled the twisted knot of her own emotions. She covered the last few inches of space between them and wound her arms around him. Solid and big and hard, he took her breath away. He made her excited and alive and she wanted to rub herself up against him.

She opened her mouth against his back, the thin linen shirt no barrier to the heat from his skin. She dug her teeth into the hard muscle. His grunt and filthy curse made her smile. "I'm distracted too. All I can think of is that I want a repeat of that night. A hundred repeats. Here. Now."

She didn't know when he turned. Or when he pulled her to him. Or how it was that he maneuvered them into the wide window nook and then she was atop him, her legs splayed across his lap with her arms around his neck.

All she knew was the jolting sensation of his mouth against hers. *Finally.* Of the heat and hardness of him enveloping her. Of the sweet, sharp taste of him reaching out into all her limbs like tendrils of magic.

Her rib cage expanded as if it couldn't hold her thumping heart, her blood sang. She moaned when he thrust his tongue into her mouth, and chased hers. When his big hands enveloped her waist and tugged her against him. When he groaned into her mouth when she licked him.

This kiss was nothing like the ones at the party. Those had been sweeter, exploratory, a benediction. She realized, panting now, how gentle he'd been with her that night. How much control he'd exerted, how much he'd let her set the pace. How much he had made it all about her. It had been an introduction to the pleasure he could weave using her own body. It had been soft and inviting and full of promises.

This kiss…was the exact opposite. This kiss simply

took. With nips and bold strokes, this kiss claimed her. *He* claimed her. There was no leash on his hunger. No soft invitation to feast on him. No playing nice for the wide-eyed virgin. This time, he gave her his rough need, his desperate bites, his urgent, panting groans.

He licked and nipped and soothed, leaving no doubt as to how much he wanted her. How easily he could steal her breath and give her his own back.

He wasn't gentle with her—not his lips on hers, not his fingers on her hips, not his body when he flipped her over and lay her down on the bed against the fluffy cushions. And Naina loved it all. Loved that she'd brought him to this desperation with just her words.

He knelt over her, between her legs, his gaze drinking her in. "Can I touch you?"

He asked in such a quiet yet fierce voice that Naina shamelessly blurted out, "Yes, please." She licked her lips. "Sometimes I wonder if that evening was a dream."

"I do too. And I want to know so badly that it wasn't."

"Yes, please," she said again and he laughed.

"These shorts have been driving me crazy," he said, before yanking them down.

And then he made love to her with his fingers.

All Naina knew from the moment his fingers disappeared under the seam of her panties was pure pleasure. First soft and slow, like the wings of a butterfly, to deep and visceral, until she was chasing his hand in pursuit of the peak.

And through it all, he learned about her. Watching every expression on her face, listening to every gasp, asking her what felt better, what she wanted more of, what would push her over the edge.

By the time she was fragmenting into a thousand shards, Naina felt as he'd bound her to him permanently.

She could imagine no other man showing her this care. No other man watching her with such ferocity. No other man putting her needs first.

Their foreheads leaning against each other's, their breaths were a harsh symphony. Her sex still pulsed from her orgasm but Naina wanted more already. She wanted everything. And she was beginning to realize that everything with this man could literally mean her...*everything.* Her mind, body and soul.

But even that stray thought couldn't dull the impulse to touch him. To know him. To learn what gave him just as much pleasure.

"You know what I regretted most about that night?"

His gaze jerked to her, his brows drawing into a scowl. "What?"

Pushing herself up onto her elbows, she snuck her hands under his shirt. "That I hardly touched you at all. That I just lay back and let you...do all the work. Today, I want to rectify that."

"I will let you have your way with me. To an extent," he added.

Naina rolled her eyes at his arrogance, refusing to let him deny her this.

Warm, taut skin greeted her questing, hungry fingers. She traced the ridge of his abdominal muscles, up his defined pectorals. Some instinct she didn't even know she had made her alternately scrape her nails against the smooth skin and then pull through the rough trail of hair. Up and down, she ran her fingers.

Head thrown back, he let her have fun. Let her have her way with him. A profusion of joy and warmth filled her to see him submit to her this way. This all-powerful man to the entire world, and with her...he was Vikram. Just Vikram who liked old songs and tart retorts and rough kisses and her. He was this way only with her, and it was the biggest joy she'd ever known.

The corded muscles in his neck stood out. Pushing herself up even further, Naina pressed her open mouth against the hollow of his neck and licked him. His arm came around her waist immediately, holding her up while she feasted on the jut of his shoulders, the pulse at his neck. Always watching out for her.

His innate concern only twisted the hunger more tightly inside her. She wanted to crawl into his heart and burrow there. Clasping his cheeks with her palms, she sucked his plush lower lip into her mouth. "I told Ajay he was getting this curve of yours all wrong," she whispered.

He raised a brow.

"When he was drawing you," she clarified.

He still glared. And then he sighed.

"I don't want to hear his name right now, Dream Girl." He tugged at her lower lip with his teeth in retaliation and she moaned at the sharp sting. The sheer heaven of his caresses pulsed even brighter in contrast. He soothed the tiny hurt by blowing on it, his eyes raking over her face. "I don't want him drawing you anymore. That picture of you…it was brilliant. And it felt like he achieved that only because he knows you so well."

Her eyes wide, she stared at him. "You're serious."

He hummed his assent against the shell of her ear.

"I find I'm very possessive over you, Dream Girl. The fact that he laughs with you, that he shares his talent with you…that he knows you so well, while I watch on like a spectator, wanting so badly to be the one to be next to you…it's hard for me to reconcile at my age what a sore loser I am. So take pity on me and refrain from any more midnight trysts with him."

She giggled and traced the lines around his mouth.

"You're not that old. And it wasn't a midnight tryst. We were watching one of your films. He idolizes you."

He simply shrugged. As if this didn't make a whole lot of difference. Suddenly serious, he cupped her cheek. "You're one of those people to whom everyone is drawn. I'm realizing that now. I was wrong to assume you're a pushover."

She plunged her fingers into his hair and sighed. "Ajay and I are just friends. We laugh a lot and—"

"Ah…there's the rub, Dream Girl. It's not that I don't trust you. It's just that I…"

"You're what?" she said when he trailed off, caught by the expression in his eyes. It was unreadable. Suddenly, it felt as if she couldn't reach him. As if he'd drawn himself behind a curtain she couldn't open.

"I'm selfish, especially it seems, when it comes to you. I don't want just your kisses and your moans. I want your tart comebacks, your hopes and fears, your laughter, your dreams…" Holding her gaze, he ran his big palm over her neck, to the valley between her breasts, to her belly and finally, to cup her mound. "…your everything." He pulled away, and she felt the loss of his touch like an ache. "I want you too much, this too much. And in my experience that's never a good thing."

"Speak for yourself," she said, not liking his tone or the bleak look in his eyes.

Determined to erase his sudden doubts, she slowly kissed his jaw. Dotted a line of open kisses to his mouth. This time, it was she that took. She who kissed and nipped and bit and licked until they were panting against each other. It was she who controlled his pleasure, she who chased his tongue in his mouth, she that became the aggressor. And she loved it.

She pulled his skin between her teeth, while sending

her fingers back down, past the waistband of his trousers, to his throbbing erection. The hardness of him against her palm had her moaning out loud.

With a boldness she'd discovered she loved within herself, Naina scooted closer, until his thigh was pushing up against her core. She traced the shape of his shaft through his jeans, up and down, cupping and stroking, reveling in the tight tension that deepened in his body as she caressed him.

She had done this to him. Her.

"Inside me, please," she begged, beyond reason now. Beyond caring that Zara Khan or anyone else could walk in here and find them like this. All she wanted was to feel him inside her again. to experience his thick heat moving faster and harder, to hear him finding his ultimate pleasure with that hoarse grunt in his throat.

When her fingers reached for his zipper, his fingers tightened on her wrist. Stalling her. Stopping her.

"What are you doing?" she said, falling back onto the pillows, her tone sharp to cover the sudden shaft of fear.

Gaze lit with some unreadable emotion, he held her arms above her head. Bending down, he took her mouth in a rough tangle of a kiss that left her breathless but was in utter contrast to what he said next. "We should stop now."

She jerked her hands away from his grip. "Why?"

"I need a moment to…collect myself. A few days to process this. It's the consequence of being a man of a certain age."

She widened her eyes, forcing humor into her tone. "Oh, you mean you might not be able to…perform?"

He nipped the lush mound of her palm and then soothed it with a kiss. "No, you minx." He sat back on the bed, his expression thoughtful. "Technically, you still work for me and I swore to myself a long time ago that I…would never repeat any of my father's actions, including sleeping with an employee. Not discounting the fact that any association with me of this kind will plaster your face everywhere in the media. I…have to think of the consequences first. To me. And to you."

"Is that why you recommended me to Zara?"

He shrugged, and she knew she wasn't going to get a complete answer. "You will do well working with Zara. Especially since the replacement for my assistant will start soon anyway. And yes, I thought a little distance might be good for both of us."

"Me leaving to work for Zara was a little distance?" she asked, fighting the dark cloud that seemed to come across them all of a sudden.

"I should apologize for not discussing it with you first, but it wouldn't be honest." He rubbed his jaw, his eyes shining with unspent desire. "You always throw a wrench in the works, Dream Girl."

"Is that bad?"

"Not all the time."

"Then what is it that you have to ponder?"

"One of us needs to keep an eye on where this is going and it should be me. We need to be very careful. I don't want to hurt you, Naina."

"You would never hurt me."

His eyes gleamed in the low light. "That kind of blind trust is…dangerous. No one's worth your trust, Naina. That's what I'm trying to tell you."

"You said you wanted truth. That is my truth. I trust you absolutely. I know I'm going to sound like a heroine in one of your movies with no life before you arrived on the screen. But… I was only half-alive before that night at the ball. The sun feels brighter on my face now, the world more colorful, even my own emotions are sharper and more defined… You helped me realize who I am, and what I want, Vikram. And you're what I want now."

The more she said to convince him that she wanted him, the more he seemed to retreat. He shook his head. "You're…"

She sat up and gathered the pillow to herself as if she could protect herself against what was coming. "I'm what? Help me understand."

"You're…*you*, Naina. Your honesty, your artlessness, your innocence, you…make this very complicated."

She felt as if he was listing everything about her that made her unsuitable for him. Unsuitable and gauche and… just not enough. Anger rescued her from pathetic hope, from begging him. "What the hell does that mean?"

His silence spoke for him. His eyes said everything.

"I've made hard decisions just like you did, at a young age. When Papa passed away and I realized our home was mortgaged to the hilt, I gave up my PhD to find work to pay it back. When Maya got sick and needed round-the-clock looking after for weeks, I did it. Even though it meant canceling plans with Rohan, plans we'd made for months.

"I have lived through disappointments and hurts and setbacks just as you have.

"You don't have to protect me. From the real world. From you. From this." Frustration made her growl. "Even when I didn't admit to you that I was Dream Girl, we've been honest with each other. Whether this thing between us lasts for one night or one week or one month, all you have to do is say it's over. I can take it."

"I know that."

And yet, he didn't make a move to touch her. Stubbornly kept his distance. It was clear that something was still eating away at him. Clear that even after all this honesty, after stripping her defenses from her, after making her drop her barriers and admit to so much, he still didn't consider her his equal. He didn't consider her good enough for his sphere, for him.

"I have to be the first woman in the universe who's being rejected because the man has principles," she threw out.

"This is not a rejection, Naina."

"No?" Naina stood up on trembling legs and gathered her dignity. Seeing that she had just humped his thigh like a dog in heat, it was a little hard. "Was it just a power trip then? Making me admit how much I wanted you, giving me that orgasm without letting me give you pleasure in return…was it all just to prove that you have this…power over me? To prove to yourself that you can win me from some other guy?"

He flinched and she felt a moment's satisfaction that she had wounded him. It was fleeting though, for it wasn't in her nature to hurt anyone. And she didn't want to hurt him, of all people. She wanted to be a part of his life for as long as he'd allow, and he was taking that away from her.

"You know me better than that, Naina," he finally said. Still not touching her. Still not moving.

"I thought so too. But I've been proven wrong before. Maybe you're right and I will always be a little too naïve and little too foolish when it comes to men."

He called her name as she left the room but she refused to listen to him and his great principles anymore. She wasn't going to cry over him. She wasn't.

She had gambled everything and she'd lost. That's all this was. That's all it had to be. And yet, she couldn't help but like the man a little more for sticking to his own damned rules.

CHAPTER TEN

NAINA WAS TYPING away at her laptop in her bedroom, with a steaming cup of chai and a plate of samosas, while the rest of the team got dressed for the awards show to which they'd all been given free passes, thanks to Vikram's generosity.

It would be a frivolous, fun evening but the last thing she wanted was to be reminded why she didn't belong in the same sphere as Vikram, to see him and Zara on display for the entire world to see.

It had been three days since their showdown. Three days in which Naina had stubbornly stayed. Because leaving would have meant running away and letting him win.

He'd wanted to simply remove her from her role as his assistant, supposedly to give him time to work out how to manage any personal relationship they might have. But the reality was, she would be out of sight, out of mind. Apparently, she could be just as bloodthirsty when it came to arrogant men who made executive decisions for her.

In the stark light of day, she'd even succeeded in convincing herself that she'd had a fortunate escape. A man who could exert such self-control at that level, a man who could pull away that easily in the middle of lovemaking when he so badly wanted her—and Naina knew how desperately he'd wanted her...how could he ever feel comfortable with the strength of her emotions?

But when night fell and she heard him come into the villa long after she'd retired, when she heard his footsteps pause outside her room, when she remembered catching him looking at her as they worked, as if he couldn't get enough, when their hands touched innocently and lingered, she fell right back into the pit.

Fool that she was, she'd even deprived herself of Ajay's company. Not to pacify Vikram but because Ajay saw too much. The last thing she needed was to be pitied over Vikram's rejection of her.

It was his loss.

If she said that enough times in her head, she was going to believe it. Soon.

The silver lining however had been the camaraderie that built between her and Zara. True to Naina's first impression, the actress was down-to-earth and kind—mythical qualities in the industry. She had insisted Naina join her for her dinner last night, and just for that, she had all Naina's gratitude.

She had a feeling Zara knew most of what went down between her and Vikram. At dinner, she'd said, "The world is built for men to take it from us, Naina. Vicky is a good guy. But don't change, even for him. Don't let him take a single thing more than you're willing to give. Not your tears, not your joy, not your ambition."

"He doesn't want anything from me," Naina had replied, still smarting. "I'm not sophisticated enough to play his game."

Zara had squeezed her hand. "What is sophistication but a mask against hurt? You caught his interest because you're genuinely you. You can learn to play games but do you think we can all become a more honest version of ourselves, like you? Listen to your heart. You know him better than anyone."

"You're closer to him than anyone else. Even his family." Naina was ashamed to hear the hint of jealousy seep into her words.

Zara, the lovely woman that she was, just smiled. "We've been good friends for a long time, yes. But I've never seen him the way he is with you. You get to see the real Vikram, the Vikram even he doesn't know exists, methinks. And there's nothing more threatening to a powerful man than the unknown."

Naina didn't know what to make of that. Weighing it up, she thought Zara's insight might be useful. Naina wasn't a pushover, but Vikram had made her realize she could do a better job of establishing her own boundaries. Of giving her own wishes and dreams as much weight as she did Jaya Ma or Maya's. Of learning to love without fear.

She couldn't help seeing everything through the lens of his words now, herself included. She had always operated out of a worry that she'd disappoint everyone around her and that had to end.

This morning, she'd asked Zara if her job offer was still open and accepted it. Even in this, the blasted man had been right.

Why should Naina change the course of her whole life because of him? She resolved to speak to Jaya Ma about Papa's debts as soon as she returned home and persuade her that they should sell the house to pay them all off.

She'd clung to it only because she'd had memories of Mama and Papa living there. But Papa would never have wanted the house or his debts to become a millstone around her neck. To stop her from moving forward in life. Once again, Vikram had been right.

A knock sounded at her door. Naina opened it to see

one of the staff members standing there with a luxury designer shopping bag hanging from her fingers. Before she could reply, the woman thrust the bag into Naina's fingers and left.

Shaking her head, Naina pulled out the contents of the bag. A beautiful pale yellow dress slithered out from between layers of expensive tissue paper. Her mouth falling open, Naina tentatively unfolded the gown. Weightless and silky, the long gown caressed her fingers, instantly lifting her mood. The corset had been embroidered with hundreds of beads and then the dress flared at the hips in a high-low hem.

On impulse, Naina held it against herself in front of the mirror. It would fit perfectly. She smiled at her reflection. Further inspection revealed no note but a velvet case that made her heart thump. She opened it to find an intricately twisted white gold necklace with delicate white stones that would glimmer against her skin.

Zara had already offered to lend her an outfit, although Naina had refused. She should've known Zara wouldn't simply leave it at that.

With the dress and jewelry in hand, she didn't even have the excuse of not having anything good enough to wear to hobnob with the A-listers.

She'd been prepared to have a fling with the sexiest Bollywood star in history three days ago. She'd even talked about the script ideas she had for the project with Zara just yesterday. After months of grieving for her father and having lost her way for a while, she'd finally found her stride.

She wasn't going to spend tonight moping in her room. It didn't matter if she wasn't good enough for Vikram Raawal.

She was good enough for herself.

* * *

He hadn't thought she would come. He had fiercely hoped though and that had been a distasteful experience. He'd never in his life hoped for someone else's actions to make his day better.

But then Naina had already changed so many things. Burned so many assumptions he'd lived with down to the ground. The challenge lay in understanding which emotions could be managed or willed away and what needed to be indulged, within the limits he set for himself.

From the moment he had seen her on the flight, laughing with Ajay, he'd known things were changing. Day after day, he'd been telling himself that this lingering…madness, because he still wasn't sure what to call it, over his innocent, too-good-to-be-true assistant would go away.

It hadn't. And to continue to lie to oneself was both foolish and dangerous. When he'd seen her late at night alone with Ajay, he'd realized that the time to do nothing had already passed. If he didn't act quickly, he would fall into a pit of his own making.

If he didn't take things into his control…his emotions would begin to rule him. His everyday life, from the smallest minutiae to the biggest decisions about family, career, even the house he lived in, would become ruled by his need for her. His entire life would be defined by how he felt rather than what he did, at the mercy of someone else's fickle emotions and that was unacceptable to him.

Not that he believed for one second that Naina was fickle.

I was only half-alive before that night at the ball… God, the woman had no idea how incredibly addictive her particular brand of honesty was. Of how easily she shackled him with those artless words. She wore her heart in her eyes and Vikram wanted it so badly. He wanted how she looked at him to last forever, he wanted to be the hero she thought he was.

He saw now what an utter disaster it would have been for Zara and him to get married. They'd never been attracted to one another and he could only thank God she'd had the sense to turn him down. It wouldn't have been the explosive minefield of his own parents' marriage, to be sure. But there also wouldn't have been an iota of challenge in it either. Not a single spark of this excitement he felt as he stood there just contemplating what Naina would say next.

Or do next.

He and Zara were too alike. Too controlling. Too used to having their own way to let anything exciting grow between them. Maybe even too flawed for life to be anything but another cycle of that rote existence that had been gnawing at him of late.

All he needed to do now was course correct. A marriage where his heart wasn't involved but his body was, where he was absolutely certain of his wife's loyalty and trust... that was the ideal solution for him. Naina was the answer he hadn't realized he needed. She made all the dissatisfaction, the lingering restlessness of the last year disappear like sunlight cutting through fog.

Admitting it to himself brought an intense relief shuddering through his body.

In just a few short weeks, she'd made him uncomfortably aware of how possessive he could be, of how much he wanted to rearrange her entire life and everyone revolving around her in their comfortable orbits, just so that she could never be hurt again. Of how much he wanted to protect her from the world, and sometimes even from herself. What better way to do it than to look after her for the rest of their lives?

He'd spent three days keeping his distance from her, weighing the odds and ends of the entire thing and finally reached a decision, a decision that would serve both of them well. Once he made up his mind, Vikram never regretted or second-guessed himself. Never looked back.

All that was left was to convince her.

He stayed behind a pillar and watched her as she flitted from group to group on Ajay's arm, looking like a beautiful butterfly.

The silky yellow dress was perfect for Naina's petite figure, and the diamonds at her throat only emphasized the sparkle in her eyes. He loved that she was wearing an outfit that he'd particularly chosen for her. It was an underhanded way of getting her to accept it, thinking it was from Zara rather than him, but he'd so wanted to spoil her. Wanted to give her everything she could ever want.

Even here, among so many beautiful people, there was something innately different about her. Something that snared his attention from the moment she walked in and held it. Not that he doubted his attraction to her, or the depth of his need for her.

She was his. Only his.

Naina was more than glad she'd come tonight. She'd thoroughly enjoyed the performances by some of the most noted Bollywood stars and musicians. Had laughed her heart out at one comedy skit that had satirized Vikram amongst other actors and actresses.

Naina had enjoyed drinking champagne that tasted like rainbows, eating delicacy after delicacy dripping in butter, dragging poor Ajay to the dance floor and shaking it up to some fast numbers.

She'd spotted Virat, who'd flown in for the show, and waved at him from a distance, not eager to impose. He'd walked over anyway and hugged her, genuine affection in his eyes. She'd even been a reluctant witness to the awkward tension when Virat and Zara had come face-to-face. Vikram must truly have the emotional range of a spoon if he thought these two simply didn't like each other. Naina felt as if she'd been standing in a minefield of unspoken words and longing.

Through all the excited gasps and unbelievable star sightings, she was aware of where Vikram was every single moment. Aware of her speeding pulse any time he was nearby.

It was supposed to have been only a fling if he'd agreed, wasn't it? And yet, she constantly felt as if she'd lost more than that. More than just laughter and the chance for some spectacular sex.

No. He had taken a part of her with him whether she'd been willing to give it or not.

The thought didn't bring the frantic fear she'd expected, however. Like she'd told him, she had lived through harder times. Meeting Vikram had only made her stronger and she would survive this too.

While most of the team were living it up and celeb-spotting as if their lives depended on it, Naina followed his every movement from when he'd showed up at the stage to announce an award to the edge of the dance floor later with a drink in hand.

It was hard to see him with Zara, touching her casually, cocking his head close when she whispered something, draping his arm around her waist for a photo op...

Now that she understood their relationship better, it was also clear that what Zara and he shared was affection, even love, yes. But not romantic love. Anyone with a little sense could see that but of course the press always wanted to speculate about the couple regardless.

The bungalow where the after-party was held had a lounge with floor-to-ceiling glass walls all around offering a spectacular view of the ocean, with people spilling out into the garden and the marquee. Small crowds huddled under the gazebo, in the upstairs balconies, and some lounged by the infinity pool. Lanterns placed artistically lit up pathways everywhere.

It was entirely a different sphere of life, and she'd recklessly tangled with the uncrowned king of it all. She smiled at the vain thought even as she saw more than one beautiful woman sidle up to him.

Having fun at the party while he was an out-of-her-league Bollywood star was one thing, but standing near him, knowing that she'd seen a part of him that no one else had, while he joined their team and complimented Mrs. Sharma on her pretty sari and teased Ajay on his awful dance movies…was quite another.

She both hoped he'd ignore her and prayed he wouldn't. The man was turning her into a certifiable mental case.

"You look lovely tonight, Ms. Menon," he said suddenly.

Six pair of eyes turned to her, as if to appraise the truthfulness of his comment. Her heart took a little tumble as his gaze found hers. "Thank you," she said primly, knowing from the glint in his eyes that this wasn't the simple kindness he'd offered everyone else. Which was in itself unusual. He wasn't the type to engage in casual chitchat with his team. Or anyone for that matter.

"That dress is quite different from your usual colorful skirts."

For a horrific second, she thought he was mocking her style.

She ran a hand over her belly nervously. "Yes." Something in his gaze made her spine stiffen. Why was she letting him drive this conversation? "But then, this isn't my usual playground, is it? I had to borrow pretty feathers to cover up my usual artless style and my far-too-honest mouth. It's been made very clear to me—"

"Ahh...so then that red lipstick isn't quite doing its job." His gaze flicked to her full, lush mouth for a second. "It certainly fooled me."

"That I'm not sophisticated enough," she finished lamely.

"While I love your usual colorful skirts and dangling *jhumkas*, I have to say you rock this look too. Not that I'm surprised."

Her pulse raced as she realized he was not being facetious. "Thank you."

"Who said you're not sophisticated enough?" Mrs. Sharma jumped to her defense like the mama bear she was.

Naina shrugged. "Never mind, Mrs. Sharma. It's okay," she said, scooting closer to the other young guy on their team—a total idiot whom Naina usually avoided like the plague—and tangled her arm through his.

Two could play at this game. She would play so many games that Vikram would forget what artless and honest meant.

"I don't really have the taste for the high life. Too fickle for me. I'm happy where I belong."

The idiot took his chance and pulled her closer to his side, his muscled arm tight around her waist, smooshing her boob into his side. Naina thought she might throw up a little in her mouth.

Vikram on the other hand looked as if he wanted to separate the guy's arm from its socket. But such a vulgar display, she knew, was limited to his movies. Messy emotions had no place in his cultured, controlled existence.

But when he looked back at her, while the team saw their grumpy boss with a polite smile on his face, Naina saw something else. He hadn't succeeded in obliterating every emotion right then. His tight jaw, the way his teeth gripped his lower lip told her that.

"You clearly can move through worlds, Ms. Menon. Masked or unmasked, no man worth his salt could fail to recognize that you're the real thing."

Every word hit Naina like a fist to her heart, vibrating in her very cells.

If there was any doubt left among her team that this wasn't a usual interaction, that comment put paid to it. They stared in stunned disbelief at the raw, genuine emotion ringing in his words.

Did he want the team to gossip about them? Now, when she was on the verge of leaving? Why was he torturing her like this?

"Far too real then," she said, self-mockery filling her words. "And here I always thought I was not enough. Apparently, the opposite's the problem."

"Naina, *beta*, what in the world are you talking about?" Mrs. Sharma interrupted, her gaze swinging between her and Vikram.

Naina searched for something to say. "I think I will go thank Ms. Khan again. She was kind enough to lend me this dress and the necklace."

"I can't believe Ms. Khan let you borrow an expensive diamond necklace like that," Mrs. Sharma piped up, envy in her tone. "Be careful with it, *beta*."

"Oh, these are not real diamonds. They're..."

Mr. Sharma peered at her neck. "My dear girl, I would say those are one hundred percent real diamonds. And exquisite ones too. I should know. I was a jeweler's apprentice in another life."

Naina could have kissed Mr. Sharma's cheek for dropping that tidbit and pulling the team's attention away from her for a moment. Because she was sure her shock was written on her face.

Why would Zara let her borrow real diamonds? And now that she thought about it, why would she even own a dress that fit Naina's petite form when she was tall and statuesque? Why would…

She jerked her gaze to Vikram. One look at those falsely innocent eyes and the truth hit her. He had sent the dress and the diamonds to her!

A designer dress and real diamonds… What was he thinking? And why?

Anger diluted the stupid hope building in her chest. Hope was dangerous, hope made her weak.

She wanted to grab his arm and drag him through the curious spectators to demand what his game was. She wanted to tell the entire world and all the beautiful women that had made eyes at him that he was hers. She wanted to tell him, in front of this whole crowd, that she knew the real man, that she loved him for who he was beneath the mask of the Bollywood star, that she…

She loved him. So much that it stole her breath.

"Naina, what is it? You look…pale," he said, a sudden seriousness to his tone. All manner of formality was gone, all the false charm and teasing buried beneath genuine concern.

Naina heard Mrs. Sharma agree through the sudden pounding in her head.

She stared at him anew, her breath seesawing through her. Big and broad, he filled her entire vision and yet, she had no need to see or hear the rest of the world. In his beautiful eyes that saw so much and betrayed so little, in that sensual mouth that smiled far too infrequently, in the sharp nose that quivered to betray him when he wanted to remain serious with her, her entire world was in this man.

She was in love with Vikram.

A half sob, half laugh erupted from her mouth.

Scowl deepening, he took her arm and dragged her away from the avidly watching team members, his gaze not wavering from her. "I'll take you back to the resort. If you still don't feel better, we can call Dr. Mehta—"

"I'm not unwell."

"There's nothing wrong with being looked over."

His hand around her elbow, he walked her to the front of the bungalow and stuffed her into his car.

"You can't just ditch Ms. Khan." Something about the resolute set of his jaw made Naina look back. "I'm enjoying the party. I don't want to leave."

"Enough, Naina. You've already proved that you can stick it to me."

"You've made your decision, Mr. Raawal," she said, stubbornly. "You need to stop hovering around me as if you were my…keeper."

"Yes, I have made a decision."

Even without that statement, Naina got it. He had made a decision. It had been in his eyes when he'd complimented her. Because he didn't do anything without forethought. Without weighing everything.

Her pulse raced as she wondered what it was. If she could bear to be sane when she heard it.

"I don't think we should be alone right now," Naina protested, when they arrived at the resort. It felt as if the entire world had fallen quiet so that the only sound to be heard far and wide was the thudding of her heart.

His mouth flinched, his fingers tight on the steering wheel. "You sound as if you're terrified of me."

"I am." When he jerked his gaze to her, his mouth a flat line, she amended her answer. She could wound this man, she was realizing. "Not of you, exactly."

She sat like a doll while he undid her seat belt in quick movements. She went with him when he took her down the walkway to the villa they shared, straight through to her bedroom.

"Now, how about you tell me what's really wrong." His gaze ran over her face. "You still look like you're in shock."

How could she fall for a man who could control his desire and feelings as if he had access to an on/off switch? Who didn't even have an affair without calculating all the pros and cons?

She was never going to get over him, because even in this fog of fear, she knew no one would top Vikram for her. No one would know her or like her or care for her more than he did. Because he did, she knew that. Despite his own reservations. But by the same measure, would he always deny even the possibility of them being together long-term?

"I *have* received a shock," she finally mumbled.

"Did someone say something to you?"

She shook her head, one tear rolling down her cheek.

"Tell me what's bothering you."

His gentle tone made the feeling in her chest swell, until she couldn't breathe. No one had ever paid so much attention to her well-being. Not even Papa.

"Come, Dream Girl. I know I'm not a real hero but I can fix anything for you. I want to fix it for you."

"I just realized that I've fallen in love. With you." She wiped the tear from her cheek and laughed. "With the arrogant, dominating, I-make-my-own-rules Vikram Raawal, who can't even have a fling with me because it breaks his rules."

His head jerked back, his shock clear in those beautiful eyes. "What?"

Naina fell to her bed and buried her face in her hands.

"And I just told you, didn't I? Not that it makes any difference."

"You think it makes no difference to me to know that you love me?" Those simple words sounded unusual on his tongue.

"Not in the big scheme of things, no. You abhor the entire concept of love. I know you well enough for that. And by blurting it out like that, I only opened myself to your ridicule. To you pushing me away again."

He knelt in front of her and tipped her chin up. Those eyes were tender, his knuckles gentle on her cheek. As if she were precious. As if he were afraid he would mar her with his touch.

This big man, on his knees in front of her, the look in his eyes…it was an image she would never forget.

And Naina knew that while he might never love her, he did care about her. He had kept his distance not because it was easy for him but because he'd thought it was the right thing to do while she worked for him. Not because she wasn't good enough.

Because Vikram always did the right thing, did his duty. Whether it was hard, or inconvenient or even if it meant denying himself happiness.

"I would never ever ridicule you. Never. What you have told me is a gift, Naina. Believe me, cold and calculating as I am, even I recognize it.

"Your words are a gift, Dream Girl. One I'm not sure I even deserve."

"Is it?"

"Absolutely. And even before you told me this, I had my plans for you."

"Like sneakily sending me a dress and diamonds?" She pressed her fingers to the warm stones at her throat. "Why, Vikram? I don't understand."

"I wanted you to have what you needed to go to the party."

She nodded, realizing how simple it was to him. She was now under the umbrella of protection Vikram Raawal extended. Whether she asked for it or not, he would always care about her. Give her whatever she asked. Except…himself. "You should know when I say I love you, I… I have no expectations of you. It is simply a fact. Like I love my stepmother and Maya and my neighbor's old dog Vicky."

"How charming that your neighbor's dog is named after me." He held her gaze as his own widened. "You named him, didn't you?"

She nodded and Vikram laughed. The joy in his chest was indescribable.

He had a feeling he could spend half a lifetime with her and she would still make him laugh. She'd give him more than he'd ever imagined he could take for himself. She'd already given him a future he looked forward to like he'd never done before.

And her love was a gift he would cherish. A privilege he would never take for granted. He would give her everything in return, everything he was capable of giving.

"That's the difference between you and me, Dream Girl. Because I do have expectations. Of this. Of us. A whole world of them."

She raised her face and pinned him with that stormy gaze. As if she meant to see into his very soul. As if she already could. "So you do want to be with me?"

He laughed again, to cover up the urgency he felt. Even his breathing felt shallow—his reaction to losing control of this thing between them. "Is that what you want to call it? Being with each other?" He searched for ways to say it right. "I want more than you can imagine. I want everything, Naina.

"I want you to be my wife."

The entire world seemed to have fallen silent at his admission. He couldn't even hear the waves outside beneath the dull thundering in his ears. He felt vulnerable, and he didn't like it one bit. But just this once, he promised himself. Just this once and she would give him everything in return.

"Have I rendered you mute, Dream Girl?"

She raised her gaze to his, her hands slowly coming to cradle his cheek. "Are you sure? You know you..."

"Would I offer you marriage if all I wanted was to scratch an itch?"

"No. Of course not, but...this is a...complete..."

Her swift intake of breath made him smile. Impatience fluttered through him, but he curbed it.

She turned her head, and moonlight gilded the tip of her nose, the curve of her cheek. In that moment, she was truly the most beautiful thing he had ever seen.

He pushed himself to his feet, settled down next to her and pulled her to him. She let him arrange her to his satisfaction, her curvy body settling against him with a sensual slide that made his heartbeat jump. Her palms landed against his chest, her face half hidden in the curve of his neck.

"Talk to me, Naina. Tell me what you're thinking. Don't ever take away your words," he said, burying his nose in her hair. She smelled like coconuts and lemon and something so incredibly luscious that desire began a beat in his veins. Just the graze of her body, the scent of her skin was enough to drown him in memories of their time together.

Of the incredible pleasure he'd found with her. Of the utter feeling of peace he'd felt holding her in his arms.

Small fingers rubbed at his chest, the weight of her voluptuous breasts against his ribs incredibly arousing. "You can have anyone, any woman in the world. And I'm just..." She laughed and it was the sweetest sound he'd ever heard. "I mean, not that I'm not great. I'm just not particularly beautiful or brave or ambitious or smart or fierce or..."

"Watch out what you say about my girl," he said, hearing the thread of ache buried deep in those words. It wasn't exactly insecurity. It was a question that had never been answered by people who should have, a question that gained more and more control over one's life the longer it went unaddressed.

"I'm so...ordinary, Vikram. Very much so. Nothing..."

"I'd like to point out that everything you've said is wrong."

"How?" she said, the word so full of hope that he had to consider his words carefully.

"Firstly, the idea that I could have any woman I wanted is such ridiculous thinking. I'm really disappointed you haven't already deconstructed such an arbitrary, archaic thought, as if women were meant to be simply...had." She giggled and pinched him and Vikram felt as if the entire world was in his arms right then. "Secondly, if I've learned one thing in life—and since I'm more than a decade older than you, you have to admit that I've seen and heard and done more things in my life than you have—"

"Oh, God, I can see you're going to use this to dominate every argument we will have..." she muttered into his chest, her mouth a warm, open pocket against his throat.

"It is in the ordinary that life and magic happen. Thirdly, all that is completely moot because I don't want anyone else. I want you, Dream Girl. Only you."

He could feel her softening against his words, against his touch. Against him. He nuzzled his nose into her face.

"But, Vikram…"

"Shh… Dream Girl," he said, pressing his mouth to the corner of hers. That quieted her immediately. "Do you believe that if I give you my word, I'd never ever break it?"

"Absolutely. From the first moment."

"Good. Now believe me when I say you've given me a future that I never allowed myself to even imagine I could have."

He opened his mouth and whispered against the silky soft skin of her jaw, loving the taste of her on his tongue. "So think of this. Take your time. I trust you, too, Naina. I trust that once you make a commitment to me, you will keep it. And I have never trusted anyone like that ever before."

Slowly, against his body's every wish, he untangled her from him. Or him from her. And stood up.

She frowned. "You're leaving?"

She looked so forlorn that he took her hand in his and pressed his mouth to the soft skin at her wrist. Her pulse moved through him like a song, sending his heart into overdrive. "You have a lot to think on. I…don't want to persuade you in any way. And if I stay, I will." He cursed and she looked at him with those wide eyes. "I will use the hunger I see in your eyes to persuade you to do anything.

"And I don't want to. So even as it kills me, I'm going to walk away, Dream Girl. Come to me when you're ready.

"Come to me, be my wife and I'll lay the entire world at your feet."

CHAPTER ELEVEN

NAINA TWISTED THE knob on the door and went in without knocking. It hadn't been more than a few hours. She hadn't gotten a wink of sleep and she knew she wasn't going to.

When she'd seen dawn paint the sky a brilliant pink, she'd given up and gotten out of bed. It wasn't as if she had to think and decide. She wasn't like him. She already knew her heart. She knew that while he would never say the words she longed to hear, this was enough for her. What he could give was more than enough.

He wasn't sleeping either. He was sitting upright on a huge bed in the center of the room holding the latest version of the script, bifocal glasses perched on his face, looking utterly cute. Bare shoulders and lightly haired chest on display made her swallow.

She stood like that, with her back pressed to the hard wood, her hands folded at her midriff. Suddenly, she felt strangely shy. For all that they'd been so intimate with each other at the ball, it had been in the dark of the night. In a way, it had even been easier. Easier to shed her inhibitions, easier to live in that moment, because at the end of it, she'd known she was going home alone. There had only been pleasure.

This intimacy, however, was different. This had vulnerability and awkwardness and tenderness and the slow burn of desire. Of anticipation.

When his gaze swept over her from her hair, into which she'd slathered that awful conditioning oil, to her bare feet, she realized she still had on her old oversized T-shirt and she'd taken her bra off as always. Thank God she'd at least washed her face and was blessed with good skin.

He put away the script and took off his glasses. Pushing up on the bed, he folded his arms behind his head and gave her the once-over again. The sheet slipped downward to reveal the happy trail on his abdomen and the waistband of his pajamas.

God, she could just lick him up when he looked like that.

"Are you planning to stay by the door all night?"

"I barged in to tell you my decision."

"And?"

"I realized belatedly that maybe I should have dressed up for the occasion."

"Dressed up?"

"Not formally, I mean. Just worn something silky and not applied this oil thing to my hair."

His mouth twitched. "Do you own silky somethings?"

"Not really."

"Is that oil thing so repellent?"

"Of course not. It doesn't have any scent at all. Don't you dare laugh at me, Vikram. My curls go haywire if I don't tame them at night."

"I wouldn't dare laugh at you, Naina." He sighed. And that broad, hard chest flexed impressively. "You...every time I think I know you, you surprise me some more. You make me laugh, Dream Girl. Now how about you tell me what's going on in that head?"

"I'm saying yes. To your proposal. I want to be your

wife. I couldn't sleep and I really wanted to come in here and tell you. And now, now I feel like I should've worn something sexier or put makeup on or just...you know, done something to mark the occasion as special."

"You make everything special, Naina. Haven't you got that yet?"

Naina shook her head. She knew she was being stubborn, but she couldn't help it. "It's not every day an ordinary girl gets proposed to, is it? You're the stuff of dreams, Vikram. I have this...crazy, overwhelming urge to make this night different for you. When you're a crotchety ninety-year-old man, I want you to think back on this night and go...yippee!"

A wicked light shone in his eyes. "So what I'm getting is that you really want to wow me?"

She nodded.

"Take that T-shirt off, then. Only if you're comfortable, that is. You always have to tell me what is okay and what is not, Naina."

Vikram had barely finished his sentence before she caught the hem of the tee and pulled it up over her head. The movement loosened the clip in her hair and even in their tamed state, her curls framed her face.

His breath slammed into Vikram's throat as he greedily studied this woman who was going to bring him to his knees very soon. He wanted to be on his knees right now, pressing his face into her cute belly button and even lower. He wanted to fill his every breath with the scent of her arousal.

Her skin was smooth and silky. Her breasts full and high, her waist tiny. White cotton panties made her brown skin gleam. She lifted both her arms to pull her hair back and that pushed up her breasts even more. His erection pressed upward, his breath shallow.

"I think I know what would make tonight special for you," she said, while he drank in her stunning curvy body.

"What?" he said, his voice hoarse.

"That night at the ball, you gave me a fantasy evening. I want to return the favor. I…want this time to be all about you."

Vikram pushed away the soft duvet and straightened up some more. "My pleasure is in you finding yours, Naina."

"No, Vikram." She pouted and he wanted to sink his teeth into that lip. "Don't be a gentleman. Don't treat me with kid gloves, please. This is as much about me as it is about you. How do you like it best?"

He saw it then—her vulnerability when it came to him. Because she thought herself not particularly beautiful compared to the women of his circle. God, if only he could make her see how he saw her, right then. How gloriously fierce and sexy she looked.

Since he couldn't, he decided to give her what she was asking for. To show her how much he wanted her.

"Fast and hard," he whispered without a beat. "But not without you climaxing first."

She nodded seriously, as if he was giving her life-saving instructions. "So what should I do first?"

"Are you wet for me, Dream Girl?"

Pink streaked her cheeks and the Neanderthal in him loved that only he saw her like this. But she didn't let her obvious shyness stop her. Slowly, she sank her fingers under the cotton of her panties, her brow furrowed in concentration.

"Oh…" she whispered and it went straight to his shaft. Hell, forget fast and hard, he was going to embarrass himself at this rate. "I'm very wet," she said with a languorous smile.

He patted the place next to him. And she came. Once

she lay down on the bed, he pushed her thighs wide and rolled to lie between them. He sank one hand into her hair and pulled up her face and took her mouth in a blisteringly hungry kiss. True to her word, she gave as good as she got.

She thrust her tongue into his mouth and licked him, her soft groans falling on his skin like sizzling raindrops. He pulled away, and leaned his forehead against hers. "Naina, this is definitely what you want?"

Clear brown eyes looked into his, and he wondered if she could really see into his soul. God, this woman made him hard with just one look. And she understood what he was asking too.

That this wasn't just about tonight. This was about their entire lives together, enmeshed. This was a commitment he would never break. And he needed to know she knew that.

She clasped his cheek and yet the tenderness didn't break the heat of the moment. "I want to marry you, Vikram. I want to spend the rest of my life with you. I'm going to be your hot, only seventy-eight-year-old wife when you're that crotchety ninety-year-old."

And then he didn't wait. He gave them both what they wanted.

He pushed off his pajamas and thrust into her wet heat in one deep stroke that sent her spine arching toward him like a bolt of lightning.

He let her get used to him for a few seconds and stayed still, while busying his mouth with the elegant line of her neck, the thrust of her breasts. He licked her nipple before drawing it deep into his mouth. Her hands in his hair told her how much she liked it.

With increasingly loud moans, she goaded him on. He pulled out and thrust back in and she groaned again.

He brought her hand to where they were joined. Eyes

wide, she looked down and then back up at him. "Touch yourself. Tell me when you're close."

She nodded, and Vikram filled his hands with her buttocks and dragged her even closer. Tilting her hips just a little, he pistoned in and out of her, desire a clamoring shout in his veins now. And she never looked away from him.

Finally, when she threw her head back and clenched against him in ecstasy, he let the last thread of his control fracture.

Naina woke up when she felt a hard arm around her waist, constricting her movements.

"A stampeding elephant moves less than you when you sleep," a voice whispered at her ear and she smiled.

Slowly, she turned, and there he was, lying on his side, looking down at her.

A burst of joy filled her chest. "Maybe we can sleep in different bedrooms like the maharajas and maharanis of the past. You can come visit me whenever you're in the mood."

He scowled. She giggled and tapped his brow.

He caught her finger and tugged it into his mouth. He licked the pad and sucked on her finger and Naina wiggled under the sheet covering them. She sent her hands on a quest and found warm, rough velvety skin. She stroked him to her heart's content—the silky hair, the taut nipples, the slab of his abdominal muscles, and further down...

He caught her wrist, and stilled her. He turned her until her back was to him and cradled her face in his hand. At her bottom, he was rock-hard. She gasped in a breath, ready again. Ready for whatever he wanted.

With his thigh tucked between hers, the pressure at her

core was delicious. His fingers played with her nipple, sending arrows of want deep down.

"That's not the kind of marriage I want," he whispered, licking the rim of her ear.

"No?"

He bit the soft shell. "Remember when you said you were called old-fashioned and that it was an arbitrary construct forcibly put on women?"

"I can't believe you remember all my lectures."

"Every word, Dream Girl. But I have no problem admitting that I am terribly old-fashioned. I want the world and its myriad, talented artists and set designers to know you're mine. I believe in claiming what's mine."

She turned around in his arms. "I…we don't have to rush into this, do we?"

"That's a relative term. We don't have to get married tomorrow, as much as I want to. Daadi will never forgive me. Say at the end of next month, when she's home from London?"

"I just need time to…"

"Decide?"

"No. To…take this all in."

When he scowled, she went for his mouth. Softly. Slowly. In a sensuous whisper. Almost a supplication. She rubbed her mouth against his, and stilled. And he understood the stillness. That first slide of their lips breathed through him, memories of that first evening only amplifying the sensation now.

Her tongue tentatively licking at his lower lip, pleading for entry rather than barging in. And when he did, with a harsh exhale, the tip of her tongue swirled against his, and then retreated. And then she did it all over again.

In and out, tease and taunt, lick here and a nip there, she wrung slow, soft pleasure out of him until he was panting. But he let her. He let her take whatever she wanted, however she wanted him. He let her explore and seek and retreat and revel in the simple kiss.

"You're all I want, Vikram," Naina whispered against his swollen lips. "It's not even like I want a big wedding. As long as Jaya Ma and Maya can make it, I'm okay with anything."

"Good," he whispered, the scowl disappearing.

Naina turned around again and nudged at the hardness with her bum. "Now will you just show me how it's possible this way?"

He laughed against her back and it was like a symphony playing over her skin. He lifted her leg and pushed in slowly from behind and Naina thought she might die from the onslaught of pleasure.

"Let me guess," she said, her breath seesawing through her, with his every firm thrust. "This is your favorite position."

His hand sneaked down from between her breasts, over her belly to unerringly land on her nub. He flicked it and she felt fire rain down her belly. "How do you know?" he asked, working her with a practiced ease that she was so incredibly grateful for.

"You have all the control like this."

He dug his teeth into her shoulder, counteracting the rivulets of pleasure pooling down at her sex. "True, Dream Girl. But I would never cheat you out of your pleasure."

As his thrusts became faster, he turned her face and kissed her and Naina knew, as she climaxed more fiercely than ever before, that he would always keep his word.

CHAPTER TWELVE

"I THINK THE script is brilliant. You've outdone yourself, bhai," Virat said over the video call, his fingers still shuffling the pages on the desk in front of him and making notes.

Vikram smiled, feeling more than a sliver of satisfaction at hearing the awe in his brother's words. It wasn't that he didn't trust his own intuition. But he had spent most of his career making movies for commercial success and he'd begun to doubt his vision. He'd started this concept as an homage to his grandfather but it had become his own soul project.

Today instead of feeling the sensation of having shackles around him whenever he contemplated a new project, Vikram felt a simple joy. Saving his parents from definite ruin had cost him a lot of his artistic integrity. And yet for Virat and Anya and even his parents' sake, Vikram knew he would make the same choices all over again.

"And yet you continue to slash it with that awful red pen of yours."

Virat looked up and frowned slightly. "Okay, so don't rain down fury on me. But there's just one element missing. And no, I still can't figure out what it is. Just give me another week to sit on this, yeah?"

Vikram nodded, even as he remembered that Naina

had said she knew what was missing. She didn't know a lot about making movies and yet, he trusted her intuition when it came to people. She was also one of the few people who would give him her honest opinion, who challenged him to look past his own blind spots.

Look at how easily she'd woven herself into the fabric of his own life.

In just nine days, he'd already gotten used to waking up with her curled up against him. It was disconcerting to say the least that after thirty-six years, someone could become so addictive in the matter of a few days. But he had no other word that would fit what was happening.

Marriage had seemed like something that would only work for him with someone like Zara, who would never ask him for more than he'd give. And Naina didn't either. And yet, he often woke up in the middle of the night to realize she had a way of taking what he wasn't even sure he could give.

There was a magical, addictive quality to their union that did…give him pause. Once she was his wife, that strangeness would become normal, he reassured himself. Naina was so far away from any life partner he'd imagined in his wildest dreams that the novelty of it was bound to go to his head.

"I'm surprised you're still in the Maldives when everyone else has flown home."

Vikram shrugged. "Aren't you the one who's always saying I need to relax more? Go with the flow?"

"But it's not just the island paradise that's wrought this difference. You're smiling and you didn't even yell at me when I said I needed time to sit with the script and make changes to it. Even Anya said you sounded different on your call with her."

"I trust your judgment, Virat. I know I have made you

doubt that before, both professionally and personally, and I apologize for it."

Virat blew out a breath. "I guess we're doing this then. Then I apologize for attacking you like I did last time. I'm not unaware, nor is Anya, of how much you've given us at great personal cost to yourself, *bhai*.

"It's not a debt I can ever repay."

Vikram swallowed the lump in his throat. He simply nodded, glad that they had sorted their differences. Oh, they would absolutely butt heads again—they were far too different in their temperaments not to, but things would be okay between them.

"Come, *bhai*, spill it," Virat prompted again.

"I'm engaged," Vikram said simply.

A stillness came over his brother's features, all the more disturbing since Virat had always been a ball of fiery energy from childhood. Every school had thrown him out, every teacher raised their hands when it had come to him. Even as an adult, there was a sense of constant motion, an excessive energy about his brother that Vikram always found disconcerting. And yet now…it was as if he'd pulled a shroud over himself, masking the real him.

But Vikram knew his brother well. Very well. They were comrades who'd lived through the war zone that had been their parents' marriage.

Virat wasn't simply angry at his announcement. It was something else. Something Vikram wasn't sure even his brother understood.

"You said proposing to Zara had been an impulse. A mistake. You said you'd been relieved when she turned you down. God, *bhai*, don't tell me she's accepted you after all. You're not right for each other."

He knew he was being a beast but Vikram wanted confirmation of the sudden doubt niggling at him. "Are you so sure about that, Virat?"

His brother pushed a shaking hand through his hair suddenly looking sick to his stomach, and Vikram realized he'd gone too far. That whatever was between Zara and Virat was no joking matter. "It's Naina," he said, eager now to remove that devastated look from Virat's eyes. "Not Zara. Like I said, that was just a momentary madness."

Virat's jaw dropped. "Naina as in Ms. Menon who shattered your ego, the Naina that you hired to be your temporary PA?"

Vikram laughed. "Yes. That Naina."

Virat leaned into the camera, as if to get a better look at Vikram. *"Bhai*...you're serious?"

Vikram simply nodded. "We haven't made it public yet. So keep it to yourself."

"She's not your type."

"I was unaware I had a type," he said flatly.

"She's innocent and full of heart, and one of a kind."

Vikram didn't like the admiration in Virat's voice. Even though he knew his brother was teasing him now. And that every word was true. "She's also undemanding, low maintenance and yes, she's honest about what she feels for me and she's never going to break my trust."

"You're marrying the poor woman because she's low maintenance?" His brother sounded appalled.

"I'm marrying her because she doesn't play games like everyone else in our industry, Virat. Naina knows my shortcomings, knows exactly what I can and can't give her and yet, she's all in. After all the drama of Papa and Mama's marriage, this is exactly the kind of—"

"Bhai..."

Vikram didn't need the warning from Virat. His skin

prickled. He hung up the call and turned around to find Naina standing at the entrance to the room.

Her eyes looked even wider than usual, the acute hurt in them pinning him to the spot.

"You wanted to marry Zara?"

He hated feeling defensive and yet she made him feel it. "It was just a crazy, impulsive thing. I didn't really mean it."

"But you don't do crazy impulsive things. You weigh your every word and action. So...what happened?"

"We don't need a postmortem of it, Naina."

"You proposed to your best friend. It had to have meant something. Even for you."

"Even for me?"

"Yes, you."

"I had a rough year. Call it a midlife crisis. I asked her one evening and she laughed it off and that was that. Really, Naina, you're making too much of this."

"Oh, yeah, I forgot. I'm supposed to be undemanding. Low maintenance. I'm supposed to give you all my trust and come running when you whistle, so that you can throw me a treat and then walk away when you're done. I'm not supposed to create drama. That last one is my most attractive quality to you, isn't it?"

Vikram rubbed his hand over his face and cursed. He hadn't meant for it to sound like a dismissal. Or a cruelly neat summary of what role she filled in his life. It had been a glib, defensive thing to say to Virat. Because how could he explain to his brother what he felt for her when he didn't understand it himself? When he didn't really trust it? When the fear of one day losing her kept him up at night?

"I will apologize if the way I said it hurt you. But it's not far from the truth, Naina. What we have is—"

"Am I just a replacement for Zara since she turned you

down? Because I have to tell you, you're getting a bad bargain, Vikram."

Vikram could feel himself shaking, losing control of this. "You're insulting not just yourself with that ridiculous comparison, but me too. And the commitment we've made to each other."

She met his gaze and nodded but he saw that they weren't done. He could see the same fears he felt in her eyes. "You're right. I know that you and Zara are best friends. I know that and yet…" Confusion and something like grief suffused her features. "Please tell me this was before you met me at the ball. Before we slept with each other."

"If it's just to keep your timeline straight, yes, it was before I met you. Before you came into my life. Before you—"

"So why hide it from me then?"

"I didn't hide it as much as I decided it was irrelevant to us. I still stand by that decision."

"And that should be enough for me?" she said, tilting her chin in challenge.

"Yes."

She sat down and pushed the tangled mass of her hair away from her face. "I thought you were one person who would never hurt me. I didn't even care that you…"

"That I what?" Vikram felt like he was standing on the edge of a cliff, blindfolded, completely unaware of how deep the gorge below was.

"That you didn't love me back. I was okay with it, honestly. I know you're not given to sweet words and sugary declarations but your actions said enough for me. I was more than happy with the fact that you wanted me in your life forever. That you…"

"I still do," he said, a shaft of fear cracking through the shell he kept around himself.

The power this woman could wield over him sent him into a cold sweat. And fear was something he'd always hated. Despised. It made his words curt. "So the question to ask is have *you* changed your mind?"

And she responded to that harshness, her mouth flinching. Her eyes widening further. Her fingers in her lap tangled and untangled. "No, yes. I don't know. All I know is that I need to rethink this. I need to—"

"Rethink what? God, Naina, look at me and say whatever the hell is going on in that head of yours."

"I don't know if I can marry you." She spat the words out and he could see the anger in her now. But it didn't touch him. Couldn't touch him.

If it did, he would be lost. And despite everything life had thrown at him, he had never allowed anything to make him into that lost creature that depended on someone else for its emotional well-being, like his father had his mother. "Either it's a yes or a no."

Naina saw the instant the shutter fell down over his features. As if it was simply a matter of pulling down a curtain. She suddenly wished she'd gone into his arms. When he touched her, when he held her, it felt like nothing and no one could hurt her. Like nothing could ever come between them.

"I love you, Vikram. So much. That's what makes this complicated."

"You have a funny way of showing you love me, Dream Girl. Just like the entire world."

"You're right. That you proposed to Zara in a crazy moment doesn't change anything. Maybe you hid it from me because it's such an uncharacteristic thing for you to have done. Because you hate weaknesses, don't you? You'd hate for anybody to think you needed someone in your life. But I do understand one thing now."

"And what is that?"

"That this marriage would mean completely different things to us both. For me, it meant entering into a holy bond with a man I love, and trust. A man who'd give me his highest commitment.

"But for you, it's a way of locking me down. A way of having what you want without the messy tangle of emotions to impede you. A way of giving me everything, the entire world, without actually giving me the one thing you should give.

"You're a businessman in this too, Vikram, as you are in everything you do. I'm a no-risk investment. That's why this is easy for you.

"I was awed by the fact that not only did you want to be with me but that you wanted to spend your whole life with me. I thought that was the ultimate commitment. For all the clever words you give me, I'm never going to be your equal in our marriage because you'll always hold part of yourself back. Because you have nothing to lose by marrying me and everything to gain.

"I deserve more than that. So I need time and distance from you to properly think this over. I need to—"

"Distance and time are not going to change a thing. I had years to become what I am today, Naina. This is another foolish demand of so-called romantic love…this expectation that people will change for you, that suddenly they can grow new personalities, that one morning, I'll wake up and absolutely believe in love…is downright ridiculous. You're giving up what's real, what's here, for some fantasy version of life that's not true."

She nodded then. "You truly think this is only about three little words? Or about asking you to change for me?"

"Then what the hell is it that you want from me?"

"Nothing. I do love you. I'll always love you because you made me love myself, Vikram. You gave me myself back. No one else did that for me. And if I agree to marry you knowing what I do now, if I continue this pattern of loving you so much, worried that I might lose you at some point because you don't feel the same, then I'm right back where I started. Do you see?

"This is me doing what you're always urging me to do—protecting myself from hurt. From people who would use my love and affection to achieve what they want, what's best for them.

"See, what you've been preaching to me all along has finally sunk in. I'm doing what's best for me."

She turned away from him, every inch of her trembling. Every cell in her hoping that he would swallow the distance between them and take her into his arms. But also just as terrified that if he did, she wouldn't be able to help herself from going back to him.

In her misery, it took her a few minutes to hear the silence behind her. She'd thought it would hurt less if she was the one who walked away first. Instead of being the one who was always left behind.

Her limbs shaking, Naina realized it made no difference at all. It still hurt like hell.

CHAPTER THIRTEEN

VIKRAM PUSHED HIS hand into his shaving kit looking for the card he'd stuck in there. He usually immediately saved an important contact on his phone but then, he wasn't his normal self anymore.

Something sharp pricked his finger and he pulled back with a filthy curse. A drop of blood welled up on his skin. He pressed a cotton ball against it and upended the leather shaving bag onto the black marble countertop.

A black metal dangly earring with tiny fake pearls shining around the base winked at him.

"I got this one at a street bazar in Hyderabad when I lived there one summer."

He picked up the *jhumka* and smiled. God, he couldn't believe he remembered every detail of her bargaining with some bloke in her funny dialect of Hindi. Naina had told him the story behind every pair of earrings one night when he'd complained about her things being everywhere.

Colorful scarves on different drafts of the script. Tubes of lipstick—always some gorgeous shade of red—seemed to multiply and take over among his clothes. She'd completely taken over his bedroom and he knew now, his heart.

He'd threatened to throw them all away if one more earring stuck into his backside at night and she'd been truly horrified. When he'd arrogantly reassured her that she'd have her pick of rare gems and jewelry to replace these ones, she'd been close to tears. So he had kissed her, promising to never throw anything of hers away.

"I know it's hard for you to understand, Vikram. But I don't want anything from you. Do you get that?"

He'd shaken his head. Because he didn't. Because he wanted to shower her with everything money could buy. He wanted her to live in the lap of luxury and never worry about another loan payment. But every time the matter of finances came up, she'd shut him down.

"The whole world is going to say I've landed myself a nice upgraded lifestyle. But your standing in the world, your various mansions, your cars, even your star power... they are all just window dressing, Vikram. The real you that only I get to see, the man beneath the megastar...that's my prize. You're my true prize."

He'd said nothing in return to her. On guard, constantly wondering what she'd demand if he said those things. He'd shown her instead with his kisses and his mouth and his fingers, driving her higher and higher and higher and then holding her tightly when she fell. She'd told him again and again, making herself vulnerable to him even while he continued to protect himself.

"I'm a no-risk investment," she'd said on that last day, and he realized now how right she had been. *"For all the clever words you give me, I'll never be your equal in our marriage, because you'll always hold part of yourself back."*

No, she was wrong about that. Those were only the lies he'd told himself.

Even when he hadn't recognized it, he'd been falling for Naina. God, he'd fallen for her so hard that very first time when she'd torn into him. When she'd told him so clearly what she thought he could be if he tried to change.

He just hadn't accepted it.

Two weeks since she'd walked out on him and yet she'd already left her mark on him. Already changed him in ways he was only realizing now.

Take for example the call he had received yesterday from his parents. They were going to celebrate their fortieth wedding anniversary in a fortnight's time with a huge bash, he'd been informed, and would Vikram please approve the budget and the event planner they were planning to hire and release the funds.

So he wished both his parents all the fun planning the party in such a polite note, released the funds and hung up the call without any questions, or demands or ultimatums.

His mother had called him back within minutes, inquiring if he was unwell.

He laughed now, wondering why he hadn't seen it this way before. He had built enough of a fortune that his parents could throw a bash or two and not make a dent in it. As for how they'd conduct themselves in front of the media and the others in the industry, nothing he said or did was going to change them now. When they hadn't all his life.

People that were important to him knew of him from his own reputation, his work ethic, his word. Nothing they did or said was going to change the path of his life. Not anymore now, and not for the past fifteen years.

It was as if a tremendous weight had been lifted off his shoulders. As if some invisible chains that had been binding him had suddenly been yanked off and he was free now.

Free to move forward.

Free to live his own life.

Free to pursue his own future with the woman he loved with all his heart.

* * *

The party was in full swing by the time Naina walked through the lavishly decorated foyer. She rubbed her hand down the pale pink sleeveless blouse she'd worn over another long cotton white skirt embroidered with beautiful yellow flowers. Jaya Ma and Maya had been horrified when she'd defiantly refused to dress up for an evening hobnobbing with the royalty of Bollywood.

This was the second party she was walking into at a Raawal residence. But this time, she was here as herself. Just Naina. Simply Naina.

The Naina who took risks.

The Naina who liked helping people.

The Naina who sometimes loved too much.

She wasn't here to impress anyone or to make herself feel better or to catch anyone's eye. She was here for herself. To make connections. To build a career at her own, slow pace. To live her life to the fullest.

When Virat had called her and insisted that she attend the anniversary party of his parents, she'd instantly agreed. Caught him by surprise. Because, of course, he knew his brother and she had been together. And that they had fallen apart just as spectacularly.

Virat wasn't inviting her as a favor or because he felt sorry for her. He was inviting her because she was part of the team now. She was officially part of Raawal House's Magnum Opus. And now she was working for Zara Khan, who'd been given the role in the film that Vikram had intended, she was going to see Vikram on the sets of the biopic anyway. Better to get used to seeing him. Of longing for him. Of wishing things had been different.

Because as much as the anger and hurt had slowly fallen away, the love she felt for him had stayed. And she'd made her peace with it.

In the meantime, she was going to stay right there and maximize her career opportunities. And try to help her stepmother a little with her own career, if she could. It wasn't as if Jaya Ma was not talented. She, like Naina herself, simply needed more opportunities, more exposure.

"You okay, *beta*?" her stepmother whispered in her ear and Naina nodded.

They circulated through the main lounge and the back garden and then lined up to greet the family. The bouquet of flowers she'd brought as a gift felt extra heavy in her damp hands as Naina craned her head to look at the family members greeting the guests. Neither Virat nor Vikram were present. But Daadiji was, newly arrived from London.

Naina swallowed when Vikram's mother's gaze, then her husband's, suddenly fell on her. Then Daadiji waved at her with a broad smile. One by one, it seemed as if all the crowd were craning their heads to look at her. Strangers, acquaintances, there was no one who wasn't staring in her direction, mouths agog, expressions full of awe.

A sudden silence fell over the crowd as if someone had sent a signal. For a hysterical second, Naina wondered if she was in a nightmare. Was she naked? Had she walked in with her face pack still on?

She freed one hand and tried to reach for her stepmother. Her arm met empty air. Even Jaya Ma had ditched her. She swallowed and looked up at the beautiful crystal chandelier on the high ceiling and she saw Zara standing on the upper balcony, with Virat by her side. Zara looked as though she had tears in her eyes and Virat...he gave Naina an encouraging nod.

And then into the silence came that old Tamil song. Her mother's favorite. Her own eyes now full of tears, she simply stood there, letting the song seep into her. Letting it wash away all the sadness in her heart and filling it with fresh, bursting hope.

Because she knew then. She knew why they were all looking at her. Knew why her soul felt as if it had been slammed with an awareness she couldn't deny.

Heart in her throat, Naina turned. Empty space greeted her until she looked down.

He was there—her very own hero. On his knees. In front of the entire world. Because Naina had no doubt this would be all over the internet in a few minutes.

Vikram Raawal on his knees for a very ordinary girl. Vikram Raawal in love. The Vikram Raawal who'd always walked the line of propriety with iron-clad rules.

Her breath slammed into her with such force that Naina thought she might just melt into a puddle.

In a half white kurta with gold piping at the Nehru collar, with his unruly hair pushed away to reveal those aristocratic features, he was broad and big and so gorgeous and...

And in his hands was a small velvet box with a ring that looked like a family heirloom that could probably be dated back a thousand years. A small oval ruby nestled amidst tiny diamonds...

Tears fell over her cheeks making the diamonds flicker extra hard. She shook her head, hating that she was making a mess of her face.

"Won't you look at me, Dream Girl?"

There was no charm, no mockery, only tenderness in his voice. Nothing but unadulterated emotion. Such need that it made his voice hoarse.

And she finally met his gaze. "I... I never said you had to do this. I never demanded that you prove anything to me. Never."

"Ahh...but I promised myself I'd always give you more

than you ask, Naina. I never want you to doubt me again. Never doubt that you and only you have everything of me. Everything, including my heart.

"This is the ring that Daadu gave Daadi. I asked her for it because I thought I needed all the luck I can get and she gave it to us with all her blessings. But if you don't like it—"

"I love it," she whispered, because she did.

He looked at her with such naked adoration in his eyes that Naina swallowed. "I'm all in, Dream Girl.

"You could walk away from here without another backward look and I would still love you. They could all laugh at the cliché I've become and I would still love you. Twenty years later, I could be the worst-case scenario for every Romeo out there...stories and songs could be written about me—horrible rap songs, and Virat will probably make a movie about all this, just to get back at me and I would still absolutely love you."

And then Naina was laughing and crying, because God, she loved this man so much.

"Whether you say yes or not, I will love you from now to forever, Naina. Forgive this old guy for not being wise enough to see it sooner."

"Stop it," she said, smacking him on the shoulder. "You're not old. And you're just imperfectly perfect."

"Virat told me that you were the one who tweaked the film's storyline in the end."

"I...the more I read it, the more I realized it had no true happy ending." She pressed her hand to his mouth. "I know you want to make this a serious movie but who said historical sagas that show the Independence Movement shouldn't also have a little happiness too, Vikram? It doesn't have to have such a bleak landscape to be taken seriously.

"I know your grandfather didn't actually meet and fall

in love with your grandmother until later on. But why can't you tweak the timing in the film a little and give them both the happy-ever-after they deserve?"

He laughed and shook his head. "I think that ending makes it shine, Dream Girl. I just wondered why you didn't come and tell me?"

"Because I didn't want to take anything away from what you've already achieved, Vikram. And I never want you to think I'm in this for the opportunities you could give me."

"I never thought that, Dream Girl. Ever."

"I knew Virat would give me an objective opinion of my idea. And Zara's already arranged for me to talk to another producer about another script idea I have. I can't tell you how excited I am. And it's all thanks to you."

"I didn't do anything," he said.

"You set me on this path. You gave me the initial push and the confidence."

"You're the one who's saving me," he said "From myself. From a world that sometimes only takes and doesn't give back. From a life that was nothing but an endless cycle of loneliness and broken promises.

"You're my always and forever. My new beginning and my happy-ever-after. My very own love story. Will you marry me, Naina?

"Because my life is nothing but a cheap, commercial sellout without you by my side, Dream Girl."

She went close to him and he buried his face in her belly. She dropped the bouquet and buried her fingers in his hair thinking her heart might just explode with all the happiness filling it. "Yes, I will marry you, Vikram. And for the rest of my life, I will love you. I will never doubt you. And I…" Her knees did finally give in.

And he caught her, her real hero.

Naina fell into his arms, his mouth claiming hers with

a need that quivered through her entire body. Applause
broke out around them. She heard Daadiji and Zara and
Virat cheering and Jaya Ma screaming, "That's my step-
daughter. That's my girl," at the top of her voice.

She laughed into his kiss and he bit her gently and then
he was putting the ring on her finger and Naina was terrified that it might all be just a dream. She laughed a lot,
they both touched Daadiji's feet, Virat squeezed her into a
bone-cracking hug and Zara kissed her cheek and hugged
Vikram.

His mother, even more beautiful up close, kept snatch-
ing looks at her son as he looked at Naina. Waiting to be
introduced. Naina felt a flicker of shame lick up her cheeks.
God, this had been their anniversary party and Vikram
had just simply hijacked it.

She walked up to Mrs. Raawal and introduced herself,
knowing Vikram wouldn't be able to avoid his mother after
that. His arm came around her waist not two seconds later.

"I'm sorry for…interrupting your party, Mrs. Raawal.
I'm…"

"Oh, please. I didn't mind at all. In fact, whatever the
reason my son wanted to prove to you that he loves you,
I'm glad for it. I got to see up close just how much he
adores you." She offered her cheek and Naina dutifully
kissed it. "And please call me Vandana."

"Will you bring her to meet us properly after the party?"
she asked her son, a wealth of hope in her eyes. "I would
like to get to know this girl who's made my son so happy."

Naina squeezed Vikram's hand for all she was worth
when she saw the instant refusal on his lips. He pressed
a kiss to her temple and smiled. His expression and his
words when he turned to her were tempered. And Naina
had never been so proud of this man she loved. "Not just
yet, but soon, Mama. I want her to myself for a little while."

Mrs. Raawal nodded and kissed Naina's cheek. "Welcome to the family, Naina. I have no words to tell you how glad we are that you're in his life."

Naina swallowed at the open ache in her eyes. They left in a whirlwind of camera flashes from a myriad of mobile phones. But instead of driving across the city to his own home, they stopped at Zara's flat for the night. Which was much closer.

Once they entered Zara's expansive flat, Naina turned to him. "I'm... I have no words. I know you hate that kind of drama and invasion into your private life... I never needed it, Vikram. I just wanted your love." She pressed her hand and her mouth to his chest, loving the tight squeeze of his arms around her.

"I know you didn't ask for it. But you deserve it, Dream Girl. You're the best thing that walked into my life and I will constantly try to let everyone know, including you, how much I love you, and you'll just have to put up with that."

"I love you too," Naina whispered, knowing that she finally had her very own hero.

* * * * *

HIS SCANDALOUS CHRISTMAS PRINCESS

CAITLIN CREWS

CHAPTER ONE

MELODY SKYROS HAD entertained herself for years by imagining that, at any moment, she could embrace her true destiny, become a deadly assassin, and go on a targeted killing spree of only those who really, really deserved it.

But that wouldn't be ladylike.

She had trained in various martial arts for years. In secret, thanks to one of her gently bred, blue-blooded mother's few acts of marital defiance. Because Melody's notoriously unpleasant father, aristocrat and media magnate Aristotle Skyros, could never know that his despised second daughter was receiving anything but the basic comportment classes expected of Idylla's lofty patricians, who cluttered up the ancient island kingdom with enough hereditary snobbishness to fill the gleaming Aegean Sea.

Aristotle could certainly never know that a daughter of his had been training less in how to sit gracefully at a formal dinner and more in how to neutralize multiple attackers with her fingertips.

He had never forgiven her for being born flawed. He never would. Melody was blind and therefore useless to him——except as a weapon to wield against those who actually cared about her.

Melody's earliest, happiest daydreams of what she could do with the lethal skills she was learning and then mastering had all been focused on ridding the world of Aristotle.

Who most definitely deserved it.

But her older sister Calista had handled her father, shockingly enough. Calista, born perfect enough to please Aristotle, had worked her way up to become her father's second in the family corporation, all with an eye toward beating him at his own game. And sure enough, she'd embarrassed and humiliated him by having him removed from his own board and summarily fired from his position as CEO two days ago.

This was in no way as neat, clean, or personally satisfying a solution as an assassination, in Melody's opinion.

Especially when Melody was the one who had to pay the price of Aristotle's embarrassment.

Though the price in question had its own rewards, she could admit.

Because tonight she had a new target in mind: His Royal Highness Prince Griffin of Idylla, who was her brand-new brother-in-law, since her sister had married King Orion the night before.

That was bad enough. Melody was still having trouble processing what else the famously oversexed and dissipated Griffin was. To her, personally.

Because it had all happened so fast. Too fast. *Dizzyingly* fast.

After Calista had become the Queen, the King had swept her off to the tune of cheers and much merriment as the clock in the palace struck midnight. Christmas Eve had ended, Christmas had begun. Glad tidings were exchanged on high, as befit the traditional, arranged marriage of an Idyllian king that Melody knew included deep and genuine emotion on both sides.

It only took a few moments in Orion and Calista's presence to *feel* how much they adored each other. A good and proper fairy tale that the whole kingdom could rejoice in and a balm for a nation wearied by the squalid, scandalous antics of Orion's predecessor, the deeply polluted King Max.

Orion had promised—since long before he took the throne—that his reign would be scandal-free.

When a palace aide had come to escort her away, Melody had assumed she'd be packed off home to her parents' house, where her father would no doubt be up waiting for her—keen to make her tell him every detail about the wedding and then punish her for attending it. She'd been looking forward to it, as matching wits with her father was one of her favorite games. He always assumed he was the smartest man in any room when, in fact, he was woefully unarmed.

Instead, she had been whisked off to a suite in the palace, something she found pleasant enough until she realized she'd been *locked in.* And come morning, her sister had emerged from what should have been newly wedded bliss to make her *announcements.*

"This is about making sure you're free, Melody," she'd said over breakfast. Sternly. Taking to her new role a bit too eagerly, in Melody's view. They'd sat in a private salon so sunny that Melody had leaned back in her chair, the bitter coffee she preferred between her hands, and tilted her face toward the heat of it.

"Are you sure? Because to me it sounds like a royal decree. *Your Majesty.*"

"It's both."

Calista sounded the way she always did, stressed and *sisterly* and racked with *grave concerns.* Melody never had the heart to tell her that she enjoyed her life a whole lot more than anyone—including Calista, who unlike the rest loved her dearly and was thus forgiven her unnecessary *concern*—seemed to imagine. That didn't suit most people's view of what blindness must be like, Melody was well aware. She had learned to keep it to herself.

"I appreciate your help, of course," Melody had told her. "But I don't need it. You shouldn't be worrying about such things, Calista. It's the first day of your new life as the Queen of Idylla, all hail. Not to mention, it's Christmas."

"I know it's Christmas," Calista had retorted, but her voice was softer. "And once a few practicalities are sorted out, I promise you that we'll celebrate the way we always do."

"You mean, with Father drunk and belligerent, shouting down the place around our ears while we all cower until January?" Melody had laughed. "As appealing as that sounds, maybe it's time for new traditions."

"But tonight is the Christmas ball," Calista had continued, sounding ever more dogged. Melody could feel the daggers her older sister was glaring at her, and, she could admit, took pleasure in remaining as placid and unbothered as possible. Because it annoyed Calista so deeply and obviously. "And I want to give you a gift that no one, least of all Father, can ever take back."

That Melody had not wanted this gift was neither here nor there.

"I think I'd rather take my chances with Father's temper," Melody had said when Calista had told her what she wanted Melody to do.

What she, as Queen, had *decreed* Melody *would* do, that was.

"You can't," her sister had replied. "If you go home again he will ship you off to one of those institutions he's been threatening you with for years. It might as well be a prison, Melody! And it's unlikely that he will ever let you out again. Do you hear me?"

"My ears work perfectly well, Calista. As I think you know."

But the new Queen had made up her mind.

That was how Melody had found herself in the arms of Prince Griffin, Idylla's so-called *charming rogue* as he led her in an excruciatingly formal and horrifically *long* dance in the Grand Ballroom of the palace.

Prince Griffin, who was forgiven his many sins and trespasses in the style of his father because he was considered *delightful*, for reasons unclear to Melody.

Prince Griffin, who had declared he planned to turn over a new leaf to better support his brother back during coronation season, but had taken his sweet time in the turning.

Prince Griffin, her new assassination target.

And to her dismay, as of an hour or so ago, her husband.

Melody had considered knifing him in the back at the altar, for the poetry of it all, but Prince Griffin—renowned across the land for his cavorting about with any and all women, his cheerful debauchery, and his disinterest in the usual charitable pursuits of royalty that were usually erected to cover up the consequences of the first two—was under the impression that he was Melody's…protector.

She would have been only too happy to disabuse him of this notion. But that, too, had been forbidden.

By yet another royal decree.

"Don't be absurd," Melody had said, while she'd stood gamely still in another of the palace's innumerable salons. She'd been subjecting herself to a phalanx of dressmakers, all of whom poked and prodded and pinned her into a dress she had not wanted to wear at all, and certainly not after the extraordinarily formal Christmas lunch she'd eaten her way through. "I have no need or desire for protection. Prince Griffin's or anyone else's."

Her sister and her new husband had been there, lounging about in their post-Christmas luncheon haze. And perhaps post–private time haze as well, though Melody knew her supposedly hard-as-nails, professional sister was enormously missish about such things. At least to Melody.

As if her eyes were the not the only thing that did not function as expected.

Everything smelled sugary and sweet, floating up toward the high ceilings. And over the mutterings of the vicious dressmakers and their sharp, cruel pins she could hear various rustles from the settee the King and his new Queen sat upon. Telling her there was a lot of *touching*. Perhaps more touching than had been seen in the palace for some time.

"I know you don't need any protection," Calista had replied, but in a tone of voice that suggested to Melody that her sister was rolling her eyes. "But it's not about you, you see."

"The forced wedding I want no part of is not about

me?" Melody asked. Rhetorically, obviously. "And here I thought it was meant to answer my dreams of becoming a princess at last. Not a dream I've ever had, to be clear."

She heard her sister sigh. She heard the King shift position.

Orion was a different order of man than Melody's father. Or his own father, come to that, or the country could never have embraced him. Not after the things Terrible King Max had done and laughed about when they'd turned up in the tabloids, as they inevitably did. That Orion was fully in control of himself—and therefore everything else—was palpable. Comforting in a king.

As someone who'd spent her entire life learning how to control herself in various ways, physical and mental and more, Melody was forced to admire him.

"Your sister has regaled me with tales of your abilities," Orion had said then. Melody had felt the astonishing urge to offer him the appropriate obeisance. Not that she could with so many people around her, pinning and prodding and demanding she remain still. She was surprised she even had the urge to drop a curtsy, but there it was. The first time in her whole life she'd actually felt decidedly patriotic. "And I'm delighted that my brother will take such a remarkable woman as his bride. But you must understand something about Griffin."

Melody had felt certain that she understood Prince Griffin all too well. The spare had not followed in the footsteps of the heir. Griffin had always preferred gambling halls, the beds of unsuitable women, and any other form of debauchery available to him. And as a royal prince, there was very little that was *not* available to him. He was not the sort of man who would require *work* to figure out. Melody had been bored of him and his high-profile antics long before she'd ever met him.

This was something she would have said happily to her sister. But Orion was not only the King, he was Griffin's brother. So, uncharacteristically, she'd remained politely silent.

"He has always played a certain role, particularly with women," said the King, and somehow, Melody had kept herself from letting out an inelegant snort. *A certain role* was one way to describe an unrepentant libertine who had spent the better part of his life knee-deep in conquests. "But with you, he is…different."

This was true, but not for the reasons Orion likely imagined. It had always amused Melody to cringe about and act as if she might crumble to dust if someone paid attention to her. It gave her great satisfaction to allow people she could easily have maimed to fawn all over her and treat her as if she was too damaged to sit without assistance,

In other words, she'd long enjoyed acting the part of damaged goods.

The first time she'd met Prince Griffin, it had been second nature to act as if his mere presence was enough to give her the vapors. As if her blindness made her timid and she could do nothing but quail and cower.

Melody did so enjoy being underestimated.

Until now.

"I would take it as a personal favor if you would allow my brother to imagine that he can, in fact, protect you. Not because you need protection, but because I believe it would do him good to indulge that feeling." Orion sighed. "I ask you this, not as your King, but as his brother."

What could Melody do with that but acquiesce?

She had not knifed Prince Griffin at the altar, though it had caused her pain to refrain. She had even smiled— if tremulously, the way the person the Prince thought she was would smile, surely—though that was something she usually avoided doing in public. Her father always raged at her that she should smile more, so, naturally, she had taken it upon herself to smile as seldomly as possible. When Prince Griffin had finally led her into the ballroom, it was as his supposedly submissive and overwhelmed wife. His charity case.

It had been the longest, strangest Christmas of Melody's life.

So long and so strange that she found herself almost nostalgic for the usual Skyros family Christmases past. Idyllians tended to reserve the gift-giving for Boxing Day and then again in January on Epiphany, the feast of the three wise men. Christmas was for the traditional breads, walnuts, and pork or lamb, depending on the family. In her own family, Christmas was one of the few occasions Melody's mother insisted her father acknowledge that Melody existed, which made for a long, fraught, unpleasant meal that likely gave everyone indigestion, reliably left at least one member of the family in tears, and inevitably ended with smashed china and threats.

That sounded like a lovely Christmas carol in comparison to this, she thought as she was introduced to the King, the palace, and then the watching nation as the kingdom's newest Princess.

Then came the interminable dancing.

"You are remarkably good at this," the Prince told her, as he waltzed them both around and around and around.

Melody was entirely too aware of the pressure of so many pairs of eyes on them. The *weight* of it all. And the murmuring and whispering and muffled laughter, snaking about beneath the music, as all the gathered Idyllian nobles attempted to come to terms with what shouldn't have been possible.

Everybody's favorite prince, married to the damaged, discarded, scandalous-by-virtue-of-her-notable-imperfections daughter of the already highly questionable Skyros family. Yes, Calista had done well for herself. But Aristotle was a stain on the kingdom. Everyone agreed—until they wanted to do business with him.

Well. Not any longer, perhaps. There was that silver lining to hold on to.

Melody found dancing silly. It was so much more pleasurable—and effective—to fight. But the simpering creature, fragile and overwhelmed, that she was playing tonight would never think such a thing.

Nor have the tools to fight in the first place, she reminded herself.

She shivered dramatically, hoping Prince Griffin would imagine it was fear.

"I hope I don't embarrass you," she said, in a quavering sort of voice. The kind of voice she liked to use around her father, mostly because it always made her sister laugh. And usually also made her father choke with rage that such a daughter had been inflicted upon him. "I couldn't bear it if I embarrassed you."

Prince Griffin was tall. His shoulder was broad and remarkably firm to the touch. Much as his mouth had been when he'd kissed her, swift and perfunctory, as the wedding ceremony had ended. The hand that grasped hers was large, and dwarfed her fingers in a manner both powerful and gentle. Its mate was splayed across her back, pressing heat into her with every step of the dance.

Years ago, when she and her sister were still teenagers, Calista had spent untold hours describing various members of the royal and aristocratic circles their family moved in. Painting each and every character for Melody, who had her own impressions of them based on how they took up space, how they breathed, how they fidgeted and smelled. But even if Calista had not exhaustively detailed Prince Griffin's wicked gaze and shockingly sensual mouth long ago, these things were apparent in the way he carried himself. The way he spoke, his voice rich and deep. And more curious, capable of stirring up something...electrical.

Deep within her.

Melody didn't know what to make of that.

"You could never embarrass me," Prince Griffin said gallantly. "I have spent far too many years embarrassing myself."

And while part of Melody wanted to laugh at that, there was another part of her that... shuddered. Deep inside, where that electricity seemed to hum louder than before.

It was almost alarming.

The orchestra was still playing. And as was tradition and ancient royal protocol, the newlyweds were required to dance to the bitter end. On display, so all of Idylla could form its own conclusions about the new couple before the tabloids took them apart come morning.

Given that Melody was the daughter of a media king who had long trafficked in tabloids as a matter of course and a means to shame his enemies and rivals, she expected there would be quite the tabloid commotion tomorrow. On Boxing Day, when the whole of the island would be tucked up at home opening gifts, stuffing themselves with food, and perfectly situated to read, watch, and judge.

Judgment being the foremost occupation of most of the island's citizens, as far as Melody had ever been able to tell.

The dance finally ended. Mercifully.

But Prince Griffin did not release Melody's hand.

Instead, he placed it in the crook of his elbow, a courtly sort of gesture that Melody, by rights, should have found annoying. She did find it annoying, she assured herself. She did not need to be ushered about like an invalid. She only used a cane sparingly—and usually for effect—having spent so many years working to hone her other senses and her spatial awareness through martial arts. Because she loved the notion that she could be as graceful as any other Idyllian lady, when and if she wished.

She reminded herself that tonight's show of weakness wasn't about her. It was about the man beside her, who needed the King to intercede on his behalf. Who needed his brother to not only arrange his marriage, but make his new wife complicit in pulling one over on him. For his own good.

Something in Melody twisted a bit at that. She knew the particular, crushing weight of *her own good* better than most. It had threatened to flatten her for most of her life.

But she reminded herself that Prince Griffin was a stranger. That she had done what was asked of her, that was all. He was the King's brother—but *she* was nothing but the King's lowly subject.

That didn't make the twist in her belly go away. But it helped.

The night wore on. Griffin stayed at her side, which meant Melody had no choice but to smile. To simper. To pretend to be *overwrought* by her remarkable elevation in status.

When instead, what she really was, she found, was… entertained.

Not just by this stranger, this husband foisted upon her, who acted as if she needed him to dote on her in this way. But by all the women who contrived reasons to swan up and *congratulate* Prince Griffin on his nuptials.

And it was him they were congratulating, Melody was well aware. Not her. They all seemed to suffer from the same common ailment—the notion that because Melody couldn't see them, she also couldn't hear them.

They came to him in clouds of scent, their voices dripping with greed. Malicious intent. And when aimed at Melody, nothing short of pure disdain.

"I'm so deeply happy for you, Your Royal Highness," they would flutter at him. "But how hard it is to imagine one such as you truly off the market."

"Do you mean the local farmers' markets?" Melody would ask, disingenuously. And tried to beam just slightly angled away from the direction of whatever woman stood before her. "I am told they've made such a difference in the city center. So festive, particularly at this time of year."

Perhaps her favorite part of the whole thing was standing there in the aftermath of such fatuous statements, feeling the reaction all around her.

Oh, yes, she was enjoying herself.

She would never have chosen to marry of her own volition. But having been forced into it, and having received an order from King Orion to play a part, Melody found the whole thing far more amusing than she'd expected.

Until the trumpets blared and it was her turn to be swept out of the ballroom by her royal husband.

Melody wanted to complain at length to her sister, because no one else knew her well enough to listen to her without simultaneously pitying her in some way she would likely find deeply tiresome. But the Queen was not available for sisterly grousing, leaving Melody to surrender herself to this last part of the royal marriage ritual while keeping her feelings to herself.

She thought this particular part of the traditional Idyllian royal wedding was cringeworthy. Everyone stood about as if they were in some medieval keep, cheering on the bridegroom as he ushered his new wife off to what they claimed was *happy-after-ever*.

What they meant was *the marital bed*.

Melody had never understood these strange architectures erected around sex. In the case of a royal wedding, everyone pretended it was about courtly manners. Or ceremony. Or tradition itself, as if the fact people had long done something meant everyone must forever carry on doing it.

But at the end of all the theatrics, it was about sex. It was always about sex. It amused her to no end that *she* seemed to be the only person capable of seeing that.

Prince Griffin drew her along with him and because Melody could not comment on this the way she would have liked, she had no choice but to...allow it.

And there was suddenly nothing to concentrate on but him. Awareness swept over her, whether she wanted it or not.

He was hot to the touch. Too hot. He had a hand splayed at her low back again and she wished he would remove it, because it was far too…confusing.

Distracting.

She told herself it was because they were climbing stairs. That was why she seemed to be heating up, almost steaming. But deep inside, low in her belly, it was if her body was far more exultantly medieval than she'd ever imagined possible.

He moved with a certain quiet power that made the fine hairs on the back of her neck prickle. Because she recognized it. He was…contained. Not quite what he seemed on the surface. And she could feel that so distinctly it was as if he was making announcements to that effect as he led her away from the crowd.

He kept a firm, if gentle, hold of her, as if she needed help navigating through the wide corridors of the palace and their acres and acres of gleaming, empty marble. He did not make small talk, and when she noticed that, it made all the strange things churning about inside her start to glow.

Because the character of Prince Griffin that everybody knew so well had never let a moment go by without filling it with sound of his own voice. Everyone knew that. Notorious charmers were rarely shy and retiring.

Not that she thought the real Prince Griffin, whoever he might be, was *shy*. The quality of his silence was different than that. It was too confident. Too secure.

She could feel it in the way he guided her, with an ease that suggested he'd spent the bulk of his life matching his pace to hers and maneuvering her where he wanted her, and this wasn't the first night he'd ever done so. It felt so natural it was almost as if she was leading the way.

Melody understood, deep in her bones, that this was not a man to be trifled with.

But she couldn't make that odd glimmer of understanding work with the fact he was *Prince Griffin,* so she shoved it aside. And pretended she was flushed from the walking in such a cumbersome gown, nothing more.

Instead of taking her toward the guest suite where she'd been put up the night before, he headed in a completely different direction. And paying attention to him was too disconcerting, so instead, she paid attention to the direction they moved in. A long walk, then left. Down a set of stairs, then out into a courtyard. There was a fountain making noise, and she could hear the sound of the water bounce back from the walls.

Then she remembered. Prince Griffin did not live in a wing of the palace, the way his brother did. He maintained his own residence on the far side of the palace grounds.

She could feel the press of the December night, chilly for Idylla, though mitigated by blasts of heat at equal intervals as they walked. Heaters, no doubt. Because royal personages could not be expected to suffer the travails of weather.

Melody wanted to laugh at that. But didn't, because it occurred to her that she was now one of those royal personages. Like it or not.

Then they were inside again. His home, she understood. Hers, now. There was the scent of him, or something that reminded her of him. A certain richness, a hint of intensity. She could sense walls around her, suggesting an entry hall, and then a room. He led her to a couch, placing her hand on the arm and encouraging her to sit. She ran her fingers over the wide arm of the couch, done up in a deep, sumptuous leather. Then she sank down on the seat, tossing the skirt of her enormous dress out as she settled into place, and getting a sense of the width of the couch as she did.

And then she listened.

Her husband moved almost silently. So silently, in fact, that it once again made her shiver in the grip of too much awareness. She had the sense of him prowling, and he was...

Not the same, here.

Away from the crowds, something in her whispered.

Was this where Prince Griffin was truly himself? Whatever that meant?

That electric charge deep inside her connected again, lighting her up. Sending heat and flame and something else shivering through all parts of her body, making her want to leap to her feet to do something to dispel it—

But instead, she reminded herself to be meek. This was not where *she* could be herself. She could only play her prescribed part, as ordered. Melody bowed her head.

And listened as her surprisingly formidable Prince— her husband, God help her—fixed himself a drink. Then one for her too, she corrected herself, as she heard ice hit heavy crystal for a second time.

Sure enough, he was soon beside her again, pressing a cool tumbler into her palm.

"I thought we could both use a bit of whiskey," he said, in a low sort of growl that bore almost no resemblance at all to the cultured, charming, carefree tone he'd used in the ballroom as all those women had vied for his attention.

It was fascinating. *He* was.

Melody felt herself flush.

"I want you to be comfortable here," Prince Griffin told her, still sounding growly, but with a more formal note mixed in. "And you have nothing to fear from me. I do not intend to…insist upon any marital rights."

Her flush deepened. She told herself it was outrage that he would even mention *marital rights* in the twenty-first century. But she knew better.

If she was outraged at anything, it was that he'd apparently decided his own wife didn't merit the same sexual attention he was literally famous for flinging about like it was confetti. Without even asking if, perhaps, she might like to partake of the one thing he was widely held to be any good at.

"Why not?" Melody demanded. Then remembered herself. She tried to exude innocence and fragility, and only hoped she didn't look constipated in the process. "Forgive me if I'm misunderstanding the situation we find ourselves in here. But I thought the entire purpose of these royal weddings with all the protocol and the carrying on about bloodlines and history was the sex?"

CHAPTER TWO

HIS ROYAL HIGHNESS, Prince Griffin of Idylla, could not possibly have heard his frail and fragile new bride correctly.

He stared down at her, trying to make sense of the question that was, as far as he could tell, still hanging in the air between them. Filling up his private study, stealing all the air out of the room, and most disconcertingly by far, centering itself between his legs.

Where, it appeared, his body had already decided that he was attracted to his wife.

Wildly attracted.

Griffin was appalled.

At himself for proving, as ever, he was more monster than man.

Lady Melody Skyros was not only a gently reared noblewoman, deserving of his respect and care. She was not merely one of Idylla's sweet young things whose mothers plotted exquisite marriages like something out of a period film while their fathers vied for power and influence. She was also blind. His choosing to marry her was, as he was well aware, an act of largesse that palace insiders believed would redeem him in one fell swoop in the eyes of the populace.

She was his redemption, in other words.

Griffin did not want to think about sex. Not with her. Not near her.

His tawdry exploits were in the past. Melody was his future.

The past was dirty, just as he'd liked it, but the future—as he'd promised his brother—would be squeaky clean.

Griffin was many things and pretended to be many more, but his word was his bond. Always.

And when he slipped and thought about sex in the presence of this woman he barely knew who was now his for all time, it became entirely too difficult to keep ignoring the fact that she was beautiful.

Inarguably, impossibly, shockingly beautiful.

The kind of beautiful that could, if he let it, lead straight to very bad decisions on Griffin's part. The sort of decisions he absolutely could not permit himself to make any longer. He'd promised Orion those days were behind him.

Because they were, he assured himself. Sternly. This was Orion's squeaky-clean new future and Griffin had vowed he would do his part.

Even if his part meant living like a monk in the presence of an angel.

"I cannot have heard you correctly," he managed to say, clenching his tumbler of whiskey tight in his hand.

Too tight.

"Sex leading to the required royal heirs, of course," Melody said in that same sweet voice that matched her name and seemed to get tangled up inside him. "I am given to understand that every person on the island of Idylla with even the faintest trace of noble blood thinks of nothing *but* heirs."

Griffin coughed. He forced himself to look away. He even went and sat down in the chair across from her to put some more distance between them, but that was not an improvement.

The view was still the same.

Lady Melody was widely held to be the embarrassment of her family. The Skyros Scandal—though it was not so much that she was personally scandalous as that her obvious imperfections had so clearly and deeply offended her father. Because heaven forfend any creature on this island be anything less than physically perfect. Especially if that creature happened to be related to a bottom-feeder like Aristotle Skyros who trafficked in the mythic beauty of the Idyllian population.

A myth his own media outlets perpetuated, naturally.

And all the while he'd had his own blind daughter locked away, out of view unless absolutely unavoidable.

Rumors had always swirled about the younger, lesser Skyros daughter. Was she misshapen? Incapable of human interaction? One salacious story had claimed, for years, that the ironically named youngest child of well-known snob Aristotle was, in fact, a monster he kept chained up in his basement. Her sister had been in the public eye from a young age, following in her father's footsteps and rising in the Skyros family empire. And then, of course, her father and the former King had arranged to marry Calista to Orion in a seedy little conspiracy of force.

It was as if Calista had to shine all the brighter—all the way to the throne—to divert attention from the whispers of deformities and insanities and monstrous rampages in the dark of night.

Even when Melody had appeared at the series of balls

leading up to her sister's wedding on Christmas Eve—
notably neither deformed nor monstrous—the gossip
had continued.

All absurd, of course, but Idylla was a relatively small
island. Where larger kingdoms had cities, the people
here had their stories.

Griffin had expected that perhaps Melody would not
have the polish of her older sister. Who could? Calista
was in so many ways a sharpened blade. Anyone would
seem rough around the edges in comparison.

But today there was no escaping the truth.

Melody was a vision.

He had seen her from across a ballroom, once or
twice, as a distant curiosity. And up close only once before. That time her blond hair had cascaded all around
her while huddled in a chair, trying to make herself invisible while her sister prepared to become Queen. His
memory of her at that brief meeting—a bit like an ur-
chin, Eponine to the gills—had stayed with him over this
last, strange week, when it became clear that he could
no longer put off doing his duty.

And it had been that memory that made him feel…
not resigned, exactly, to this plan of his brother's that
he'd vowed to support. Griffin had no wish to marry.
But if it turned out that he must do so anyway, he found
he could see his way clear to marrying a woebegone
creature like the one he'd seen that day. A victim to her
overbearing father, the subject of idle gossip and absurd
stories. Blind, ignored, possibly even abused.

He would *elevate* her, he had told himself grandly
even last night. He would *take care* of her. There would
be no lies like the ones that had shaped his life—not in
his marriage. And perhaps, somewhere deep inside him-

self, he would find something soft after all these years of bitterness and hardness. Something that might bloom instead of wither.

Something good, even in him.

A thing he'd lost so long ago that he'd begun to think it, too, was nothing more than a myth. But then his bride had appeared down at the other end of the long aisle of the Grand Cathedral. And she had walked the length of it on his brother's arm, far too graceful for a charity case. Far too...frothy.

Beneath her veil, he'd expected to find the sad, cringing waif he'd met so briefly once before.

But instead, there had been...this.

Her.

Melody, something in him whispered.

All that blond hair gleamed gold, piled on top of her head and fixed into place with gleaming precious stones set on elegant combs that gave the impression of a tiara without actually using one. A tiara could make an ordinary face exciting, simply by adding all that light and sparkle, but Melody's face was already exquisite. Heart-shaped, with eyes that he had half expected—based on what, he didn't know—to be clouded over. Strange in some way. But instead, they gleamed like his beloved sea. And her neck was a graceful, aristocratic line, signposting the rest of her slender, supple form beneath the dress she wore that was more like spun sugar than fabric.

She looked like a fairy tale.

And Griffin did not believe in fairy tales.

Eyes like the ocean, lips like rubies—and what the hell was he doing?

"I have no particular need of heirs," he managed

to say, recollecting himself. And more important, the vows he'd made to protect this woman from harm— and himself. "And therefore no need to marry to procure them."

Much less to procure access to the mechanism by which heirs were produced.

Did Melody not know who he was?

If there had been witnesses to this conversation, which there mercifully were not, they would not have believed it. *The* Prince Griffin, reduced to this state? After his years in the military alone, when he had faced far greater challenges than a beautiful woman who wished to talk about sex he would not be having with her.

To say nothing of his dedication to sampling as many women as possible, and not to *talk*.

About *heirs*.

Until tonight, he would have said that there was no way a woman could surprise him. No chance.

And yet here he was.

"That can't be true, Your Royal Highness."

His bride managed to sound as if the gently chiding statement was actually a question. Her face was tilted toward the tumbler she held in her delicate hands, where a ring that had once been his mother's dwarfed her slender finger. It was not the ring his despised father had given his poor mother on the occasion of their traditionally arranged royal wedding. This ring, she had told him long before her sad end, had been handed down through her own aristocratic family. It had once belonged to his great-great-grandmother, herself a great favorite of a long-gone Idyllian prince.

It felt like a talisman. When Orion had announced Griffin's time was up, he'd gone and found the ring, pleased with its weight, its heft. It was a recognizable gift of his esteem that he could bestow upon this charity case of his, bedecking her and marking her as his own.

Last night, his final evening as a free man, he had rather liked imagining it on her finger. It had felt like an internal settling within him. A quiet reckoning. He had felt ready—almost eager—to begin this next chapter.

In which he would play a new role. That of a good man like his brother, rather than the kingdom's favorite scoundrel.

Griffin had been *alight* with his own nascent virtue.

Yet something about this woman and that ring *here*, in his private study where she spoke of sex and not gratitude, moved through him…differently.

And felt too much like heat.

Griffin shoved that aside as best he could. "I am many things, Lady Melody. There is no pretending otherwise. But I am not a liar."

A curious sort of smile curved her lips, though she kept her face tilted toward the glass she held. Angled so he could not quite read her expression.

"And I am not a lady." Her smile looked innocent again. Very nearly tremulous. He found himself frowning, as if something about her wasn't quite tracking. "As of tonight I am Her Royal Highness, Princess Melody of Idylla. Your brother said so himself."

"Indeed you are."

"I will confess to you that I did not harbor secret dreams of becoming a princess. I am told most girls do, but then, I was never much like *most girls*."

Griffin thought of monsters and dark basements, images that did not fit with the elegant creature before him, all gold and ivory and that mysterious curve to her mouth besides. "I should hope not. I doubt I could bring myself to marry *most girls*."

He expected her to flush with pleasure. For her smile to tip over into something…more recognizable, maybe. Certainly more pleased with her circumstances. Or him. Or even herself.

But it stayed as it was. Innocent and yet…not.

And that ring on her hand like a harbinger.

Griffin was no doubt overwrought. He tossed back the healthy measure of the whiskey in his glass and ordered himself to stop looking for myth when there was nothing but a marriage. What did he expect? He had never been married before. It was not an institution he had ever intended to experience personally. Not after witnessing his parents' ritual abuse of the sanctity of their own union.

Or, as he liked to call it, his fondest childhood memories. All of them lies of one sort or another.

And if *he* was finding forbearance hard to come by tonight, what must it be like for Melody? She might not have been chained in a basement, but she had been sheltered all the same. In the most literal sense.

He needed to think less about his own contradictory feelings and more about what she must be feeling, ripped out of the only home she knew. Even if that home had been with the vile Aristotle Skyros, change was always hard.

Griffin ordered himself to be benevolent.

Wasn't that the point of all this?

"I know that wedding nights are more typically spent in baser pursuits," he said, aware as he spoke that it was still as if he was…outside his skin somehow. He rubbed at his face, suddenly more relieved than he should have been that this new bride of his who was unsettling him so comprehensively couldn't actually *see* her handiwork. He knew he should have hated himself for that, but there was far too long a list already. "But that is not something that need concern us. I will not impose upon you, if you were worried. You can rest easy on that score."

There was a pause.

Griffin heard a loud noise and it took him far too long to realize it was his own pulse, a racket in his ears.

As if he was the person panicked tonight. He, who was renowned for his calm under any and all pressures.

His bride curved her lips into something small and demure. "You are too good."

He found himself studying her again, because he didn't believe that smile. Not when she'd sounded so... dry. Or was he imbuing her with a personality that would better suit that heat in him that he was doing his best to keep tamped down?

You're terrible at charity, Griffin growled at himself, which was not exactly news. *The poor thing is no doubt petrified. Focus on that, not yourself, if you can.*

"I'm aware I have a certain reputation," he said, as gently as he could. Because perhaps it was best to address everything head-on. To have the sort of conversation most people—even people in arranged marriages like his—surely had before taking their vows, even if the topic was business or wealth and property consolidation in lieu of poetry or romance. Not that it mattered much when the end result would be the same. "I want to make sure you know that you will never have to bear the burden of it."

"Is it burdensome?" Again, that dry tone when her face better resembled that of a distant saint carved into marble. Or, more likely, he was hallucinating that contradition in her because he was self-serving to the core. If Griffin had any virtue at all, it was that he knew himself too well. "I was always under the impression that you enjoyed yourself. Thoroughly."

"The burden was not mine, Melody." Her name in his mouth…did not help. "It was my brother's. He wished to promise the kingdom that the royal family was reformed. But it was not Orion who needed reforming."

"You are very kind to reorder your life to please your brother. Even if he is the King."

"I was under the impression you did much the same for your sister."

"Didn't you hear?" Melody's voice was light. Yet ironic, he would have said—had she been anyone else. "She was doing me the favor."

"The honor is mine," he said, inclining his head slightly as if she could see his courtly gestures.

He knew she couldn't. Yet the way she tilted her head slightly to one side almost made him wonder.

"You are too kind, Your Royal Highness."

"We are wed." His voice was starched straight through. "You must call me Griffin."

"Griffin, then."

And they both sat there a moment. She looked as remote as she did beautiful. He found himself wondering what on earth he'd gotten himself into.

He did not think about the way she'd said his name.

Melody turned her glass in her hand, but not as if she was fidgeting. It was more as if she was…considering it. That didn't make sense. "If our marriage is in name only, does that mean that you will continue your… ah… exploits as before?"

For a moment, Griffin forgot who she was. For a moment, this was no more and no less than a dance he knew far better than the waltz they'd performed in front of the world.

All his good intentions seemed to ignite.

"Are you asking me if I intend to keep my wedding vows?" he asked with a certain silken menace. "Or are you more interested in discussing my exploits?"

As if she was the latest woman auditioning to warm his bed, and nothing more.

He could feel his pulse again, greedy and intent. And across from him, he was sure he saw a flicker of something sensual move across her face, lighting her up and making every last muscle in his body tighten—

But he was mistaken. He had to be.

Because, while he watched, she seemed to shrink there across from him. No saintliness, no sensuality, only a crumpling in on herself.

It was unbearable.

He was truly everything they said he was, and more. Bitter as that was, Griffin had no choice but to accept it.

Look at what you're doing here, he growled at himself. *You can't help yourself.*

"Am I allowed to question you?" Her voice was the same thread of sound he remembered from before, when he'd seen his future Queen's blind waif of a sister and had found himself seized with the uncharacteristic urge to protect her. "I'm so sorry. I'm afraid I hardly know how to handle myself in the presence of a man of your stature. Or at all. I must confess to you that I have not often been in…anyone's company, really."

She sounded plaintive. Uncertain and overwhelmed. By contrast, Griffin felt himself relax. He felt on solid ground again.

This, he could do. He was not a monster like his father. King Max had been a dark man, bent and determined to demean and degrade, use and discard. He had been venal and greedy.

Griffin was none of those things. He indulged in his sins, yes. But he didn't wield them as weapons.

Looking at this lovely, infinitely breakable creature who had become his wife, he reminded himself that this was his chance. At last he, too, could be virtuous.

Without actually having to dedicate himself to all those tiresome years of self-control and abstinent moral rectitude that defined his brother.

All he needed to do was be kind.

Surely even he could manage that.

"You can do or say whatever you like," he assured her, almost indulgently. "This is your home now. And to make it more appealing for you, your sister made certain that I engaged your favorite aide to ease the transition. I hope that, in time, you will be happy here." He reminded himself that he was not taking in a delicate boarder. He was talking about a marriage. "With me."

Melody cleared her throat delicately. "My aide?"

"I'm told she was responsible for privately tutoring you in all the tedious rules of Idyllian comportment. And then stayed on afterward as you enjoyed her companionship."

His bride's face glowed. Again, Griffin felt filled with a new sort of joy.

He could do this. He could be the man he'd never been.

"I enjoy her companionship very much," Melody said, emotion clear in her voice.

When she sat up straight again, Griffin felt as if he'd won something.

"Inside the walls of this house, you can do as you please," he told her. "Think of it as yours. You will have your own apartments. All the independence you might crave. All I ask is that outside these walls, you never let anyone know the truth about our relationship."

The glow on her face faded a bit, and he disliked it. Intensely.

"But everyone will know the truth as soon as you return to your usual…pursuits." She did not *quite* shrug. "People like to gossip in general, I think, but gossiping about you is a national pastime."

It was said so innocently. He couldn't possibly object.

And still, his grip on his tumbler was so tight that he was briefly concerned that he would shatter the glass.

Because no one seemed to think he would keep his word. Not Orion. Not his lovely new wife.

Not you? asked a voice inside him. Mocking him.

Reminding him who he really was.

"I will not be returning to any 'pursuits,'" he gritted out.

Quite apart from having made vows to Melody, he had made a promise to his brother. His King.

Griffin released his grip on the glass, his gaze on his bride. "Idylla has seen more than its share of scandals. There will be no more. Not if I have anything to say about it."

And his new bride bent her head as if to curtsy before him, small and meek, and why was he having trouble with that? Why was he looking for more?

"Then it is as good as done," she said softly. As if she was in danger of being carried off by the next breeze. "I am sure of it."

Griffin told himself he was, too.

CHAPTER THREE

MELODY AND HER brand-new, confusing stranger of a husband were summoned—invited, she kept reminding herself, though did it count as an invitation when it couldn't be refused?—to a "cozy" Boxing Day morning with Their Royal Majesties, King Orion and Queen Calista of Idylla.

In the palace proper, which was unlikely to be *cozy* in any way. By definition.

Then again, it wasn't as if the holiday had ever been filled with anything resembling cheer in her parents' house, either. Or coziness. Or much in the way of goodwill toward men—or anyone.

"I trust you find everything in your rooms acceptable," Griffin said when he came to collect her outside said rooms. "You must let the staff know if anything does not suit you."

Even his voice sounded stiff and gruffly awkward. Melody wasn't the least surprised to find that when he once again guided her hand to grip his elbow, his entire body could have been confused for a column of granite.

As if he was the one who was out of place here, in this own home, instead of her.

Oddly, this made her feel more comfortable.

"I'm overcome by your generosity, Your Royal Highness," she said in as decent an impression of his wooden formality as she could muster up.

And then tried to remind herself that she was supposed to be awash in all her fraudulent cringing as he led her back toward the palace.

Half of her attention was on the route Griffin took, different from the night before. He went out the side of his house—*their* house, she corrected herself—and led her back into the courtyard that separated his residence from the palace. Melody breathed in deep, enjoying the faint, salt sting of the ocean breeze tinged with hints of far-off storms. And reveled in the chill in the air, in case she'd forgotten that it was December. She noticed the blasts of heat again, placed at clever intervals, just when she thought the winter chill might penetrate her skin.

She was keenly aware that Griffin was walking at a deeply sedate pace that was almost certainly for her benefit, as he was far too tall. With, presumably, the long legs to match. He couldn't possibly consider this *procession* a reasonable pace. Melody tried to tell herself that it was kind of him to slow down in a misguided attempt to cater to her needs, whether she actually needed him to do it or not. It was something she ought to appreciate, surely.

It wasn't as if she'd had a lot of kindness, particularly from men. She ought to have been basking in any faint sign of it.

But she couldn't quite get there. Because the rest of her attention was focused on the deeply pleasurable, if unconventional, wedding night she'd had.

Griffin had delivered her to her rooms and then left her to her own devices. That had included a tray of food from his kitchens that she tore into the moment she finally freed herself from that enormous gown. Only when she'd finally eaten enough to stave off the hollow feeling in her belly after a long day of performing her fragility did she and Fen, her sensei and friend since Melody was small, set about learning each and every contour of her new home.

Fen had been old and wizened when she'd started teaching Melody at the tender age of seven, or so she liked to claim. And as each year passed, she became more and more herself. *Earning the right to her bones*, she liked to say.

And what her bones liked the most that night was making sure Melody could navigate the house she found herself in with as much silent ease as she had her parents' home.

They'd started in Melody's rooms and then, when the household had gone quiet for the night, had fanned out to the rest of Prince Griffin's domain, taking it room by room, chamber by chamber, until Melody had memorized the layout of her new home as best she could on an initial sweep.

Then she and Fen had returned to their upgraded royal apartments and settled into their new and improved life of luxury.

"I am all right with this Prince," Fen said happily as she'd gone off to her own private room in Melody's suite. "So far."

"As am I," Melody had murmured as Fen's footsteps faded away, leaving her to her lovely new bedchamber, stocked with quietly elegant furnishings that warmed beneath her hands and complete with an honest-to-God four-poster bed with a princess canopy.

Nothing Melody had ever wanted or dreamed of, necessarily. But she was happy to have it all the same, and with so little required of her in return.

This morning, both she and Fen had revised their charitable opinions somewhat when they'd discovered that in her new role as a royal princess, Melody was no longer expected or encouraged to dress herself.

Her staff—because, apparently, she had a *staff* in the royal version of her life—had first appeared to hover about and smother her with unsolicited and unnecessary help while she'd tried to get out of her wedding dress. They'd appeared again that morning, three relentlessly cheerful women who would not take no for an answer. Instead, they'd bustled ferociously around the vast apartment, which would have resulted in their quick and merciless deaths at Melody's hand had they not come bearing a tray of Idyllian pastries to complement the thick, rich coffee that had far more in common with traditional Greek coffee than the milky, frothy concoctions preferred in other places. Or so Melody had read.

Even Fen's dark mutterings of the dire consequences she might mete out for waking her were soothed away with an infusion of caffeine. And lashings of butter and dough.

Melody had found that shoving bits of heavenly pastry in her mouth was the only way that she could make it through the experience of having more women flutter about her. Dressing her as if she was an oversize doll. It was creepy.

"I am only going to my sister's house," she said at one point, when she could no longer keep her words trapped inside her. And what came out was far more polite than what still lurked around in there. "We've spent many,

many hours together wearing only our pajamas. I'm not sure this level of preparation is called for."

"I can't imagine that anyone would wish to go before Their Royal Majesties without looking their absolute best," one of the women said. Mildly enough.

"I would *die*," declared another.

And that was how Melody found herself slicked into her princessy place all over again.

She did not need to take stock of Prince Griffin to understand—merely from the elbow she held as he led her into the palace at a snail's pace—that he was kitted out much the same. The coat beneath her fingers had a luxuriant richness that seemed to meld with the hardness of his forearm. And if she listened, she could hear his military medals clink about on his lapel.

Her marriage might turn out to be fine. It was already better than she'd imagined, because Melody had never dreamed that she'd be left to her own devices. She never had been before. That was all good news.

But she worried that the studied formality of royal life might kill her.

"Do you always dress in formal clothes to visit your brother?" she asked as they moved into the part of the palace she recognized. The private royal apartments, where her sister now lived.

"Only when there is a photo opportunity," Griffin replied, and Melody found she liked his voice almost too much. It cast the same spell his physical presence did, as if there was a force field that emanated from it—from him—and surrounded the both of them when he spoke to her that way. Low and dark. Inviting. "And when it comes to things like national holidays, you can be certain that there will always be a photo opportunity."

"I will make a note," Melody said, without thinking, because she was still caught up on his *voice*.

Because if she'd been thinking, she certainly wouldn't have used that tone. It was far too sharp and dry and revealing of her actual personality.

She could feel his gaze on her, measuring. Aware, perhaps, that there was more to her than the role she played.

And they couldn't have that. So Melody clung to him instead, letting out a breath on a shuddery sort of high-pitched sigh.

"I'm so terrified I'll do something wrong," she lied. She endeavored to sound as feeble as possible. "There's a reason my father has always preferred to keep me out of the public eye."

Griffin stopped moving, forcing her to stop, too. She instantly balanced evenly on her feet, before it occurred to her that perhaps she should be feeble in gait as well. So she made a small production of tripping into him, which accomplished what she wanted.

He caught her. Easily and swiftly. Then held her up with an arm wrapped carefully around her back.

Melody told herself she should have laughed at that. Or wanted to laugh.

Instead, she could feel her whole body hum in response to that coiled, whipcord strength of his. To the heat of his body making her feel overly warm, everywhere. To the fascinatingly foreign and relentlessly male length of his torso pressed against her.

Oh, my.

"You will not be locked away ever again," Griffin told her fiercely. "You are a royal princess of Idylla, Melody. And more important still, my wife. If any accommodations need to be made, I promise you, it will be the world who accommodates you this time."

And all she could do was stand there with her face tilted up to his, her mouth slightly ajar in astonishment. Possibly in more than astonishment, though she couldn't say she fully knew what *more* was.

She could feel the flush that started deep and low in her belly flood through her, heating her up everywhere else. She could even feel it splashed all over her face when she'd spent long years learning to control her expressions.

But however she looked—no doubt flustered beyond repair—it clearly worked for Griffin. Melody told herself that was all that mattered.

Because he took her hands in his, solicitously.

She assured herself that what she felt was delight that her display of feminine weakness was doing its good work. And not…a different sort of feminine weakness altogether.

"You are safe now," he told her. "I promise."

And the oddest thing happened.

Melody, who had not felt truly unsafe in too many years to count—no matter what her sister thought about her prospects—felt a warm and happy sort of glow burst into bloom inside her.

As if she had needed saving.

And more, as if the promises of a strange prince who had been as forced into this marriage as she was meant anything to her. When…how could they?

Griffin stood there for a moment, his big, hard hands making her infinitely capable ones feel small and delicate. Something that should have appalled her—but it didn't. It really didn't.

While she was still trying to sort that out, he led her down the hall, murmuring his greetings to various staff members and royal guards as he passed. All while Melody clung to him, told herself she wasn't shivering slightly in reaction, and tried to sort out what was happening inside of her.

There was something about Prince Griffin. He was so...male. So big, so strong. So determined to protect her whether she needed his protection or not.

Melody liked it.

She more than liked it.

Because not only was she filled with that marvelous sense of warmth again, there was that other heat again. That electric invitation winding itself around and around inside of her, part of that shivering thing and more, too. It sank low in her belly and set up a kind of pulse, and she knew that was all about him. It was because of him.

Melody was used to cataloging every stray feeling that moved through her body. She had a highly developed sense of where she was in space and knew how to find her feet and her balance. She also knew how to connect to herself, and knew from discussions with her sister and Fen that this was a skill the sighted often ignored because they took visual cues as gospel. Melody preferred using all the senses available to her, not just one.

And still, she had never felt quite like this.

Her thighs seemed to whisper to each other as she walked. Between her legs she felt...heavy. Damp. There was an odd kind of prickling sensation working its way all over her skin. Her breasts—packaged into what her staff had assured her was a charming royal blue something or other that brought out her eyes, oh, joy—felt swollen.

Even her own palm seemed to generate more heat than it should, there where she clung to his elbow.

Whatever this was, Melody thought, she wanted more of it.

And then, with no little pomp and circumstance on the part of the palace staff, they were ushered into the presence of the King and Queen of Idylla.

Melody would have charged straight in to Calista, but she felt her husband pause. And understood what he was about even as he did it. She heard his heels come together, and felt it as he began to execute the quick bow that protocol demanded upon greeting the monarch for the first time in a day.

Accordingly, she snapped out her own curtsy.

And would have felt deeply silly had she not heard her sister huff out what sounded a lot like a laugh.

"Congratulations, Griffin," Calista said. "You've changed my sister overnight when I would have said that was impossible. Apparently all it took was a quick royal marriage to make her the proper Idyllian aristocrat we always hoped was lurking in there."

"You know you prefer it when I'm feral," Melody replied airily. The way she would have if they were alone. But, of course, they were not alone, so she forced herself to make a simpering little noise as punctuation. "I only hope that I am not too embarrassingly improper now that our circumstances have changed so much."

Her sister laughed again at that, even as Griffin murmured something soothing, and then there were more staff members everywhere. An endless amount of arranging and rearranging of the two royal couples on this or that bit of furniture in what Griffin told her—without her asking, as if he was attempting to be attuned to her needs—was the King's private parlor.

Approximately twelve thousand supposedly candid photographs later, the staff retreated, tables of food were wheeled in and their real Boxing Day could commence.

But Melody found that she was less interested in opening gifts than usual, because given her preferences, she would have continued to explore the wonder that was Prince Griffin's muscular forearm.

"Are you all right?" Calista asked in an undertone, when the gift-giving had finished and there was nothing left but the eating. And then more eating. The royal brothers were off in the far corner of the room, talking to each other near the windows that let in the sea air, already warmer and sweeter than before. "Did anything happen last night?"

"Many things happened last night, Calista. I was bartered off to a playboy prince as a kind of Christmas offering to the nation. Perhaps you heard."

"I don't mean the wedding. It was a glorious ceremony, you know. Christmas lights everywhere and you shining in the middle of it all." She sighed a little. Happily, Melody thought. "I meant after that, when he took you home."

Melody liked the idea of shining brighter than Christmas. It seemed to connect with that new, shivery electricity she could still feel low in her belly. She wanted to press her hands against her own abdomen to feel it, the way she'd experimented with electric things when she'd been young. To feel that hum. That buzz.

Then the burn.

And now, because of Griffin, it was inside her.

Waiting, she thought.

"Are you asking if my husband hauled me back to my brand-new home and plundered his newly acquired bounty?" Melody asked her sister dryly. "I think you'll find he's entitled to do precisely that, according to ancient Idyllian law. Fen looked it up to make sure."

Calista gripped her wrist. "He didn't…?"

"Of course not."

Melody went to lounge back against the settee where they sat, but stopped quickly when the dress she was wearing made that entirely too uncomfortable. Not if she wanted to also breathe. So she stayed where she was, straight-backed and formal, and after a moment, thought that was just as well. Talking with Calista, it was too easy to forget herself. And she shouldn't assume Griffin wasn't paying attention.

There was more to him than he pretended there was. She could feel it.

She reminded herself to keep her voice low.

"If he'd tried I would have maimed him," she said cheerfully.

"I think it's easy to assume that you might act a certain way in a certain situation when you imagine it from a distance," Calista said carefully. "But then, when the situation actually arises in real life, it might prove to be far more overwhelming than you expect."

That got Melody's attention. "I'm now a little more worried about your wedding night."

"I know you can take care of yourself," her big sister said, in a fierce undertone. "I'm hoping you didn't have to, that's all. Griffin has never struck me as the kind of man who would take something that wasn't offered to him, but you never know, do you?"

Melody's experience with men had almost exclusively

been with her father. As Griffin was nothing like Aristotle, praise the heavens, she had personally been struck by...that, really. What he wasn't. *Who* he wasn't.

When she instead considered who he *was*, everything went electric.

"He was a perfect gentleman," Melody told Calista, and didn't quite manage to keep the note of complaint out of her voice. "What did you expect, with me playing this role? He thinks I might blow away in the faintest breeze. He would have to literally be a monster to force himself upon a creature he believes is so fragile."

Beside her, her sister made a funny noise. "Do you sound...unhappy about that? Or have I had too much sugar?"

"He has no intention of touching me," Melody said, as if she was making a proclamation. A quiet proclamation. She listened for a moment, making sure she could hear the low rumble of two male voices, still far enough away from the couch where she and Calista sat that there was no chance she'd be overheard. "I asked how we would produce heirs if there was no touching, and he didn't seem concerned about bulking up his part of the line of succession."

"Good," Calista retorted. "You hardly know him. No reason to rush into anything. You have your entire marriage for that."

"I'm sure we'll develop a beautiful friendship," Melody muttered. "But to be honest, I'm really much more interested in sex."

She heard Calista choke. "Excellent news on that front, then. You happen to be married to perhaps the most sexually experienced man in the whole of Europe."

"Sad, then, that he has decided he will never insult me

with his touch." Melody sighed. "I have graduated from my own, personal, lifelong convent at last to discover that I've been sent to carry on more of the same in Prince Griffin's private monastery. It doesn't really seem fair."

"Our parents' house is many things, but I wouldn't call it a *convent*."

"That is likely because you were allowed to leave it. As you wished. Without any fears that you might put off the neighbors with your imperfections."

There was a small silence, and Melody instantly felt guilty. It wasn't Calista's fault that her father was who he was or that he'd always treated Melody so appallingly. And yet she knew full well her sister felt somehow responsible for it. For *her*.

"That wasn't meant to be an attack," she said. "Just a statement of fact."

Calista coughed, delicately. "Well. The thing is, Griffin is a man."

"I'm aware of that." Melody frowned. "Wait. What do you mean, exactly?"

"I mean that you've been particularly adept at using your body since you were a kid. And not to generalize hideously about my new brother-in-law, but he has always freely admitted that he's drawn to women who know how to use their bodies. Just...in a different way than you're used to using it."

It took her a moment. "Seduce him, you mean."

"Why not?" Calista asked. Across the room, the male voices got louder. And began moving closer. Calista leaned closer to Melody, speaking quickly. "What do you have to lose? If he gets overly excited you can kill him with one hand. Why not take the opportunity to play?"

Why not, indeed? Melody asked herself later, when,

filled with too many pastries, cakes, and squares of baklava oozing with honey, Griffin led her back to their new home.

"What do you normally do for Christmas dinner?" she asked, when they arrived in his entry hall. *Their* entry hall, she corrected herself.

"Are you hungry?" He sounded amazed.

"Not in the least. But I will be. Later."

"Well. Typically I have a light supper before…" He cleared his throat. "But, of course, I have no plans to go out this evening. I would be delighted if you would join me for a meal."

"Wonderful," she replied, smiling up at him.

As if he'd handed her the heavens instead of agreeing to share a meal with her. One he would clearly not be cooking himself.

Not that it mattered. She was pleased all the same.

Though, then, it was nothing short of torturous to allow him to carefully lead her back to her suite, clearly under the impression that she couldn't find her own way. And that even if she could, she was so breakable that she might crack into shards without his supervision.

There had been a great many years that she'd lain in her bed in her father's house as a girl, dreaming of one day being treated as if she was precious and perhaps fashioned from spun glass. Not a *princess*. But more the way Calista had been treated.

She wished she could go back in time and tell that girl how annoying it was.

"Thank you for a lovely Boxing Day, Melody," Griffin said in that marvelous voice of his that rumbled through her, collecting between her legs. "I am honored that I got to spend it with you."

Melody had the ridiculous urge to curtsy. And curtailed it. Barely.

"I am, too," she replied, laying it on a bit thick. In her opinion, she sounded more tearful than anything else.

"I will see you this evening, then," he said, in that rich, heady way of his.

"Yes," she whispered.

Melody slipped into her suite, then stood there, her back to the door she closed behind her. She heard the sound of Griffin's steps receding down the corridor. And then, moments later, the faint brush of a footstep at the end of her own entry hall.

Fen.

"Have you ever seduced a man?" she asked her sensei.

"Naturally," Fen replied, sounding unfazed.

Because Fen was always unfazed.

"You need to teach me how," Melody said. Because Fen was her sensei, yes, but she had also long been Melody's partner in crime when it came to quietly, secretly, making the embarrassing scandal of the Skyros family into a whole lot more then met the eye.

Pun intended.

"Very well, then," Fen said in her usual way, stern and sedate at once. "We have work to do."

CHAPTER FOUR

LATER THAT EVENING, Griffin waited for his bride with his back to the cozy, intimate dining area he'd had his staff prepare with this holiday supper he'd told her was his tradition. They'd run with it, festooning the room with evergreen boughs that made the air smell crisp and sweet, and small, twinkling lights better suited to more northern climates.

The truth was, Griffin had no such tradition.

Historically, Boxing Day was what he considered the finish line of the deeply tedious run of holiday balls that characterized the last bit of each year. It was an Idyllian tradition. Every week, another holiday ball. All of which he, as a royal prince, was expected to attend. For years he had performed this duty *at* his father, who had stopped asking Griffin to do anything—because Griffin would refuse him. On principle.

But he would happily walk over burning embers for his brother.

It often felt as if he had, come Christmas. The good news was, after his final command appearance for the traditional Boxing Day photos the palace liked to release, he was free to do as he liked until New Year's Eve.

And what Griffin liked usually involved rounds of

debauchery to balance out so many weeks of tedious duty and responsibility.

There would be no more of that, obviously. That was the promise he'd made.

That was the promise he would keep.

Griffin might have felt a faint pang at that, but he ignored it. He gazed out toward the sea instead. His residence sat up on the same hill with the rest of the palace complex and, on clear days, offered him sweeping views of whitewashed buildings with the Aegean forever beckoning in the distance. Tonight there were only the bright lights of the island's only real city and the brooding dark of the sea beyond.

A match for the brooding dark within him—but he was ridding himself of that, too. Griffin had been so many versions of himself in this life already. A doting son to a fragile mother. A rebellious son to a despised father. An avid student, a clever soldier, a playboy prince. What was one more role?

A protector, this time.

This time Griffin intended to get it right.

He heard a sound behind him as the door was opened and his bride was led inside. *His bride.* His *wife.*

Griffin still wasn't used to those terms, but when he turned to face her, he forgot whatever pangs he might have had for careless nights with reckless people. Because Melody seemed to blot out any memories he might have had. Simply by entering the room.

He imagined that if it was daylight, she might block out the sun.

"I hope I'm not dressed inappropriately," she said in that breathy voice that made him want to conquer dragons and raze cities on her behalf. With his own two hands.

Melody looked frail and uncertain as she clung to the arm of her aide. The other woman was dressed all in black and held herself still in a manner that poked at him. *Too still*, something in him warned, as if he was still in the military. The aide was of indeterminate age and bowed slightly at the sight of him. Very slightly. And she did not smile.

But he dismissed that odd, poking feeling, because he was far more consumed with Melody.

"The staff who dressed me claimed that you'd said it was casual, but I don't know what casual means in a royal palace—"

"You look beautiful, Melody," Griffin assured her.

It was a throwaway remark. He would have said it to anyone so jittery and overwhelmed in his presence.

But in her case, he found he meant it.

Profoundly.

Gone was the pretty dress she'd worn earlier and the careful hair, fixed *just so* to look splendidly effortless in photos. Tonight, she wore what passed for casual in his circles. What looked like a whisper soft cashmere sweater over elegant trousers in a lustrous black. Her hair was down, but not in the wild way he'd seen it once before. It looked silky and smooth, and he had the near ungovernable urge to get his hands in it. To hold all that sunshine and gold in his palms and watch it slip through his fingers.

He tried to shove that unhelpful urge away.

"Do you require your aide's assistance to eat?" he asked.

Courteously, he thought. And yet he could have sworn that both of the women's expressions...changed. Tightened, almost.

"She can manage," the older woman said.

A bit forbiddingly, to Griffin's mind. Then, not waiting to be dismissed as she technically should have, she bowed her way out of his presence. And the room.

When the door closed behind her aide, Melody took a step—

And Griffin cursed himself for not moving sooner as he sprang across the room to take hold of her arm.

"We don't want you to trip, Melody," he said, as gently as he could.

"You are too kind," she replied.

Sweetly.

Too sweetly, something in him muttered, but he ignored that, too. How could his frail and breakable bride be *too* sweet when she could barely function without assistance?

He steered her, not to the table waiting for them, but out to the balcony where torches flickered against the December darkness.

"I thought it would be nice to sit outside tonight," he said stiffly. Because his wife was the only woman he'd ever met who he didn't instinctively know how to charm, and that was a prickly sort of realization. He didn't care for it. "We can have a glass of wine before we eat, if that appeals."

"That sounds like a wonderful idea," Melody said in her soft, gentle way. "I love torches."

Griffin paused in the act of helping her to the balcony's casual, comfortable seating area. "How do you...?"

And then watched, thunderstruck, as she laughed.

Silvery, like the moon. Like starlight.

"I can smell them," she told him. "And if you listen closely, you can hear the flames flicker in the wind."

But he was too busy questioning why his heart was galloping around his chest when all she'd done was laugh. *At* him.

He busied himself pouring out two glasses of the wine he'd requested from his cellars, then he went back to sit with her. There on the same comfortable bench near the torches that it had never occurred to him to listen to. Or smell.

Though he did then. And imagined he always would, now.

"I want to ask you a favor," his wife said after a moment, during which time he absolutely did not study the way she pressed her wineglass to that full lower lip of hers, slow and sensual.

"Anything," he said.

Hoping he sounded gallant instead of…obsessed.

Melody smiled, looking pleased. "My sister described you to me a long time ago. Your features, I mean. Calista told me all the girls swooned over the Royal Princes and she made sure I knew what you two looked like so I could swoon along with the best of them."

"And did you?" Once again, he found that when he was close to her it was difficult to recall why, exactly, he couldn't treat her the way he would any other beautiful woman. "Swoon. Over me. If you swooned over Orion, you're welcome to keep that to yourself."

"I was never one for swooning." She smiled after she said it, and he instantly forgot that oddly brisk note in her voice he'd thought he heard. "That was a very long time ago, though. And now we're married."

"Indeed we are."

"This time," she said, her voice hardly more than a whisper. So soft he had to angle himself closer to her to make sure he heard her. "This time I want to see you for myself."

She leaned in as she spoke, making him wonder why he'd chosen to torture himself like this, by sitting in close range. And then forgetting he'd ever questioned such a thing, because the scent of her swirled around him… and bludgeoned him.

Melody smelled sharp and sweet. Tart apples and brown sugar. And it took more self-control than Griffin thought he'd ever employed in his life to keep his hands to himself.

Though he couldn't seem to do much about his body's reaction.

"You can do anything you like," he managed to say when he was reasonably certain he could sound like something other than a slavering beast. "But I'll confess I don't know quite what you mean."

She smiled, her eyes so blue, that it was hard to believe she couldn't see him already. When he felt so *obvious*. He, who had never been any such thing in his life. He, who had made a career out of sampling any morsel that crossed his path, always letting them down so easily that they tended to trail about after him ever after. He, who had never been *obvious* because, it occurred to him, he hadn't really felt much one way or the other.

Before.

Who could have guessed that wanting something he couldn't have would *burn* like this? Brighter than the dancing flames that surrounded them?

And he tried to ignore the deeply male part of him that, because she was burned so brightly into his head, wanted to be the same for her.

God, the way he *wanted* the one woman he should have desired only to place behind protective glass.

Griffin was forced to acknowledge that he was far more like his father, the degenerate King Max, than he had ever wanted to admit.

Melody lifted one of her graceful hands off of her wineglass, then held it between them with her palm facing him.

"This is how I see." Her head tilted to one side, sending her hair cascading over her shoulder and that scent of hers dancing all around him. Griffin breathed in, deep, like he wanted to drown himself in her. He did. "Do you mind?"

His throat was tight. And he was harder than he thought he'd ever been. His sex was ready. *He* was ready. He could feel the pulse of his need, deep and low and insistent.

He should have been ashamed.

Yet he was...not.

"I would be delighted," he managed to get out, in a gravelly voice that no doubt betrayed him.

But he couldn't think of things like shame. Not when Melody was leaning closer. Shifting her body so that her thigh was pressed against his. Torturing him—

"Would you hold this?" she asked, in that same soft, sweet voice.

Reminding him who she was.

And who, by contrast, *he* was.

Griffin took her wineglass from her. He ordered the beast in him back to its cage. And recited the promises he'd made—to his brother, to this woman, to himself— like a prayer as he gripped both glasses. Much too tightly.

Not that he expected prayers to help him. Not after the sins he'd committed—and gleefully.

Then he watched, transfixed, as she lifted her hands and carefully fit them to either side of his face.

The shock of it was like a blow.

He felt his pulse gallop. She was touching him, her hands cool against his jaw, while he could do nothing but burn. Her face was close to his, and that was another kind of heat. The scent of her filled his senses. Her hair, her skin, the soft curves in her lean frame.

But he didn't move. He didn't dare.

She moved her head as if she was listening to something far away. A faint frown line appeared between her brows.

Griffin died a thousand deaths, yet somehow—*somehow*—kept his hands to himself.

And slowly, almost reverently, Melody began to move her hands as if he was made of Braille and she was reading every word.

Griffin had seen every possible sexy thing there was. He'd had them acted out upon him and acted them out in return. Yet he had never in his life seen anything sexier than this.

Than her.

Princess Melody, his bride, focusing on him with such intensity that he was sure if he squinted he would be able to see the force of all that concentration in a shimmering, electric arc between them. As if every light touch of her graceful fingers against his jaw, his cheekbones, the bridge and then the line of his nose, spread light.

She traced his eyebrows and his temples. She smoothed her fingers through his hair as if she'd read his mind and knew what he longed to do with hers. She found his mouth and traced her fingertips over his lips, seemingly heedless of the greedy flare of heat that kicked up inside him.

He shoved it back down. Or he tried.

Melody shifted beside him, and he couldn't decide if it was a blessing or a curse that he was still holding on to both of their wineglasses. Surely it was a curse that he couldn't put his hands on her as she performed this oddly hushed and seemingly sacred act.

That was the blessing, too, he knew.

Because she was looking at him, that was all. She wasn't trying to seduce him. And in return, he wanted to devour her.

Melody didn't stop at his face. Almost dreamily, her hands drifted down to learn the column of his neck, that betraying pulse, and the width of his shoulders. He wore only a light sweater himself and found he missed the faint abrasion of her fingertips against his bare skin. She learned every muscle in each of his arms, then moved back to his chest. Her brow still furrowed, she used the whole of each palm to trace his pectoral muscles, then the ridged abdomen below.

And then slowly, with that same fierce look of concentration that had him hard enough to burst, she climbed her way back up again for one last pass.

Her face was so close to his. It was unbearable. And Melody moved a hand as if she knew what she was doing. As if she was deliberately positioning her palm she could pull his head to hers—

But she didn't.

It was an agony. He was *in agony.*

She stopped, her lips a scant centimeter from his—

"Thank you," she said, her voice that soft wisp of sound.

He barely heard it over the thundering inside of him. The clenching, near-unmanageable need.

"Melody…" Griffin began, though he had no idea what he planned to say.

Or if instead he might beg.

He, who had never begged because there had never been a need. Because he had never, in all his life, had occasion to want.

Not when everything was provided to him on a procession of silver platters. Not when any need or desire was met before he bothered to express it.

Griffin couldn't identify, at first, the thing that swelled in him when she dropped her hand. Then sat back, moving away from him, letting the December night back in between them.

Longing, he thought. *This is* longing.

In something that might have been astonishment, had it been less… bright.

Her smile made the stars seem like diamonds made of paste. "Now we see each other."

"You can see me anytime you like," he told her, and he was appalled by the sound of his own voice. His need so naked, so unmistakable, that he was surprised his shy and sheltered bride didn't recoil.

Griffin pressed her wineglass back into her hand, waited until she gripped it, then stood.

Deeply glad she couldn't see him wince as the heaviness of his sex…protested.

He moved to the balcony rail, entirely too aware that he was reacting as if she'd attacked him.

How he wished she would.

"I can't imagine what it is to be blind," he said then. Formally. Because he thought he ought to say something, if only to cover his reaction to her. "I'm sorry."

"I don't know what it is to see," Melody replied, smiling. "I can't accept your apology when I never lost my sight. I suppose I could sit about mourning something I never had, but what would be the point?"

"That sounds very healthy, Melody. I admire you."

"Do you? Why?"

It was possible that all that unfamiliar longing and need charging around inside of him was making him see things that weren't there, but for a bizarre moment, Griffin could have sworn that she was…issuing him a challenge.

There was something in the way she was sitting there, holding herself so still. There was something about the way her face tipped toward his, an expression he couldn't possibly be reading correctly on her lovely, innocent, guileless face.

Almost as if she was preparing herself to take some kind of swing—

But that was absurd.

This women needed his protection. She couldn't challenge a stray summer breeze, much less a man who still trained at military fitness levels to keep himself in fighting shape.

What Griffin needed to do, he acknowledged with a certain grimness, was accept the fact that his body was a lustful thing that wanted to drag his bride down to his level so he need not keep all the promises he'd made.

Accept it, get rid of it, and move on.

"I admire any person who handles adversity with such equanimity," he said after a moment.

He needed to get a grip on himself.

Now.

This was not an opponent of some kind. This was his fragile, virtuous, helpless bride. Who had not touched him because she'd *wanted* to set him on fire.

That was an unfortunate side effect.

One that should have embarrassed him, as it highlighted that despite the trappings of his overtly civilized life, at heart he was nothing but a beast. Nothing but greed straight through, a slave to his own passions, like the father he despised.

She had been trying to see him, not seduce him. He should have been disgusted at his own response.

No more, Griffin vowed to himself. Again.

And made himself go and take his seat once more because he, by God, would be the master of his own flesh.

Melody inclined her head, demurely enough to make him question ever seeing anything but that in the way she held herself. "And I admire you."

He laughed, lounging back because this felt like familiar ground. "What is there to admire? I'm afraid I'm concocted of silver spoons, hereditary fortunes, and an entire lifestyle I did nothing to earn."

"Yes, but who would truly wish to be a royal?" Her smile was so gentle there was no reason he should feel the sharp edge of it rake over him. "It might be a pretty prison cell, or so I hear. But it's still a prison cell, isn't it?"

"It is an honor to represent Idylla and support my brother in all his works," Griffin said by rote.

It wasn't that he didn't mean it. He did.

But that didn't mean there weren't…textures to the words that formed the boundaries of his life. The simplest words, he'd found, always had the greatest complications lurking right there in plain sight.

"Of course you do," Melody said. Still with that smile. "I was lucky to avoid the bulk of my father's attention, if Calista's experiences are anything to go by. Being his favorite came with its own price tag, there's no denying it. It's not hard to imagine what being Crown Prince to King Max must have entailed."

"Heavy lies the crown," Griffin replied, lightly enough. "Which is one reason I have always preferred to keep my own marvelous princely brow smooth and unencumbered."

Next to him, Melody shifted. And leaned in.

And Griffin was a connoisseur of women. They flocked about him and he had long taken pride in the fact that while he frequently and enthusiastically indulged, he truly enjoyed those indulgences. He didn't have a type. He didn't have hierarchies. He wasn't attempting to put notches on his bedpost or prove anything to anyone. He simply loved women and loved being with them, whatever that looked like.

Yet here, now, as Melody swayed closer to him as if she planned to kiss him at last, Griffin felt like an untried innocent. A chaste virgin without a shred of control.

He wanted his hands on her.

He *wanted* and he didn't have the slightest idea what to *do* with it.

Inside him, storms and fires swept this way and that. It was cataclysmic. It was *too much*—

Griffin was somehow out of his depth when he would have said that was impossible. And all Melody did was sway ever closer…

Her scent, her warmth, wrapped around him like a fist.

He could remember, too intensely, the perfunctory kiss he'd delivered at the altar. It had been little more than a brush of lips and yet it *burned in him*—

God help him, but he wanted a proper taste.

But when she was so close that not kissing her seemed like an offense, what Melody did instead of put him out of his misery was...lift her hand.

Then, unerringly, find his forehead.

She traced her way down his to the furrow between his brows.

"Not so smooth and unencumbered, I think," she murmured.

It took some thousand years or so for her words to penetrate the wild drumming of his heart, the matching beat in his sex. The wildfire inside him, wicked and raging.

Melody's smile was cool. Almost as if she knew. "Maybe all lives have their hardships, Griffin. Maybe crowns aren't required."

CHAPTER FIVE

MELODY WOKE UP the next morning in a confused, grumpy rush, because there were voices and commotion and she could tell from the state of her own sleepiness that it was much too early.

Much too early.

She had never been a morning person. One of the benefits of having spent most of her life shut away from the sort of people her father wished to impress—meaning, everyone—was that she could keep her own hours. And did.

"No time to waste!" came a voice that reminded her entirely too much of the governesses she and Calista had suffered through when they were young. Brisk and self-important, every last one of them. "There are already too many appointments for one day!"

Melody lay face down, enveloped in the deep embrace of the glorious featherbed piled high with soft linens and fluffy down, as befit a royal princess's bedchamber. She had never felt quite so pampered in her life and intended to lie about, enjoying it, for as long as she could.

She had not, as she sometimes liked to pretend on the few occasions she was allowed to interact with people outside her immediate family, been forced to sleep on a pallet on the floor in her parents' dungeon. Her father was cruel, her mother weak, certainly. But on the off chance that Melody might ever compare notes with any other member of the Idyllian aristocracy, they'd made certain that while her rooms were far away from the rest in the sprawling Skyros villa—lest her father find himself forced to come face-to-face with Melody against his will, which was to say, ever—the rooms were appropriately outfitted.

Also, they did not have a dungeon. Aristotle preferred to imprison his daughters in a more lasting cage of disdain, rage, and insult.

Melody's ascension to the palace was not exactly the rags-to-riches story all the papers were claiming it was. She'd laughed over all the local articles that had called her Cinderella after her sudden Christmas wedding, making her screen reader repeat it again and again. Still, fairy tale or not, Melody found the accommodations of her new life as a princess nothing short of splendid.

She did not want to crawl out of her bed. She did not even wish to turn over. Particularly not when she was—despite the enduring embrace of the glorious featherbed—not nearly as well rested as she would have liked.

That was what happened when a person went and played seduction games with Prince Griffin, ate entirely too much rich food, pretended that it was all in aid of celebrating the holiday—and then was forced to allow him to escort her back to her rooms when even she could feel that the hour was too late and the tension between them too intense.

She hadn't expected the intensity, she could admit.

And when she had finally made it into her rooms,

she'd been forced to endure a lecture from Fen about her deficiencies as a seductress.

I could have seduced him ten times already, for all you know, she'd told the older woman.

If you had seduced him even once, you would be in his bed, not yours, Fen had retorted, her voice as pointed as one of her lightning-fast jabs.

"I am still sleeping," Melody announced now, more to her pillow than to the new voice still bustling around her room. Slinging open the curtains and stoking the fire, if the obnoxious noises being made were any indication.

"I'm afraid not, Your Royal Highness." And it was amazing how the voice made Melody's new title into the sharp lash of something unpleasant, like a whip. "A private citizen might enjoy these days off between Boxing Day and the new year, but that is not the way of the palace."

Melody burrowed deeper into her covers, and did not offer to introduce the intruder to the way of the fist as she wanted to do with every cell in her body.

"No, thank you," she said, again, with her face half-buried in the pillow. "Go away."

She was drifting back into blessed sleep within seconds, settling even deeper into the sweet clutch of her marvelous bed—

Until the covers, impossibly, were ripped off of her body, exposing her to the still chilly air of the bed-chamber.

Melody felt murderous.

She flipped over, prepared to leap up and attack the woman that she could sense hovering there at the end of the bed, clearly overly impressed with herself—as any fool might be when they did not understand the consequences of their actions—

But she remembered herself just in time.

Melody was not herself. Not here. Back at her parents' house, she'd been taking care of herself for years and was accordingly left alone. *Here* she was a fragile, cringing, trembling little thing who would not, for example, catapult herself out of the bed and kick the person standing at the foot of it in the face.

She made herself breathe until the urge to attack faded. Then she shoved the great mass of her hair back and tried to school her expression into something appropriately deferential.

"I don't know who you are," she said quietly, yet with perhaps too much fury lingering there in her voice. She cleared her throat. "But you should know that I take my sleep very seriously."

"I am Madame Constantinople Dupree," came the voice once again, redolent with self-satisfaction. "I'm the foremost expert on courtly manners in the whole of Europe and have been gifted to you, Your Royal Highness, by His Royal Majesty King Orion himself."

"A gift for the girl who has everything," Melody murmured.

Not as nicely as she should have.

"I am led to understand that your manners are above reproach, which I will take the liberty to doubt, as I have never taught you."

"I did manage to marry a prince," Melody countered, and had to order herself to release the tension in her body, because this was no time to be wound like a spring, ready to attack. It would get her nowhere.

No matter how satisfying it might have been.

Madame Constantinople Dupree sniffed with pointed disdain. "A prince is but a man, Your Royal Highness. And it is not the men of society you need concern yourself with on your first day of social calls. You should be so lucky! Alas, it is the aristocratic women who will be coming to vet you today, I am afraid."

"Are you?" Melody shrugged before she thought better of it, and tried to pull off a bit of a cringe at the end of it. "I am not afraid of a collection of silly women who speak of nothing but last night's parties."

"You should be," Madame retorted with another sniff. "Believe me when I tell you that even if they have not sampled Prince Griffin's legendary charm personally, there will be no reason whatsoever for them to go easy on you."

"Save that I outrank them."

In return to what she'd thought was a winning argument by any measure, Melody heard a light, brittle sort of laugh. It reminded her so much of the sort of sound she'd been letting out herself since her wedding that she was forced to take more notice than she might have otherwise.

"My dear child." And she could hear things she didn't want in the other woman's voice, then. A seriousness. And an underlying bedrock of certainty. "Society's most fearsome women are coming to pay their respects to a new member of the royal family. Which you should be aware means they would love nothing more than to pick clean your bones, slay you alive, and destroy your reputation. Preferably over a lovely cream tea, with a charming smile attached. Never, ever underestimate the ruthlessness of a woman who seemingly speaks of nothing. She is almost certainly deliberately hiding her power, and a hidden power is nearly always far more dangerous."

Melody sat a bit straighter at that, for she knew it to be true of herself. Why not the great many aristocratic ladies she had never bothered to study, thinking them anything but worthy opponents? She should have known better after witnessing her sister's struggles over the years. Not all fights used the weapons she'd been training with for a lifetime.

But that didn't mean Melody intended to lose.

"It can't be that bad, can it?" she asked. "A bit of palace intrigue, perhaps? A few salacious rumors?"

"Whatever you are imagining, Your Royal Highness," replied Madame Constantinople Dupree, severely, "it will be worse. Much worse. And yet here you are, still abed in your nightgown, when we ought to be preparing you for war."

"War?" That sounded a lot more fun than the day Melody had imagined, but she reminded herself to shrivel a bit, like a frightened creature might. "I don't know…"

The other woman sighed. "They told me you were a frail, fragile little thing. Rest assured, that can only work in your favor. But we must act now."

"Very well, then," Melody said, with exaggerated bravery. And was certain she could hear Fen's snort of laughter from the hall. "War it is."

Accordingly, she surrendered herself to the brisk morning schedule outlined by Madame, who did not pretend to be anything less than a humorless drill sergeant. She allowed herself to be marched off to the shower, then whisked into the chair that she'd discovered during her explorations last night, sat before a vanity table. Inaptly named for a blind woman, perhaps, who could be vain in all manner of ways that did not involve mirrors, but she doubted that Madame Constantinople Dupree would find such commentary amusing.

As she sat there, letting servants buzz around her, breakfast was brought to her. And Melody was deeply unimpressed to discover it was little more than a hard roll to go along with her coffee.

"I prefer my breakfasts not to suggest that I might have woken up to find myself incarcerated," Melody muttered. To Fen, who had brought her the tray and who was currently pretending she didn't speak the local language—one of her preferred places to hide herself in the presence of others. None of whom, apparently, ever bothered to discover that she was, in fact, an Idyllian native. "Though I think they serve better food in jail."

"You may have as luxurious a breakfast as you wish, Your Royal Highness," Madame said in a forbidding tone from somewhere behind Melody. Once again wielding Melody's new title like a sword. "But I should warn you that you will be eating all day."

"That's the first thing you've said about the day ahead of me that sounds the least bit enjoyable," Melody retorted, because she hadn't yet had enough coffee to think better of it.

"Nothing about today will be enjoyable," came the swift, brisk reply. "You will be judged on what you eat along with everything else. How you sit. How you respond. How you laugh. How you hold your hands. You must view today as a comprehensive exam, Your Royal Highness. One from which it is extremely likely that you will emerge with dire marks from all involved."

"Will all these ladies pelt me with their tea sandwiches?" Melody asked dryly. Too dryly, she understood, when Fen refilled her coffee without her having to ask. "Sling pots of clotted cream at my head?"

It was difficult to pay attention to things like the expression she ought to have had on her face, or the tremulous tone she ought to have been using, when her staff was careening all around her. They were troweling on cosmetics she had no way of knowing if she liked or not and doing acrobatic things with her hair, all while Madame stood behind her, radiating disapproval.

It was only Fen's cough, in fact, that reminded her to shift her body language into something that made sense for the character she was meant to be playing here. To round her shoulders and make herself small instead of entertaining little fantasies of what it might be like to bat away clotted cream weapons, and expose her real self to any soft, pampered, vicious society ladies who imagined they could bully her in some way.

That would be satisfying, but foolish. And not at all the strategy that she was supposed to be employing. By decree of the monarch himself, in case she'd forgotten.

"I understand that this seems silly to you," Madame was saying in a tone that made it clear she did not, in fact, understand. Or wish to understand. "You've led a very sheltered life, after all. Protected from the intricacies of life at court."

That was not how Melody would have described her life, but she told herself to let that go. If anything, she should have been amused that after being considered the great, humiliating scandal of the Skyros family— something that couldn't be true, by definition, if she was now a member of the royal family and sister to the new Queen—there was already a new, usable fiction to explain why it was that she had been so seldom seen or heard from her whole life.

"Yes," she murmured, striving to sound overwhelmed rather than entertained. "Very sheltered."

"In a perfect world, I would have had months to prepare you," Madame said, reprovingly. "Years. Instead, I have but hours." She sighed. Heavily. "We will do the best we can."

"It is just…" Melody paused, because the woman tugging on her hair did something that made her eyes water. She blew out a breath as if that was emotion, not a sting. "The Prince did not say anything about this. He didn't even tell me there was anything for me to do today."

That was true, of course. But it was also true that she'd said it that way deliberately, to encourage them all to believe that she enjoyed a great intimacy with the husband she barely knew. The sort a newlywed bride ought to enjoy.

The sort everyone would assume she enjoyed, in all senses of the term, because it was Griffin.

"Prince Griffin enjoys the affection of the nation," Madame said with another helping of that severity. "He has spent a lifetime cultivating the goodwill of his people. He also enjoys the advantage of having been born royal. None of these advantages are yours, if you will forgive me."

Melody smiled demurely. "Of course. I am cognizant of my own deficiencies. How could I not be?"

But the joke was on her, because Madame did not rush to assure her that she was in no way deficient, the way regular, sighted people normally did in the face of any direct or indirect reference to her blindness.

"I'm glad to hear it," the older woman said instead.

Stoutly. Forcing Melody to respect her, despite herself. "What you can expect are packs of hyenas, parading about as if they truly wish you might become friends one day. They do not wish this. You will be given no benefit of any doubt. You will be accorded zero room to maneuver or grow. They will come in prepared to eviscerate you. And will take pleasure in the fact that they might do so to your face, without you any the wiser."

For the first time, Melody felt something inside her... shift. The way it did when she was preparing herself to step into the ring. To fight with Fen, who never gave her any quarter.

"I am not as unaware of what goes on around me as people might imagine," she said quietly.

"I am thrilled," Madame replied. "This is the first cause for optimism I have had since I entered your bedchamber."

And hours later, when Madame was cautiously optimistic but in no way satisfied, she ushered Melody from her own apartments to a set of rooms she and Fen had explored on her wedding night. Her formal reception rooms, she was told today.

For her sins.

"You have forty-five minutes before your first guest," Madame said briskly. "Is that enough time?"

"For what?"

Melody felt deeply grateful that she'd spent the bulk of her life studying the things she had. With Fen, who had never allowed her the luxury of self-pity. Because she could not imagine, otherwise, how she would have handled the morning she'd had. Madame was not a martial artist. But she was a sensei all the same, and had somehow managed to instill in Melody a deep appreciation for the finer nuances of snooty aristocratic behavior that she'd never before possessed.

It will not be enough to play the innocent, she'd said gravely. And more than once.

But I am innocent, Melody had replied.

Evenly at first. Then, as the hours dragged by, with far less equanimity.

Innocence is blood in the water, Madame had retorted. *Do not fool yourself on that score. You will find it is preferable to outswim the sharks than to hope they are taken aback by innocence.*

Madame threw open the doors to the reception room and ushered Melody inside, Fen walking silently behind her.

"You must use this time to familiarize yourself with this room. I assume from the way you moved around your bedchamber and the rest of your apartments that you have a system for doing so. The more comfortable you are, the less ammunition you will give your enemies. Do you understand me?"

"Completely," Melody replied.

She and Fen used their forty-five minutes wisely.

And by the time Madame returned, announcing that the onslaught was to begin, Melody was as primed as if she was preparing to grapple.

Which was good, because grapple she did.

They came at her in order of rank. Something Melody had deliberately not concerned herself with in all her days, because what was the point, though she had received quite a crash course on Idyllian nobility today.

It was a parade of ladies with various titles, all of which they waved about them like taunts. Some were kind. Some pretended to be kind. Still others engaged in actual taunts, as if they did not expect that Prince Griffin's unexpected bride would be capable of telling the difference.

Melody could tell which ones had sampled her husband. Which ones had only wished they might. And which still intended to get their claws into him, despite his marriage.

She supposed another woman might dislike knowing such things.

But not Melody.

The more these women showed themselves to her, thinking she couldn't see who they really were, the more power she had over them.

"I cannot imagine how overwhelmed you must feel," cooed an openly poisonous member of the lesser aristocracy. Married to a minor lord, she nonetheless carried herself as if she had the consequence of a queen. *The* Queen.

From this, Melody was given to understand two things. First, that Lady Breanna was very beautiful. Second, that Breanna was not happy to discover that Melody was not disfigured, as some had liked to whisper to explain her absence from public events over the years.

Expectations were power, too, if a person knew how to use them. Melody did.

"How lovely of you to worry about me," Melody replied sweetly. "But there is no need for concern. I like to think that I've been training my whole life to step into this role."

"It appears that the Skyros family took their *education* far more seriously than some," came the arch reply. "I assume there were more opportunities to…ah, *study* than the rest of us were accorded."

Even if Melody had not received a morning-long crash course in how to handle just that sort of elegant poison masquerading as a conversation, she would have known that she was being attacked.

"Surely it is the role of any Idyllian citizen to support the royal family." She kept her voice friendly, as Madame had advised. Because it was always better to keep them guessing, the other woman had said. Making Fen guffaw, then pretend it was a cough. "That was how my sister and I were raised, in any event."

The only interest Aristotle Skyros had ever had in the royal family was how to rope the previous King into marrying off Orion. To Calista, so that Aristotle might therefore wield a greater influence over King and country. But that did not fit with Melody's performance here, of virtue masquerading as patriotism, all wrapped up in a shy smile.

"Indeed," trilled Lady Breanna. "As were we all. But I will confess, I don't think there's a soul on the island who is not *enchanted* to discover that Prince Griffin truly has the heart of gold we always suspected he did."

It was the same checklist that, by now, had been waved in front of Melody a thousand times today already. Her family was grasping and unworthy. She was out of her depth to a laughable degree. And, not least, Griffin himself had only condescended to stoop to taking a creature like *Melody Skyros* as his bride as an act of selfless charity.

Granted, that was all true. Particularly the last, but that didn't mean Melody had to like the way these horrible women threw it in her face.

Each and every one of them. With glee.

She leaned in. "I'm not sure he was thinking with his

heart, Lady Breanna." She could feel the other woman's bristling outrage, so she decided she might as well stick the knife in. "I suspect it was a rather different organ altogether."

And it wasn't until the doors closed behind Lady Breanna and her sputtering indignation—likely because she had designs on Prince Griffin's organ herself—that Melody allowed herself a deeply inelegant cackle.

Madame would not approve.

The doors opened again and Melody tried to compose herself.

But she knew, almost instantly, that it wasn't another insipid well-bred lady come to offer her a raft of backhanded compliments.

She could feel the sheer male power, ruthless and intoxicating, like an abrupt change in temperature. It emanated from him, so that even if she hadn't heard the particular cadence of his steps—so familiar to her now—she would have known.

"Do not stop laughing on my account." Griffin's voice was low. Deep. Rough in a way that made her think of decidedly un-aristocratic things. And made her body hum in response, as if they were already doing them. "It makes you sound like a different woman altogether."

Melody knew she should have wilted. Curled into a soft little ball in need of his care, the way she was supposed to do. But something in her rebelled.

Maybe it was all the hours she'd spent today playing princess games. Maybe it was Griffin himself, bringing all that brooding, storming *maleness* in with him as he flung himself onto what she knew was a frilly, feminine little settee across from her.

She tried to imagine that. A man like him, so big, so

hard, so deliciously male, overpowering that frilly piece of furniture without even trying.

A shudder seemed to come from deep inside her, wrecking her.

Or it would have wrecked her, she corrected herself. But she couldn't be wrecked. Not by hours of polite torture and not by him.

"As it happens," she said, because she couldn't resist, even when she knew she should have, "I believe I am a different woman, Your Royal Highness. I've been required to sit here for hours, smiling merrily while all your ex-lovers lined up to make sure I knew the precise length and breadth of your…"

She paused, deliberately.

He went still.

Dangerously still, but her trouble was, she liked that.

"*Reputation,*" Melody supplied, at last. Innocently. "Your reputation. And better still, how true it still is today."

CHAPTER SIX

FOR A MOMENT, Griffin was certain he hadn't heard her correctly.

Not when his Princess sat before him, looking as fresh and pure as if she had just that moment descended from the clouds above, harp in one hand and halo attached.

Melody was radiant. She had spent hours in a pit of venomous snakes, and yet she sat there before him looking sweet and virtuous and wholly unfazed.

Even as she spoke of his *reputation*.

He eyed her a little more closely. She was dressed in what might as well have been battle armor. Her wedding dress had been a glorious confection, a fairy tale in fabric. The casual sophistication of the night before was left to his memories—and the filthy, erotic dreams of her that had kept him up half the night, to his shame. But today's ensemble was deceptively simple. The elegance was in the details. Not trying too hard—which the more vicious would have used as reason enough to sniff about her—and not trying too little, either, which would have branded her as haughty by some and unfit for her position by others.

Even her hair managed to look effortless yet sophisticated at once. It was tamed and swept back from her face, highlighting the perfection of her aristocratic bone structure. Her makeup was subtle, and instead of dramatic jewelry to proclaim her position, she had only demure hints of sparkle at her ears and the hollow of her throat.

Then again, the ring he'd put on her hand spoke loudly enough.

And the dress she wore was a masterpiece. Griffin imagined that he would see a great many dresses cut precisely like this on the island's fashionable ladies within the next few months. It was perfectly feminine, yet authoritative. It announced not only the elevation of Melody's rank, but signaled her ease with her new role. It was both more than a shift and less than a gown, showing off the heartbreaking beauty of her form while remaining modest enough to win the approval of even the most ferocious society matron.

He found he was...proud.

"I should have prepared you for what would happen today," he said, and then stared down at his hand, astonished to find he was pressing it against his chest. Because something there...ached. "I apologize that I did not. If I am honest, it never occurred to me that they would force this protocol upon you. I assumed you were relaxing into your new role, in private."

He had also been far too busy frothing about in the grip of his own demons. Not that he planned to share that with his innocent bride.

Who seemed to *glow* at him. "I'm actually pleased you did not prepare me."

Melody sat with her legs together and her ankles demurely crossed, a vision of propriety. Her hands were folded in her lap, gracefully, and he found himself staring at them—remembering how it had felt to have those very hands all over him.

And the fire that had kept him up half the night surged back to life. Flames licked over him while all of that *want* tumbled through him, making him edgy with need.

Making him think he might burn to ash if he couldn't get *his* hands on *her*—

Griffin didn't know what he might have done then. And he would never know, because the staff was all around them, seamlessly clearing away one set of tea things and bringing another to take its place.

And Melody looked as if she was staring right at him with her eyes like the sea in summer, when, of course, she wasn't.

That thing in his chest unfurled and ached all the more.

"You should not be pleased," he told her, and only when he heard his own voice did he realize how tense he was. He ordered himself to find his way back to the charm he was known for. "We have been married less than two days and I have already failed you."

"Not at all," his bride told him, her voice far airier than his. "It was far more fun to do it blind."

For a moment, he could only stare at her. Slowly, Griffin blinked.

Then watched, while that ache in his chest hitched and turned into something far hotter, as she smiled.

Wickedly.

He had the lowering, white-hot notion that if they'd been truly alone in this room, he would have ignored the table between them and gotten his hands on her at last. He would have taken her, there and then, any way he could.

It was that wickedness in her lovely smile.

It was the way it changed her. Altered her face, making her look almost as if…

But then she laughed again, and this time, she sounded as innocent as ever. As pure and good.

Untouchable, something in him complained.

When he had vowed to protect her, not defile her. She was goodness personified. She deserved more than… him.

"I shouldn't say things like that," Melody said brightly, then laughed again. A tinkling sort of laugh, like a bell, that made him think of the sorts of churches he never entered. Griffin tried to ignore the lick of flames inside him. He tried to shame himself for all this greed, but failed. "Madame Constantinople Dupree was very clear on this point. But she did tell me that a little bit of firmness, just the faintest hint, wouldn't go awry."

"They eat sweetness for breakfast," Griffin agreed, trying to shift to make himself comfortable. But she was still sitting there before him, looking every inch the Princess, and he was undone. And uncomfortable. "And regurgitate it as a scandal whenever possible."

"Then I already have a leg up," she said, almost merrily. "As, being your foremost work of charity, I'm already scandalous."

There was nothing specifically untrue about that statement. There were many reasons that Melody was the right choice for him, forcing him to keep the promises he'd made to his brother in more ways than one. Married, settled, scandal-free and bonus, yes, his choice of the hidden Skyros sister had instantly made him seem far better than he was.

There was absolutely no reason that should sit on him, a heavy weight he couldn't seem to dislodge.

"What you are," he said, with more temper than should have been involved, surely, "is my wife. A royal princess. Should anyone treat you as something less than that, whether or not your tone is something less than polite will be the least of their concerns."

Melody smiled and this time, sadly, without that wickedness. "Can you imagine? A royal prince charges forth to defend his wife from passive aggressive comments… I can see the papers now. It would cause a terrible ruckus and neither one of us would look good at the end of it, would we?"

He considered her for a moment, realizing that this was yet another version of his wife. Every time he saw her, it was as if she was someone else.

If he was any kind of a man, that should probably not excite him as much as it did.

But he found her fascinating.

"I did not marry you to force you into society battles," he said, because though she sat there looking as if she was perfectly happy to let the silence between them drag on forever, he found he was not. "There are no winners. Only Pyrrhic victories if you're very lucky. And everyone walks away stained."

"Are you stained, then?"

Griffin was glad she couldn't see the bitter twist to his lips. "Unto my soul."

Melody inclined her head. "That sounds unpleasant. You must know that there are solutions to that problem."

"Are there indeed?" He could think of several things that would feel like solutions. To him, anyway. "And what would you know of stains—or society, for that matter?"

"Only that it is the women who bear the brunt of both," she corrected him softly. "Men are allowed to be stained, aren't they? It gives them a certain appeal. Women, by contrast, must make certain they are spotless and beyond reproach. Or appear so."

She sounded as if she was parroting a hymnal. "We are not so medieval in Idylla these days, Melody."

"Perhaps you are not, Your Royal Highness," she retorted. And once again, he was sure there was more to her than manners and innocence. It was that flash of something like temper. It was the hint of *more*—but no. He merely wanted her, that was all. He needed to get used to that novelty. "You can act as you please. And do. Had I been in any doubt on that score, a number of your admirers came here today for the express purpose of letting me know exactly how many stains your soul bears. But naturally I cannot behave in a similar manner."

"Because you are a married woman, Melody." He told himself that wasn't temper that worked its way over him. Through him. Griffin did not lose his temper—ever, and certainly not around women. "My wife, in case you forgot."

"I didn't forget." Her expression was polite. Mild, even. And if he wasn't mistaken, faintly amused. He had no idea what to do with that. Or with her. "I was only making a point."

She turned her head away from him then, and he had the odd sensation that he was watching her...change. Especially when she seemed to cower where she sat.

"I only hoped to...not embarrass you," she said in a

wispy voice. "I'm sorry if I failed. My father could have told you that was inevitable."

Griffin told himself he should feel nothing but the urge to protect her. From the world. From her odious father. From himself.

But instead, what he wanted most was to touch her. To feel her beneath his hands. To see the truth of her the way she'd seen him—because he couldn't quite believe what he saw before him. He couldn't make sense of it. Of her.

If she was as frail and beset as she looked just now, how could she possibly have fended off the fangs of so many society women?

You only wish she was secretly strong and capable, a voice in him chided. *So you could stop pretending to be good.*

He cleared his throat. "I regret that you were put through that. I apologize if you found it an ordeal."

"You have a past. I understand that." She turned her face back toward him. "Should we pretend that you do not?"

He had been about to say something similar. And found he didn't like it much when it came out of her mouth.

"I would prefer that you not be confronted with anything you find unpleasant," he managed to say.

"Goodness. I didn't realize that was on offer." Again, she smiled, and he began to understand how she'd held her own today. "I rather thought that this was a life we were going to have to lead, together. For who among us lives a life devoid of unpleasantness? Even in a palace?"

She should have been soft. Yielding. In tears.

That she was not seemed to lick its way beneath his skin. It…bothered him.

"I cannot tell if this is all a mask for your rage or if you truly are as unbothered as you seem," he said instead of addressing all those half-notions he was sure would sound like so much wishful thinking if he said them out loud.

His wife—his Princess, chosen for her fragility—smiled. And did not look in any way fragile. "I'm an open book."

"Perhaps. But not in any language I speak."

Her head tilted to one side. "Do you speak many languages, then?"

Was he relieved that she was changing the subject? Shouldn't he have been?

"I speak a great number of languages." Griffin shrugged that off even as he said it, because it was second nature to live down to any and all expectations. "I spend half my time conversing with dignitaries from various countries. It's easy to pick up a few things."

"And here I thought that conversing was not exactly your most notable people skill."

He thought he ought to apologize. But he'd already done that.

Her smile changed yet again. He found he was becoming obsessed with it. Soft and innocent when everything in him was wicked.

Or, like now, as if he entertained her.

"I don't begrudge you your past," Melody said. "Surely we can indulge each other in that."

"Do you have a great many lovers in your past, then?" he asked before he thought better of it.

Because the truth was, he was surprised to discover, that he did not feel indulgent on that topic.

At all.

Her smile seemed edgier, though he could have sworn nothing about it had changed. "It would be a sad life indeed without a few great loves scattered about."

Griffin opened his mouth to reply to that, but then stopped. He reminded himself that he was meant to be charming, for god's sake. "A great love could be a book. I think, somehow, that you would be less...whatever you are had you been faced with my library today."

"Is your library digitized? Because if not, I'm afraid, Your Royal Highness, that it's only a room to me."

"It is not digitized, no." Griffin was ashamed to realize he hadn't even thought about that. He pulled out his mobile and fired off a message to his chief aide. "But it will be."

"Wonderful," Melody said.

When he looked up from his mobile, she was lifting the teapot and pouring out tea for both of them, then replacing it, all with an ease of movement that would have convinced him that she couldn't possibly be blind if he didn't know otherwise. She picked up her tea, and sat back in her chair, sipping at it.

"Never fear," she said. Calmly. Softly. Because he was making things up in his head to cater to his sex. He knew that. "Whether you make your library accessible for me or not, I have no intention of parading a selection of lovers in front of you. I think we both know that would be frowned upon by every last citizen of the kingdom."

Innocent. Pleasantly intelligent. In no way the sort of wicked, fallen woman that he considered his real type. She deserved better than him, better than the man he really was. He had vowed to give her the Prince he ought to have been instead.

And he would do that, even if it killed him.

He would.

"I am a man with a rich and complicated past," Griffin told her, because she ought to hear that from him as well as in the form of a thousand inevitable barbs from others. "If your past is also rich and complicated, I can hardly complain."

Something he had always believed in, as a matter of fact. Fervently.

But saying those words…hurt. It was like the syllables curdled his mouth.

"You are so progressive, so open-minded and modern," she murmured. And if it had been anyone but Melody, he would have been sure that note he heard in her voice was sarcasm. But she smiled at him, beatifically, and he tried to shake it off and accept that she was who she was supposed to be—not who he *wanted* her to be. "My great loves are not men. You have nothing to fear. I come before you untouched and virginal, because nothing will please the crowds more than a man of great experience with a woman of none. Is that not so?"

Griffin was becoming increasingly tired of the way she did that. Ripping the ground out from beneath him when he was used to being in control of his surroundings. Spinning the world around and around on its axis until he was dizzy. He studied her as he lounged there opposite her on an uncomfortably spindly piece of furniture that he suspected had been deliberately chosen to make the parade of overtly curious society ladies ache a bit as they flung their daggers at the new Princess.

What he didn't know was whether Melody herself was responsible for that sort of thing. Or if she was simply being guided, lamb to the slaughter, straight into the heart of the schemes and scandals of Idyllian society.

More than that, he couldn't tell which he wanted it to be. Did he want a fragile innocent who he truly believed would bring out the heretofore unknown decency in him? Or did he want what the fire in him wanted—a far more complicated creature, capable of defending herself from the onslaught of would-be rivals and all manner of wickedness with what looked like carefree ease?

He knew what he *should* want.

But that seemed to do absolutely nothing to cure the way his blood pumped hot. Or the erotic images that poured through his head the way they had last night, with the same results.

Griffin was burning alive.

"I'm afraid that your long day of torture will extend into the evening," he told her when he could speak. "We have an intimate dinner party to attend. And by intimate, I'm speaking in terms of the standards of the palace. Twenty people, or so. Thirty at the most."

"Just a few friends, then."

Was he smiling—a real smile? Extraordinary. "Never make the mistake of thinking that any of these people are your friends. Especially if it feels like they are."

He meant that as a throwaway remark. To go along with this surprisingly uncomfortable discussion. Because that's what it was, he admitted. That feeling clanging around inside him. It was pure, undiluted discomfort. He didn't like the idea of vipers like Lady Breanna—who he'd had the misfortune of seeing as she exited—sitting here and sniping at his bride.

Across from him, Melody tilted her head toward him in that way that made him feel more examined, more *visible*, than the regard of any other person he'd ever met.

"I had no idea," she said. As if she pitied him.

Griffin wanted to run from the room, and that was so uncharacteristic it rooted him to the spot.

"About what?"

And he was not pleased that he sounded gruff. Bothered.

"I take loneliness for granted," Melody said quietly, and again, something…shifted.

They were sitting in the formal reception room of his residence. It was among the prettiest rooms in the whole of his house, which was not a mistake. It had been designed to let in the light and the sea, so anyone who entered felt instantly steeped in the glory of Idylla.

He certainly did. It was as if the sea and the sky surrounded her like a halo and lifted her up, making her something celestial.

Griffin had taken advantage of this room himself, upon occasion, but Melody somehow made it look natural. As if the room had been built specifically to showcase her glory.

And he did not think that it was a trick of the light that made the staff waiting against the wall seem to disappear. It was the huskiness of Melody's voice.

She sounded as if she was telling him a deep truth rarely spoken.

Griffin found he was very nearly holding his breath. His heart pounded. He did not know what to *do* with himself.

"I don't mean to suggest that I didn't enjoy my childhood, because I did." Melody toyed with the delicate teacup in its saucer, held neatly in her lap. "Yes, my father was unpleasant, but as we've already established, life is not meant to be a parade of pleasantries. Still, I did not make friends the way my sister did. It was not encouraged. I grew used to my own company at an early age. But this cannot be a surprise. You know how I was raised."

"An insult that will be addressed," Griffin found himself saying, low and dark. "I promise you that."

He had the impression she was studying him, in her way. She sat so still. She seemed to be listening so intently he was sure she could hear that wild heartbeat of his.

"I imagine it's as easy to feel alone when your public life is relentless as it is when you are confined to solitude," she said after a moment. "It's just that no one thinks of it that way."

Griffin wanted to laugh that off. The way he would have at any other time.

But there was something about the way the air felt tight between them. There was the memory of her fingers moving over his face, making him feel naked. Still. The way she saw him, here and now, in a way that had nothing to do with the masks he wore for the world. The roles he played. The Prince Griffin he'd made into a performance.

"I grew accustomed to the contours and duties of my life long ago," he said. Stiffly. "I do not require sympathy for that. I'm well aware that my life is made up of great privilege. It should come as no surprise there are prices to pay for an accident of birth."

"You have gone to such lengths to pretend otherwise."

It wasn't an accusation. Griffin could have handled an accusation. He could have dealt with an undercurrent of dry wit or an arched brow. That would have put them back onto familiar ground. He would have known what to *do*.

Instead, he sat forward, and somehow managed not to reach across the narrow little table between them to take her hand. To toy with the ring he'd slid there himself.

"It is not that I was pretending," he told her, though she was a virtual stranger and no matter that he was married to her. "It was that Orion's role was always so clear. And I…had no wish to compete with him. It seemed easier not to try."

He had never said something like that before. Not out loud. Not to someone else.

Across from him, Melody leaned forward and put her tea back onto the table before her with a decisive *click*. She stayed like that, leaning forward. Closing the distance between them enough that if he'd only reached out, he could touch her at last.

He didn't.

Griffin had no idea how, but he didn't.

Even though the look on her face was so intense it made him imagine what it would be like to slide deep inside her. To claim her.

To know her the way she seemed, too easily, to know the parts of him he'd never let out in the light.

"What would happen if neither one of us pretended to be anything we were not?" Melody asked.

And the things Griffin yearned for then didn't make sense to him. It was as if they were someone else's dreams, but they starred him, and her, and not only in his bed. She made him want more than her body. She made him want *her*. And a whole life filled with the things other men deserved, but he never had. It was a violent, clattering thing inside him, loud and discordant.

That was what he told himself.

Because he hadn't been lying to her when he'd told

her he'd never considered the issue of heirs. He'd never wanted any part of that mess, being a product of it himself.

Griffin didn't understand why, looking at this woman who should have been nothing to him but a kept promise, all those things that had never appealed to him before suddenly seemed…beautiful.

But in the next moment, he shook it off.

And laughed.

Loud enough to chase the clatter away.

"That seems a little one-sided," he said, relaxing into his seat as if it was comfortable. Because that was one of his talents—he could make himself relaxed and boneless anywhere. He excelled at it, in fact. "What could you possibly have to hide?"

And it wasn't until later that he would realize he recognized the look on her face then. It wasn't until later that he would put it into context.

She laughed, too, but only after a moment.

Only after she looked—for the briefest moment—as if he'd slapped her.

CHAPTER SEVEN

THE SO-CALLED INTIMATE dinner party was both boring and thrilling, which didn't surprise Melody in the least. Not after a lifetime of hearing Calista's stories about such gatherings. All that hostile gentility over the soup course, animosity disguised in airy chatter about nothing, and blood feuds concealed in manners so fine they squeaked.

"You appear to be enjoying yourself far too much," her sister murmured when the women repaired en masse to one of the salons, an archaic custom Calista had always claimed to enjoy as it permitted a glimpse at the real faces of women who preferred to act out characters in the presence of men.

"*Enjoy* is a strong word," Melody replied. She sat with her sister on one of the salon's many couches, thereby giving the rest of the women tacit permission to sit as well. "It's informative, isn't it, these awkward gatherings of so many soft creatures."

Calista made a reproving sort of sound. "They only appear soft, Melody. When it suits them. Beware the talons beneath."

Melody knew that she and her sister had very different definitions of softness. But as Calista shifted into her queenly hostess duties, Melody settled back against her seat and tried to exude it. She tried to look shy and fragile and all the rest of the things she was supposed to be— *soft* chief among them. She had already met most of the women who were now fluttering around Calista, jockeying for position and pretending their only goals were sudden, bosom friendships with the brand-new Queen. And while she found a measure of enjoyment in pretending she really hadn't noticed all the slings and arrows these same women had thrown at her in their private audiences earlier—and continued to throw out in their usual understated ways—she spent most of her time sitting softly at her sister's side. Fuming.

At herself.

She didn't know what had come over her this afternoon. She blamed it on back-to-back tea skirmishes with Idylla's viper class, which would surely make anyone loopy. That was the only reason she could think of to explain why she'd actually tried to *build a bridge* with Prince Griffin.

And had basically admitted to him that she was hiding things, though he hadn't picked up on it.

That didn't mean he wouldn't.

Melody could not pretend she knew her husband very well. How could she when she was acting a part herself? But she knew already that whatever else Griffin was, and whatever he might like to pretend in public, he was nowhere near as foolish as the tabloids liked to claim.

He was far too self-aware, for one thing.

And tonight, as she sat about attempting to look overset and trembly while surrounded by so many high-placed members of society—all of them chattering about nothing in particular while political and powerful undercurrents flowed as freely as the wine—Melody was forced to conclude that he was a whole lot more than that, too.

The way she had the day of their wedding when she'd first noticed that leashed power in him, such a surprise in a man who acted as if all he was, ever, was *charming*.

"You seem subdued," Griffin said when the dinner party finally ended and he was once again walking her slowly back through the palace. *Guiding* her as if, left to her own devices, she might topple over, hit the marble floors, and stay there until discovered. "I hope you didn't find the night too taxing."

Melody fought back a flash of irritation. *No,* she wanted to snap at him, *I do not feel overtaxed. I feel bored out of my skull.*

As anyone would, should they find themselves called upon to play a hapless ninny.

But she didn't say any of that, and not only because she had been asked to keep him in the dark—to keep him like this. The unlikely champion of the most inadvertently scandalous heiress in the kingdom.

"I was thinking about you, actually," Melody said instead.

Her hand gripped his elbow, so she could feel the kind of shock that went through him. It rippled in him, there beneath her fingers. She wanted, more than anything, to…lean in. To follow that shock, that reaction, and see where it went.

That was how she'd learned the shape of the world. She touched it. Traced it. Felt the heat of a thing, or its coldness. If it was hard or soft, pliable or unyielding. Fen had spent years guiding these explorations, explaining what figures of speech meant, and giving Melody touchstones.

But that wasn't how she wanted to touch Griffin. Not exactly.

She wanted to touch him to learn, certainly. Melody had not had the opportunity to touch many men. There was a novelty factor.

Still, she knew that mostly, she wanted to put her hands on him because touching him made her *feel things*. She wanted to explore it. She wanted all those things she'd read about and more, the opportunity to practice them the way she did her forms and strikes. Until there were no mysteries, only sensation.

But she supposed that even if she wasn't pretending to be someone she wasn't, that sort of thing would almost surely be frowned upon out in the halls of the palace. There was always protocol to consider—that and all the other things Madame Constantinople Dupree had banged on about this morning.

"You were thinking about me?" Griffin laughed, another thing Melody could feel vibrate through him. And through her. "That's a shallow pool, I think you'll find."

"That's what's so fascinating." He opened the door to the courtyard and led her through it, and something about the cool air on her face made her distinctly aware of how overheated she was. As if her body was taking in all those vibrations and sensations between them, charging her up, and making her glow with it. The way the lightbulbs she'd cupped as a child had, buzzing faintly until they grew too hot to hold. "I think everyone sitting at that table tonight actually believes that about you."

"I beg your pardon?"

He slowed, which shouldn't have been possible. As they were already nearly crawling. But for once, Melody didn't mind his deliberate, overly careful steps. She could feel the expanse of the courtyard all around them. And the density of the December air, pressing in. It made her feel as if the night was wrapped tight around them, threaded through with intermittent bursts of heat.

Not all of that from the evenly spaced heaters.

"I have no idea what they see, of course," she told him. "I assume you laugh and smile and do all the usual things with your face."

"The usual things…" he repeated, as if she'd said something shocking. "Forgive me, but how do you know what things people do with their faces?"

"How do you think?"

Melody laughed, but not because she was amused. Not really. It was more like there was a steam rising in her and she had to let it out as if she was a kettle set to boil. And her own laugh, the faint and tinkling one she was allowed while she stayed true to her character, should have reminded her what was at stake here.

But she still lifted her free hand. And without questioning her motives—because she already knew perfectly well they were not the least bit pure, because she was not the character she was playing—she slid her palm over his mouth.

That sensual, firm mouth of his that made her whole body shiver into a kind of tight, hot awareness.

"Say my name," she told him.

A soft order, but an order all the same. After she said it, it occurred to her that perhaps this frail, wispy creature she was pretending she was would not be standing about issuing orders to a prince. But it was too late.

"Melody," Griffin said.

And she couldn't tell which made her feel more raw. The brush of his lips against her palm, making her dizzy.

Or that note in his voice, a warning and yet something darker, something sweeter, at the same time.

"Now frown and say it," she said.

And Griffin complied, sending more sensation soaring through her, shooting out from her palm and finding all the places where she was the most feminine, the most entranced by him. Her breasts. Her belly. That slick heat between her legs.

Her voice hardly sounded like hers. "Once more, with a smile."

And that time, it was as if he said her name directly into the molten core of her.

Melody didn't know what to do with that kind of storm. That kind of need. The wallop of it that nearly took her knees out from under her—when she had learned how to balance while standing in the Aegean, either maintaining her connection to the shifting sands beneath her or getting tumbled by the waves.

This was far more difficult than that.

"Is that how you learned?" Griffin asked, his tempting, fascinating mouth brushing against her palm and sending impossible licks of flame spiraling into every part of her.

It took Melody longer than it should have to drop her hand.

"People's words sound different depending on what they're doing with their faces," she told him, unable to tell if she sounded fluttery or forthright because of the noise in her head. The pounding of her pulse and worse, the way it streaked all the way through her to lodge in the place she was softest. "And the more you listen for such things, the more you pick up on the subtleties. Calista and I used to hide in our parents' drawing room, where they would have their strange little parties that were almost always power trips of one sort or another. And afterward, we would parse everything we'd heard and everything she'd seen, so that I could get better at picking up on inflections. I got very good at it."

She could feel the weight of his stare, then. Probably because the trembling fawn of a charity princess she was meant to be would no doubt faint dead away before she'd indicate that she might have any skills at all. But there was no taking it back.

Deep down, she could admit, she didn't want to take it back.

You don't want his pity, do you? a snide voice inside her taunted her, sounding entirely too much like her father. *You little fool. You want the most famous Lothario in ten kingdoms to* admire *you.* You.

Melody could fight anything—except the obnoxious voices in her own head. But she could ignore them.

"I think you're the one who's fascinating, Melody," Griffin said, but there was that gallant note in his voice again. So carefully courteous that it bordered on condescending, to her mind. "To have achieved any of the things that you have strikes me as nothing short of a miracle."

Whatever, Gaston, she thought grumpily.

"It's not a miracle," she said, perhaps a little too crossly. "I didn't have a choice. The more blind I looked, the more it offended my father. It was simple math. The better I got at acting as if I had my sight, the easier it would be all around."

"And again." Griffin's voice was like a shudder in bones. "I do not intend to let that behavior on your father's part slide."

"My father has already been amply punished for his sins," Melody said impatiently. "In the only way he is likely to notice. He's lost his company. He's been cast out of the highest circles of power in the land. The daughter he attempted to control defied him, the daughter he preferred to ignore has been elevated to spite him. For my part, I would prefer to pretend as if I don't know he's alive. Repayment in kind, if you will."

"I had no idea you were so… cold."

Griffin sounded both as if he admired that and was confused by it.

Melody was straying off course, but she couldn't seem to help herself. She could have corrected it then, before he had time to really think about how different she was acting. She could have toppled over into a swoon, or started cowering before him… But she couldn't quite bring herself to do any of those things.

This character she was playing was beginning to feel like a chokehold.

"Tonight, all those people sat there, thinking they knew you," she said instead, though she knew better than to indulge herself in this. Why couldn't she seem to stop? "I assume you must put on a good show. But I could hear you. I heard the way you directed the conversation—a perfect counterpoint to whatever your brother was saying. When you got loud, it was so he could speak quietly with whoever was nearest him. When you were outrageous, or entertaining, it was to allow him to continue discussions he didn't want the others overhearing. Quite a team, aren't you?"

Griffin had gone stiff again. "I made a vow long ago to serve my brother's interests as my own." His voice was made of steel, much like his arm. "We are all we have."

"I don't understand how the whole nation doesn't re-alize what a team you are. Instead, article after article witters on about how he is good and you are bad. Light and dark, day and night. As if you could have one with-out the other."

"Melody." And there was a different note in his voice then, something male and warm. She itched to put up her palm and *feel* the way he said it. "Are you...defend-ing my honor? I must tell you, this is an exercise in fu-tility at best."

"I vowed to honor you, did I not? There on an altar before the King and all the world. Surely defending that honor is implied."

"I like this fierceness in you, Princess." Griffin was shifting, reminding her that they'd stopped on their walk across the courtyard. That they were out in the night, the sea air batting at them, and still. Still, between them, this beguiling heat that was making her...foolish. "I like it very much."

His hands moved to grip her upper arms, and Melody knew well the language of *grips*. Holds and releases. The way that bodies moved together and apart, in an end-less dance of forms that could be meditation in practice and violence on the street. She knew how to fall. How to fight. How to use every inch of her body as a weapon.

But this was...something else.

This was a melting, a melding.

She felt as if she was dissolving, as if the hard heat in his palms was changing the very composition of her body. As if it was streaking inside, and making her some-thing different. Something new.

Something better, a new voice inside her whispered.

She could feel it—*him*—everywhere.

"Why do you feel you must hide?" she asked him.

He made a low sort of noise, as if she'd landed a gut punch. "I don't consider it hiding. Light and dark, day and night—these aren't insults. And it has always been easier, where there is already a bright sun, to become the moon instead."

"Does your brother know?" It was difficult to concentrate already. And when he began to move his thumbs up and down over her upper arms, almost absently… Well. Melody couldn't stop the goose bumps that rose everywhere he touched. Or the shiver that wound around and around inside her, showing no signs of stopping. "Or does he think what everyone else does—that his only brother is a committed degenerate like your father? Only, somehow, more popular than King Max ever was. As if by magic."

She should not be speaking to him like this. Melody knew she shouldn't. She owed her sister her loyalty, and by extension, her sister's husband. Calista wanted this marriage for Melody's sake, to keep her safe. Just as Melody wanted her own situation to be stable and her person protected well enough—not because she felt unsafe, but because it made Calista feel better. She understood all this.

More, she had agreed to all this.

But nothing had prepared her for the *heat*. Griffin's thumbs moved almost convulsively against her arms and that was the only thing she could seem to keep in her head.

"Do not mistake the matter." Griffin's voice was almost indistinguishable, then, from the night air that moved around them. But inside her, every word was almost too hot to bear. "I was reckless and heedless by choice. Hedonistic and no doubt remarkably asinine. I enjoyed my youth, Melody. And as long as my father was alive, there was no possibility that I could ever catch up to his level of seedy, irresponsible behavior. Just as there was no possibility that I could ever compete for Orion's halo."

"Why must there be catching up or competing?"

"I did not *pretend* to be badly behaved, Melody," Griffin told her, as if the words stuck in his throat. "I *enjoyed* being badly behaved."

"Yes, yes," she said quietly. "You cut a swathe through the female population, sampling supermodels like candy. I know."

His grip tightened almost imperceptibly, but she felt it. And thrilled to it.

"I am beginning to find it concerning that you are the only citizen in the kingdom who has no problem whatsoever with my…appetites."

"Perhaps because I appear to be the only citizen in the country who also knows the rest of the story," Melody threw back at him, perhaps a bit recklessly. "However you might have fed those appetites, it was never at the expense of the palace. You never made yourself a liability—not even to your father, who certainly wouldn't have noticed."

She couldn't seem to *think* with his hands on her, skin to skin. It was too…encroaching. It seemed to get into everything, leaving nothing but flames behind.

"A happy accident," Griffin said, his voice a quiet warning. "Nothing more."

"I don't think so. I think you are far more in control of yourself and this reputation of yours than you wish to admit."

"That would be a true Idyllian scandal." Griffin's face was closer to hers, then. And the way he was gripping her, she had no option but to rise up on her toes. No option and no desire whatsoever to do anything but that. "And that cannot happen, Melody. No more scandals. My brother has decreed it."

He was so close, now, that she couldn't seem to keep herself from touching him. She ran her hands lightly over his chest, finding the lapels of the coat he wore, and better yet, his hard pectoral muscles beneath.

And inside herself, felt nothing but fire.

"Everybody knows that you married a charity case like me to make yourself look like a good man," she said. "To medicate against the possibility of any scandal, ever. They took pleasure in telling me so today, over and over again."

"If I can give you any piece of advice, Princess, it would be this. Never listen to the opinions of snakes. Especially when you have not solicited them."

"But that's not the real truth, is it?" Her voice was a whisper, at odds with the crash and burn inside her, her pounding heart, the giddy rush of her blood. "The real truth is that, deep down, you've always been a good man."

"You are sweet and naive," he growled at her, and she could *feel* his words against her own lips. "Innocent and almost unimaginably vulnerable. Especially here, in this palace of games and pretenses."

Melody wanted to show him exactly how wrong he was about that, but somehow, she couldn't seem to move. As if he was in control of her body, not her.

Something that should have alarmed her. When instead it made her...lightheaded.

"But beyond all of that," Griffin kept on, his voice laced with heat just like she was, and something like greed, "you're also wrong. You have no idea the things I want to do to you."

"Then do them," Melody managed to say. "I dare you."

"Careful what you wish for, wife."

There was too much heat and noise inside her, making her limbs feel heavy. She felt sluggish. And yet, at the same time, hectic.

It was as if she had a sudden fever. She even felt weak.

But not, she understood in the next moment, in any way ill.

And there would never be a better time than this. So much for attempting seduction, she thought. Fen was right. She was terrible at it. It was high time she tried a more direct approach.

Following an urge so overwhelming it hurt, Melody closed that last, scant bit of space between them and pressed her lips to his.

She remembered their perfunctory kiss at the altar. She'd had the impression of firmness, maleness, but that was all.

This was different.

Griffin went still. Radically still.

And she could feel the heat in him, all that marvelous, leashed power, while he held himself back as if he was afraid of hurting her. Or overwhelming her.

Melody, on the other hand, was not afraid at all.

She slid her hands up to loop them around the strong column of his neck.

And then…she played.

Once, when she'd been a teenager, she'd kissed one

of the statues that lined the atrium in her father's house. Because it was shaped like a man, and Calista had told her about kissing. Melody had wanted to know what it was like.

She remembered the cool marble. The impenetrable seam between those fine, chiseled lips.

This was like that and not like that at all.

Because Griffin was alive. Hard, yes, but not like marble.

He was so much better than stone.

So she entertained herself. She kissed him, angling her head this way, then that. But it was not until she slipped her tongue against that same seam, just to taste him better, that she shuddered.

"You have no idea how to kiss, do you?" His voice was raw. A scrape against the night, and deep into her, too.

"Teach me," she whispered.

Griffin made another one of those low, shockingly male noises that made everything inside her burn hotter. While between her legs, she felt slippery.

His hands moved from her shoulders and she protested that with a little noise, but only until he took her face between his palms.

Then Prince Griffin, Idylla's favorite scourge, set his mouth to hers.

And devoured her.

It was like falling. It was like tumbling through space, caught up in the waves of the sea and tossed this way and that, but it didn't ever end.

What he did to her mouth bore no resemblance to the kisses she'd given him, sweeping them away in a blaze of fire.

Griffin used his tongue, his teeth. He ate at her mouth,

sometimes making more of those lush, dirty sounds that made her ache. That made this strange fever burn hotter, leaving her weaker and desperate for more.

Melody's life was built around sensation. What she could touch, what she could feel.

Nothing had ever prepared her for this.

For a mouth on hers, the scrape of his tongue, and the glory of the flames that licked all over her.

She was made new. She was forever changed.

She met the thrust of his wicked tongue, pressing herself against him with sheer, heady abandon, because every touch made it better. Hotter.

So much wilder and all-consuming than she'd ever imagined.

And she thought she might be perfectly happy to die like this—

But he stopped.

Griffin tore his mouth from hers, and then rested his forehead there, pressed against hers. It was a new spark. A different, quieter fire.

"I don't want to stop," she managed to pant out, surprised to hear she sounded as out of breath as if she'd just survived one of Fen's more brutal training sessions.

She could feel the change in his body, in the way he held her. He set her away from him, as if he was deliberately creating space. And then maintaining it.

"That should never have happened," he said, stiffly.

But Melody could hear what lay beneath it. All that same heat that was still storming through her, still making her burn with that wildfire that was only his. Why would anyone step away from that?

"Why ever not?" she asked, genuinely confused. "Aren't we supposed to be married?"

Griffin was turning her when she didn't wish to be turned. But there was no fighting it unless she intended to truly fight, so she allowed it. He tucked her hand back in his elbow and then, suddenly, he was walking her across the courtyard at a brisk pace he'd never used before.

As if he couldn't wait to be rid of her.

Melody didn't like the way that notion twisted around inside her.

"Am I to take the silence as an indication that we are not, in fact, married?" she asked tartly.

And as she did, wondered when exactly it was she'd last pretended to be the wife the King and her own sister had asked her to be. When had she last cowered or cringed?

But she couldn't bring herself to do it. Not now.

Not when she could taste him.

Griffin did not speak again until he'd marched her to the door of her room.

"That should not have happened," he said again. Stiffly. Formally. Annoyingly. "It will not happen again. You have my word."

"I don't want your word."

"Nonetheless, it is yours. I keep my promises, Melody." She could hear the storm in him then, dark and ferocious. It made her heart clench tight in her chest. "Whatever else might be true about me, I keep my promises."

"As good men do," she whispered, though she shouldn't have.

Griffin made a low noise, but he did not reply. Instead, he turned swiftly and left her there, half fire and half fury, to burn out on her own.

CHAPTER EIGHT

THE WIFE HE'D never wanted and shouldn't have noticed much now he had her…was driving him mad.

It was the morning of New Year's Eve. As was his time-honored tradition, Griffin was chasing out the old year with the kind of punishing workout he usually reserved for whipping himself into shape after disappearing into too much debauchery for too long. Who could have predicted that a spate of abstinence would make the particular punishment he doled out to himself on this day…worse?

He ran faster, as if—with enough intensity and speed—he could outrun it.

Her.

It was one of the island's rare stormy days, keeping him cooped up inside when he would have much preferred to run up and down the hill from the palace to the beach. He liked the palace's private access road that ensured he could test himself as he pleased without causing a public commotion. He liked to tell himself bracing stories about his desire to pit himself against the elements, and that wasn't entirely untrue.

But a deeper truth was that his house had never felt so small, when he knew full well it could happily sleep eighteen.

Because Melody was everywhere. Even here, in the gym he doubted she'd set foot in, he was sure that he could catch her scent in the air. Or hear a hint of her laughter.

She was a ghost, haunting him wherever he went. And the worst part of that was that she was not dead like the others who called his name on dark nights. She was fully alive, flesh and blood, and living under the same roof.

"I was given to understand that this would be a sophisticated arrangement," he'd said coldly one night.

His nightly ritual of sitting in his study, brooding out the windows, and *not* drinking himself into oblivion because he was past that now he was married, had been interrupted. Again.

By the unsolicited appearance of his wife.

Griffin had not been pleased to discover that she did not need to be guided around the house, carefully ushered from room to room—and, more importantly, more easily left in said rooms. It turned out she could find her way on her own, which meant she…did.

"I think it would be difficult to get more sophisticated than the Idyllian Royal Palace," Melody had replied airily, standing there in the doorway as if she intended to become a fixture. "Isn't that, more or less, the definition of royalty? Sophistication by default and decree?"

"I was referring to our marriage." And the sound of his own, tight voice hadn't helped Griffin any. His bride was an onslaught all her own. "You have an entire wing of the house. Why aren't you in it?"

"You know why not."

She'd smiled at him, sweet and guileless the way she always did, though he knew better, now.

Melody might look like an angel, but she wasn't one.

Or more precisely, she had no desire to remain one.

"I have already told you that there will be no repeat of that unfortunate night in the courtyard," he'd told her with all the suppressed outrage he had in him. Because that had been a close call. Too close. He should never have allowed himself to succumb to temptation. He was furious with himself. And she didn't help matters. "There is no requirement that I produce an heir, Melody. Therefore there's absolutely no need for this marriage to be consummated."

"But—"

"You have already tried every possible method to convince me otherwise," he'd gritted out.

He'd stood up from his chair because it was entirely likely that she would try one of her other tricks, as she liked to do. The night she'd come and settled herself in his lap. The night she'd come wearing what she'd tried to claim was merely her usual nightgown, sheer and see-through and—but he refused to go there.

His bride might not fear his appetites, but he did. "If you will not protect your own virtue, I must."

"I'm more concerned about yours," she'd replied, there in the doorway with one hand against the door-jamb and the light playing over her lithe, lean figure—

Stop. Now.

"No need," he'd growled at her. "I possess none whatsoever."

"I only mean that this sudden valiant attempt at abstinence might actually do you harm." She'd tilted her head in that way he knew, now—though he still couldn't quite believe it—meant mischief. "Aren't you afraid that it will all go…blue?"

"I doubt very much you know what *blue* is," he'd all but barked at her.

Only to see, in return, a wicked smile take over her lush mouth. "I feel confident, however, that in this case I know what it does."

On his treadmill now, staring out at the sullen rain that pounded against the windows before him and stole his usual view of the ocean, Griffin picked up his speed.

But it didn't help. Nothing did. He might not have *gone blue*, as Melody had so inelegantly put it, but he wasn't right. He wasn't secure at last in his own goodness and virtuousness, which was the entire point of this exercise.

He could *taste* her, still. He woke in the night with the sheets twisted around him and his sex hard and heavy. While images that ought to have shamed him shined too bright and too real in his head.

God help him, it had barely been a week.

After he finished punishing his body, he tried a cold shower. But it turned out even frigid temperatures didn't help. His whole body turned blue beneath the icy spray—except one, specific part.

As usual.

While he dressed, then had his breakfast and spoke with his staff about the usual concerns he intended to ignore, Griffin accepted the fact that there was a part of him that liked the fact this wasn't easy. That the wife he hadn't chosen was more to him, already, than a piece of furniture or an inherited heirloom he was expected to care for, like all the rest littered about this house. That she had turned out to be far more of a temptation than he'd anticipated when he'd acquiesced to the marriage Orion had been threatening since his coronation.

He'd expended a lot of effort convincing the world that he'd allowed that particular part to lead him around for years. When, in truth, he'd simply indulged himself without limits, because he could. Now fiction had become fact and indulgence was out of the question.

Griffin supposed that was poetic. And no one had ever claimed poetry was meant to be *comfortable*.

If being a good man was easy, he told himself—sternly—as he headed toward the palace proper, there would be more of them in the world.

"Your marriage was meant to settle you," Orion said, sounding entirely too amused, when Griffin presented himself in his office. "I must tell you that you do not look particularly settled."

"On the contrary, brother." Griffin stalked to his preferred chair before the fire and draped himself across it like the libertine he'd been for years. And ignored how little he wished to lounge about bonelessly these days when everything inside him was so…fraught. "I have never been more at ease."

Orion's lips twitched. "Clearly."

"And what of your marriage?" Griffin asked. Demanded, really—taking advantage of the relationship only he had with Idylla's moral, upstanding, remote new King. "You've only been married one week. Most newlyweds would be off on a honeymoon somewhere, reveling in their new commitments in the time-honored fashion. Instead, you must host the traditional banquet and ball tonight and, as ever, ransom yourself to the demands of your duty."

"Is that an inquiry into my well-being?" His brother eyed him, seeing far too much, Griffin was afraid. "Or a complaint about your own situation? I didn't realize you and Melody enjoyed the sort of relationship that would require what a honeymoon normally delivers."

And the dark look Orion threw his way, as if Griffin's reputation swirled around him like a thick winter cloak…rankled.

Despite himself, Griffin could hear Melody's voice from that night in the courtyard that he was trying so desperately to forget.

Why must there be catching up or competing? she'd asked.

Why indeed.

And suddenly, on this final day of a strange year, it seemed important to him to find out—once and for all—if Orion was aware that Griffin *chose* to be dark to his light. That it wasn't who he was, it was who he had become. Deliberately.

Certainly, he had been exuberant in his youth. He had also had a decorated military career, something that would have been impossible had he spent even half as much time whoring about as it was reputed he had. And he had gone out of his way to downplay his military experience in all the interviews he gave, because that wasn't what the kingdom wanted from the second royal son. They had Orion for sober responsibility and the hope of a brighter future.

They wanted the spare to be *fun*.

"Do you imagine that I'm incapable of controlling myself if I wish it?" he asked.

Not nearly as lightly as he should have done.

His brother laughed. "I have no doubt that you *could* control yourself, Griffin. I do wonder whether or not you *will*."

"You asked me to marry a sheltered innocent who

knows little of the world and even less of men, unless you count her loathsome father, which I do not," Griffin growled. "No, Orion, I do not require an extended honeymoon to slake my lust all over her fragile body. But thank you for thinking the best of me."

Orion lifted his head and fixed that particular stare on him that usually encouraged his underlings to… rethink.

But he had already committed himself to this ill-considered course, so Griffin stayed as he was, lounged out in a chair before his brother's fire. The very picture of careless indolence and self-indulgence.

He was good at that.

"I don't believe I accused you of anything," Orion said after a moment. The offended monarch in his gaze, if not in his voice. Not quite. "Is that a guilty conscience talking?"

Griffin had been about to apologize. But now…he thought again. "I'm astonished you think I have a conscience. Surely not. After all, the whole of Europe knows I am little more than a cardboard cutout replacement of our late, unlamented father."

Orion only eyed him. And then, after a moment far more tense than it should have been, sighed. "I know you'll keep your promise to me, Griffin. As you have kept every promise you ever made to me. It is the Queen who is less certain."

"Perhaps if she had spent less time writing tabloid stories about my exploits across the years she would have less to worry about now."

He expected his brother to bristle at that, but Orion only smiled. He stood from his desk, and came over to the fire. Then he took the seat opposite as if settling in for a cozy chat, and all of this was so unlike his usually grim, workaholic brother that Griffin found himself…thrown.

A sensation he ought to have been used to, after all the time he'd spent with his bride lately.

Because unless he was mistaken, his brother, the uptight King, looked…relaxed.

"I told her something similar myself," Orion was saying, still smiling. "But you've met Calista, of course. She can't be *told* something."

But Griffin noticed that his brother sounded affectionate when he said that. As if that was not a flaw in his Queen, but a virtue.

He couldn't take that on board. Not from Orion, who had made a great many sweeping statements about the obedience he would expect from the woman he'd been required to marry, thanks to a deal their father had made. Threats of imprisonment on remote islands and so on, should Calista fail to fall in line. Griffin hardly knew what to do with evidence of *affection*.

He returned instead to the matter at hand. "Does Calista truly believe I will harm her sister?"

"Of course not," Orion said, so easily and so swiftly—so matter-of-factly—that something inside Griffin twisted in on itself.

He understood that if his brother had answered in any other way, or taken time to think it over, it would have irreparably damaged something in him. And that understanding landed in him with the full force of a blow.

It took him a moment to realize Orion was studying him. "It is the habit of a lifetime, nothing more, to concern herself with her sister's affairs. Calista has always seen herself as Melody's champion. And how do you find her? Your wife, I mean. Not mine." His smile took on a different sheen. "How is she adapting?"

"She's been blind since birth, Orion," Griffin said gruffly. "There was no *adaption*, only her life. She has never had to find something that was lost."

And he bit back what he'd been about to say—which was that Melody was perfect to him as she was. Maddening, yes. Shockingly uninterested in his notable good works on her behalf and not at all what he'd expected. But there was not one thing *wrong* with her.

Not a single, solitary deficiency.

He tasted copper and made himself smile instead. "I think she's doing beautifully."

"I am pleased to hear it. Calista will also be pleased."

"I live to serve."

As this was, in fact, true, Griffin could see no reason why it all seemed liked a collar around his neck just then. He told himself it was the constraints of duty, that was all. He would happily kill for his brother. But that was a different thing entirely than day in, day out, dutiful appearances.

Or marriages.

"I will see you later tonight," he said stiffly to Orion, unwinding himself from his chair and standing as if he meant to leave.

The stranger who now inhabited his brother's body, relaxed and at his ease, only lifted a brow. "You cannot be serious. Why on earth would you attend the New Year's ball?"

Griffin stopped on his way to the door, surprised. "Do I not always attend the New Year's ball?"

"Because you could have nothing better to do than dance attendance on your family when you were single.

You are no longer single." His smile shifted and his gaze sharpened. "Perhaps you and your new wife can continue to…not have your honeymoon."

And Griffin did not precisely bare his teeth at his brother, his liege and King. But he wouldn't call it a smile, either.

He took his time heading back across the wet, cold courtyard to his house, where his staff was no doubt fluttering about, forever in the process of attempting to corral him into attending some or other dull function he wished to avoid.

The thought of it, in fact, made him move a little quicker, because he couldn't think of anything he would like better just then. A bit of corralling. Duties he was forced against his will to perform—it all sounded like bliss because it wasn't mooning about over his wife like a lovesick calf.

God help him, he'd become the very thing he hated. Soft and sentimental.

Too much like his mother.

When Griffin knew better than to allow such weakness in him. The former Queen had been no match for horrid King Max. He had been neither faithful to her nor particularly solicitous where she was concerned, and she had wilted in such conditions. Griffin's earliest memories were of her tears.

And then of the sad, lonely way she'd escaped her fate—taking her own life.

Whatever Griffin had become, he had chosen it. He had embraced it. Unlike his mother, so incapable of rising to the challenge of her tumultuous marriage, Griffin had met his role and made it his own. He was not and never had been a victim of circumstance.

Until now.

He had been so sure he knew what he was getting into. He had met Calista's sister once before, and she'd seemed so small and slight to him. She had cowered in her chair, half-feral with her hair like a curtain, and he'd thought—very distinctly—that she needed someone to take care of her.

Not himself, mind.

But when his brother had suggested—in that way of his that was not, in fact, a suggestion—that Griffin make good on his promise, and quickly, and with Melody, he had warmed to the idea.

He could prove, at last, that he could care for something so tender, so delicate. That he was better than the role he'd played all these years. That he was as in control of leaving his disreputable past behind as he'd been in creating his reputation in the first place.

What he hadn't counted on was Melody.

The rain had soaked him through on his walk back across the courtyard. He took his time changing, then made his way to his offices. But when he arrived, it was to discover that his staff had dispersed into the wet afternoon.

"You always dismiss the staff on New Year's Eve," his personal aide said, sounding baffled. And looking at him as if he'd come in with a selection of extra heads.

"Things have changed," Griffin said, attempting to sound dignified.

Or he had, which was far more disconcerting.

His aide gazed back at him. "Would you like me to call them all back, Your Royal Highness?"

This time, there was no doubt about it. Griffin was not

smiling. He was grimacing and trying to put a spin on it. "Of course not. You might as well take off yourself."

And then, for the first time in as long as he could remember, Griffin found himself…at loose ends.

It was humbling, really, to consider what a huge amount of time and energy it had taken to conduct his life and affairs as he had before. Or so he was forced to assume, since the lack of his usually overstuffed and heaving social life seem to echo in him like an abyss this afternoon.

Then again, perhaps he was brooding again. Because all the parties he'd used to attend were still occurring, in their usual forms. He had made stern announcements that he was to be left alone after his marriage, that was all, and he was a royal prince. His announcements held some weight for those who wished to curry his favor,

That didn't mean *he* couldn't dip into his old life as he pleased. If he pleased.

But even as he thought that, Griffin realized it wasn't what he wanted. The parties. The people. The endless jostling for his attention that, if it suited him, he pretended to believe was genuine feeling. He stood in his ancient house, the rain beating against the windows and gray straight through, and tried to imagine immersing himself in that world again. The world he'd considered his before Christmas.

Now it seemed like someone else's memory, fading quickly into insignificance no matter how he tried to draw it back.

Not only because he'd made a promise to his brother to avoid scandal.

It was her. It was Melody.

She'd kissed him, out there in the dark. She'd put her

hand over his mouth. She made him ache, she disturbed his sleep, and he did not understand how this woman who could quite literally not see him…saw him best of all.

Griffin was a man with so many acquaintances, so many so-called friends. He had famously never met a stranger.

But he had always felt like one.

Until the least likely person in all the world…recognized him, somehow.

He didn't understand it.

But Griffin accepted the fact that left with nothing ahead of him tonight but empty hours, the ceaseless rain, and the dawning of a new year whether the world was ready or not, the only thing he was at all interested in doing was finding his wife. And that somehow, this thing that should have been anathema to him—his arranged marriage to a woman he should have had no interest in at all—in no way felt like a downgrade from his usual activities.

He decided he might as well embrace it.

He wouldn't touch her, Griffin assured himself as he found himself prowling through the halls of this sprawling, empty house. He didn't need to be led about by his desires after all these years of pretending he was a slave to them. He had no intention of allowing such a thing. But that didn't mean he couldn't…talk to her.

The simple truth was that he'd never met another person like Melody.

Because there was no other person like Melody.

As he walked, the rain beat against the windows as if it was washing off the year. And Griffin thought of how he'd wanted nothing more than to take apart his brother for suggesting that Melody was in some way impaired.

When Griffin knew better.

He had been sitting at pompous, tedious dinner tables like the one the other night his whole life. Not once had anyone seen the faintest shred of anything in him he did not wish them to see. But she had.

She had seen *him*.

Then he'd tasted her. Barely.

But one taste of Melody, and Griffin was changed. Rocked. Reduced to cold showers and long runs, neither of which helped at all.

It was as if he'd never kissed a woman before.

He was not focusing on that, he told himself sternly as he found his way to her wing of the house. He would go to her, that was all. Ask her if she wished to join him for a drink. Tea, perhaps, if that was what she fancied on a gloomy evening like this one.

They would talk. She would once again prove herself far more mysterious than she ought to have been. And if, deep down, he acknowledged that the prospect of having tea with his almost completely untouched bride was far more appealing to him than any of the parties he knew were raging across the island right now—or would be, should he call and indicate an interest in attending one—

Well. That was no one's business but his.

He was headed toward her bedchamber when he paused. A strange noise reached his ears, rising now and again over the sound of the rain outside. A curious thump. Then another. A kind of…gasp.

Following the sound, he walked farther down the hall toward what had once been a conservatory for a long-ago princess who had preferred to secrete herself amongst her plants and herbs rather than spend her days ingratiating herself at court. Griffin had always felt a bond with his ancestress, though he had no affinity for plants and hadn't been inside the conservatory in years.

But there was no mistaking the fact that the noises he heard came from within.

An exhalation. A grunt. Something that sounded heavy, hitting the floor.

He eased open the door, wondering if his aide had been mistaken and there were still staff about the place, engaged in renovations of some kind. Not that he could recall authorizing any—but then, sometimes his staff took matters in their own hands rather than bother him with minutiae.

The door opened soundlessly, though it wouldn't have mattered if he'd slammed it open. And shouted while he was at it.

Because what was happening inside did not stop.

Griffin stood there, dumbfounded, as he attempted to make sense of what he saw. What was occurring right in front of him.

He couldn't.

It simply wouldn't penetrate.

Because it was impossible that his sweet, fragile, occasionally mischievous but clearly trembling and terrified wife, who also happened to be blind was...

Fighting.

There was no other word to describe it, inconceivable as it should have been.

Melody and that aide of hers were engaged in a lethal hand-to-hand battle, and Griffin might have hurled himself forth, thinking Melody under attack—

But she was landing her fair share of blows. She was attacking whenever she had an opening. With precision and clear intent.

It looked almost like an elegant dance. They threw each other, grappled on the floor, punched and kicked and never took their attention off of each other.

His bride, who clung to his arm as if an ocean breeze might carry her off, flipped in the air. She aimed her kick at the other woman's face, and when her opponent ducked, corrected in midair and then took them both down.

Punch, block, kick.

There was not one part of Melody that trembled.

And all the things Griffin had been blocking out seemed to flood in on him then. The way she'd seemed to challenge him, then cowered in the next moment. How lithe she was, how deceptively lean. How remarkably at ease with herself, as after her day of tea with society's worst, when any truly fragile creature would have crumbled. The muscles in her arms he'd felt and then dismissed, telling himself that was likely part of some or other therapeutic thing he'd assumed she must do.

This did not look therapeutic. It looked like art.

Melody not only didn't tremble, she was magnificent. Every kick, every strike, told him truths about who she was. Every easy, offhanded flip from the ground to her feet showed him that she had been hiding in plain sight from the start.

He could feel that beat in him like the drums of war.

But what he focused on most, just now, was that whatever else Melody was—chief among those things a liar— she was not fragile.

She was not breakable.

She was not any of the things she'd pretended to be. None of the indisputable things that had kept him in check.

Griffin felt the hold he'd had on himself crack into

pieces, then disintegrate. There and then, like so much ash in the wind.

He didn't think he'd moved, or made a sound, but he must have. Because one moment, the two women were engaged in the most elegant brawl he'd ever seen. Then next, they froze, both of their heads whipping in his direction.

And he knew that his bride could not see him. His head knew that. But his body reacted as if those lovely sea-colored eyes were moving all over him the way he knew his own gaze moved over her.

"Prince Griffin," said her aide, not quite landing the appropriate bow.

But Griffin's eyes were on Melody.

Who, for the first time since he'd met her, looked utterly out of her depth. He could see the difference now, and maybe one day it would be funny, how deeply she'd deceived him. How she'd played the blind girl he'd expected to see, and he'd seen only that.

But he rather doubted he would ever find anything funny again.

"Griffin," Melody whispered. His name almost a question. Her voice shaky, and this time, not because she was acting.

He could see that clearly.

And despite himself, despite how little humor he found in this—or because of it—he laughed.

It was a dark thing, wild and stirring, bursting out from the deepest part of him.

"My poor, deluded wife," he said, hardly aware of what he was doing, so focused was he on her. On how she stood in a fighting stance, not cowering or collapsing or trembling at all. The lies she'd told him battered at him, but now he knew the truth. He could feel that like her hands wrapped tight around his sex, as if the only thing he'd ever been was an animal. But this time, he did nothing to hold himself in check. "You should have known better. I might have been better than I pretended to be, but I was never all that good."

"I don't know what that means."

And something in him roared in triumph that she sounded off balance. That she wasn't quite so sure of him, after all. He wondered if she would try her act again. If she would cower or cringe, or do any of those other things he now saw, so clearly he couldn't believe he'd ever fallen for it—had been fake.

Lies in the flesh.

He'd seen what he'd wanted to see. But now he saw her.

There was no going back from that. God help them both.

"You will," he told her, menace and need warring inside him and turning into fire. "You'd better prepare yourself, Princess. Because I was happy to protect an innocent, but that's not you, is it?"

"Griffin…" she began, but his name in her mouth only made it worse.

He heard it as an invitation he intended to take.

"I have no reason at all to protect a liar," he told her, while the fire in him burned bright and tasted like victory. At last. "Least of all from myself."

CHAPTER NINE

MELODY COULD FEEL a beating thing, a wild exultation *this close* to panic and yet not quite, and couldn't tell if it was her heart or his.

"Leave us," Griffin ordered Fen, his footsteps ominous against the polished floor as he moved further into the room. Melody could feel him coming like a storm. "The Princess and I need to discuss a few things. In private."

"Perhaps it would be better if I stayed," Fen replied.

It made a deep sort of shiver rattle its way deep into Melody's bones. Because Fen was the least nurturing creature Melody knew, and given who she knew, that was saying something.

This could only mean it was worse than it seemed.

Her own heart beat so hard then, so loud, she thought it might leave a scar on the outside of her chest.

And still his footsteps came closer. Melody tried to imagine what Griffin must look like, bearing down on her. That beautiful face she'd felt beneath her hands taut and grim. Both of them unchained, finally, from this game they'd been playing all the while.

If the normally unflappable Fen was apprehensive, Melody should have been terrified.

But she knew that wasn't the thing that bloomed inside her, thick and ripe.

"I'll be fine," she murmured to Fen. "Truly."

She had no idea if that was true, so she did what she could to stand balanced on her bare feet. Ready for whatever might come at her—or ready to counterattack, anyway, which amounted to the same thing. She'd learned to punch and kick quickly, as all white belts did. It had taken her a great many more years to learn how to be still.

To wait.

"Godspeed, then," Fen muttered from beside her.

Melody didn't try to find her way back into the weak little character she'd been playing. She doubted it would work this time.

And on a deeper level, she didn't want to.

Because she wanted him to see *her* for once.

Had she sensed him? Had that been why she'd felt so much fierce joy in this particular session? Why she'd jumped higher, punched better? Had she known all along he was here?

Melody knew he was here now, certainly. She could *feel* him as he stalked toward her, temper and heat. And she couldn't bring herself to shrink back down into palatable size.

She had no idea what to do with the storms she could feel snap and howl around them, but she knew she couldn't pretend any longer. It already felt like years since she'd agreed to play her role. Decades since she'd found the whole thing amusing.

Something in her whispered that she would pay for this, later—

But she heard Fen close the door.

And in the next second, Griffin was there.

Right there, looming over her, wrapping the storm tight around them both.

Melody should have been afraid. But instead, she felt as if she was expanding. As if her ribs couldn't contain all the things she felt, and none of them was fear.

"It never fit, did it?" Griffin seethed at her. She could hear rain pounding down against the great domed ceiling, high above. But here, between them, there was nothing but thunder. "All this time, you were playing me. Letting me think I was protecting you when it seems, Princess, that you could take on the better part of the Royal Guard without breaking a sweat."

"Only if they got lippy with me," she replied.

The way she would reply to anyone. No breathiness. No cloying sweetness.

No act.

He laughed again, that wild, dangerous sound, as if he relished this as much as she did. No mask. None of that tinkling, polite, brittle laughter. No pretending she was meek when she was anything but.

"Did you have any intention of telling me the truth?" he demanded, his voice soft and close.

She didn't mistake the softness for weakness. Not when she could hear the fire in it. And could feel it crackling all over her skin.

"Because here is what I think you do not realize, my innocent bride." She expected him to grip her again, with those marvelously hard hands of his, but he didn't. Griffin prowled around her instead, walking in a tight circle. And she could feel, too distinctly, the touch of his gaze on every part of her. She felt a flush wash over her, head to toe and back again. "Or is that also a lie?"

"My innocence or our marriage?" she asked, though

it took her a moment to track what he was saying when she was far too caught up in the thunder. The fury.

His voice was a lash. "Pick one."

"I never had the luxury of being innocent," Melody told him. She concentrated on her stance. Feet on the ground, knees soft, hands loose at her sides. "Not in my father's house. He didn't get to be the King of Tabloid Filth by prizing purity. But there are different ways to lose innocence, aren't there?"

"I am primarily concerned with one."

Melody sighed. "No, despite training like this since I was very small, I am still in possession of a hymen and the virginity to match. A treasure beyond all others, or so I have been led to believe. Though I should say that this is mostly by default."

"Default?"

"I will confess to you, Your Royal Highness, that had I been given the opportunity or permitted the company of men, I would have handed off my precious treasure long ago. Sex always sounded far more interesting than random hoarding."

She heard what sounded almost like another laugh, as if he couldn't believe she'd said that. "Tell me—what did you hope to gain by pretending you were a fragile thing I might break if I looked at you directly?"

The exhilaration in her burned hotter. "I thought we covered this already. Beauty and the Beast, of course. Everybody loves a fairy tale. Particularly with sad little virgins, for some reason." She shrugged, too aware of his scrutiny. Her skin felt stretched tight and far too hot. "I'm afraid I don't make these rules."

"Did you really believe that I would fall for this?"

That sounded rougher. Darker. "For the rest of our natural lives?"

Had she believed that? The truth was, Melody could hardly recall her life before this. Before him. Marrying him had changed everything. It had liberated her from her parents' house. It had opened up her world—even if, regrettably, it had mostly been opened to poisonous society types and tedious stately dinners. It had taught her that she, too, could yearn not only for concepts like freedom but for one very specific man. His flesh. His mouth. *Him.*

She hadn't known any of that when she'd walked down that aisle. How could she have?

And more, how could she have imagined this *need* inside her—that made her want nothing more than to tear aside the pretense and show him who she was, no matter what happened?

Calista has always told you that you were reckless, Melody reminded herself. *Apparently she was right.*

"It isn't about what I believed," Melody said. Carefully. She tracked him as he came back around to face her once more, seething and furious and deliciously male. "It's what you wanted to believe. I'm not the one who needs this fairy tale, Griffin. You do."

"Haven't you heard?" And he was even closer then. He was so *big*, the blaze of his temper so hot, that she could sense a kind of humming in what scant inches he'd left between them. She could feel that humming inside her, marking her, thrilling her, making her tremble. "There are fairy tales to go around in Idylla these days. The King has made it so. No one will pay the slightest bit of attention if this one turns out a little tarnished."

His hand came to her nape, tugging her head to his.

And then—at last—his mouth came down on hers.

Claiming her.

Possessing her.

Taking the storm that raged around them and pouring it into her, then making it worse. Or better. Or both at once, leaving her spinning even as she clutched at his shirt to keep herself upright.

Because his kiss was an onslaught. A form of attack. Melody knew that.

But she thought she might die if he stopped.

He kissed her and he kissed her, and the way he plundered her mouth bore no resemblance to those kisses in the courtyard.

She shook, and this time out of a different kind of fear. She wasn't afraid of him. But he was…unleashed. And despite all her talk, she had no idea if she could handle all the raw power and sensuality that poured out of him, and into her.

No matter how much she wanted exactly that.

Melody was wearing loose workout pants and a close-fitting T-shirt, because she and Fen had agreed that there was no point raising suspicions by bringing any actual, formal gear. And it had been so interesting to train like that, in light, stretchy fabrics that allowed her a different understanding of the things her body could do.

And now, that same performance fabric offered no barrier whatsoever to the man who lifted her up, held her high against his chest, and then pulled her legs around his waist to settle her there. Wrapped around him like the vines that circled the columns in her parents' atrium.

Never once lifting his mouth from hers.

For long, desperate, drugging moments, it was like a battle. Melody fought him, though she hardly knew why. Only that she liked the familiarity of a fight. And she wanted to get closer. Deeper. Wilder.

She wanted things she couldn't name.

Griffin bore her across the room, toward the furniture that she and Fen had pushed back into the embrace of the plants, the way they always did when they trained in here. Then he took her down with him, so her back was pressed into one of the low couches.

But he came down with her.

Her legs were still wrapped around him. Her mouth was still fused to his. And as he settled, hard and huge between her legs, that relentlessly masculine part of him pressed tight against the place she ached the most, something in her…

Changed.

Surrendered, something in her whispered, though she wouldn't know. She never had before.

But she shifted, so quickly it made her dizzy, from the kind of fight she'd always known and loved and considered a part of who she was to…a melting thing.

A sweet, wildfire burst of molten release all through her body.

"Hold on, Princess," Griffin growled, his mouth moving from hers to find its way down her neck, finding her pulse and toying with it until she shuddered. "You might know how to fight. But this is my game, and I know how to win."

And then he took her over.

There was no other way to put it. No other way to feel. She was melting and melting, and he conquered her.

Thank God.

His hands moved with skill and certainty. He pulled the shirt she wore up and over her head, pausing to shrug his off, too. Then he pressed his naked chest against hers, and that…was a delight. A mad, careening bloom of sensation.

Her nipples hardened at the contact, and then he used his palms there, as if he was trying to see the expression that she would make.

And her breasts responded, the proud ridges standing tall.

He laughed at that, a wicked sound.

Then he used his mouth.

And Melody…lost track of herself.

There was only sensation. There was only fire and need. He stripped her, pulling off her loose pants, and making a deep noise in his throat when she was naked before him. He took a moment while she shook, lying there before him, and it was only when he returned to her that she realized he'd taken his own remaining clothes off, too.

And then…it was a symphony. His body was so different from hers. His hair-roughened chest, so heavy and solid. The lean, hot weight of him, bigger and broader and all of it somehow delightful and perfect and alien and *right*.

He took his mouth and his hands to every part of her. Every last millimeter of her flesh, until she was thrashing, her head back and her fingers gripping whatever part of him she could reach.

Melody was already moaning when he got to that slick place between her legs. He traced her wetness with his fingers. Then he tasted her with his mouth.

Then he claimed her, completely, burying his head between her legs, eating her whole until Melody exploded.

She hadn't understood.

And she was sobbing, so she couldn't tell him. She writhed and she bucked, and all Griffin did was hold her down and lick into her, until she exploded once more.

She hadn't *understood*. It had been like colors, the things she'd read about flower petals blooming and little deaths and a great many waves washing over and over and over a person who was likely shaking while it happened. She'd comprehended the *idea*. She'd known the *concept*.

But what Griffin did to her was not a *notion*. It was flesh. Blood. It was her bones like jelly and her body no longer hers, no control and no desire for any. It was *yes* and *more*, salt and tears, and a joy so intense it took her breath.

And then, as he found his way up the length of her body again, he used his fingers. It was a revelation made of flame and steel. No longer testing her wetness, but this time, finding his way inside her. Melody felt the stretch. The faint burn.

But she couldn't analyze it. She couldn't catalog the particular sensations the way she always did, then file them away with the rest.

Melody didn't want to learn the shape of him. She wanted to lose herself in him, or she already had, and there was nothing to do but allow it.

To glory in it.

To surrender herself completely and worry about it later.

He began to thrust in and out of her with his fingers, and that was so amazing, so astonishing, that Melody didn't know what to do with herself. She was making noises she didn't recognize. She flushed, hot and red, like a fever—but this one felt almost too good to bear.

But her hips seemed to know things she didn't, rising to meet those hard, seeking fingers. His mouth was at her neck. She felt the graze of his teeth on her collarbone.

And everything was this. The rise, the fall. The thrust of his fingers deep into her body. Steel and fire, flesh and blood. His mouth a hot demand. Her own sounds a betrayal and a song at once to this rough, wondrous music.

Then, finally, Griffin took her mouth again, kissing her deeply. Until his tongue mimicked the thrust and retreat of his fingers, and that was too much.

It was all *too much*—

And this latest explosion made her stiffen, everywhere, until she thought she might shatter.

Then she did shatter.

And when she was herself again, Griffin was gathering her beneath him. He pulled her knees up and wide.

Melody could feel something wider and blunter than his fingers press against her softness. And she knew.

She had wanted this. She had dreamed of sex, that funny word that seemed so strange and sharp when all of this was…hot and physical, wide and deep. It was everything and too much and not enough. It was flesh and fantasy, surrender and hope. It was—

Griffin twisted his hips and thrust his way deep inside her.

And this time as she bucked against him, it wasn't another one of those explosions. It was a different shattering—and the shock of pain.

She blew out a breath, then another, and his hands were at the sides of her face, brushing her hair back.

"Breathe," he ordered her. "The pain will ebb."

She obeyed him. She believed him.

Melody tried to pull in a breath, then let it out again, but he was on top of her. He must have been holding himself up on his elbows, but that didn't take away from the press of him. That huge male body of his was sprawled out on top of her, holding her where she was. Keeping her there.

More than that, anchoring her in that place where they were connected.

Griffin seemed content to hold himself there forever. Something about that made her...not anxious. Nothing like anxious. But still, she wriggled her hips, experimentally.

Sensation walloped her, raw and huge, and she froze again. And panted a little.

But almost in the next moment, she tried again.

It was the same, only this time she was sure that there was something in the punch of it that she liked. Or wanted to like.

Melody knew pain, after all. She remembered the first time she'd been hit in the face—the shock of it, the emotional response. And then, years later and a great many more strikes and blows to the face—because that was how a person trained—it wasn't as if getting hit changed any.

What changed was that she knew how to take it.

And here, now, she figured she should apply the same principle. Lean into the sensation and find out what it was.

So she did. And the more she moved her hips, the more the intensity changed. It didn't lessen, but it didn't stay put. It seemed to move through her until she felt it, everywhere. And there between her legs, she couldn't decide if she was sore or scared or gluttonous.

The more she moved, the better it felt.

"Better?" Griffin asked, his voice a rough, spicy growl that merged with the sensations inside her and made them...*more*.

"Better," she managed to say. "Good."

He made another low noise. Then he gathered her in his arms again, dropped his face to her neck, and began to move.

First slow. Easy.

But every time she adapted, raising her hips to meet his thrusts, he changed the rhythm. Faster. Harder. Deeper.

It was too much. It was not enough.

She wrapped her legs around his waist again, not sure if she wanted more or if she wanted to hold herself together somehow, and he grunted his approval. And somehow that let her surrender all over again, losing herself in the building storm.

He found her breasts with his mouth, and still that pounding. That rattling, slick, intense thrust and retreat.

And the more she gave, the better it got.

Until eventually, everything began to tighten again. Everything focused on the place where they were joined, and it got wilder, and hotter, and too intense—

And she was suddenly afraid that whatever was coming for her, she couldn't take. She couldn't fight it. She couldn't *survive* it.

"Melody," Griffin said at her ear, his voice dark and wicked and beautiful. "Let it happen."

And it was as if she was waiting for that. For him to make her feel safe again, even in this.

She felt the punch of it first, a wallop that should have made her cry. Or perhaps she was crying already, but she didn't care, because her body was arching up into it. The rattle and the roll, the madness and glory rocked through her then.

Making her fall apart even as she was, for the first time in this searing heat, whole.

And still he pumped himself into her, thrust after thrust, until he roared out her name.

Then together they shook, and together they fell, and then, for a long while, there was nothing but breath.

And even that seemed near to impossible. Too much to bear.

The world crept back in. It felt aggressive.

Everything was different now. And yet, as far as Melody could tell, great swaths of the population ran around doing this all the time. So much and so often that they grew bored of it, or opted out, or any number of other things she hadn't really understood when she'd read about them and certainly couldn't imagine *now*.

It was physically painful to remind herself that if even a tiny fraction of the stories told about Prince Griffin were true, *he* went about doing exactly this the way some people brushed their hair or had a bath.

The world no longer felt aggressive. It was crushing.

"Well," Melody said brightly, though he was still sprawled over her. She couldn't tell which one of their hearts was pounding so hard it hurt, but she had a good idea. "Thank you. I was beginning to think I would die without ever understanding what sex was."

Griffin shifted and once more she felt his hand on her face, brushing back her hair. She was tempted to imagine that was tenderness. She felt herself melt all over again.

But when he spoke, his voice was all condemnation. "You have no idea what sex is. That was a palate cleanser. Did I not tell you to hold on?"

"Yes, but—"

There was that laughter again, dangerous and wild. It swept over her, making her skin prickle. "We're just getting started."

And he was still so deep inside her, it was like they were one.

She didn't mean to make the sound she did, something like surrender.

"I'm going to take you apart, Melody," Griffin said softly, a kind of dark promise. And she could feel him grow even harder, again, deep in the clutch of her body. As if every part of her, inside and out, was his. "Lie by lie. Until I'm done."

CHAPTER TEN

"HAD I KNOWN what the process of exposing lies entailed," Melody said some weeks later, "whether of omission or otherwise, I would have made it clear from the start that I was keeping things from you. The very first night, in fact."

She was exultantly naked, stretched out in Prince Griffin's bed, the wildfire within her sated. For the moment. A state she'd found herself in almost constantly as the first weeks of the new year wore on.

It was already the best year of her life.

Melody reached out with her hand across the rumpled sheets, searching for that glorious indentation that was Griffin's spine. She had come to a deep appreciation of a man's back. *His* back, to be more precise. She had clung to that back, dug her nails into it, drummed her heels against it. She had kissed her way across one side, then the other.

Thinking about the things she'd done made her want to do them all over again.

Griffin sat on the edge of his bed as he often did, and though she could feel that same dark, brooding force field of his all around them, she found it difficult to hold onto much of anything but joy. Until these weeks, she'd had no idea that joy could be a physical thing. It could surge in her veins, flood her whole body. It could sing in her chest and set fire to her limbs.

Oh, yes. This was a marvelous year, indeed.

She found him, and felt that humming electricity arc between them, the way it always did. Melody blew out a soft little breath at the buzz of it. Then she traced a lazy pattern over those powerful, hard muscles, down to the place where his hard, honed body met the surface of his wide mattress. A body so different from her own. She thought she could spend a lifetime reveling in their differences and never tire of it.

It was convenient that a lifetime was what they'd both signed up for, then.

Tonight had been like any other night in her new life as a royal princess. They had gone out to yet another engagement, the way they did most nights of the week. One thing that had changed, though Melody was not entirely certain what it meant, was that when home they no longer had their meals together. Griffin no longer doted on her, gallant and courteous, or walked her places at his snail's pace.

Which was not to say he was rude. But if she was to look for him, then find him in the house of an evening, Griffin no longer wasted time talking.

At first that had suited her. Having discovered the astonishing truth about sex, and how endlessly magnificent it was, all she wanted to do was drown herself in it.

Her new husband had been only too happy to oblige, despite his initial talk of lies and taking her apart. She chalked that up to the intensity of it all. All these weeks of it and she still didn't *quite* believe that she could really live through it, until she did.

It was like suddenly learning, after all this time, that she had access to a brand-new sense. All that sensuality, all that heat and greed and fire, worked together to make her feel like the four she already used were... different with him. Better when they were naked and he was inside her.

She almost felt she had never known her body until now.

As January wore on, however, Melody had begun to notice things other than screaming his name and exploding into sensation—though slowly, she could admit. The fact he no longer seemed interested in conversation, for example, when before it had been as if her every word had fascinated him.

Tonight she'd spent the long evening out at another formal dinner, paying attention to the interesting undercurrents swirling all around them. But when she'd tried to describe them to Griffin on their drive back to the palace, he had instead pulled her over his lap, got his hands beneath her skirts, and had her sobbing out his name instead.

Once inside their home, he had carried her upstairs to his rooms. He had stripped her naked and had taken her once more, hard and fast against the wall of his overlarge shower while the water beat at them, enveloping them in a slick embrace of steam.

She hardly remembered how they had gotten back to his bed, where she knew she'd slept for a time, only to wake when he pulled her close once more, surging into her before she was fully awake the way they'd discovered she liked a little too much.

A person could cry out so much and so long that it no longer left her voice husky in the mornings, it turned out.

Melody couldn't think of another way she might have learned that. And now she couldn't really imagine her life if she *hadn't* discovered that.

It was still the middle of the night. Griffin's royal bedchamber, where Melody spent most of her time these days, had walls of windowed doors on three sides and no curtains. The morning sun poured in, warming and waking her each day, usually to discover him gone and the bed cold.

There was no warmth on her face now. And he was still there.

And when he did not respond to her hand on him, it occurred to Melody that perhaps it was finally time to pay attention to more than the things they could do to each other's bodies.

Or you could press yourself against him and kiss his neck, and see how quickly you find yourself beneath him, she argued.

But it was one thing to find herself so sensually overwhelmed that her skin felt too sensitive. It was something else to deliberately avoid a topic because she'd grown accustomed to sensitive skin, and wanted only more of it.

"Is something the matter?" she made herself ask.

"Go back to sleep, Melody," Griffin ordered her, his voice low.

She sat up instead, dropping her hand from his back, which felt like a grievous loss. "If that was meant to be soothing, it failed."

"Heaven forfend that I fail you in some way. Can the foundations of our marriage based on lies survive? Unless, of course, I make you come again."

Something inside Melody twisted at that, a sharp and

unpleasant flash too close to actual pain. He sounded darker than usual. Forbidding, even.

She began to count back. And as she turned over these past weeks in her head, she realized with some shock that he had changed completely on New Year's Eve. Night and day, in fact, while she'd trailed around after him, desperate for more.

It was like when she'd learned to read Braille. It had opened up a whole new world, and she'd wanted to do absolutely nothing else but explore.

Possibly that made her something less than the ideal wife. She sat straighter and decided she would make up for that now. Since Griffin had obviously done all these things before, it stood to reason he hadn't been quite so drunk with the joy of it.

Though she would have sworn he had been.

"What if, for a change, we had a conversation?" she suggested.

And a cold sort of flush washed over her when she heard his short, bitter laugh.

"What is there to discuss?" Griffin's voice was even darker and more forbidding than before. "You lied to me. That's the beginning and the end of everything."

Melody wished she had paid a little more attention over the years to her sister and the relationships Calista had spent so much time building, buttressing, or fixing. But she hadn't. She'd had no expectation that she would ever have those things, and besides, she'd always found Calista's friendships, contacts, and endless talk of networking…silly, at best. It was nothing but games and misdirection.

Melody preferred the simple eloquence of a fist. A kick.

But now there was a heaviness in the room, his words felt like a bruise, and she had no idea what she was doing.

"I have already told you why." Or she had tried. She had not told him that his brother had personally asked her to pretend she was fragile, as even she with her inadequate grasp of relationships had concluded that would not help anyone. "I had no idea what kind of man you were. Or how you would treat me. Of course I kept a few tricks up my sleeve."

"I would not call what you did 'a few tricks,' Melody. What you did—everything you did—was a carefully calibrated misrepresentation of who you are. There's not one fragile bone in your body."

He had turned while he spoke and now he crawled over her. Melody fell back, though she could have fought to stay upright, because her body wanted nothing more than to surrender to him. To whatever he threw at her. Again and again and again.

She could feel the cage of his arms, and then the weight of him, pressing her down into the mattress. And surely there was nothing wrong with this. With them. Maybe this was how relationships were built—using whatever common language was available, and this was theirs.

Melody had long since become fluent.

Between them, she could feel the heavy weight of his arousal that she was beginning to think filled him with despair even as it made her shiver with delight.

"Aren't you pleased?" she whispered then, her lips near his. "Isn't it more fun to make each other shake instead of worrying that I might shatter without warning?"

"I detest liars," he said, a growl against her mouth. "There is not a single member of my family who did not lie to me. And now you, too. The woman I will be tied to for the rest of my days."

She shifted her hips, smiling at his sharp intake of breath.

"And you, of course, are a beacon of honesty at all times," she murmured. "Even when, for example, you pretended for years to be dissolute and shallow when you are neither of those things. Not entirely."

"You have no idea what you're talking about."

"Griffin—" she began, and this time without the complication of her hips, or her soft heat against the steel of him.

But he didn't allow it.

He kissed her fiercely, wildly. And despite herself and her notion that she ought to *do something more* the way a wife surely did, Melody thrilled to it.

The way she always did.

Griffin flipped her over, muttering dark demands into her ear as the huge, hard heat of him slid home. Melody groaned.

And he took her that way, a ferocious claiming, without another word.

The next time she woke up, the morning light was pouring in. It danced over her skin, spreading its warmth wherever it touched, but Griffin was nowhere to be found.

Melody wanted to go and find him, to demand that he explain to her what was happening. What she'd missed. Her heart was pounding too hard, as if she was exercising when all she was doing was lying in a bed, alone.

But she made herself breathe. She made herself think.

And reminded herself that strategy won far more fights than brute force ever did.

So instead of forcing the issue, she would train. And wait.

That night, her staff dressed her in yet another one of the ensembles that, in all likelihood, the Idyllian press would fawn over tomorrow. It was another thing Melody had come to accept as these weeks rolled along.

Because while Melody had lost herself completely in carnal delights, Idylla had also fallen in love. With their King and Queen, who everyone agreed were a bright new light, sweeping out King Max's darkness. And more, with Prince Griffin, whose sudden Christmas switch from bad boy to besotted husband set the island to fluttering and swooning.

Still.

Melody herself was considered fragile, certainly. But the public loved her. For every aristocratic woman who delivered backhanded compliments, Melody was seen as being that much closer to full-on sainthood. *An angel of redemption*, the papers cried.

Her staff had taken to dressing her accordingly.

"What am I wearing?" she asked Fen on her way out.

"A halo," her friend replied, laughter in her voice. "As always."

"I am your redemption, apparently," Melody told Griffin later, in yet another car on the way to yet another engagement.

A moment she had chosen precisely because he could not silence her the way he normally did. Not if he wanted to parade her into the dinner looking like an angel. Smudged lips and wild hair would not give quite the same impression.

She could tell from the tension in the car that he knew it.

Griffin was sprawled out across his side of the plush back seat, taking up far too much of the available space and brooding so loudly Melody was surprised the driver couldn't hear it through the glass.

"It's a nice story," he said. Eventually and with ill grace. "But I think we both know the truth."

Melody found she was growing weary of this. There were so many more enjoyable things they could be discussing. Like what he did to keep his body in such delicious shape. Or what else he could teach her. She found it an endless delight that she'd married a man who had quite literally done it all, and could show her.

"What does it matter if I am less breakable than you imagined?" She had to remind herself to keep her impatience out of her voice. Somehow she knew he would not appreciate it. That, in turn, might possibly lead to less sex, and she couldn't have that. *Focus*, she ordered herself. "You were famous for how much sex you had. Quality and quantity, apparently. Surely you cannot have imagined that you would spend the rest of your life as a monk?"

"I wanted to," he bit out, shocking Melody so deeply that her half-formed decision to interrogate him...disappeared.

"But why? Why would anyone want that?"

"Not all of us are granted the opportunity to pretend that we are holy, clean, and pure." Something dark and painful was between them then, and laced through his voice. The car felt hot with it. "I don't expect you to understand."

"But I do." She reached out a hand, meaning to touch him. His face, or his chest—but he grabbed her hand in midair, stopping her. Melody curled her fingers over his, then, and held on. "Do you know what it's like to be held up as a symbol for others when all you really want is the luxury to be a person like anyone else?"

"Do *I*? You forget who I am. Do *you*, Melody?"

"I have always been my father's excuse," Melody shot back at him, still holding his hand in the space between them, gripping his fingers tightly. "His embarrassment or his curse, depending on the year. Meanwhile, my sister watched me train for years and knew full well that I have always been capable of defending myself. More, she knew I enjoyed doing it. Yet somehow, my life became her burden to bear. A problem she was required to solve, whether I felt I required a solution or not."

"You cannot possibly compare our experiences." His words were like bullets. "My life has been a public spectacle outside my control since my mother showed me to the world from the palace balcony two days after my birth."

"You think I don't know what it's like to forever live according to others' expectations?" Melody laughed. "I don't consider myself disfigured, disabled, or any of the other words people use to describe things they don't understand. I am me. And still, I was asked to hide that. To play up what everyone else thinks is a liability. To make sure that everyone around me, especially you, would treat me as an object of pity instead of a woman. What else do you think a saint *is*?"

His hand tightened against hers. She could feel his pulse, hard and hot.

"These past weeks, I thought that finally I'd been given the opportunity to be everything I am to a person who isn't Fen," Melody continued, her voice a little more intense than it should have been. A little too intense to pretend she wasn't emotionally involved in this, like it or not. "I like to play games, I'll admit. But I thought we stopped. Yet we didn't, did we? You called me a liar, and ever since, you've cut what we could be in half. If you can't protect me, you deflect with sex. If you no longer think I might fall apart, you take me apart, but only in one way. There's a name for this, you know."

"You can call it what it is. Consequences," he gritted out. "The consequences of your actions and nothing more."

"Or, possibly, something like a madonna/whore complex. Just throwing that out there."

"I don't have a complex," Griffin growled. "What I have is a fake marriage."

He dropped her hand.

Melody wanted to reach out again, but she didn't. And it hurt.

Try some strategy, she snapped at herself. *Unless you want him to keep treating you like this.*

"But you have always had a fake marriage and you have always known that it would be exactly that," she said. Reasonably, in her opinion. "You married a perfect stranger by order of the King himself, on scant notice and with no opportunity for argument. How did you think that would play out?"

"I married a half-feral waif who had been locked away in a basement and needed rescuing. I made her a princess." Griffin's voice was darker than she'd ever heard it, and still it hummed in her, bright the way she thought light should be. "Only to discover she was neither of those things, never was, and never will be."

"Then what am I?" she asked as the car slowed. She

could feel Griffin gathering himself, putting his public mask back into place, and she wanted to rip off whatever halo she was meant to be wearing and toss it. At him. "Because I would have thought that a secret ninja princess would be the perfect companion for the kingdom's favorite Prince, who covers what good he does with all that charm and too many playboy antics. A secret saint all his own."

"Secrets are nothing more and nothing less than a sickness waiting to claim its casualties," came Griffin's reply, as if it was torn from him. "And there is no time for ninjas tonight, Melody, secret or otherwise. The ambassador wants nothing more than to tell happy stories of hope and redemption, just as my brother does. Our only obligation is to embody those stories in public, lies or no lies."

"You do know that it is possible to do both," Melody said. The car stopped. She heard the driver open his door. And told herself the drumming of her pulse was something other than a strange panic at these things he was saying. "Surely you and I decide what our marriage is in private, no matter what show we must put on for the world. I don't believe you need redemption, Griffin. And if you do, why must it only come with abstinence? Why can you only be a good man if you're denying yourself—"

"Because there are consequences for actions," he threw at her, and he sounded so…stark. "There is always a price to be paid, Melody. Maybe your life has been sheltered in such a way that you have never had to learn this lesson. But you will now. You should never have lied to me. But you did. We are what *you* made us."

"I'm not the one who put me on a pedestal in the first

place," Melody said softly. "You did. You wanted me to be a saint so you could be, too. Now you blame me for falling when I am who I ever was."

"A lie," he growled. He leaned closer, and she thought she felt his lips at her temple, a brush of heat that made her think of loss and fire, need and grief. "What you are, Melody, is a lie."

She knew she had his attention now, electric and intense. Melody could feel the full impact of it on her, like hands pressed tight to her skin, seeing things she would have preferred to keep hidden.

"Maybe I am." She shook her head. "But Griffin... If you don't have someone to blame, who are you?"

CHAPTER ELEVEN

HER QUESTION HAUNTED him.

Griffin felt he should have been used to that by now. Everything involving Melody was a haunting of one form or another. First he'd wanted nothing but to put his hands on her. Wanting had kept him awake, made his days an exquisite torture, and taught him precisely what kind of man he was. Now he wished only that he could lose himself in the madness and heat they generated between them. He told himself it was better that way. That it was all there was and ever had been.

He should have been happy.

Griffin was an unlikely monk, and well he knew it. It was a role that could never have fit well, and he'd found it almost unbearably suffocating in the course of a single week. *One single week*, he growled at himself, lest he was tempted to forget.

To make up for it, he'd spent these weeks since discovering Melody's perfidy doing little more than teaching her one sin after the next.

But it turned out that wasn't enough, either.

He had taken her home from the ambassador's house that night, forestalling any further commentary or haunting questions on her part the same way he always did.

Because he called her a liar, he knew full well she was one—but their bodies fit together like magic.

And despite himself, Griffin knew full well there was no greater honesty, no sweeter truth, than the spells they cast together. Over and over again.

Until he was having trouble remembering why it was he couldn't let himself trust what he felt. When they were naked, fused into one. Slick and hot and so perfect together it sometimes hurt.

"Your marriage has been even more successful than we dreamed," his brother told him one pretty day. "I must congratulate you on a job well done."

It was the end of January and the brothers stood out on the palace balcony, which had long been used for any number of official appearances from the royal family. His parents had stood right here and presented each of their sons, the heir and the spare in turn, to the nation with all attendant fanfare. Griffin liked to tell himself it was his earliest memory when, in truth, he suspected he'd seen the photographs and newsreel and had incorporated them as a personal recollection he could not possibly have had at two days old. But a grand presentation to an adoring crowd was as good an origin story as any for the kingdom's charming rogue of a prince, he'd always thought.

Though it seemed to scrape at him today.

"I'm delighted, as ever, that my personal life can serve the crown," Griffin replied to his brother.

And though he'd intended that to come out with a certain dark humor, he could tell he missed the mark. Orion's gaze slid to him, then returned to the crowd. They both stood at attention, waving, while below the crowds chanted and cheered. Griffin kept his usual public smile plastered to his face and, today, found it a chore.

"Is there trouble in your personal life?" Orion asked mildly. *The King* asked, Griffin corrected himself. "Anything I should know?"

"I suspect you already know," Griffin retorted. Again, more harshly than necessary. And certainly more harshly than was wise out here in public, where there were always telephoto lenses.

He remembered Melody's words in the car that night. *What do you think a saint is?* she'd demanded, throwing the question at him with the first real spark of temper he'd seen in her. Something he should have celebrated, because wasn't that what he'd claimed he wanted? Honesty no matter the cost?

Today it felt like a price too steep to pay. All of it.

Orion didn't reply, too busy waving while below, the Royal Guard performed a particular march to celebrate Idylla's Armed Forces. Griffin regretted saying anything. More than that, he regretted that he no longer seemed to have control over himself. He knew whose fault that was.

Who are you? Melody had asked him. *If you have no one else to blame?*

He couldn't seem to shift that question off of him. It sat on him like a weight, thick and heavy.

When the event was finished and it was time to retreat back into the palace, he found himself hoping that some crisis had cropped up and Orion's aides would sweep him off to tend to important matters of state.

No such luck.

"What is it you think I know?" Orion asked, dismissing the staff waiting for him with a flick of his finger.

Griffin took his time facing his brother. His King.

"You too?" he asked. Lightly, he told himself, though there was too much ice in it. He shook his head. "Is there no end to the lies you plan to tell me, brother?"

Orion stiffened. "I don't think I—"

"I understand your need to protect me when we were young," Griffin said stiffly, aware that he was crossing a long-held line. Knocking down a wall the two of them had left standing between them for a reason. "The responsibilities of your position have always come with all kinds of knowledge I doubt you wanted yourself. I don't blame you for not sharing things out of a need to shoulder the greater share of the burden. It is why you are already a great king. But this? Asking my wife to lie to her own husband? How can you possibly imagine that falls within your purview?"

To his astonishment, his brother looked stricken.

"At first I thought it was a lie perpetrated on you as well," Griffin forged on, not waiting to hear what Orion might offer as a defense. "That it was Calista who advised her sister to hide the truth about herself. I would put nothing past the Skyros family, after all. But I quickly realized that Calista was not her father or you would not have married her. Because I trust *you* enough to know your own wife."

He realized as he said it that he had not spoken so harshly to his brother since long before Orion took the throne. But he did nothing to walk it back.

"I don't think you understand," Orion began, in that careful voice that won over fractious members of his court and made his ministers sigh with pleasure.

Griffin was not appeased. "You are mistaken. I understand completely." He raised a brow, his gaze steady. "You don't trust me to keep my promises, though I have never broken them. You know how I feel about lies, and yet you did this anyway. I have always thought that I was lucky because whatever service I provide my King is part of the joy I have in my brother. Thank you, Orion, for proving that joy is a one-way street. It is better to know that than not."

Orion stood as if facing a firing squad. "That is not what I was doing. I didn't think of it as a lie. It was a bit of misdirection, that's all. Nothing more and nothing less than the harmless white lies anyone tells at the beginning of a relationship."

"It was not up to you to decide," Griffin bit.

"I am your brother first," Orion said, his voice rough. And nothing like careful. "Always."

"Alas, Your Majesty, I don't believe you," Griffin shot back.

And then, deliberately, performed a deep sort of bow more appropriate for lowly servants in the presence of the monarch than the King's blood. To his mind, underscoring the truth of their relationship. It was royal. It was municipal. But Griffin was a servant to the crown more than he was a brother to a king, and he needed to remember that.

Then he turned, quitting the room before he began to say even more things he shouldn't. He could feel them all bubbling up inside him, making a mockery of the character he'd spent a lifetime building, then playing. He was meant to be relaxed, at ease. He was the foil to his brother's upright morality.

But who was he when there was no one to blame?

He tried to shove that question out of his head, but his walk back through the palace made it impossible.

Griffin had grown up here. He'd spent his life in these very halls. And yet all he could see today was Melody.

Melody clinging to his arm when he now knew she could probably run down these halls without incident. Melody tipping her face toward his. Melody with her hand over his mouth, telling him to smile, to frown.

Melody everywhere, like a tune stuck in his head. Giving him no quarter and no peace.

He let himself into the side door of his house and then stopped, listening for her. Listening to see if he could tell where she was and what she was doing that easily, because he persisted in imagining that if he knew what she was doing he wouldn't feel this *need* to go and see it for himself.

Yet once again, loath as he was to admit it, he felt drawn to her. As if he no longer had control over himself.

As if he couldn't stop himself from shoving his fingers deep into his own wounds.

Griffin took the stairs two at a time, choosing not to question his haste. His abominable *need*.

And he found her in her reception rooms, tending to the daily work of the social calls he suspected she found as tedious as he always had. He nodded curtly at the guards outside her door, then stepped inside without making a sound.

His wife—his secret ninja princess, as she called herself, and he should not find that so charming—was sitting on her usual settee, bathed in all that golden light. Griffin told himself that her inescapable beauty, her sheer perfection, shouldn't make such a racket inside him. He told himself he wanted it to go away.

It is only sadness, he told himself.

Because he knew the truth. Because it was lies. Because *she* was.

But when he looked at her, all he saw was her radiance.

As bright and as beautiful as any truth.

And it did not seem to matter how many sins Griffin taught her or how many times he practiced them upon her. It did not seem to matter how many times she broke apart in his hands, or screamed out his name, or rode him to a wild finish as if she was the one teaching him each and every one of the carnal delights he'd thought he'd mastered.

None of it touched her.

Melody was holding a cup and saucer before her in a crisp, elegant manner that made the two women sitting across from her seem almost embarrassingly gauche in comparison. And all she was doing was sitting there. Listening.

"I beg your pardon," she said softly when the woman who had been speaking paused to take a bite of one of her tea biscuits. "But I believe my husband has need of me."

When Griffin would have said she could not possibly know he was there.

And then it was all exclamations and fluttering as the two women—who he was certain he knew, though he found he could not focus long enough to identify them— scurried from the room in clouds of overexcited tittering.

"You do not normally show your face at these calls," Melody said when they were gone. Griffin indicated with a nod of his head that the remaining staff should leave, too. "Lady Marisol and her sister will dine out on your appearance for weeks."

"I don't know why I'm here," he ground out when they were alone.

Against his will.

Melody rose, then, nimbly moving around the furniture and making for him, unerringly.

Griffin still wasn't used to it. There was still something inside him that expected her to trip. To fall. Or to at least *look* as if she wasn't quite so sure of herself.

To need you, something in him suggested.

"There's nothing I can do about the fact I deceived you, Griffin," Melody said softly when she came to a stop before him. "I would apologize, but I'm afraid I'm not as sorry as you might wish me to be. In my position, I suspect you would have done the same thing."

Griffin didn't want to hear that. And he didn't want to think about it too closely, either, because he was afraid she was right. Arranged marriages weren't particularly out of the ordinary in his world. It was a widely accepted practice not only in Idylla, but in many royal and aristocratic circles around the globe. But it was different to walk into one as a woman.

Of course it was. Especially if that woman was blind.

"It had nothing to do with you," Melody continued as if she'd read his mind. "For all I knew, I was jumping from one fire to another. I don't regret protecting myself. I would do it again."

"Thank you for your honesty," he managed to say. And then, because he couldn't help himself, "Even if it is a bit late in the game."

And something in him seemed to shatter, even as he stood there. It was her scent, crisp and sweet at once. It was the smile he'd failed to keep on his face before the crowds. It was her, all of it, and now he knew her too well. The warmth of her skin. That smooth, glorious curve of her hip that could cause war and peace alike, and often did. The crushed velvet of her nipples and the strength in her thighs, particularly when she gripped him tight.

He knew too much.

And still Melody stood before him, something almost like a smile shaping her lips, her eyes so wide and the endless blue of the sea.

Griffin wanted things he shouldn't. Things he couldn't understand.

It never got better, that wanting. It only grew more intense. She was *doing this to him*, and still, she looked like an angel.

"It doesn't have to be like this," she said softly. "Does it? Can't we make it what we want it to be?"

"You don't understand."

Griffin expected her to sigh at that, the way she often did. Argue, maybe.

He could have handled that much better.

What she did instead was to reach over and slide her hand over his heart, as if she could hear the way it beat, jagged and painful.

"I want to understand, Griffin," she said softly. "But I can't unless you tell me."

"It was my mother," he said, when he was certain he had no intention of speaking. It was as if the words were torn from him, and once spoken, he couldn't seem to stop.

He put his hand over hers, there against his chest, intending to peel hers away.

But he didn't.

Before him, Melody simply waited. Still and yet engaged. No longer pretending to cower or shake, and that seemed to punch in him. He would never have told this story to a fragile creature. It would never have occurred to him.

Melody was anything but.

"She used to tell me I was her favorite," he heard himself say, his voice as rusty as the words seemed when he'd kept them inside so long. "My brother had belonged to the crown since birth, but I was her friend. Her *buddy*."

God, how he'd always hated that word.

"As the years went by, she became more pale. Brittle, almost, the longer she stayed married to my father. She told me only I made her smile. Only I tethered her here."

Melody made a soft sound of distress. "That seems like an unfair burden to place on a child."

"Whether it was or was not, it was the only thing that kept her with us." Griffin ran his free hand over his face. "Everybody knows that my mother took her own life. But they act as if that was out of the ordinary for her. As if it was a one-time mistake gone too far." He shook his head, his throat suddenly thick. "It wasn't."

Melody only murmured his name. And he suddenly felt that her palm, lying there and holding his heart in place, was the only reason he was still standing upright. Telling this story he'd never told. The story he'd vowed he would never tell.

"She tried again and again," Griffin said, unable to stop himself. "And sooner or later, if someone wishes to go, they will. No matter how carefully guarded. No matter how loved."

"It's not your fault, Griffin," Melody whispered.

He looked at her, fiercely glad she couldn't see the emotion he feared was far too obvious, all over his face.

Even as he was convinced that somehow, she knew anyway.

"I'm afraid you're wrong about that," he said, his voice steady with the conviction of all these years. The scar of it. What it had meant to him. What it made him. "My brother found her. But I left her. She promised me she would not do it, and fool that I was, I believed her. *And I left her.*"

Somehow, it seemed as if Melody's palm against his chest grew harder. Hotter. And there was something about the expression she wore that made a low sort of shudder move in him. *Protective*, something in him whispered.

But he thrust that aside.

"The only other person I have actively tried to care for in my life is you," Griffin told her, because what did it matter now? Why not lay all of this out, this grief and betrayal, so that at last what was between them would be clear?

Unmistakable.

And then, maybe, he could go about the business of putting himself back together when he still didn't quite understand how he came to be so broken in the first place.

"You're focused on the fact that I am not as weak as you expected me to be," Melody said, a faint crease appearing between her brows, making her look fierce. "But you made me feel safe. Me, Griffin. When I have never felt such a thing, anywhere. Or with anyone."

He wanted to hold on to that. He wanted it to mean something. When would he stop with all this fruitless *wanting*?

She blew out a breath. "No one fights the way I do,

consistently and with years of intense practice, because they already feel safe. I thought the only way I could ever feel like that was if I was actively attacking someone. If I was winning a real fight. But all you had to do was treat me as if I was fragile. As if I might be precious. And there it was."

This was excruciating.

"It was a lie," he gritted out.

"But don't you see?" She shook her head, that hand on him seeming to pin him to the wall when he wasn't touching it. "What would it really mean if you had saved a weak and fragile creature, more breakable than glass? Anyone could save such a girl. I could save twenty with my hands tied behind my back. Surely the victory is greater when the need is less."

He reached out to touch her, but only to grip her shoulders so he could set her away from him. Because he *wanted*, God how he *wanted*, and he knew better than that.

Telling Melody the story of his mother reminded him, forcefully, of the one inescapable truth he never should have let himself forget.

He had left his own mother to die.

What he had left was a promise to his brother and a wife he was sworn to protect, no matter what. He deserved nothing more.

And that meant, no matter who he blamed or how he felt about it, that first and foremost he needed to protect Melody from himself.

Especially if she was foolish enough to feel safe in his presence.

"I never should have touched you," he told her, almost formally. "I betrayed both you and myself when I allowed the truth of who you are to cloud my judgment."

"That did not feel like a cloud to me, Griffin. It felt like clarity."

He ignored that. This was about keeping his promise to himself—the one he'd made the morning his mother had been found. That never again would he let anyone too close to him. Not when it was so clear that he couldn't be trusted.

"We will return to our initial arrangement. Wiser, I hope."

"We can't return to me cowering and cringing and you imagining that's real," Melody replied, matter-of-factly. And it kicked about inside him, the way she said such things. With total conviction and absolutely no fear. "So what is there to return to?"

"Something more civil than this," he blurted out. "The way marriages between people like us have always been."

Melody considered him for a moment that seemed to stretch out. And ache.

"If you make yourself a priest, riddled with the glory of your abstinence, would that make up for it, do you think?"

He stiffened as if she'd shot him. Some part of him would have preferred it if she had. He thought of the knife he'd carried in his boot since his soldier days, and how easy it would be to simply take it out, hand it to her, and let her do her worst. How much quicker and more elegant.

At least then there would be no waiting. No quiet tyranny of day after day of *wanting* all these things he couldn't have.

No more of this, he ordered himself. It was time to retreat into duty. Into the ascetic life he'd planned to live once he married. No scandals, no secrets, and none of this ruinous *passion.* That was a risk other men might take, but not him.

He should have known better. He had.

Now it was time to enforce it.

"You wanted to understand and I have told you," he said, scowling at her even as he drew himself up. She might think there was clarity in the way they'd come together, that howling, greedy madness, but he knew better. Clarity was clean. It was a kept promise, not a messy vow. "And it doesn't matter if you agree with my reasoning or not, Melody. This is how it will be."

He heard the ring of finality in his own voice and, for the first time since he'd seen a wild and cringing creature in his soon-to-be sister-in-law's company, thought he might actually be himself again. It was a gift.

He told himself it was a gift he wanted.

"Because you are the Prince?" Melody asked, a strange note in her voice. "You think you can order me around?"

"That and because I'm bigger than you. Either way, this ends here."

Griffin picked her up and set her back another few feet, so there could be no argument. And no possible impediment to him walking out of this room and into a quieter, more reasonable future.

"I hope that in time you'll see the beauty of this arrangement and understand the need for—" he began as he made for the door.

But the world was upended.

Something hit him, hard.

Then he could do nothing but lie there, blinking, as it slowly dawned on him that he was...on the floor.

He was on the floor of the main reception room, in fact. And his angel of a wife was standing over him, her hands in a position even he could see was decidedly martial.

More critical, to his mind, was the foot at his neck.

Not *quite* applying pressure.

Melody's hair had fallen down around her, and he was reminded once again of the first glimpse he'd had of her. His Eponine, and why was it he had forgotten that Eponine was more feral than sweet?

It was only as his heart thundered in his chest and the breath came back to him that he understood what must have happened.

"Did you...*throw* me?" he demanded, feeling tautly stretched between temper and astonishment, there on his back on the floor at her feet. And a host of other things he dared not name.

"You might be bigger than me, Your Royal Highness," Melody said, cool and calm as if she tossed men of his size this way and that all day long. "But might is only right if it actually works. Otherwise it's little more than ballast and can only make a hard fall hurt more. As perhaps you've discovered."

His head was spinning, and he wanted to blame the fall he'd taken, but he suspected it was her. Just her. "Melody—"

This time, astonishment warred with sheer outrage as she applied pressure, lowering her foot as if to cut off his airway.

And the look on her face told him she just might do it.

"Enough talking, Griffin," she said, like a queen commanding the peasants. "It's my turn."

CHAPTER TWELVE

"IF I WERE YOU," Griffin seethed at her, simmering there beneath her foot in all of his male glory, "I would think very carefully about your next move."

Melody could feel a different kind of electricity in him. A kind of shock, climbing up her leg and fanning out to take over the whole of her body. It had been something like instinct to reach for him, to throw him.

To show him that unlike everyone else in his life, *she* would not be so easily dismissed by the kingdom's favorite Prince.

They were his press, his adoring public, even his brother. She was his wife.

Maybe it was time to show him what that meant. What she wanted it to mean, anyway.

"What makes you think I haven't already thought through my next move?" she asked, taking pleasure in the mildness of her voice. In the fact she wasn't breathing heavily after that throw, while his chest was still rising and falling rapidly. "If I were *you,* I might issue fewer threats after finding myself on my back, clearly no match for a woman one third my size."

"Is this the romantic poetry that you hope will change

my mind and lure me back to your bed?" Griffin asked acidly. "It leaves something to be desired."

"Not all of us had access to your educational opportunities," Melody said, and even laughed. A real laugh, for a change, because they were alone and she'd thrown him and what point was there in wearing masks at this point? "While you were comparing and contrasting sonnets in fine universities, I was learning the poetry of movement. And of stillness. Better still, how to make myself unseen—especially when standing in full view."

He vibrated beneath her, temper and steel, and it moved through her like a caress. "You are not the only person who had to learn such things. And if you do not remove your foot from my throat, I cannot be held accountable for my actions."

Melody did not remove her foot. If anything, she applied more pressure.

"I am not the one dead set on pretending we are so different that we must exist in a monastic marriage for the rest of our days," she threw at him, fiercely. "Do you really think I don't understand grief? Do you imagine I didn't spend my youth tearing myself apart, wondering why it was I had been born with an affliction I couldn't hide? How hard do you suppose it was to choose to love my sister when it would have been so much easier to hate her, simply for being all that I am not?"

His hard fingers laced around her ankle, but she still didn't move her foot. "I hope you're not suggesting I'm jealous of my brother. Nothing could be further from the truth."

Melody was so used to hiding. To pretending to be less than she was.

But Griffin had taught her that there was no level of

intensity he couldn't meet. And that was the Griffin she believed—the man who was as wrecked as she was, but still reached for more. The man who held her so close she felt as if she was inside him, too. The real Prince, dark and stirring and, most of all, hers.

She was tired of hiding. Of fighting on mats, with Fen, and never for herself.

Never for what mattered the most.

That ended here.

"What I'm suggesting is that each and every one of us is filled with the same dark mazes, Griffin," she said then, the intensity of her feelings making her voice shake. "It doesn't make us special. It doesn't make us different or unique. What makes a person is what they do with the darkness inside of them. Because you can dress it up in any pretty words you like. You can blame your mother. You can claim you blame yourself. But at the end of the day, you and I both know that the real reason you want to keep us in these boxes of yours is because you're afraid. Of *us,* Griffin."

"If you do not remove your foot," he bit out, sounding far more vicious than before, "I will stop treating you with the courtesy my wife deserves and instead treat you to the sorts of things I learned when I was a soldier. You do not want that."

"I welcome it," Melody shot right back. "You speak of honesty? Then fight me. *Me*, the person who's right here in this room with you. Don't hide behind old promises and ancient guilt when you know as well as I do that what is between us is extraordinary."

She felt his hands grip her ankle tighter, and not entirely gently.

It thrilled her.

"I do not wish to be indelicate," Griffin hurled at her, and she could feel the great blaze of him, there beneath her foot. She could feel it race up her limbs, making her shiver. Making her wet. Making her that much more determined to get through to him. "But you are not in a position to judge, Melody. You lack context."

"You're going to have to do better than that," she chided him. "Do you really think that you can insult me? My father is inferior to you in every conceivable way, save one. When it comes to insults, Aristotle Skyros is truly peerless."

Below her, she could feel the tension in Griffin tighten. He had to be reaching his breaking point, she thought.

And in the next moment, he moved.

It was sheer joy.

He tried to simply shove her away, moving her foot as if he could move her body that easily. Succumbing to that belief in his own superior power that Fen had always taught her about. *Even if they see what you can do, they will not believe it*, the older woman had told her. *It will not make sense to them. They will assume that because they are bigger they will always be stronger. That is a weapon. Your weapon.*

Melody broke his hold and flipped backward, hampered only slightly by the dress she wore. Despite the dress throwing off her form, she landed nimbly and evenly, laughing as her feet hit the ground.

"Come now, Griffin," she scolded him. "You're going to have to do better than that."

"I'm not going to fight you," he said stiffly.

"Why ever not? Are you afraid that I will best you? You should be."

He made a noise like thunder. "What will happen, Melody, is that I will hurt you!"

She danced closer. And then she punched him, hard. Right in the solar plexus.

And waited until he pulled a ragged breath back in.

"No," she said, steadily. Intently. "You won't."

"I won't fight you," Griffin gritted out. "No matter the provocation."

"No sex." Melody kept her hands up as if, at any moment, she might strike him again. "No sparring. What remains, then, in this imaginary marriage you intend for us to have?"

"I don't care," he growled at her. "Just so long as it does not—"

"Hurt?" she prompted him. "But I think it will, Griffin. I am certain of it."

And this time, when she danced close again, she ducked beneath his arms. And stayed there, flush against his chest, her palms flat against the steel of his pectoral muscles.

"Melody…"

Her name was a warning.

"Here is a greater hurt, then," she said softly. "I love you, Griffin."

And for a long moment, he was silent. Still. Beneath her hand, his heart pounded, but it was as if he was once again made of stone. Impossible marble beneath her palms.

Deep inside her, something started to crack. Because if she could not reach him, then what? Had she truly exchanged one prison for another after all? She hadn't wanted to believe it.

"No," Griffin said at last. She had begun to worry he

would not speak at all. And he sounded tortured when he did, making that cracking inside her go deeper. Wider. "You cannot. That is a darkness no one can penetrate, I promise you."

"I'm not afraid of darkness," she whispered. "I live there."

"Melody." Another warning, though this one more broken. "You don't know what you're saying."

"Close your eyes." And then she checked that he'd obeyed her, lifting her hands and sliding them over his eyes. She pulled in a breath, holding them there. "Stop worrying about the darkness. Think about your heart. Listen to your breath. To the sea outside, far below. To me, Griffin."

"Melody..."

But this time her name was more like a song.

She shifted up on her toes, closer to him, glorying as ever in the way their bodies fit so perfectly together. Whether they were dancing, fighting, or exploring each other on his wide bed, it was always like this.

As if they had always been meant to find each other.

"Feel this," she whispered, and then she kissed him.

And Melody knew how to kiss him now. How to tease him, how to tempt him. How to make them both shudder.

How to turn want into need, heat into fire.

She kissed him again and again, and she wasn't surprised when Griffin shifted, kissing her back. Taking control.

His hands moved into her hair, sinking in to hold her where he wanted her.

"This is not darkness," she said, tearing her mouth from his. "This is love, Griffin. I suspect it always has been."

He dropped his head closer to hers, but he did not open his eyes beneath her palms.

"I wanted to give you the Prince, not the dissipated lout," he told her, there against her mouth. "And maybe it was easier to pretend it was the lie that made the difference. But it's *me*, Melody. I don't know how to be whole. I am one or the other, never both, and you deserve more than that. You deserve a real life. You deserve love."

"I deserve the life I've chosen. With the only man I will ever love." He tried to pull away but she slid her hands down to grip his neck, and held on. "You don't scare me. Your dark, your light, they are all *Griffin* to me. You speak pretty words and you make the crowds laugh, but all I hear is your heart. I always have. I always will."

She felt that cracking thing inside her, or maybe he was the one who shook.

Or perhaps this was the earthquake they'd generated, a tsunami not far behind, and as long as they were together like this—still that perfect fit—she couldn't say she minded.

"I couldn't live with myself," Griffin managed to say, "if I lost you too."

And the cracking, the shaking, intensified, but she wasn't afraid of it any longer.

"There is a simple solution to that," Melody told him. "Live with me without any rules. Love me without any boundaries. Forever, Griffin, so neither one of us ever loses."

And for a long moment, she didn't know if she'd reached him. She could feel the fight in him. The battle. Earthquakes and tsunamis, tornadoes and storms.

But he didn't pull away.

"You have no idea how much I want to believe that I might be capable of such things," he said as if each word cost him. As if they hurt. "How much I wish that somehow, I could even pretend to give you what you deserve."

"You have already made the scandalous Skyros sister a royal princess," Melody said, smiling against his mouth. "It seems to me there is no magic you can't perform."

She felt the fight in him...shift. Like the tide going out. His arms moved, but only to hold her.

"What am I to do with you?" he asked quietly.

And Melody's smile was so wide then, it threatened to split open her face. "I've already told you. No monasteries. No lies. We will do what we must outside these doors, but in here, when it's just you and me, why can't we be only and always who we are?"

"Why not indeed?"

Then Griffin was kissing her again, over and over. And when he shifted, lifting her into his arms, she thought he would carry her to one of the couches—but he didn't.

He shouldered his way through the doors, and carried her through the halls of their home, taking her to his bedroom.

"I've been playing a role my whole life," he told her as he set her down beside his massive bed. "I don't want to play it with you any longer. But I warn you, once I start this thing with you, I fear I will never stop."

"What do you think forever means?" she asked him, that smile still on her face as if it would never leave.

Griffin knelt down, his hands spanning her hips in a possessive grip that made her feel something like giddy.

"Princess Melody," he said, his voice deep and formal and the most beautiful thing she had ever heard, "I thought taking you as my wife was an act of charity, and it was. But it was not me who was bestowing that charity. It was you. I cannot compartmentalize myself with you. I cannot pretend. I want everything or nothing. And nothing will not do."

"I love you," she said. "And think, Griffin. We've only just started. We have our entire lives ahead of us."

"And with you, I want it all." He leaned forward and pressed a kiss to her belly, its own kind of promise. "With you, I will risk anything. Family. Happiness. Love."

Love. The word was like fire in her.

But the more she burned, the more it felt like pure joy, until she thought she might burst with it.

"Prince Griffin." And Melody's voice was thick, because these were vows. This was their real wedding, right here, where their true communion had begun. "With you, I can see. The life we will live. The family we will raise. The love that will grow stronger, day by day."

"Year by year," Griffin agreed, his voice rough with the same emotion that coursed through her veins.

"Because if it doesn't…" Melody promised him softly, sinking down on her knees before him and smiling all the wider. "Trust me, my beloved Prince. Feet on your throat will be the least of your concerns."

"I can't wait," Griffin said, and then he gathered her in his arms, took her to their bed, and got started on their real marriage, there and then.

CHAPTER THIRTEEN

OVER THE YEARS, Griffin learned many things about the woman he had imagined he was saving—only to discover that all along, he was the one who needed it more.

He had learned the safer she felt, and the more comfortable in his presence, the wilder and brighter the joy. Just as he had learned that she was in no way a morning person and should always be approached with caution and coffee.

Not in that order.

He moved her into his suite, not the least bit interested in the normal way things were done in marriages like theirs. The real truth was that there were no marriages like theirs. And while he and Melody could play any role the palace required, in this house, what they were first and foremost was in love.

Love, Griffin found, changed everything.

He found his way back to his brother, because he understood, now, the things that love could make a person do. He understood that Orion had thought he was helping, not hindering.

And he forgave not only his mother for leaving, but himself, too.

The joy got wilder and brighter all the time.

He and Orion, without consulting their brides, took it upon themselves to suggest—in no uncertain terms—that Aristotle Skyros remove himself from Idylla. For good.

"You cannot banish me," the horrible man seethed at his King.

"And he will not, as he is a good and benevolent king," Griffin replied, all idleness until he met the despised man's gaze. "But I do not think you would like it should the rest of the royal family feel compelled to take matters into their own hands."

Aristotle slunk off, never to be heard from again. It was impossible not to view his departure from the island—and his daughter's lives—as a triumph of epic proportions. Especially when his wife remained behind.

And Griffin watched as time did what nothing else could have. He would not call it a true healing, necessarily. But when Calista started giving Apollonia grandchildren, a mother found her way back to the daughters she had abandoned.

"I will never trust her," Calista said with a sniff after her first child was born, sitting in the private parlor where the four of them often gathered.

Melody shrugged. "I have always liked her more than you. She was kind enough."

"*Kind enough* is not kind." Calista smiled down at the newborn Crown Prince while beside her, Orion looked besotted. The Queen gazed at her sister. "Though I will admit, even she blooms without Father around."

"So would a desert," Melody replied.

And later, when they were alone, Griffin showed Melody precisely what he thought about *kind enough*. By being first deliciously cruel.

Then so kind she screamed.

"I think I'm ready for the next adventure," Melody said one night, when they had been married for five glorious years.

"You may have any adventure you like," Griffin told her with that gallantry that made her smile. And call him *Gaston*. "You already have."

They spent the bulk of their time dutifully representing the interests of the crown. They were mindful of their responsibilities. But they also took long, significant breaks, where they pleased no one at all but themselves.

Melody had wanted to explore the world, and he had taken her wherever she wished to go. They had jumped from planes, hiked up mountains, swum with dolphins. Griffin had lived more since he'd met Melody than the whole of his previous life.

The longer they stayed together, the deeper and better it got.

"I hope you mean that," Melody said then. They lay in their bed, the soft Aegean breezes playing over their naked skin.

She nestled against him. Then smiled.

With an innocence that struck fear into his heart.

Because whatever else his beautiful Princess was, a secret ninja or a wildly creative lover, she was never innocent.

"Tell me what you want and I will give it to you," he declared.

"You already have," Melody said quietly. "And in about seven months, you can meet him yourself."

Griffin thought that his heart could never beat that hard again. That he could never love more than he already did.

He kept thinking it, and he was always wrong.

As Melody proved twice more. Two perfect princes and one remarkable princess filled this house of ghosts with laughter, bloodcurdling screams, and joy.

So much joy, it hurt.

You missed all this, Mother, Griffin thought years later.

All three children had been settled into their beds, some with tears and some with grace. And his wife appeared before him on her soundless, careful feet, her hair the way he loved it, wild all around her.

Fifteen years had passed since the day he'd carried her here from the reception rooms where the local ladies had long since learned not to poke at Princess Melody. Since the day they'd stopped being two and had become one, at last.

Since the day their true marriage had begun, and changed everything.

"I hope you locked them in," he said, grinning as she came to him. "Hellions."

"There is no point. It would work for one night only, and then Fen would teach them all how to break out. But I've thrown the bolt on *our* door, never fear."

"My beautiful, perfect wife." Griffin gathered her to him, holding her in his arms. "My Princess. What would I have done if I'd never found you? Who would I be?"

"Let's never find out," Melody said.

Then she wrapped herself around him, making that

same, sweet fire burn bright between them, the way it always did.

And always would, hot enough to propel them straight on into forever.

Over and over again.

* * * * *

MILLS & BOON

Coming next month

AN HEIR CLAIMED BY CHRISTMAS
Clare Connelly

'I will never understand how you could choose to keep me out of his life.'

Annie's eyes swept shut. 'It wasn't an easy decision.'

'Yet you made it, every day. Even when you were struggling, and I could have made your life so much easier.'

That drew her attention. 'You think this is going to make my life easier?' A furrow developed between her brows. 'Moving to another country, *marrying* you?'

His eyes roamed her face, as though he could read things in her expression that she didn't know were there. As though her words had a secret meaning.

'Yes.'

For some reason, the confidence of his reply gave her courage. One of them, at least, seemed certain they were doing the right thing.

'What if we can't make this work, Dimitrios?'

His eyes narrowed a little. 'We will.'

It was so blithely self-assured, coming from a man who had always achieved anything he set out to, that Annie's lips curled upwards in a small smile. 'Marriage is difficult and Max is young—only six. Presuming you intend for our marriage to last until he's eighteen, that's twelve years of living together, pretending we're something we're not. I don't know about you, but the strain of that feels unbearable.'

'You're wrong on several counts, Annabelle.' He leaned forward, the noise of his movement drawing her attention, the proximity of his body making her pulse spark to life with renewed fervour. 'I intend for our marriage to be real in every way—meaning for as long as we both shall live. As for pretending we're something we're not, we don't need to do that.'

Her heart had started to beat faster. Her breath was thin. 'What exactly does a 'real' marriage mean?'

'That we become a family. We live together. we share a bedroom, a bed, we raise our son as parents. It means you have my full support in every way.'

It was too much. Too much kindness and too much expectation. She'd thought he would be angry with her when he learned the truth, and that she could have handled. If he'd wanted to fight, she could have fought, but this was impossible to combat. The idea of sharing his bed…

'Sharing a home is one thing, but as for the rest—'

'You object to being a family?'

He was being deliberately obtuse.

She forced herself to be brave and say what was on her mind. 'You think I'm going to fall back into bed with you after this many years, just because we have a son together?'

His smile was mocking, his eyes teasing. 'No, Annabelle. I think you're going to fall back into bed with me because you still want me as much as you did then. You don't need to pretend sleeping with me will be a hardship.'

Her jaw dropped and she sucked in a harsh gulp of air. 'You are so arrogant.'

His laugh was soft, his shoulders lifting in a broad shrug. 'Yes.' His eyes narrowed. 'But am I wrong?'

Continue reading
AN HEIR CLAIMED BY CHRISTMAS
Clare Connelly

Available next month
www.millsandboon.co.uk

Copyright ©2020 by Clare Connelly

COMING SOON!

We really hope you enjoyed reading this book.
If you're looking for more romance, be sure to
head to the shops when new books are
available on

Thursday 12th
November

To see which titles are coming soon, please visit

millsandboon.co.uk/nextmonth

MILLS & BOON

LET'S TALK

Romance

For exclusive extracts, competitions and special offers, find us online:

- facebook.com/millsandboon
- @MillsandBoon
- @MillsandBoonUK

Get in touch on 01413 063232

For all the latest titles coming soon, visit
millsandboon.co.uk/nextmonth

WANT EVEN MORE

ROMANCE?

SUBSCRIBE AND SAVE TODAY!

'Mills & Boon books, the perfect way to escape for an hour or so.'

MISS W. DYER

'Excellent service, promptly delivered and very good subscription choices.'

MISS A. PEARSON

'You get fantastic special offers and the chance to get books before they hit the shops.'

MRS V. HALL

Visit millsandboon.co.uk/Subscribe and save on brand new books.

MILLS & BOON
A ROMANCE FOR EVERY READER

- **FREE** delivery direct to your door

- **EXCLUSIVE** offers every month

- **SAVE** up to 25% on pre-paid subscriptions

SUBSCRIBE AND SAVE

millsandboon.co.uk/Subscribe

MILLS & BOON

THE HEART OF ROMANCE

A ROMANCE FOR EVERY KIND OF READER

ODERN

Prepare to be swept off your feet by sophisticated, sexy and seductive heroes, in some of the world's most glamourous and romantic locations, where power and passion collide.
8 stories per month.

STORICAL

Escape with historical heroes from time gone by. Whether your passion is for wicked Regency Rakes, muscled Vikings or rugged Highlanders, awaken the romance of the past.
6 stories per month.

EDICAL

Set your pulse racing with dedicated, delectable doctors in the high-pressure world of medicine, where emotions run high and passion, comfort and love are the best medicine.
6 stories per month.

ue Love

Celebrate true love with tender stories of heartfelt romance, from the rush of falling in love to the joy a new baby can bring, and a focus on the emotional heart of a relationship.
8 stories per month.

Desire

Indulge in secrets and scandal, intense drama and plenty of sizzling hot action with powerful and passionate heroes who have it all: wealth, status, good looks…everything but the right woman.
6 stories per month.

EROES

Experience all the excitement of a gripping thriller, with an intense romance at its heart. Resourceful, true-to-life women and strong, fearless men face danger and desire - a killer combination!
8 stories per month.

DARE

Sensual love stories featuring smart, sassy heroines you'd want as a best friend, and compelling intense heroes who are worthy of them.
4 stories per month.

To see which titles are coming soon, please visit

millsandboon.co.uk/nextmonth

JOIN US ON SOCIAL MEDIA!

Stay up to date with our latest releases, author news and gossip, special offers and discounts, and all the behind-the-scenes action from Mills & Boon...

 millsandboon

 millsandboonuk

 millsandboon

It might just be true love...

GET YOUR ROMANCE FIX!

MILLS & BOON
— blog —

Get the latest romance news, exclusive author interviews, story extracts and much more!

blog.millsandboon.co.uk

MILLS & BOON

HEROES

At Your Service

Experience all the excitement of a gripping thriller, with an intense romance at its heart. Resourceful, true-to-life women and strong, fearless men face danger and desire - a killer combination!

Eight Heroes stories published every month, find them all

millsandboon.co.uk

MILLS & BOON
DARE

Sexy. Passionate. Bold.

Sensual love stories featuring smart, sassy heroines you'd want as a best friend, and compelling intense heroes who are worthy of them.

ur DARE stories published every month, find them all at:

millsandboon.co.uk